I0717024

Portals:

Book Six

Legions & Liches

Travis I. Sivart

Portals: Book 6 – Legions & Liches

Travis I. Sivart

Portals: Book 6, Legions & Liches

Copyright © 2024 Travis I. Sivart

All rights reserved.

ISBN: 978-1-954214-81-1

Talk of the Tavern Publishing Group

Portals: Book 6 – Legions & Liches

Travis I. Sivart

Dedication

To my wife, who's crazy enough to support my crazy dreams.

Portals: Book 6 – Legions & Liches

Table of Contents

Travis I. Sivart

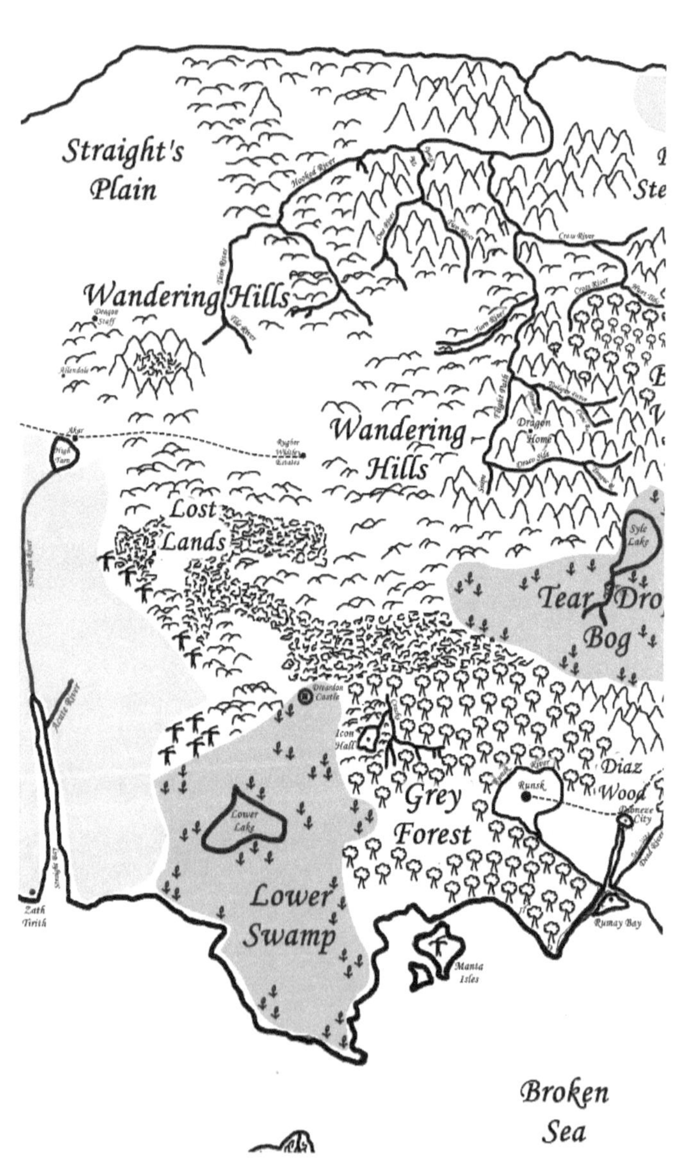
Straight's
Plain
Wandering Hills
Dragon Staff
Aftendale
Akyr
High Tarn
Rygher Valley Estates
Wandering Hills
Hooked River
Tarn River
Cross River
Cross River
Dragon Home
Draco Side
Syle Lake
Tear Drop Bog
Lost Lands
Straights River
Acute River
Drandon Castle
Icon Hall
Grey Forest
Diaz Wood
Runsk
Ebneze City
Lower Lake
Zath Tirith
Straights GD
Lower Swamp
Manta Isles
Runay Bay
Broken Sea

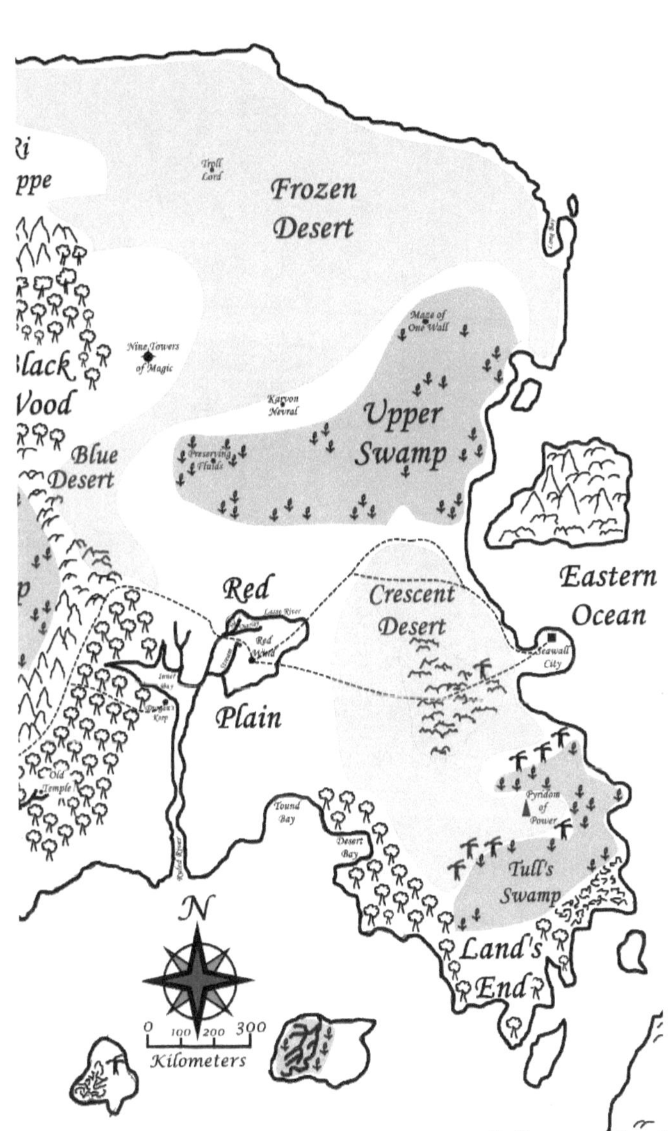

Troll Lord
Frozen Desert
Long Bay
Maze of One Wall
Black Wood
Nine Towers of Magic
Ri ppe
Kayon Nevral
Upper Swamp
Preserving Fluids
Blue Desert
Eastern Ocean
Red
Lasso River
Outlay
Red World
Crescent Desert
Inner Bay
Seawall City
Plain
Dunlun's Keep
Pyridom of Power
Old Temple
Tound Bay
Gold River
Desert Bay
Tull's Swamp
Land's End
N
0 100 200 300
Kilometers

Portals: Book 6 – Legions & Liches

Prologue

Jack sighed as he surveyed the group in the common room of the Traveller's Inn. They were a fine and swarthy bunch of misfits and miscreants. He'd worked with each of them on many occasions, and they were closer to being family than customers.

He knew when each and every one of them came to the Traveller's Inn because he'd invited them. Maybe not outright. Sometimes the inn had a mind of its own and did things with no input from Jack. But it was because of *his* choices and judgment the doors of the dimension hopping hostel opened to the others in the room. But couldn't pinpoint when they'd become more than people he knew.

Running his hand over the well-worn surface of a table, Jack looked past the people to the inn and tavern that became his home, his vehicle, and his prison. The ever-changing inn and tavern had taken on the appearance of a run-of-the-mill Old English pub. Dark wood with brass accents was the prime décor, and the fireplace centered on the wall across from the polished bar, tables and chairs scattered around the room.

Jack wasn't trapped here and could travel of his own accord, moving through time and space to different realities. After all, that's how he'd met everyone in the room. But he didn't do it as much since he'd screwed up and broken the world of Aetheria. Since then, he'd become its self-appointed protector.

His gaze wandered over the dozen and a half people in the room. Each had been there for him and had a drive to help others, though not in the same ways he did.

Behind the bar was the ever-present Cogsley, an automaton with what appeared to be a lightbulb for a head, and tux and tails—including the requisite top hat perched atop his glass dome—was his usual fashion. Beside him, just outside of the bar, was Cogsley's constant companion Golem FloorSweeper. The hulking automaton always looked a bit depressed and moved around their chores with slumped shoulders and downcast eyes, if you could call the rough shaped indents such. The terracotta-colored golem was unfinished, undecided what their final form, gender, or name would be.

These two were the backbone and heart of the inn. They never ventured out, or at least not for long periods. They took care of the place and were the only ones Jack hadn't invited in. As best he could tell, the inn created them as an extension of itself.

Hugh Blueaxe, a big man with blue-tinted skin, stood in the back of the room, an enormous double-bladed axe leaning against his thigh. He'd been coming to the tavern since the Talisman was banished from the skies above Aetheria. Hugh was chatting amicably with Nomed, a demon half-breed with a runner's build and an overfondness for 1990s dance-club leather. He had a muscular runner's build that belied his ability to use the double-handed sword slung across his back.

Nomed was a schemer, a trickster, and an agent of chaos. He manipulated kings and kingdoms and loved the game. But he fought against his demonic heritage by using it to trip up others of his kind and their plots. Hugh was a gladiator (Jack thought he had been, at least) who later became a homeless man close to death.

After succumbing to an illness that caused undeath, Hugh was brought back and imbued with magics that changed him into what he was now.

Wanderly, the halfling who could whistle up a literal storm, was playing dice at a table with Darome the gnome. The latter fancied himself a top-notch illusionist and dressed the part with purple robes and a conical hat covered with suns, stars, and moons. Durg, the half-ogre bodyguard of the gnome, towered over the two but stared longingly at the kegs behind the bar.

Wanderly was a wild card who stuck his nose where it didn't belong, but had the innocence and wonder of a child. He was the original caretaker of the inn, by Jack's appointment, and helped it become what it is today.

Darome and his bodyguard, Durg, were a combination of magic and brute force. The gnome always strived for more knowledge and power, but squandered it in lending a hand to the little person who needed help.

The elder Professor Elementius sat across from his young and enthusiastic scribe, Tilbert, quietly lecturing about some vague topic while gesticulating passionately. Jack had brought in these two to document the travels of the inn and the people within. They were constant fixtures, never seeming to leave, though Elementius had connections to a network of magical colleges somewhere.

Suykimo, Elizabeth, and Zachary sat together in a booth at the back of the room. Elizabeth was her usual self, a well-groomed and mannered lady of the lower aristocracy. She'd been a nursemaid before striking out on her own and meeting the other two. Suykimo watched Jack, his almond-shaped eyes sharp and knowing. The man was part human and part aeifain or dasism, one of the elvish types. He was wise and patient and was a quiet but solid companion. Zachary sat beside the other two, bristling with weapons. He was the muscle of the three, but was also often the impetus that lent action to their cautious knowledge.

Two younger folks sat at the bar, Spencer and Trudy Tridington. They were twins and Jack had been a good friend of their uncle, who'd discovered shadow horrors trying to creep and slither into the world. He'd watched the twins grow up as they inherited the dark mantle of monster hunters and traveled the world to stop the Eldritch forces seeking entry.

Croaker Norge slouched in a chair in front of the fire, his feet on the stone hearth in front of the crackling blaze. A pipe stuck out from under the brim of his tilted fedora, and he crossed his arms on his stomach. Sitting backwards in the chair beside him was Kitty, her silver cannon-like arm glinting in the flame's glow as she whispered to him while pointing at a window.

Croaker was a detective wrapped in wrinkled brown clothes. He was a whiz at creating gadgets and had lived in more than one timeline. He adopted Kitty, taking her in like a long-lost niece. Croaker might have complained about her pink hair, tattoos, piercings, and sharp tongue, but he adored her and doted on her.

Jack took a deep breath and stepped to the edge of the raised platform that the outermost tables were on. He lifted his drink, swallowing down the last dibbles of whiskey, then brought the empty glass down on the railing three times. All eyes turned to him.

"There's something big coming," Jack said, bringing the soft murmur of conversation to a halt, "and I need everyone up to speed and ready to jump into action."

"There's always something big coming, Jack," Wanderly shouted from the bar, causing a smattering of laughter.

"Well, then we know it's not you," Croaker's growl cut through the laughter. "Now shut up and let Jack talk."

"Thank you, Croaker," Jack nodded at the man, then addressed Wanderly. "But you're not wrong. Here at the Traveller's Inn, we seek out the problems of Aetheria and help solve them. After the apocalypse caused by the comet Talisman, everything went to pot. We're running back and forth, putting out small fires constantly. But those are like a fireplace compared to the forest fire that's coming."

Jack paused and looked around the room to make sure he had everyone's attention before continuing.

"A disease has been released on Aetheria, on the continent of Teurone, and it stems from a place that has been a source of problems for thousands of years, Ez'rainia-fromton, the desert empire of the undead."

"Where Verl'zcn luk was imprisoned before escaping and stealing his godhood?" Hugh asked.

"Yeah," Nomed growled, "the same. Go on, Jack."

Everyone had their eyes on Jack, and he watched their body language as they waited. Each person leaned forward, all frivolity and joking put aside for the moment, though Darome still dropped the dice and scraped the small pile of coins to his side of the table. Wanderly didn't appear to notice, but Jack could see the curly haired man palming three of the gold kords that Darome didn't notice.

"I have agents in the field," Jack continued, "good ones. But they're down a person. They lost a good woman after they overthrew a madman trying to control magic. If they'd failed, then more than one god would have lost their power and their place in the pantheon."

"Did the woman die?" Elizabeth asked from the corner booth.

"No," Jack chuckled. "She retired and went home. Something I encourage anyone to do if they ever feel like their time here is done. When I last checked, she's living her happily ever after with a good man. At least for now. That will change soon enough, relatively speaking."

"Jack," Croaker's gravel voice came from under the brim of his hat, "can you get to the point? Why are we all here?"

"Right, and I promise I will, in just a moment." Jack paused among a chorus of sighs, groans, and patient nods. "The three…agents met one of the forces of nature. He is one of the remaining Troll Lords, and now prefers to go by the name Al. Now that they're down to only two, I need a replacement for Aiyana, the one who left."

"I'll fracking do it," Kitty stood and ran her hand down the titanium tube of her forearm. "I got the firepower and the attitude, and with Croaker having my back—"

"Sit down and shut up," Croaker grabbed Kitty's shirt and pulled her back into her chair. "Jack has a plan, and he'll let us know if it involves one of us."

"It does," Jack agreed. "It involves every one of you, but not yet. Not for this. I've chosen someone to bring over for this mission. A very capable woman who knows firepower as well as you, Kitty."

Kitty beamed, and Jack knew that the street samurai could appreciate any women stepping up to kick ass and take names.

"A military woman," Jack went on, "and smart. Oh my god, is she smart. She'll handle the other two with grace and ease. Or with mockery and teasing. But more importantly, she's just the one to bring over to face down the legions of undead about to be released on Teurone. But she's also the one to help the others protect another force of nature, Rykul the Great Bear."

"What?" Darome leapt to his feet, standing on his chair so he was Jack's height. "I thought Rykul died!"

"He did." Jack nodded. "But his essence remains and needs a home. If the liches get to him first—"

"Wait a minute," Trudy rose to her feet, hands on hips, "liches? Like super powerful undead wizards? And plural, like more than one? They're trying to take over a literal *force of nature*?"

"That's part of it," Jack sighed. "The rest is that they're releasing the disease I mentioned to turn any living being into a zombie before they're even dead."

"Ugh, yeah…" Hugh sighed and traded a look with Nomed, "I know what that's like. But Jack, are you sure you don't need us for this?"

"Positive," Jack nodded again. "I need all of you for what comes after. I'm taking the Traveller's Inn on the road through the dimensions. Something is coming, and it's plotting to take control of our inn. It wants to do what we do, but for very different reasons."

Jack let that sink in. The room was quiet, then the last person Jack would have expected it from laughed.

The laugh went from a chuckle to a rolling guffaw and changed to an uproarious, almost maniacal, laugh.

Professor Elementius quietly dictated the events to Tilbert, who typed haphazardly on his brass, fifteen key stenographer's machine to keep up. Hugh and Nomed leaned forward and looked towards the bar. Darome wobbled on his chair and toppled off it with a high-pitched yelp. Wanderly stared with wide eyes, sliding another small pile of coins off the table and into his waiting hand. Kitty gasped and Croaker lifted the brim of his hat to look. Elizabeth traded looks of wonder and concern with Zachary and Suykimo. Trudy and Spencer stared down the bar at the terracotta automaton, quaking with laughter.

"Uh oh," Durg said, tearing his eyes away from the casks of ale, "sometings berry wong."

"What I think Golem meant to say was," Cogsley said dryly, drawling out the words in his upper crust accent, "is that we hope the inn doesn't come under new management."

Chapter 1

Reggie—swashbuckler and gambler—slapped the wooden bench he straddled, causing the silver coins between him and Dandy Rym to bounce, then looked up at the man. His opponent glared back, his eyes slitted and his mouth in a tight line.

The six men around them called out support for their boss. Reggie wasn't a house favorite in this arena.

"You can't win them all, Kazzek," Dandy Rym sniffed, calling Reggie by his nom de guerre, "sometimes you must know when to walk away. At least, if you don't want to lose everything you got."

The larger crowd in the arena stands, surrounding those surrounding Reggie, gasped. Reggie opened his hand, revealing what he held, and the crowd cheered.

Dandy Rym's eyes went wide, and his hand went to his hip.

Reggie dropped his five playing cards on the bench, showing the winning hand, and smiled.

"Parsay loves you, and I'm paying for that now," Dandy sighed, dragging his coin pouch from his belt. "But we still have the bet on your little friend below."

Reggie glanced to the blood sands below where Griffon, the gnomish gladiator, faced off against a rhinoceros beetle larger than a horse. Fingering his necklace of dozens of holy symbols, Reggie muttered a prayer to Parsay, asking for luck, and to Torr to help Griffon in combat.

"The town of Arena," Dandy Rym sighed, "one giant arena, surrounded by smaller arenas. People tell stories about how a trading post grew up around the original structure, and once merchants started putting up permanent structures, someone dug a new fighting pit."

The tall man put a hand on Reggie's shoulder, and Reggie wasn't sure if it was out of camaraderie or to make sure he didn't run. The rough men—surrounding the frontier fop and the swashbuckler—snickered and tightened their little circle.

"Sometimes it was for dog fights," Dandy Rym continued, "or cockfights, but there's always room for men to fight. They settle nothing in this town without someone fighting. And this is the second part of the bet you made with me, your old crew mate."

"Well, I always liked you—" Reggie said, but Rym waved him to silence.

"You won the first part, the card game," Dandy went on as if Reggie hadn't spoken. "You know, I always wanted to beat you when we ran together, doing heists and second story jobs, but could never do it. This second part, the fight in the gladiatorial arena, and Griffon being something of a legend, is quite the thrill."

"Well, the gnome volunteered." Reggie licked his lips, wondering what his host was getting at. "And the little guy is something of an attention whore. Griffon is an incredible fighter, but also an annoying and obnoxious bastard."

He's been that way since we met, Reggie thought, *shortly after Griffon came to this world from Earth.*

Even though Reggie and Griffon were from the same country in the same world, they were from two different worlds. Reggie was from the 1930s and had retired from being an archaeologist during the golden era of archeology, dying in his bed. Griffon was a twenty-three-year-old kid from the 2020s who lived in his parents' basement and played video games all day.

In this world, they knew Reggie as Kazzek Tel Virian, a twenty-something, blond swashbuckler who once was a Robin Hood sort, but in the cities. Griffon inhabited the body of Auric, a famous gnomish gladiator who was twice the boy's human age, half his height, and ten times his skill in anything except snacking.

"I didn't want to make the bets," Reggie said, "but I need information about this disease. People are dying and it's getting worse now that the spring trade routes have reopened. After leaving Elda's Rest as the last of the winter snows melted, we followed clues about the disease, traveling west through the Wandering Hills until we reached Arena."

"Right," Dandy Rym nodded, patting Reggie's shoulder, "people are turning into the walking dead without being dead first, right? What did you call them, the 'lost folk'?"

Reggie nodded and swallowed as Griffon went down underneath the charging insect.

"And you'll get the information." Dandy Rym grinned, and it felt predatory to Reggie. "It's just a matter of you keeping that magical blade. If your little friend loses, and I think he will, I get his legendary weapon and yours. And after everything I've heard about you two and these artifacts, they'll change my world."

Griffon had already died twice, in two different worlds, and he didn't plan on doing it again. He rolled to one side, running his blade—Raven Stealer—along the underside of the immense beetle.

He called upon the cursed magic the witches had sacrificed him for and flung his hand towards the beast's head. A series of sparking explosions went off like a dozen fireworks, and he hoped it would blind the creature.

It didn't work.

Coming up from his roll outside the cage of legs, Griffon stood and the massive head of the rhinoceros beetle knocked him back. The gnome landed on his butt three paces away, but still held on to the ivory horn handle of Raven Stealer.

It's a bug. I could have told you that an illusion wouldn't work on an insect, even a giant one. Raven Stealer said in his head. *But you're very graceful when landing on your ass.*

"Bite me," Griffon retorted.

And your words are just as eloquent. The sword laughed. *You should write books.*

Griffon didn't reply, dodging another charge from the beetle. The monster left a trail of white guts behind it from the wound, but didn't slow.

Waiting until the last moment, Griffon stepped to the side and swiped through three legs on one side. The beast crashed to the ground, sliding along the red sands.

The gnome used one of the flailing stumps as a step and launched himself onto the back of the insect. Running along its shiny carapace, he stopped at the neck and rammed the sword down and into the monster's head.

You do know that beheading the beast would be more effective, don't you? Raven Stealer asked.

"Yes," Griffon grunted, "but not as good for the showmanship side of things. Listen to that crowd!"

The gnome held one hand up to the cheers of the audience, and the other on the hilt of the sword, using it to steer the massive bug as it tried to escape.

He jerked the makeshift tiller, guiding the beetle to trample the three men he'd fought in the first round of combat. The crowd loved it.

Grabbing the pommel with both hands, Griffon jerked the blade back and forth, decapitating the monster. The beast went down into the dirt and the gnome flew forward, ducking into a roll and coming up on his feet, his sword held high.

"See?" Griffon said through his wide grin. "I know what I'm doing!"

Great, Raven Stealer said sarcastically, *let's hope you know how to handle the third challenge.*

The gate in the arena's side opened and a gangly man ran out onto the sands, falling to his knees beside the beetle. He wailed, a long mournful sound, and threw his hands to the heavens.

"Aw," Griffon muttered, "now I feel a little bad."

No one is ever alone, wee one, the sword said. *Someone will always mourn, or avenge, the death of another.*

A sad, slumped goblin limped towards Griffon, head down and hands holding a water skin out.

The gladiator drank, the goblin kneeling at his feet, while arena workers came out to drag away the corpses from the first two battles.

Horns sounded once they'd cleared the field, and the goblin snatched the drained waterskin and bolted for the exit.

Six dark, sleek, low-slung forms darted out of the gate the goblin was heading for, and the goblin backpedaled and fell on his butt. Two circled the wall, moving out of the goblin's circle of vision. One creature turned towards the defenseless prey.

Iridescent scales covered the new beasts, with triple ridges running down their backs. Pointed snouts—bracketed by two smooth tentacles on each side—showed a prehensile tongue ending in short, cilium-like tendrils sliding over dozens of teeth.

Leaping on the goblin, claws pinned him to the ground, and the beast tore out the creature's stomach.

The crowd rose to its feet, cheering.

"People are so finicky," Griffon grumbled. "They did that for me a few minutes ago. What are these crocodile-wolf things, anyway?"

Vunteres, Raven Stealer gave an impressed mental whistle, *pack hunters who are armored, smart, and single-minded in the kill.*

Griffon said nothing as three of the vunteres shot towards him, two angling to each side to flank him. The third one came straight down the middle.

The gladiator inside Griffon came to life, not so much in his head, but in his actions. This was something the gnome became used to since inhabiting this body. Sometimes he was all Griffon, and other times the body of Auric, the gnomish gladiator, took over. Usually in fights, and sometimes when dealing with plants. The previous soul—or spirit, or whatever—was a hardcore anthophile, and loved flowers and botany.

Pack tactics threaded through Griffon's awareness, and he knew the center one was a distraction to allow the other two to close for the kill.

"Two can play at that game," he muttered, throwing out more illusionary fireworks.

Blue, yellow, and green lights shot from his open palm, and Griffon threw himself into a roll to one side. He came up gripping his sword—pointing forward—and planting his feet, bracing for an impact.

The left flanking vuntere impaled itself on his blade, and Griffon danced to the side, turning the beast as the right flanking predator came down where the gnome had been a moment ago.

Pulling his weapon free, Griffon continued the momentum and beheaded the second foe. The third stood where he had started, shaking its head to clear its vision.

"Two down," Griffon giggled, reveling in the feel of battle, "and four to go."

He looked at the one over the goblin, and the beast was staring back at him, its meal forgotten. It arched its back and slunk forward, head low.

Taking advantage of the blindness of the closest one, he ran forward and hacked at the beast, cutting a line across its ribs and foreleg.

It hissed and lurched backwards, snapping at where the gladiator had been a breath before.

The goblin slayer ran at him, leaping over the injured vuntere, and Griffon readied his sword to impale it. The beast twisted in the air, landing an arm's length away, and then something hit the gnome from behind.

Griffon went down, flipping to his back and bringing his sword across his body. He gripped the blade in his free hand and jaws wrapped around the blade.

Claws raked at his midsection, his leather cuirass protecting his exposed stomach, but barely.

Jerking the blade left and right, Griffon cut into the cheeks of his foe, then twisted the blade, dislocating the creature's jaw.

The beast fell back with a gurgled screech. Griffon pushed to his feet, only to be knocked over again as the last two healthy monsters jumped on him.

The wounded two hung back as their pack mates savaged the gnome, clawing and biting at flesh exposed between pieces of armor.

You're the one who insisted on a 'classic gladiator look', Raven Stealer pointed out in his head, *saying that sandals, greaves, bracers, pauldron, and cuirass was enough protection.*

"Oh, shut up!" Griffon shouted, stabbing a vuntere in the throat with the spiral horn guard of the sword.

Grabbing a fistful of sand, he threw it into the eyes of the last uninjured one and followed it up with a sparkly light show. The fireworks refracted off the crystalline grit and Griffon imagined it must look like a fiery explosion to the watching crowd.

The beast fell back, and the gladiator leapt to his feet, laying about him with his sword, taking out the remaining monster.

Griffon was bleeding from a dozen places, his armor hanging in tatters. He limped in a circle, taking in his surroundings. The vuntere with the injured ribs and leg retreated, followed by the one with the broken jaw.

The gladiator stalked towards the injured animals, the crowd roaring, though Griffon couldn't tell if they were cheering him on or booing his magical antics. He didn't bother with showmanship this time, dispatching the one with the shredded mouth and throat first, then the limping one.

"I didn't think they allowed magic in the arena," Dandy Rym whined, "but your friend used it, anyway."

"There wasn't anything said about it being against the rules," Reggie shrugged, "so will you be honoring our agreement?"

They were in a small tent, a private room in what passed for an inn for in the tent-town of Arena. It was attached to a larger tent that was the common room, and a half dozen similar tents jutted out from the main one. These smaller areas served as private eating and sleeping quarters, and Dandy Rym had joined Griffon and Reggie in theirs.

The gnome lay in a hammock, having discarded his armor, and was rocking back and forth, clutching Raven Stealer. The myriad cuts were closed and little more than angry lines of welts.

"I first heard about this…affliction," Dandy's eyes shifted left and right, and he lowered his voice, "happening in Akar, just north of the Great Desert on the shores of the High Tarn. It's spreading from there, I think. I'd suggest going to Allendale."

"Why Allendale?" Reggie asked.

"Allendale was once well known for having many mind mages," Dandy Rym explained, "and I figure if anyone could resist a disease that turns you into a zombie when you're not dead, it's a mind mage."

"That's damn fine of you," Reggie said, holding out his hand to shake the other man's, "and I'm sorry you lost the bet."

"Oh, that's alright, Kazzek," Dandy laughed, taking Reggie's hand, "I bet good money on you and your friend. I didn't get your blades, but I'm about to be a rich man!"

"Raven Stealer healed you up nicely," Reggie gestured at Griffon's sword once Dandy Rym had left.

"Yup, old man," Griffon giggled, "my girl takes good care of me."

"Well, food is coming," Reggie said, rolling his eyes at the gnome's bravado, "and then we need to get a good night's rest. We have almost a week's travel to get to Allendale."

"Think we'll find the disease this time?" Griffon asked, pushing up on one elbow to look at Reggie.

"I hope so," Reggie sighed, "because I'm hearing more reports about this from all over."

"And you really think this is our fault?" the gnome asked.

"Yes," Reggie nodded grimly, "I think it's the disease we released when we opened that tomb in the desert before we went to the Nine Towers of Magic. You saw the warnings, and so did I."

"I didn't know it was this dangerous, or this important," Griffon said defensively, "otherwise I would've said something. I swear!"

"I know," Reggie nodded again, his face neutral, "so you say, and so you've said many times. Just eat up and get some rest. We leave at first light and hope we're in time to put that specific genie back in the bottle."

"In time for what?" Griffon mumbled quietly. "How do we put a genie back in a bottle? I think it's a bit late to do anything except for saving ourselves."

Portals: Book 6 – Legions & Liches

Chapter 2

Lieutenant Reid I. Pierce woke to the smell of smoke and the sound of screams. She lay under a pile of wet, smouldering straw. She choked on the thick, hot air and sharp bits of hay poked her through rips in her rough dress.

Images, like memories, ripped through her head, and she flinched and curled into a ball. They didn't belong to her, but they created a deep ache in her chest and head. The thoughts were recent, less than an hour ago. She was processing grief and pain by observing what happened, going over it again and again. She understood that much.

She'd been in the garden, hoeing a row for the upcoming spring planting. They were planting beans this year. Last year's crop had been sparse, but the weather was changing from the rains of fire and ash to real rain with storm clouds and water. She was excited about the planting season, and even more excited about the first harvest, though it was months away. Her mother called for her, telling her to hurry and lunch was almost ready.

Reid let the memories—if that's what they were— wash over her like a spring rain. There was a lot of work to get done before her father returned from his trip—*Where is he now? Did he survive?*—and brought the things they needed to grind wheat into flour. It was very exciting. Their little village didn't have a baker, and it would raise their status among the others, help the town grow, and build a future for her and her kids…when they came along.

The attack came suddenly, interrupting the girl's daydreams of better days ahead of her. These memories came in jagged spurts of emotion, her mind stuttering from one horrific scene to another. Hunched, segmented monsters—some sort of four-armed bug-men—rushed into the small village she called home. Their destructive rampage didn't spare anyone or anything. They threw torches onto thatched roofs and haystacks, speared sheep, and cut down the fleeing people.

Reid jerked, her hands groping her belly at the memory of a spear sliding into her gut. The flesh was whole, but puckered, and tender to the touch.

Uncurling from her fetal position and sitting up, Reid pushed the straw away from her face and collected herself. Her real self, not whatever the other images were. Her last genuine memory of her own life, her own world—instead of this stranger's shadow sharing her mind—was flying her bird, a Black Hawk helicopter, and going over a contested area. She'd felt it buck, and then…she couldn't remember what happened to her, the chopper, or Charlie, her co-pilot. She hoped the other woman was okay.

Reid shook her head, and her vision shook and tumbled. She couldn't recall anything after that moment.

She looked around at the grubby farmyard, taking in the broken split-rail fence and a wet haystack, moist with spring rains, and dying flames struggling in a half dozen places.

Brushing strands of straw away, the smell of a pigsty and other barnyard animals blended with smoke. She had a thick, unpleasant coating in her mouth, probably a mix of fear and vomit. Inspecting herself, she felt the tight pull of the healing wound on her abdomen, a pounding in her head, and the annoying urge to scratch various bug bites.

She ran her hands across her stomach again, and it was smoother than moments ago, almost like it hadn't happened.

That isn't possible, is it? She thought. *I couldn't have been injured moments ago and healed now. That's silly. I was in a chopper, flying over a desert, and now I'm in a barnyard worried about…giant, intelligent, bug-men?*

Her house was at the edge of town, and Reid looked at a dozen ramshackle huts, the majority on fire. Insectile man-beasts viciously hacked or stabbed any of her neighbors that were in the muddy street.

This isn't my world, she thought. *Is this some kind of weird dream?*

It didn't feel like a dream, though. Very real sensations washed over her, instead of the hints at something happening and her mind filling the rest like when sleeping. She wasn't an observer. She was here, in her body.

Reid looked at her clothing. She wore a dress made of coarse linen, shapeless and unflattering. Holding up her hands, she turned them back and forth. They were much darker than her own skin, which, with her Indian and Caucasian background, was a light brown. The hands she stared at were darker than her own.

Pushing to her feet, she noticed she felt heavier and taller. The ground was at least fifteen or twenty centimeters further away than normal.

Metric? She thought. *Weird, but it feels normal here. That must've been some bump to my head when the chopper got hit. Got hit? Did we get shot down?*

A woman screamed, followed by the clicking hiss of a bug man, and Reid stopped thinking. She had to get out of sight. She pushed to her feet and ran for her house, but it wasn't *her* house. It was a ramshackle hut that belonged in a third world country, not the spacious three-story home she knew. It didn't have a manicured lawn, or a circle driveway, or even a porch with lights lining the long walkway to the door.

Pushing through the blanket hanging in the entry, she slammed a rough plank door behind, and leaned against it.

"Okay," she said aloud, trying to collect her thoughts, "I spent thirteen years in the military. I majored in engineering, so I can break this down and make a plan. I minored in psychology and understand how the mind deals with trauma. I can handle this. Obviously, it's not real, but my mind is making it real. So, I'm trying to work through whatever happened when the chopper bucked. Let's go with that."

Taking a deep breath and looking around, she studied her surroundings. It was a small place with a main room that—being generous—was a living room, dining area, and kitchen all in the same space. A loft in the back was where she slept, and her parents shared the wider bed below.

But the people she thought of as her parents blended with someone who wasn't her parents. In her mind she saw her mother, glorious in a traditional sori, and her father in his crisp button-up work shirt and tie. But she also saw a dark-skinned couple. The woman was tall and thin, almost regal in what Reid could only think of as rags. The man had a wiry build but smiled a lot and laughed easily, wrinkles growing around his eyes and mouth.

The images made her head spin, and she closed her eyes to get her equilibrium. That only made it worse. Her knees buckled and her stomach roiled.

She opened her eyes.

"Let's stick with what's in front of me," she said to herself, "and handle what I can. I don't think I can stay here. So, first things first, get supplies."

Moving without thinking, she went across the room and grabbed her mother's satchel. Snatching up a thick blanket, she folded it, then rolled it tight, and put it in the bag. Then she went to the open wooden wardrobe where the family kept their clothes. She pulled an extra dress out and stuffed it into the bag, followed by a pair of her father's pants, a shirt, some undergarments, and her gown for special occasions.

She went into the kitchen, using the term loosely, and added a loaf of dark bread, dried beef, a hunk of cheese wrapped in cloth, a small bag of tea leaves, and a corked clay jug of water to her supplies. Slinging the bag over her head and shoulder, she looked around for anything else useful.

"Weapons," she muttered. "If I'm going into a world with monsters, I'll need weapons."

Scanning the room, she saw her father's spare belt with his second-best hunting knife hanging on the coat rack. Beside it were his unstrung bow and a quiver of arrows.

The memory of her father teaching her how to carve arrows and add the fletching drifted across her mind, and she shook it away. It was a good memory, one of the bonding moments, but it wasn't something to explore right now.

She'd competed in a lot of things in her life—her real life, not the one in this not-so-dream world—and archery was one of them. Reid knew how to use a bow, along with firearms, and ranked high among her peers. She had natural hand-eye coordination.

Grabbing the belt with the dagger, she pulled it around her and tucked the end through the brass loop, tucked it behind, and pushed it into the gap between, cinching it tight. She tied the quiver onto the hip opposite the knife and pulled the bow to her side, the string wrapped around the limb.

"What the hell am I doing?" Reid asked herself. "Where am I going to go when I open this door? I can't take out a dozen of those things with the arrows I have, not even if I were in protected cover where they couldn't get to me to tear me apart."

Her mind spun at the thought. The 'real world' would never have something like this, except in a movie. And in this world, she wasn't the type that would ever do anything like this.

Pushing those ideas away, she pulled open the door, then closed it again.

"String the bow, pemtie," she muttered. She'd meant to say 'dummy', but the word in her head came out as pemtie. "I'm going to live a movie for now. Maybe an action-adventure, maybe a horror movie. We'll see."

Shrugging, she pushed that aside as well. Sliding the bow between her legs, she twisted an ankle around the end and unwound the string. Bending the wood of the recurve—a bow which bent in an odd way to deliver a stronger shot—and pulled with all her strength to get the loop of the string over the tip. Settling it into the notch, she picked it up and tested the draw.

It was a heavy draw, maybe twenty-kilos, and it wouldn't be her first choice. But she knew how to pull, and how to use leverage. It might tear the bidj (another translated word, meaning crap) out of her wrist if she had poor form, but she could use it effectively.

Nocking an arrow, but leaving the bow undrawn, she opened the door with her free hand and peeked outside.

A bug man looked towards the movement of the door, and the woman brought the bow up, shifted her dominate foot back, drew the string back to her cheek, and let fly.

The arrow left her bow, smooth and straight, burying itself into the monster's chest.

"Chuz you, bug-eyed bastard," she said, the native word filling for her foreign swear word.

The beast stumbled backwards, looking down at its chest in surprise, and Reid used that distraction to step into the open and run around the building.

"Where the hell do I go now?" she whispered.

Hiding was her first impulse, and if she could make it to a stand of scrub trees in the distance, that would probably be far enough away to not be noticed.

Her second impulse was to help the people in the village. She didn't know them personally, but it felt like she did. Kohn the blacksmith was probably fighting the attackers, making a stand to protect his shop and his family of seven. Grought the 'Lord of Timber', as he called himself, would fight as well.

Names and faces flashed across her mind. Dozens of men, women, and children were dying as she debated, and she hated herself that she wasn't charging in to help them.

But if I do that, wouldn't I just die with them? She thought. *One woman against a dozen monsters—maniacal beasts with armor hide and stood a head and a half taller than most men—are not something to be taken lightly. I can fight, and probably die here, or I can run.*

Bile rose in her throat at the second idea, and she bent over dry heaved, small bits spilling across her leather shoes. It wasn't the first time today that her body had done this, and she wiped at the moist remnants of her last meal clinging to her bosom.

An enormous head leaned around the corner of the hut; the bug man she'd shot looking for their attacker.

Another arrow was flying before she could think about it, sprouting from the creature's faceted eye.

The segmented giant slapped a slim pincer to his eye, jittering backwards and falling onto the wet earth. The beast spasmed, his four arms flailing, jamming the shaft deeper into his brain.

Without thought or intention, her body took over and did what was natural.

Reid ran.

An hour later, she was still crouching and shaking in the small forest a short walk from the village. She'd played here as a child, not that long ago, while her parents gathered firewood.

"Rykul, Dragon Staff," she muttered, realizing she had been saying it repeatedly.

She rocked back and forth; her arms wrapped around her knees. The bow lay beside her, and the arrows in the quiver jabbed her in the ribs with each back-and-forth motion.

Reid made herself stop, knowing that moments of crisis were the worst time to panic. She would have time to process and evaluate later, even have a good ugly cry session. Right now, she needed to determine what was going on, and how best to keep herself safe.

"Chuz this," she said, wiping at the tears and snot on her face. "I'm better than this. I've got this. I can do this thing."

Pushing up from the dirt and leaves, Reid stood. Looking towards the west, she saw the sun would set in an hour or two.

She thought about her older sister, who loved hiking and camping. It was never Reid's thing, but her sister loved it. Between having gone with her older sister more than once and her military training, she had a good idea of how to make a campfire, though lighting it may be more of a challenge.

Gathering dry wood, small sticks and large branches, she set about to survive a chilly spring night. She only hoped that it wouldn't rain.

With her family on her mind, she set about her task. Her younger brother, with his gadgets and video games, would've never made it out here.

"Chuz, chuz, chuz," Reid swore, trying to light the wood she'd gathered.

She'd gone camping before, but someone always had a lighter, or those special little things you can light on fire, so it starts the rest of the stuff burning. Reid didn't have those things. She didn't even have matches. Her military training was more than a dozen years ago, and that training had been just a small part of it. She was a pilot, not a grunt.

Another part of her mind, though, knew something. It wasn't her conscious mind; it was that same lingering background process that ran from the village earlier. And it didn't want to freeze to death any more than she did.

Relaxing, she allowed her reflexes to take over. She found rocks, making a ring beside where she'd piled the wood. Reid added a light layer of kindling to the bottom with twigs on top. She watched as her hands worked without guidance, her body knowing exactly what to do to create a fire without any sort of accelerant or source of flame.

Twenty minutes later, Reid sat in front of a crackling campfire. It was small, with the rocks ringed close. She didn't want to light up the night and create a beacon to help anything find her.

She ate some bread, cheese, and meat. Reid only had water to drink. She'd brought tea leaves, but no pot or even a cup to heat in the coals of the fire.

Relieving herself nearby, she returned to the campsite and wrapped herself in the blanket, shivering in the chill spring air, and used her satchel as a pillow.

She was soon asleep.

Reid, waking under a blanket of frost the next morning, had conflicting thoughts as she opened her eyes. And they made her angry.

"Probably good that I'm angry. It'll help get my blood going," she said, shuffling to her feet and wrapping the blanket around herself. "First, I can't believe I'm still here. You don't take naps inside of dreams, it just didn't work that way."

She stamped her feet and moved in a small circle around the cold firepit and her meager belongings. She stretched, shoving her fists into the small of her back and rolling her head around her shoulders, and was rewarded with small popping noises.

"Second, I need to head north to Dragon Staff. Don't know how I know it, but I know it's a city and was once an outpost for the people living in the Wandering Hills. I even know they used to recruit travelers to come to their *secret hideaway*. Seems people like to believe some stupid legend that the town lured people to feed dragons. They'd slaughter the people on an altar and sacrifice them to the dragons, and in exchange, the beasts wouldn't eat the children."

Bending over, she scooped up her satchel, shoving a few things into it, including a double fistful of berries she'd found sometime yesterday.

"Dragons can't be real," she huffed. "A six-limbed reptile never existed. It's a biological impossibility."

The mind of the body she was inside of didn't want to believe they were real, but knew they were.

"Peddlers and tinkers who'd been to Dragon Staff came to the village all the time, and they said it was perfectly safe, like anywhere else. Well, as safe as the world could be nowadays. There were bandits and marauders everywhere, and I'm as likely to be attacked by a roving barbarian tribe as by trolls. But not a dragon."

There was something about Dragon Staff that was important…and the name Rykul. She couldn't remember who, or what, Rykul was, but she knew the name was important.

"That's where I'm going," she said, scooping up her bow and quiver, strapping the latter to her hip, "to Dragon Staff. Maybe I'll stop in Allendale on the way. Get some supplies and maybe some help. And, of course, to warn them of what happened in my village."

She settled her gear, wishing—not for the last time—for the sturdy and practical military belts, pouches, and packs. With a deep breath, she set out across the untamed wilderness between her village and the mythical city.

Chapter 3

The ground rumbled. The long, slow rolling motion made Griffon stumble and Reggie held out a hand to steady him.

"Did you see that?" Reggie asked, going on before Griffon could answer. "The trees outside of town barely moved except for swaying with the wind. The closer ones wobbled like unsteady drinkers reaching for the bar."

"Was that an earthquake?" Griffon shrugged off the hand and looked around.

The two stood in front of a clothier's booth in the shopping district of Allendale. Reggie insisted on getting both of them new clothes. People clustered in small groups looking up at the buildings, echoing the same discussion as the two men.

"It'll be okay," Reggie said, speaking to the woman running the booth as much as he was Griffon. "Let's just get a couple extra shirts for me, then we can go find you some new armor before going back to the Thirsty Prophet."

The gnome squinted up at Reggie.

"Changing the subject, eh? Okay, I get it. In that case, here's something; I don't know why we're staying in this dusty, tired town instead of the Citadel," Griffon complained, hooking his thumbs into his belt, and glaring at the maroon shirt Reggie was holding up to his chest. "Aiyana gave that to us to use, so we didn't need to pay for inns. And it's my fight money we're using."

"She gave it to me, not us. And we're using my money also," Reggie said absently, "you're just not used to earning money, so it makes you antsy to spend it."

"Because I lived with my parents, back home?" Griffon huffed. "I had jobs. I had lots and lots of jobs."

"But you never kept them very long," Reggie stopped, sighing. "I don't want to go through this again. We're staying in town because this is where we hear about things going on. Find the next clue to do what we need to do. The only thing I hear in the Citadel is you complaining and that wheezing snore you do. I told you to get your nose set after that goblin broke it."

"Chicks dig scars, and the broken nose makes it hard to smell your funk. And I don't know why it's our responsibility to fix this," Griffon mumbled. "We didn't make this happen."

"The women love a hero," Reggie said, changing tactics, "and the men love buying drinks for a famous gladiator. You're a bit of a legend, and since you hired that musician to write songs about you, the stories of you are traveling even further and faster."

"Yeah," Griffon said wistfully, "they do love me, don't they? And it was a bard. Ugh, I hate bards. Most annoying class in the game."

Reggie rolled his eyes and collected his shirts.

"I'll take these," he said to the merchant, "lovely stitching. I can see real craftsmanship in these, even though I think the sleeves are different lengths. Now, let's talk about price…"

While Reggie haggled, Griffon wandered away to look at the Silversmith in the next shopfront. The town had recently been rebuilt, and the shops had stalls built into the front of their small buildings. The inside was where the crafters and artisans eat, slept, and worked. The outside was for selling. On rainy days, some would let folks inside, but most didn't want strangers in their homes and businesses.

"That man loves to try and get a bargain," Griffon muttered. "It's like going yard sale-ing with my grandma. Can't he just pay what they're asking, and we can go get a steak and some fried potatoes?"

Griffon looked over the craftsman's wares without really seeing the jewelry and trinkets. He turned towards the street, his gaze gliding over the people. The clumps of townsfolk were breaking up and returning to their regular errands, the earthquake forgotten.

He watched them the same way he'd watch pats—*or patrols for the newbs*, he thought—moving along their predetermined routes programmed by the game designers.

This is one of the best video games ever, Griffon thought. *I've never seen such detail. Like, I know the NPCs do the same thing over and over, but it's a daily routine with slight variations programmed in, instead of a thirty-second loop.*

It's not a game, Raven Stealer, Griffon's magical blade made of unicorn horns, said telepathically. *But I guess it doesn't do any good to keep telling you that again and again. Sometimes I think you just continue with that delusion to frustrate me.*

Griffon smiled and looked up at the cloudless spring sky, drawing in a deep breath of crisp, cool air and letting it out slowly. Movement on a balcony across the street caught his eye, and he turned to see a burly man with a crossbow held at his side.

The man gestured at someone or something down the street with his free hand. He held up two fingers, then pointed at the stall where Reggie was bargaining with the shirt woman.

Holding onto a gutter for balance and climbing atop a rain barrel, Griffon peered in the direction the man had pointed. Two more men, both with clubs, walked in his direction. Turning back to the balcony, he saw the man lift his crossbow and aim at Reggie.

"Aw, hell," Griffon muttered, jumping to the ground.

Pushing through the crowd—a challenge with his smaller size—he swam against the current of foot traffic to get to Reggie. Glancing over his shoulder, he saw people clearing out of the way for the two toughs.

"They're gonna get to him before me," Griffon said, jumping up and down, trying to see his friend. "I need to warn him!"

Wiggling and leaping like a trout in a river, Griffon tried to catch Reggie's eye. The man was leaning over, tracing a finger down the seams of a different shirt, then pointing at the ones he was purchasing. Griffon couldn't be heard over the street noise and wasn't being seen.

"Screw this bidj," the gnome muttered.

Griffon had been learning from tomes in the Citadel. He'd started reading the books out of boredom, without much to do during the winter while on the road hunting an urban legend. Griffon enjoyed being the tank at the front of the fight, not some squishy mage hiding in the back, but he found some fun things in the spell books, so it felt different. He couldn't do much, but apparently gnomes had a knack for mind magics, specifically illusions. Calling on what he'd learned, the same sort of thing he used in the arena, he constructed an auditory illusion and targeted one of the burly men heading for Reggie.

A shrill, high-pitched scream—*The "Wilhelm Scream"*, Griffon thought proudly—cut through the murmur of the marketplace crowd, and Griffon giggled. Everyone turned toward the sound, parting like a book folding open, including Reggie.

Griffon didn't bother drawing Raven Stealer from his back. "You need to know your audience," he muttered, "and in a street brawl you don't use a sword. It's not right."

He slid one hand into a studded gladiator glove, wriggling the cestus into place, and the other into a set of brass knuckles. That was street fighting gear, and the crowd would love it.

The townsfolk moved away from the burly men with clubs, who stalked forward, looking mean. Griffon turned, looking for his friend. Reggie tossed coins to the woman and stuffed the shirts into his satchel. He casually stepped to the next booth—a farrier—and pulled a riding crop and a horseshoe from the secondhand goods table. He flexed the crop, swished it through the air, and nodded. Tucking the horseshoe into his belt, he flipped a coin to the proprietor.

Stepping into the street, Reggie held the crop in front of him at an angle like a fencing blade, facing the oncoming ruffians.

"What's this all about, gentlemen?" Reggie asked.

The men exchanged looks and stopped a half dozen paces from Reggie.

Griffon, still unnoticed, stayed close to the shops and crept moved nearer.

"We owe you," the taller, bearded man growled, "and we're going to take it out of your hide."

"No need for all that," Reggie smiled. "I'm sure you can just pay me what you owe and be on your way without the need for violence."

"You talk too much," the shorter man with a bushy moustache said, raising his club and taking a step forward.

"Wait!" Reggie held up his empty hand, causing the men to hesitate. "Wouldn't you like to get the rest?"

"The rest of what?" Moustache asked, cocking his head.

"He means the rest of our men," Beard growled. "Pretty full of himself, this one is. A good beating, and a broken jaw, should make him use less words."

"Have it your way," Reggie sighed.

Taking two long strides, the swashbuckler swished the riding crop through the air, smacking Beard across the face, across the throat with the backhand, and ended with a flourish, bringing it down on the big man's wrist.

With a yelp, Beard dropped his club.

Moustache barreled forward, and Griffon threw himself into the man's path and hunkered down. Moustache went head over teakettle, landing face first on the hard-packed dirt of the street.

Griffon leapt to his feet, throwing his arms wide as if he'd just performed a magic trick. The crowd laughed, and a few cheered. The townsfolk had formed a ragged circle around the spectacle, always eager for a distraction from their hard lives. Griffon knew that, and played upon it, hoping to grow his legend a little bit more.

Reggie stepped on the Moustache's hand and the crowd gasped as the audible crunching of bones was heard. The thug released his club, screeching and sounding a lot like the "Wilhelm Scream" Griffon conjured earlier.

Pivoting on the man's hand, Reggie pulled the horseshoe from his belt with a twirl and a spin and punched the man in the temple with it.

With a thick groan, Moustache went limp.

Turning to Beard, Reggie laid about the man's head and shoulders with the crop, leaving angry red streaks in a half dozen places. The man backpedaled, hands held up defensively, then turned to run.

"That should take care of what's owed," Reggie said smugly, then stumbled backwards in surprise, shoved backwards by Griffon.

Leaping up in front of Reggie, Griffon raised his cestus and a thunk sounded. Turning with a grin, the gladiator showed the crowd—and Reggie—the still quivering crossbow quarrel protruding from the spiked glove.

"What the hell was that?" Reggie said from the ground, looking around the crowd for the missing attacker.

"You missed one," Griffon pointed at the balcony where the third man was desperately reloading. "And you stole my thunder, jerk. I was going to put on a show for the crowd and get free drinks all night."

Reggie wasn't listening. He rose to his feet, tossed his horseshoe up and down in his hand as if testing the weight, then cocked his arm back and threw it. The iron shoe arced through the air and hit the shooter on the bridge of his nose. The man fumbled the now loaded crossbow, dropped it, tripped over it, stumbled against the rail, and toppled over the side. He landed on his back in the street, air whooshing out of him.

"And…" Griffon drew out the word, "you just did it again!"

"Indeed, I did." Reggie smirked. "Wouldn't have been sportsmanlike to just let him shoot me, would it have now?"

"Whatever," Griffon grumbled.

"I think we should depart now, though," Reggie said, craning his neck and looking around, "there isn't much by way of constables here, but someone will come looking to find who raised the rabble."

Griffon hesitated, watching the man with the broken hand crawling to the shooter. "Shouldn't we find out who these guys are first?" he asked.

"They are the Bounty Hunters of Kresk," Reggie said matter-of-factly, "and I suspect they'll send more men soon enough. We should be gone before that happens, as well."

"Oh," Griffon said, and followed Reggie dejectedly, "okay. But you do use a lot of words. Kinda annoying, you know?"

"To coin the legendary gladiator," Reggie said smugly, "whatever."

The two pushed through the thick crowd of onlookers and rapidly moved away. The townsfolk cleared a path.

"Move boy," a middle-aged man growled, jerking a young lad out of Griffon's way, "we're not wanting to upset the two who took out three thugs in a matter of moments, are we now?"

"Assassins," Griffon corrected the man, leaning close and loudly whispering conspiratorially, "and there was a half dozen more in the shadows we took out before these five.”

“I only saw three,” said the boy.

“That’s because the others are mage assassins and are—well, were—invisible,” Griffon said over his shoulder, “and we stopped them from killing three very important people. No, don’t thank us, it’s what we heroes do!”

He shouted the last sentences over his shoulder, and Griffon grinned as the buzz of a swarm of rumors took flight in the crowd.

“Why lie to them, Griffon?” Reggie sighed. “Was that really necessary?”

“People love a good story,” Griffon said, mimicking the tone Reggie often took, “and they need heroes in these dark days, sir. I am just giving them what they need and want.” He switched back to his normal, high-pitched, squeaky voice. “That’s something I learned from you.”

“Yes,” Reggie sighed again, rolling his eyes, “I picked up on that implication.”

A few turns later, Reggie stopped at a tanner’s booth. “Care to get some new armor made?” he asked.

“You know that’ll take a week or more?” Griffon huffed. “Do we have that kind of time?”

“No,” Reggie shrugged, “but we can return in a week and pick it up. If my gut is correct, we’ll have this current mystery solved and be free to come back.”

An hour later, after Griffon had been measured and sized, and Reggie had haggled over the price, the two headed for the Thirsty Prophet.

The inn was on the southern edge of Allendale and was the first they’d come across when entering town. It had been clean enough, and with reasonable prices, so Reggie decided they'd stay there.

"You know," Reggie was prattling on about the name of the inn, "they named this place after a famous prognosticator, Emerald the Drunk, who could never predict the future without first imbibing substantial amounts of spirits. He said he needed to first take in spirits before he could speak to spirits."

The blond man laughed at his own joke.

"They say he would predict the future of anyone who bought him a drink," Reggie went on, "and always had plenty of cups to help him. There was one time a troop of a Baron's men came in on their way to a campaign and bought him three bottles. They say that the things he told them led to…"

Reggie trailed off, his brisk walking pace slowing to a stop as he stared up at the clear spring sky.

"Led to what?" Griffon asked. "I usually don't care about your stories, but you can't stop there. What did it lead to?"

Reggie didn't answer, continuing to stare at a massive flock of small birds darting and spinning over the town.

"Birds?" Griffon asked. "Did you stop because they're making so much noise you didn't think everyone would be able to hear your long-winded tale?" He said the last few words in a tone mimicking Reggie's way of talking.

"They're storm swallows," Reggie pointed at the dance of the flock.

"Yeah? So?" Griffon pressed. "What about it?"

"They predict storms," Reggie said slowly, "but do you see a cloud in the sky?"

"You think it's because we were just talking about predicting the future, that these birds mean something?"

"No, but I do see where the mind might make that connection." Reggie shook his head. "Animals, you see, have a way of sensing things that you and I cannot. These particular avians excel at knowing when there has been a catastrophic change in the atmosphere, thus their name. I'm just wondering what has them all atwitter."

"Maybe Elon Musk…" Griffon smirked, and a dull rumble from the south interrupted him. He turned to look, frowning. "Another earthquake?" he suggested.

Reggie wrinkled his brow and squinted toward the sound.

"I don't think so—" his words were cutoff as a plume of earth exploded upward to the southeast, followed by a dozen others. Soil rained down in those areas and black clouds rose from scars in the land.

"What's that?" Griffon pointed at something moving.

A lone figure was running towards them. They looked exhausted and had been running for a while.

"It's a…woman," Reggie said, confused. "We should help her!"

"Why?" Griffon asked.

But Reggie was already sprinting towards the figure and didn't answer.

"Pemtie chivalry," the gnome muttered. "It's gonna get him killed someday. I miss Aiyana."

Griffon sighed and started after his companion, knowing there was no way he could keep up with the man's long strides. He'd just have to catch up.

A few minutes later he did, and Reggie had his arm around a dirty, ragged woman who carried a bow and limped. The two continued to run right past the gnome.

"What?" Griffon shouted. "Why are we still running? There's nothing chasing her!"

"Bugs," the woman panted, "are coming."

Griffon jogged to run beside the two, able to keep up because of the woman's exhaustion and injuries.

She was bleeding from a dozen bite marks on her arms and face.

"Those must be some damn mean mosquitos!" Griffon laughed.

"Those explosions we saw," Reggie said between breaths, "weren't an earthquake. They were geysers of insects. Now, run! We need to warn the town!"

The three did just that, running for the town.

Griffon looked over at the two, holding onto one another, and snorted at the difference.

Reggie was tall and lean, blond and clean. His white shirt and burgundy doublet were unstained, and his magical blade—Marcid—was a work of art. Even his satchel was tidy, made from golden leather with a dozen pockets.

The woman was a bit chubby, covered with dirt and scratches, and wore a ripped peasant dress. Her bow looked well worn, and even her sling bag was made of coarse burlap, and the stitching looked ready to split.

They made it to where a crowd had gathered behind the waist-high wall circling the edge of town, many of the people pointing behind the trio. Bells rang, and the crowd went into a panicked frenzy, running back into the safety of Allendale.

Griffon looked over his shoulder to see what had them all worked up.

The dark plumes over the pockmarks in the ground where the eruptions occurred were joining together, and they could hear a distant buzzing. Swarms of insects rose into the sky, blocking out the sun. The smaller cloud of storm swallows darted away to the west.

A line of tall, thin humanoids formed in the distance; their six limbs jointed in multiple places. Faceted eyes sparkled on their flat, oval heads as they dropped to four of their six limbs and charged forward.

Both things were coming straight at Allendale.

Chapter 4

"I guess you won't be using your new riding crop for this fight, will you, Reggie?" the gnome asked.

"No, Griffon, I will not," Reggie answered, "but I hope the locals decide that this is a fight worth getting involved in. I can't defend a whole town against a score of insect men and a sky full of droning monstrosities."

Reid watched the two, recognizing the banter. They were part of the same troop, but only Reggie had any actual experience. He was trying to relay the gravity of the situation to the little guy—Reggie had called him Griffon—without making him panic. Reggie was also ready to run rather than die on this literal hill.

"Go," the blond man turned, flapping a hand at the gawking bystanders, "get help and return with weapons, if you want your town to survive this."

Reggie was military of some sort, and probably a commander. This other guy, this gnome, he was not. He was loose and scattered, and didn't think to watch his partner's six, or think that his partner would cover his.

"What's your name, anyway?" Griffon asked.

"LT," Reid snapped without thinking.

"Elle Tee?" Griffon cocked his head and wrinkled his brow. "Are you really countryfied, and is that sweet tea, or is that initials? What do they stand for? Lotsa teeth? Liquid toast? Lava tongue?"

"Lieutenant," Reid said dryly, eyeing the small man.

"What?" Reggie asked, "And you go by the initials for a military rank? And I swear that was an American pronunciation. You're from Earth, eh?"

"Yes sir," Reid nodded, still looking at Griffon.

"What?" Griffon asked, smiling coyly. "Can't take your eyes off this steaming hot hunk of man meat?"

"Nope, sure can't." Reid said, surprising Griffon and Reggie. "And right now, I'm trying to decide if I should throw you on the ground and; one, jump your bones and have hot, sweaty sex in front of everyone; two, beat the living bidj out of you; or three, tickle you until you pee yourself, because you remind me of my baby brother. Now, and when he was an actual baby."

Both men stared at what they had thought was a quiet and meek woman for long seconds, then Reggie burst out laughing.

"Well done, LT," he said, wiping away tears from his eyes, "in one fell swoop you've shown that you were indeed a military, um, person, showed you won't put up with any lip, and brought laughter to what is otherwise and extremely tense situation."

"Thanks," her mouth quirked up in a sardonic smile, "I try."

"We only have a few minutes before the enemy arrives. Can you use that bow?" Reggie pointed at the unstring weapon.

"Yeah," she nodded. "I'd prefer a nine mil, but beggars can't be choosers."

"Personally, I like a nice pump-action shotgun, or a semi-auto rifle when I'm playing an FPS," Griffon added.

"FPS? What's that?" Reggie asked.

"First-person shooter," Reid said, still holding Griffon's gaze, "it's a type of game where you see from the eyes of the character instead of watching from outside of the body. And I was talking about real life, griefer, not some game. But when I do play FPS's, I like a nice long range sniper rifle. No need to run into a spray of bullets and blood. Only a pemtie would do that. But if that isn't available, give me something with a nice, tight three-round burst."

"Fine," Reggie interrupted their stare down, "let's get on with it then, shall we?"

Griffon looked away first, and Reid smirked, pretty sure she liked this kid. She thought she might have to smack him in the mouth a couple times over the next week or so, but she liked him.

"We just need to hold them off until the town militia arrives," Reggie explained, "or they get too close and we're about to be overrun."

"You were military also?" Reid asked, and Reggie nodded. "Where'd you serve?"

"About a century before you," Reggie smirked at her confused look. "I'll explain it all later. Now's not the time for this conversation."

"Great," Reid nodded. "I'll follow your lead this time, and when we have that conversation, we can also discuss who should be in charge."

Reggie's eyes widened a bit, then he recovered and nodded. Outlining the plan in a few sentences, he drew Marcid, Griffon drew Raven Stealer, and Reid strung her bow.

Townsfolk arrived armed with bows, spears, clubs, and a few swords. Someone handed Reid an extra quiver of arrows to supplement her dwindling supply, then the battle started.

Griffon leapt the battlement and charged into the enemy, swinging, as Reggie shouted at him to stay with the line.

Archers launched arrows high, cutting into the ranks of the enemy, and the line of townsfolk without bows shifted nervously in anticipation of joining the fight.

A dozen new men and women came out of the town, all older and dressed in commoner's clothes, but most holding wands or staves.

"Spellslingers," Reggie said when Reid looked at them curiously, "and probably the town elders or council or something like that."

Soon enough, the group proved him right as they waved their hands and guided stones, knives, and other objects into the attacking force.

Reid wasn't sure if they used telekinetic abilities, or just wind magic, but they were as effective as any militia she'd ever seen.

Within ten minutes, they had decimated the swarms of insects, the ground troops routed—all with minimal injury to the townsfolk—and the newcomers calling for a town meeting in the square.

"We expect you to be there," a grey-haired woman said, pointing at Reggie, Griffon, and Reid, "we like to know who helps our little town in a time of need, and why you'd do such a thing."

The meeting took almost an hour to organize, and the sun was high overhead by the time the elders began speaking.

"We want to reassure you, good people of Allendale," the grey-haired woman who'd spoken to the group earlier said, "that this was a fluke. A random occurrence, and that we will face any further threats together if need be."

Her voice had been amplified—by magic, Reid guessed—so everyone within a couple of blocks could hear.

"It wasn't random," Reid shouted, projecting so they heard her, using her command voice from years in the military. "These things destroyed my village between here and Akar. And I believe they're gathering to go north to Dragon Staff."

The surrounding crowd murmured, shifting uncomfortably, and all heads turned to the woman.

"There will be more," Reid continued, "and you need to be prepared."

The older woman and the gathered elders focused on the woman.

"We will be fine," the woman waved a hand, and the crowd murmured agreement, "but I encourage you to come to me if you have concerns and discuss them in private, rather than causing a panic with unfounded guesses." She said the last sentence in a tight, pointed tone, and the elder looked directly at Reid.

"Understood," Reid said, nodding once. "I will do that."

Another elder stepped forward and began speaking of how the town had always stuck together, and with the leadership of the mind mages had always been safe.

"Come on," Reid growled to Reggie and Griffon, "we need to step aside until they're done here. Then we need to follow them to wherever they meet."

"Hmph," Reggie made a non-committal grunt.

"Why?" Griffon asked, and the two looked at him. He went on. "Why should it be *we?* I mean, it wasn't we who talked to them. It was you. And we just met, and you expect us to just follow you around now? What's that all about?"

"Ah," Reggie held up a finger, forestalling any response from the woman, "allow me to explain it to him, please?"

Reggie waited for her to nod, then turned to the gnome.

"She's from Earth," he whispered, "and we're drawn together from what I've come to understand. We probably need to stick together on this one. Think of it as a quest thing in one of your games."

"Okay!" Griffon said, upbeat. "Makes sense to me."

"That easy, huh?" Reid said.

"Imma easy kinda guy, LT," Griffon winked at the woman.

Two hours later, they stood in front of a table in a large room, the twelve spellslingers sitting behind it, and a thirteenth man sitting on a raised platform in the middle. A handful of other people were in attendance, lingering in groups of two or three at the edges of the room. The grey-haired woman who'd spoken to them before stood and put her palms flat on the table, leaning out towards the small assembly.

"Most of you know me," she began, "but for the few who don't, I am Talien, second of the Council of Elders here in Allendale. The chief elder is Birch…"

She gestured to the ancient man on the raised seat in the center. "…but I will be leading this meeting. We will begin by hearing from the young lady who spoke in the town square. What is your name?"

"I am," Reid hesitated, "LT. And I know I don't look like it, but I have experience in war. These creatures, these bug-men, attacked my village and killed everyone there. I don't know why, but I feel they are heading for Dragon—"

"My god would never sanction such actions!" A man from the back of the room said, stepping to the center of the room, his words crisp and precise.

"Priest Kriksi," Talien said, "you will get a chance to speak, but we need to hear from these three first."

The priest nodded sharply, and took one step back, but didn't return to his place at the edge of the room.

"Now, you young man," Talien gestured at Reggie, "I believe you were involved with an altercation in the merchant's row earlier today. You and your gnome friend. What is your place in all this? How do you know this woman?"

"I am Reg…" Reggie hesitated as he took a step forward, then started again. "I am Kazzek Tel Virian, and this is Auric, the—"

"Griffon," Griffon interrupted. "I prefer to be called Griffon. Auric is just my gnomish name from my gladiator days. But I'm a lot more than that now."

"Fine, Griffon," Reggie went on with a sigh, "but you may have heard of us?"

"No," Talien shook her head, "should we have heard of you?"

"No, not necessarily," Reggie shrugged, "but it would have made things immeasurably easier if you had. To answer your questions, our place in this is that we try and help people and the world around us. The fight in the street was about me doing that. And I had never met this woman before coming to her aid as she ran from the attacking horde."

"Horde?" Kriksi snorted. "That's a bit of an exaggeration."

"Swarm?" Griffon suggested. "Gaggle?"

"To go on," Reggie raised his voice to talk over the other two, "I am seeking the source of a disease. A very dangerous and serious affliction that creates the lost folk, undead who become so without dying first."

"That has nothing to do with Khelikian!" Kriksi barked. "My god, the god of insects, devours the dead. She doesn't create them! These creatures were nothing I know of and did not belong to Khelikian."

"And did Khelikian have nothing to do with the swarms of giant insects during the Downfall?" Reggie spun to face the man. "Did she not create and help the mutant bugs who spat acid, burst into flames, and destroyed entire cities?"

"That was an effect of the Talisman, not Khelikian!" Kriksi spat back.

"You really wanna blame this on a comet?" Griffon sniggered. "Gods are gods and do whatever they want. They're always fighting for power between each other."

"Stop!" Talien's voice echoed throughout the chamber. "I will not have this meeting fall to bickering and accusation. This council is concerned with one thing, and one thing only. The safety of this community."

She turned to Kriksi.

"You will remain quiet until called upon," she said, quieter, "and even then, you will choose your words carefully. We know the god of insects helps with crops and soil, but she also destroys them when she sees fit. And you…"

Talien turned to address Griffon.

"…will remain silent. Your comments are not helpful. Kazzek Tel Virian, you will state your case quickly and succinctly or be removed. If you have anything further, speak your piece."

"Well," Reggie breathed, then sighed, "just that I am going into the Great Desert to find Ez'rainia-fromton to put an end to the contamination started there. That's about it."

The council studied the three in the center of the room for a long moment before Talien spoke.

"Sir," she said, "I wish you luck in your endeavors. We will do what we can to help you, for whatever you accomplish can only help us. But neither you nor your small friend seem like you are in this for the right reasons. Ah, wait before you answer. I am a mind mage and have a sense about people. I think you are both in this for the thrill or some other frivolous reason. Neither of you is the type to truly risk everything for the world. As for the young woman, it seems to me she'd be better if she stayed here and settled down rather than running off into the wilderness with you two."

She looked across the table at the small group, her lips drawn together.

"Then I believe we are finished here," Talien sat back down in her chair and folded her hands on the table, "and you are all dismissed."

"Ma'am?" Reid said, raising her hand. "May I add something?"

Talien looked at Reid, then nodded. "You may, LT. But keep it short and to the point."

"Is there a place or a person to the north named Rykul?"

"The Great Bear?" Talien leaned back, confused.

"Maybe," Reid shrugged, "but I had a…vision. Something about Rykul, and Dragon Staff—"

"Child," Talien interrupted, "Rykul was killed during the Downfall. He no longer exists in the Valley of the Bear, and all entrances into that place collapsed."

They dismissed and escorted the three to the Thirsty Prophet. Sitting around a table, sharing a meal, they ate without speaking.

"LT?" Reggie broke the silence.

"Hm?" Reid looked over at Reggie, raising an eyebrow, one elbow on the table and her hand supporting her chin.

"Will you join us on our mission?" Reggie asked.

"Like," Griffon said, "what else is she going to do? Wander around a strange new world, like someone on Star Trek who got left behind by the Enterprise? Go on a five-year mission of Discovery to seek out—"

"Okay," Reid elbowed the gnome, "we get it."

"I don't get it," Reggie said. "Was that another one of those 'pop-culture' references?"

"Yes, and don't worry about it," Reid said. "The gnome is a pemtie. As for me, well, I still think we should discuss going north. I think it has something to do with all this. But I guess I'll go along with you. I know deserts pretty well and might even be of some use to you."

Griffon opened his mouth to say something, but the door banged open. A tall, thin man bracketed by six rough-looking men stood in the doorway, framed by the setting sun. He sauntered in, tugging at the lace frills at the end of his jacket cuffs.

"Kazzek," Dandy Rym said, "You need to leave for Akar and points south, immediately! I have heard some new information that insists on all urgency!"

Chapter 5

Ahken'ho-tek stood staring at the massive stone map table, his eleven advisors arrayed around him. A thin layer of sand covered the surface, tiny figures representing troops piled to one side. A touch of magical energy would imitate any area from the maps arrayed and displayed on the walls.

The Lord of the Liches of Ez'rainia-fromton looked at the four map-covered walls, pausing a moment to study the doorway leading to the throne room. His throne since Verl'zen-luk betrayed him, the liches surrounding him, and the entire city, leaving them trapped in a prison designed for him.

He looked at the wall with the oval showing the continents of Aetheria, small plumes of smoke rising from volcanoes, and the solid mass of clouds rotating around the Regressed Continent in the southern hemisphere. His gaze wandered to the next wall and the map of Teurone, the continent they were currently on. It showed mountains and plains, as well as points of interest, including the Silver Keep, Highest Spire, the Valley of the Bear, and the Nine Towers of Magic. The last location was where the thieves had fled to, seeking to reverse machinations put into play in ages past.

Looking at the third wall, Ahken'ho-tek studied the local region. The Great Desert, the Straight River fed by the High Tarn, the Lost Lands, the Wandering

Hills, and everything else surrounding Ez'rainia-fromton. The map had changed in the ages since Ahken'ho-tek had slept. The last wall showed the ley lines intersecting with magical points, cities, well-travelled roads, rivers, and other natural features. It also showed concentrations of other magics, down to pinpoint lights of powerful magical artifacts, such as the two that the looters now possessed.

This map room was the same room, off the center of the throne room, that the pillagers had stolen the Scepter Key from. That single action had woken Ahken'ho-tek and his fellow liches, along with everything else in this cursed place, but had also locked them inside. But it didn't lock their magical energies in. Those had reached out and influenced the world.

Kenal, Master of Minions, lurched forward and pointed at the map.

"Are we ready to launch the attack?" Kenal asked, his voice echoing in the room and Ahken'ho-tek's head.

That was the thing about undead wielders of arcane forces, they had a flair for the dramatic. But it was also necessary since their vocal cords and internal organs were long desiccated.

"Yes, Kenal," Ahken'ho-tek's voice didn't echo, instead it was a dry, rasping hiss, "set the portal totems, and release the first wave upon Allendale. The enemies of the Empire shall feel our wrath again."

Six liches moved to the table to assist the Master of Minions control his enslaved army, and four watched Ahken'ho-tek, waiting to follow his lead.

The master of the long-dead empire turned and swept out of the room, moving with a grace that the others could not achieve or imitate.

Venat-fal glided beside the master, her ghostly hands clasped and her head bowed under a tattered hood.

"My Lord," the lesser lich said, her voice wispy and musical, "shall I set the workers to task?"

Ahken'ho-tek ignored her, crossing the columned throne room and taking in the chamber that housed the seat of power of a dead empire, ruled by the dead. Crystals set in the stone walls and columns glimmered, and dispersed beams of light throughout the massive space.

He'd only been awake for a few months after centuries of sleep. He couldn't remember if he slept like a living person, or if it was the sleep of the dead. He thought he'd had dreams, or memories, or his mind working while the magics of the enemy mages entrapped him, but he couldn't be sure.

Now that he'd been awakened, he no longer needed sleep or rest of any sort. He spent every available hour constructing his future, making the plans that would free him, and building resources for the next steps into the larger world outside.

He took his time ascending the steps to the throne and settling into the stone seat. Arranging his robes, Ahken'ho-tek stared down at the four liches arrayed before him, studying them.

Venat-fal was Mistress of the Stables, what they called the dull and dumb shambling dead that did the mundane, grunt tasks. She was devious, always waiting in the background for a chance to further her station.

Lepat-fal was thick, even in death, his robes gleaming with the illusion of opulence. The Master of the Unseen controlled the wraith-like beings who drained energies from the living to feed the liches and their spells.

A smaller lich grinned up at him with broken teeth. Telvak-ral always appeared eager for everything. He almost lusted for life again and was the youngest of the dead lords. He was the Guardian of the Tomes, a library of collected magical knowledge. A dusty and boring job he relished, and it made Ahken'ho-tek wonder if he'd discovered some tidbit of information and was withholding it.

The final lich waiting for his command at the foot of the throne was Chektar-ral. She appeared almost alive, her hair shining with a golden hue, though tarnished. Her magics directly tied into the ley lines, giving her the title and duties of Mistress of the Leys.

"Yes, Venat-fal, set the workers to task," Ahken'ho-tek rasped. "Send them to the furthest reaches of our tomb and have them continue clearing the entrances, so once we are able to walk the land once again, we will have no obstacles."

"The bait is set, Master," Lepat-fal said, "and the man named Reginald shall seek us to free us. He is obsessed with the visions my vessel, Thomas, set into his mind. We shall be free soon."

Ahken'ho-tek waved a hand at the lich, dismissing the statement.

"We have waited this long," the Lord of Ez'rainia-fromton hissed, "another few weeks is nothing. The final part of my plans is in motion. Now, go and leave me to consider our first conquest in the lands of the living."

The advisors left the throne room and Ahken'ho-tek waved an intricate pattern in the air. A rift appeared, a misty window showing the rolling hills around a community settling down in the twilight.

The ground erupted, and thick, dark totems grew from the holes. A swarm of hungry sturine—cat-sized, mosquito-like creatures—rose into the evening sky, angling towards the smell of people and blood. The six-limbed bug-men, vriktiri, climbed from the tunnels underneath, clambering towards the unsuspecting town of Allendale.

Dandy Rym leaned back, belching, and holding up his mug to the serving maid for a refill. His bevy of bodyguards sat at a table near the door, finishing off a platter of lamb and potatoes.

"Well, Reggie?" The fop looked across the table.

"You say, one," Reggie raised a hand and ticked off fingers, "there are undead rising in the south, coming out of the Great Desert. Two, people in Akar have been seen turning into lost folk. Three, spellslingers report huge amounts of energy being used in the desert."

Dandy nodded, rubbing his full belly.

"And that these undead are protected from magic by some force," Dandy Rym said, leaning forward, "and the further away they get from the desert, the harder they are to kill with magic."

"That doesn't make any sense," Griffon said. "You'd think they'd be tougher the closer they are to whatever is in the desert."

"Liches," Reggie muttered, clenching his pipe in his teeth and puffing, "but they may be using all the arcane energies in the area for themselves, so any walking corpses get stronger when further away from them."

"So now you're a wizard, or sorcerer, or whatever, and know about these sorts of things?" Griffon snorted. "I still say it doesn't make sense."

"I think we should get ahead of them," LT said. "Go north and see what we find there."

"No, woman!" Dandy slapped his hands on the table. "That just gives them the chance to get stronger and add to their army as they invade villages and towns."

LT stared at the man, clenching her jaw, and gripping the table.

The rest of the common room of the Thirsty Prophet had moved away from the group and the loud discussion. The townsfolk whispered in small groups, but stayed quiet enough to listen to the strangers' conversation, as well. The barkeep and serving maids gathered in a cluster near the kitchen in a heated debate, pointing toward Reggie and his table.

"It's like turning off a tap, I think," Reggie said, "if we can get to the source and stop it, cut off the head of the snake, as it were…"

Reggie's words trickled off, and he tilted his head, listening to something outside. He heard screams moments before the warning bells began ringing at the edge of the town.

"Attack from the south!" came a shout from the street. "To arms, defend Allendale, and protect your families!"

Reggie leapt to his feet, pulling his sword belt from the back of his chair and strapping it on.

Griffon sighed and slid from his seat, his hands unconsciously checking his various weapons.

LT stood and looked around uncertainly as she reached for her bow, quiver, and the short spear they had given her after the last battle. They'd also had a fresh shirt and breeches delivered, along with a comb. She'd taken a quick bath while Dandy Rym had ordered his meal, refusing to speak until he'd eaten.

She was a new woman, though still battered, and she stood straighter, her ebony skin and her sharp eyes looking healthier than they had hours before. But she still looked exhausted.

"Dandy," Reggie said, stepping towards the door, "will you and your men join us? Help us defend the town from whatever is coming?"

"Of course," the thin man said, waving the mug at the serving girl again, "let me just wrap up here. I'll pay for the meals, gather my men, and be right behind you."

Reggie looked at the man dubiously, then nodded once and headed for the door. Griffon pattered after him and LT took up the tail end.

Stepping into the night air, Reggie took stock of the situation. A thin fog crept into the streets, coating everything with a cold, clammy layer of moisture. The smell of oil and smoke wafted through the air from torches and lanterns. People ran, shouting, towards the battlement at the edge of town and others herded their families to the larger stone buildings in the center of town.

Drawing his rapier, Marcid, Reggie strode towards the sounds of the fight.

"You know," he said to Griffon, "I don't really want to fight. Never enjoyed it."

"Smart man," LT said, drawing up beside the two, "only a pemtie seeks battle."

"Hey, I like fighting," Griffon said. "It brings me the love of the little people, and I'm good at it. Not good at much else, though."

"Point made," LT grinned. "But I believe if you looked a bit deeper, you'd find you're good at a lot of things. You just don't let yourself do other things."

"I want to help people," Reggie went on with a sigh, "and if it means drawing my sword to do, then so be it."

They reached the battlement, and a line of defenders stood along the short wooden palisade. The ground trembled, and a mound of dirt poured upward at Reggie's feet. He danced backwards, moving out of the way of the dark, wooden totem rising from the earth. The soil erupted, spraying clods and small stones into the air. A hole opened near the base of the totem and an insectile head the size of a football broke through, followed by four arms.

Griffon jumped into the air, landing with both feet on the creature's head, shoving it back down. The gnome fell into the hole, catching the edges with his spread arms.

"Chuz!" he screamed. "Get me out of here! Something's grabbing my feet!"

Reggie and LT reached down, each grabbing one of the gladiator's arms and pulled him free.

Another bug man climbed out of the hole after him, followed by others as the three backpedaled.

Dropping her bow, LT gripped her short spear and thrust it forward. It was clumsy and poorly aimed, and the bug man swept it to one side, then stepped inside her range and grabbed her with two pincers-like hands, pulling her towards its maw.

A silver blade slid into the creature's eye, and Reggie kicked the beast in its midsection, knocking it back.

"Perhaps," Reggie said between thrusts, "string your bow? You have a knack for it, and you can pick them off as they come up from the hole."

LT nodded and moved to where she'd dropped the weapon. She picked it up and struggled to string it.

Griffon went into his offensive form, swinging Raven Stealer, the ivory blade singing as it cut an enemy in half.

Grinning and advancing, Griffon took his time and circled the hole to take out others who'd climbed out.

Pressing his free hand to the pommel of Marcid, Reggie felt the golden leaves of the rapier's swept hilt wrap around his other wrist, and when he pulled it away, he held a main-gauche in his off-hand. Falling into a stance, he slapped away the thin hands of an enemy, and pushed his sword between the chitinous plates of the creature's chest.

Two others came at the swashbuckler from opposite sides, and Reggie hesitated. An arrow sprouted from the midsection of one, and it stumbled backwards.

Nodding in LT's direction, he turned his attention and weapons to the second foe, cutting it down with three quick strikes.

The battle around them was in full force, new totems rising from the earth and new holes pouring enemies into the middle of the defenders. Townsfolk—grouped in threes—fought together, barely holding off the insect invaders.

"They're not killing anyone," Reggie shouted to whoever was in earshot, "they're just wounding."

"Maybe they want them alive for food," Griffon said from directly behind the swashbuckler.

"Ew," LT said from the other side, "but maybe don't say that loud enough for everyone to hear? Bad for morale."

The head of the insect man on Reggie's left exploded.

Looking in that direction, he saw a dozen small stakes tear through four others.

"The mages have arrived," he shouted, louder than before, wanting the townsfolk to hear.

A swarm of sturine dove towards the line of defenders, latching on and piercing a dozen people with sharp proboscises.

The defending line broke, scattering in all directions.

The sturine were wrenched from the townsfolks' bodies by an invisible force, bunched into a ball of squirming black forms, and slowly crushed. Blood and ichor oozed from the mass, and the smell of crushed bugs permeated the area.

The tide turned with the arrival of the mages, and the town's real militia came into the fray in formation, cutting down the invaders in swaths. The bug-men retreated, backing towards the totems, and dropping into the holes they'd emerged from. The three fought alongside the townsfolk until the last of the attackers were dead or disappeared back into the earth.

"That's seals it then," Reggie said, wiping bits of the enemy from his doublet, "we leave for the south as soon as possible. First thing in the morning, if not sooner. I think I'd like to clean up a bit right now, though."

Chapter 6

Descending the stairs, Griffon rolled his shoulders, stretching sore muscles. He slipped a hand behind him and into his waistband, scratching a butt cheek and yawning as he entered the common room. Except for a serving maid and a woman working in the kitchen, the room was deserted.

"Where is everyone?" Griffon asked the young woman, his jaw cracking as he yawned again.

"Well, Griffon," she said, "It is nearly ten of the clock in the morning. You slept quite late after all of your frivolity and shenanigans last evening. The handsome young master, Reginald, has left to answer the summons of the council. The country lass with him toddled after him, as if he'd have any interest in one such as her."

"She's okay," Griffon murmured, climbing up a barstool and sitting. "If I liked women three times my height."

"Right?" The woman giggled, a long and high-pitched noise. "She is freakishly tall, isn't she? I mean, she must be some sort of ogre half-breed."

"Okay, stop." Griffon said, really looking at the woman for the first time. "She's tall, I'm short. That's all I meant. No one's a freak. And she is not a half-breed. There's no need to be like that, alright?"

"Of course," the girl dropped her eyes and gave a small curtsey, "and I didn't mean no harm. Just having a bit of fun is all."

"Whatever, doesn't matter," Griffon sighed. "Let's start over. What's your name, and what is there to eat?"

"My name's Millie, sir. And we still have a bit of porridge in the kitchen."

"Great," the gnome smiled at the woman, his eyes wandering up and down her form, "I'll have that with something sweet. Maybe a bit of cream and honey in it?"

"Very good," she giggled. "I'll go and fetch it right away."

"One more thing," Griffon held up a finger and Millie turned towards the kitchen, "is there a couple slices of ham left over from last night?"

"I can check on that, and if there is, I shall bring it out for you," Millie smiled.

"And…" Griffon stopped her again, "maybe a couple slices of bread with butter, heated over the cook fire."

"Yes, sir," she nodded, then paused. "Anything else?"

"Now that you mention it," Griffon craned his neck over her shoulder to look into the kitchen, "maybe some of the fried potatoes from last night, a few scrambled eggs, a bit of fruit, and a glass of rum on the side?"

"Oh, is that all, then?" Millie raised her eyebrows and put her hands on her hips. "Wouldn't you also like a leg of chicken, and maybe a bit of pie, to go with all that?"

"Sounds great! Add those on also," Griffon slapped his hands together and rubbed them, "but I'll also need a cider to help wash them down!"

The serving maid turned with a huffing noise, her ponytail bouncing as the flounced into the kitchen.

Griffon watched her go, tapping his fingers on the bar top to a rhythm in his head. His mind wandered over the six months since he'd arrived in this world. He missed his world, Earth.

"Well," he drew out the muttered word, "that might be a bit of an exaggeration. I miss my video games and the internet. And toilet paper. And microwave meals. And chips and dips. They don't have that here."

"What's that?" Millie said, sashaying out of the kitchen and setting the porridge on the bar.

"Oh, nothing." Griffon sighed, pulling the bowl and spoon in front of him.

"Don't be so glum, chum," Millie flashed him a big smile. "I got your cider right here."

He settled into his first course as she went back into the kitchen, not even bothering to watch swish and sway her way out of the room. Resting his head against his hand, he spooned the runny oats into his mouth.

He'd been a hero at the Nine Towers. The ladies adored and respected him, especially the rokairn women—though he wasn't too thrilled with their beards. People greeted him warmly, asked him how he was doing, and even invited him to go places or over for meals with their families. It was weird.

Being a gladiator and loved and worshipped by thousands of fans—well, maybe hundreds, or maybe dozens—was better than a few people liking him. So, he'd left with Reggie for parts unknown on another insane quest to save the world.

"I don't care about saving the world," he muttered out loud. "People are pemtie, and most of them are bidj."

"Trying to convince yourself, little man?" Millie asked from behind him, causing him to jump in his seat.

"No." he said defensively. "They are. They always want something, never nice just to be nice."

"Are you?" she asked, winking as she wiped down a table.

He stared at her, spoon halfway to his mouth.

"Well, anyhow," she said, making her way back to the kitchen with a rag in one hand, and a bucket of soapy water in the other, "I'll bring the rest of the food out in a minute, so finish up. I gotta get all the dishes done before the lunch crowd shows up."

Maybe Millie is nice, Griffon thought, making sure not to say it out loud. *Wouldn't do to let her hear me say that, though. And I think she likes me.*

He sat up straighter as she came back into the room carrying a tray laden with steaming plates of food.

"Here you go, sweetie," she said with a smile that made Griffon sit up straight in a different way, "and you can just leave the money for the meal on the bar when you leave. Oh, and the tab for last night for you and your three friends, and that guy's bodyguards."

"What?" Griffon twitched. "Dandy Rym said he was paying for all that."

"But he didn't," she shrugged, "so someone has to pay for it."

She turned to leave, then stopped and looked over her shoulder.

"One more thing," she said, smiling again.

"Yes?" Griffon knew what was coming. She was going to flirt with him again!

"If you see your cute friend," she said with a giggle, "tell him I'll buy his next drink."

Griffon slouched as she sauntered back into the kitchen, humming a tune.

"See?" he said to himself. "Even she wants something."

He'd lost his appetite, but picked a slice of ham and shoved it into his mouth. He ate the meal, though it had lost all flavor, and dumped coins on the counter.

Griffon dropped off the stool, straightened his sword on his back, and stomped out the door. Entering the flow of traffic on the street, ready to swear at anyone who got in his way, he made his way towards the Council Hall and listened to the talk in the street.

Everyone was freaking out about the attack last night, and how a lot of the town was sick now. It was a bad omen and a horrible way to start the new year. This world's calendar started with the month Loen, and the first day of spring. It ended with a month that was neither winter nor spring, Milwen, a month for the thaw, when the weather couldn't decide.

They called it a lunar calendar, with one cycle of the moon each month and twenty-eight in each. They didn't even number the days, instead naming the four weeks. If you asked someone the date, they'd tell you the month, the week, and then the day. And their years were weird too. Griffon knew it was six thousand something, but not the exact year.

Arriving at the building he'd been heading for, Griffon saw Reggie and LT coming out of the double doors.

"Griffon!" Reggie raised a hand in greeting and appeared to be genuinely pleased to see him.

Probably wants something, too. Griffon thought.

"You've arrived at the perfect time," Reggie went on, "but first, did you sleep well and get a good meal before you wandered out to find us?"

"Yeah, I guess." Griffon shoved his hands down along his sides, seeking his pockets, but didn't have any. He settled with hooking his thumbs in his belt.

This is better anyway, he thought, *makes me look tough and heroic.*

"What's going on?" Griffon asked, lifting his chin to strike an even more impressive pose.

"We're heading south as soon as we collect our things from the Thirsty Prophet," Reggie gestured back the way Griffon had come, indicating they should do that now. "They gave LT a few things to help us out. A couple of outfits, new bowstring, that sort of stuff."

Glancing at the woman who was trailing three paces back, watching the crowd like she expected someone to jump her. He saw she had the same shirt, breeches, and spear as last night, but had a new vest, satchel, bracer on her wrist, and a pauldron that covered one of her breasts, all made of leather.

"Why the weird armor?" Griffon asked. "What good is one bracer and armor that only covers a quarter of her…chest?"

"Bows," LT spoke up, drawing closer to join the conversation, "no need for the string to tear the skin on my forearm or pop off a nipple if it catches me."

"Oh," surprised, Griffon stared at the woman's chest.

"Eyes up here, perv," LT grunted, "before I poke them out. With my spear."

"Pfft," Griffon scoffed, "you suck at combat. You showed that last night."

"She may now," Reggie interjected, stalling any confrontation, "but we shall both help her with that on our journey. We shall take turns teaching her the best way to use that spear. I think you will be exceptionally good at the task, being deft with a wide variety of weapons. How do you put it? You have skills!"

"Sure," Griffon said suspiciously, but pulling his shoulders back and unconsciously preening under the praise.

LT raised a hand to cover her mouth and a small laugh, muttering, "Oh, the fragile male ego, so easily soothed and distracted."

Reggie shot her a glance, and she dropped her hand, smiling innocently.

"Yeah, but what about figuring out who would be the leader?" Griffon shot over his shoulder. "I thought you were ex-military and couldn't be under the command of Reggie."

"I'm okay with it," she said. "It only makes sense. He has been here longer, isn't pushy about it, listens to me, doesn't stare at my boobs when I talk, and knows more about the territory and the enemy. I can handle letting him lead. For now."

Reggie laughed and threw the woman a wry smile.

"LT," he said, "when you are comfortable, I will be happy to let you lead. Some people are born leaders, and you may just be one of them. After all, you were able to set your ego aside to accept me in that role for the moment, and that says a lot."

"Why don't you tell him about the reasons behind the plan, Reginald Betancourt?" LT changed the subject in a flat voice.

"Yes, grand suggestion," Reggie nodded.

"You told her your full name?" Griffon asked.

"She wanted to know, and I saw no reason to not tell her," Reggie explained. "I also told her what I know about Kazzek Tel Virian and his history, so she knew what to expect if we ran across someone who knew me, erm, him."

"And what'd you tell her about me?" Griffon glanced sideways at the man.

"Nothing," LT growled. "Said that was *for you to do, and it wasn't his place to reveal what you may not want told to the world.*" She said the last part in a mocking imitation of Reggie, and Griffon laughed.

"That's pretty good," the gnome said. "So, what did I need to know?"

"We travel south, to Akar," Reggie fell into his storytelling voice, "checking to see the condition of the city since no merchant trains have arrived in over a week. We do what we can to help them, and then we continue on to Ez'rainia-fromton."

"Why not just use that portalling stone Aiyana gave you and go straight to the problem? Skip the middleman." Griffon looked up at the swashbuckler.

"Wait." LT stopped in her tracks, looking at Reggie. "You can do that?"

"Yes..." the man stopped also, nodded, and sighed.

"Then why don't we do that?" LT asked. "Short stuff has a point...this time."

"Because, if we can learn more about the enemy by stopping in Akar, and perhaps lend some aid if they are in dire straits, then it is the right thing to do."

LT considered this, then nodded and started walking again.

"Yep," she nodded as the other two caught up. "Sounds reasonable. That's what I like about you, old man. You always think things through."

"Heh," Griffon chuckled, "she called you old man. I do that."

"It comes with age," Reggie said, ignoring his smaller companion. "The years may or may not bring wisdom, but it does show the value of foresight, instead of hindsight. Though the latter has value, as well."

Arriving at the inn, they gathered the rest of their belongings, and headed south under the noonday sun.

Chapter 7

LT's village was in ruin. The three walked down the only road through the collection of buildings, the smell of burnt timbers and the miasma of rotting corpses filling the air. The croak of frogs and the call of birds singing the song of new life, playing counterpoint to the scene.

The trio had walked for two days, journeying south towards Akar and places between the metropolis and Allendale. Reggie had taken to giving lessons in using the short spear to LT whenever they stopped for a rest or meals, transforming Marcid into the same type of weapon.

The ground trembled. Not in the way that preceded the appearance of the totems and an attack, but more like a distant tremor.

Or maybe it's just the world shuddering at what's going on, Reid thought.

"I didn't know them, but I did." She rubbed her hands on her thighs, like she was trying to wipe something off. "Does that even make sense?"

"It does to us," Griffon shrugged.

"I've met many people who knew this body before I inhabited it," Reggie put a comforting hand on the woman's shoulder, "but most of them wanted to kill me."

"Most of them?" Griffon snorted. "Try all of them. Name one who was like, 'Oh, hi Kazzek. How've you been? Watched any good plays lately?' None. That's how many. Zero. Zip. Zilch. Nada."

"Don't be a talleywhacker," Reggie smiled at the small man.

Reid watched the exchange. It was so like her experiences in the Army. Fellow soldiers making fun of one another to help ease the stress and distract themselves from the horrors of war.

She suspected that's one of the many reasons PTSD wasn't apparent when in the field, because you had others there sharing the bad things, and helping pull you out of it with bad jokes. But the psychological wounds were still there, trying to heal. They only became scars, though. Rough mental spots that never smoothed over.

Her mind wandered to Charlie again, her co-pilot. If what these men said was true, then Reid had died. The Blackhawk helicopter—who they'd affectionately called Dilbert because of all the paperwork needing to be filled out before and after each mission—had bucked. Something had happened.

Did it go down? Or was Charlie able to keep it flying? Maybe she crashed but walked away. Or maybe she bailed. That would be okay, too. Reid just wanted Charlie to get back home to her family.

Reid didn't have family. Well, she didn't have a husband or kids. She had her parents, who always seemed disappointed that she took her degrees and joined the military. They'd pointed out that most people go into the service to get the money for a college education, then build a life after.

It hadn't been like that for Reid. She'd done college and excelled at it. Graduated in the top ten percent of her class but didn't want to be an engineer.

Or a therapist. She liked structure, which is what drew her to engineering, and the military offered clear-cut goals.

She excelled at that too, gaining recommendations that got her into flight school and promotions along the way. She'd volunteered to go overseas when the chance came up, because back home she felt like a disappointment to her parents. Not that they wanted her to settle down and give them grandkids, at least not right away. It was much more subtle than that. They were always supportive, but asked why she didn't do things differently.

Movement in Kohn's burnt-out smithy brought her back to the present. Grought, the man who ran the lumbermill, stood in the wreckage. He was pale and gaunt, his sunken eyes staring straight ahead. The blacksmith rose from the ruins behind the stout man, and the two lurched towards the group in the street.

Other forms crept from the ashes of houses and shops, limping into the street. Dozens of figures emerged, still mostly human, but with something very wrong about them.

"Ugh," Griffon said, "it's like that guy from that Stephen King movie with the messed-up animals, Pet Sematary."

Reggie jabbed the gnome in the shoulder with his elbow and drew Marcid from her scabbard.

"Get ready," Reggie said. "Looks like we're about to meet our first lost folk. They aren't just undead—"

"I know, right?" Griffon laughed. "They're all rotted and mumbling brains."

"Griffon," Reggie bit off the word, "not now. Remember, LT is new to all this, and this was her village."

"Yeah, but she wasn't really raised…" the gnome trailed off as he looked at the woman.

Reid was standing stiffly, her arms locked at her sides, staring at the villagers coming towards them.

"LT," Reggie said gently, "they're not the same people you knew. We will release them quickly. Free them so they may have a true death, rather than this half-life they now exist in."

"How do you know?" Griffon asked, this time seriously. "I mean, how do you know it isn't just like a brain disease? Like rabies or something that makes them a little crazy."

"Without a cure," Reggie breathed, "is there another option?"

Watching the people her body had grown up around stumble towards them, hands raising in front of them, vacant looks in their eyes, and drool hanging from slack jaws, Reid froze in place. She didn't really know them, but something deep inside of her did. A flood of half-memories washed over her. Images of moments with each of them. Helping old lady Mazzy carry a bucket. Getting a sweet from Conton at the spring festival. Petting the Vintel's dog when it was watching the sheep.

But now all these people were…dead…ish.

Reid could hear Reggie trying to talk to her friends, but they just kept coming, not responding to any words.

A silver sword flashed across her vision, and Mazzy went down, a cut on her throat oozing black blood. An ivory blade cut down Kohn as the gnome swirled around the man, slicing tendons and muscles in the smith's thick legs.

Then she saw her parents. They were coming out of their blackened hut, her father still wearing his best hunting knife on his hip. Her mother wore that same spring dress Reid had last seen her in, but her jaw hung crooked, knocked to one side.

"LT!" Reggie's voice broke through the fog of memories. "Defend yourself or join them! They can't hear you. They can't reason, remember, or think any longer!"

She realized she'd been shouting the names of the people her new companions were cutting down in front of her, horror locking her into inaction.

Reid had people die before. Not many, but she'd seen it when deployed. But this was different, so very personal. These people never signed up for this. They never asked or volunteered to die.

A flood of rage ripped through the woman, and she pulled it back in with a deep breath.

"I won't lose control," she said through clenched teeth, "not again. Never again."

She lowered her spear and set it at her hip in a two-handed grip like Reggie had shown her, giving her balance and strength. She took a step towards the two people who had raised her. This was like using a rifle with a bayonet. At least that's what she had told the man during training.

But it wasn't. It wasn't anything like that. She never stabbed someone she knew and loved.

The thought struck her, and she stopped for a moment. She didn't know these people any more than she knew the characters from the TV show Friends.

She grasped at that idea, putting these memories into the context of a favored series. Now she could do what needed to be done. She'd cancel the series.

Bending her knees, she thrust her spear upward into the chin of the man who *wasn't* her father, though it felt like it. She jerked the weapon left and right, tearing a gaping hole in his throat, and he stumbled to the side and fell.

Turning to the woman, who *wasn't* her mother, she jabbed the blade into the creature's chest. Screaming, she ran forward, knocking the thing down. She stood over the writhing form, pulling the spear from its chest and stabbing it over and over again. Tears blurred her vision, and she snorted back a nose full of snot between sobs.

A hand was on her shoulder, and a gentle voice was calling to her, the military her.

"LT," Reggie said again, "LT. It's okay now. It's over. You can stop. You gave the mercy they needed. Delivered the grace they deserved. They can rest now, and you can mourn them properly."

"How," she sobbed, "how do you two do it?"

Reggie patted her shoulder.

"It's easy," Griffon said in a nonchalant tone. "It's a video game."

She spun on the little man, jerking away from Reggie, her spear coming up, and taking a step forward.

The gnome took a step back, Raven Stealer coming up and knocking her weapon aside.

"It's not a video game," she shouted, "can't you see that, you chuzzing pemtie? Look around you! Does this look like *sweet graphics*? Does it smell like it? I can taste their blood in my mouth, and the ashes from the buildings! Does that feel like a video game to you? Really?"

"I don't care!" Griffon shouted back, his face growing red. "I know it's not a video game, but I need to believe it is. Otherwise, I'm going to go crazy. Does that help you?"

The gnome spun around, stomping away, swearing, and swiping at his face with the back of his hand.

"And you?" Reid said quietly, without turning around. "How do you handle it?"

Reggie took a deep breath, let it out, then spoke. "Because I must. I think of the people I'm helping survive. With each person, monster, I remove from this world…a dozen good people may have a chance at living something like a normal life. If anything in this world can be considered as such."

"I'm going to have to apologize to him," Reid sniffled, thrusting her chin at Griffon's back.

"Maybe," she could hear Reggie shrug, "or maybe not. He will adapt. There is more to that young man than most see. Definitely more than he sees in himself. But an apology wouldn't be a bad idea. He never saw death before coming here. Not actual combat, only in his games."

"He reminds me so much of my little brother," she sighed, smiling sadly. "Lost in other worlds, wanting to be anywhere except where he is. But that'll get you killed when you're in the middle of action."

Reggie moved beside her, and she saw him nod out of the corner of her eye.

"Yes," he agreed, "but he has us. And right now, that's all the three of us have. Each other."

The three spent a few hours collecting corpses and setting them alight in a mass funeral pyre. There were only twenty-three people who remained in the village, the others either killed in the original attack, or had wandered off.

Reid took down a sheep from a wandering flock, bled it on the field, and they carried it back to the charred remains of the butcher's yard to hang it, skin it, gut it, and cut away meat for dinner.

They camped using the Citadel, out of sight of the village.

The Citadel was a magical tent created by Aiyana before she left this world to return to their world. It blended with the terrain, had a full kitchen and privy, and tables that were once used for magical research. It also had beds for each of them. Sound didn't travel out of the walls, but the three could hear the spring night come to life outside.

"It's amazing," Reid said as Reggie washed the dinner dishes, "that this whole thing folds up to the size of a blanket. Where does the cast-iron pot belly stove go? And all the furniture?"

"Pocket dimension," Reggie said over his shoulder with a laugh, "at least that's how the woman who bequeathed it to me explained it."

"Magic," Griffon pouted, sitting across the tent. "That's all I need to know. Why do you need to know how everything works? Some things just work, isn't that enough?"

"It's the engineer in me," Reid sighed, walking across the room to sit in the chair beside the gnome.

"Hey," she said, poking him in the thigh.

"What?" he said sulkily, without looking at her.

"I'm sorry," she said and sighed again. "What I said before…"

"Whatever," he cut her off. "It doesn't matter."

"Yes, it does." She put her hand on his shoulder. "You guys are all I have, and I need you. I can't go pissing you off. I mean, sure, I just saw some horrible things, and did things I never would have ever imagined I'd do, but…"

"I get it," Griffon grunted.

"What I'm trying to get at is," she hesitated, "your way of looking at all this…"

She waved her hands around.

"…is pretty good. It makes sense, and it's a really cool way of dealing with these things. I wish I could be more like you."

"Short, but handsome with awesome facial hair?" Griffon asked, stroking his goatee and looking at her out of the side of his eye.

"Well," she laughed, "maybe not all that. But your ability to adjust to this world, and the way you did it, is a great way to compartmentalize things."

"What're you, a psychiatrist?" he asked.

"I could've been," she smiled. "I got a degree and everything. Instead, I decided to fly helicopters."

"That's pretty cool, though." Griffon looked at her. "Ever blow up a building?"

"That's classified, I'm afraid," she shrugged. "Can't talk about missions. Signed a paper saying I wouldn't."

"Who am I going to tell? The bug guys?" Griffon threw his hands up, smiling.

"Vriktiri," Reggie said, walking over and drying his hands on a towel.

"Bless you," Griffon said, looking up at the man.

"That's what they're called," Reggie laughed, "Talien told me. The council had done some research.

Apparently, there was an army of them in the west during the Downfall. But they didn't behave the same."

"How did they behave?" the gnome squinted at the man.

"Like a military, apparently," Reid said, dropping her hand from Griffon's shoulder and standing up. "They were well organized, incredibly so. They acted like a cohesive unit. They moved as one, as if they had the plan perfectly organized."

"A hive mind!" Griffon said. "Some of the bug guys in a game I played had that. The mobs were all linked, and if you pinged one group, the whole area started hunting your toon."

"Something like that," Reid nodded, smiling. "But these didn't do that. They acted like individuals."

"Like they were disconnected from the queen?" Griffon asked.

Reggie and Reid exchanged a look.

"Kriksi did say that Khelikian didn't behave like this," Reggie said slowly.

"Maybe something else is controlling them,' Griffon shrugged, then giggled. "Or maybe they're just bugged."

Chapter 8

"My feet hurt." Griffon shaded his eyes and looked south. "How much further is it?"

"Well, it's about two hundred kilometers total," Reggie called over his shoulder, "and we've traveled about…"

He paused, doing the math.

"I figure we've gone about at twenty-five klicks a day, so we should be halfway there." LT finished.

"Right," Reggie said, "what she said."

Griffon sighed, and the ground trembled.

"What is that?" Griffon groused. "Why does it keep doing that? I keep expecting vroom-tikis to jump out at us or something."

"Vriktiri…" Reggie corrected.

"Whatever," Griffon mumbled.

"…and I don't know," Reggie continued, "but it's getting more frequent."

"I thought it was just me," LT said, "glad to hear I'm not just being paranoid."

"Need a hug?" Griffon asked, staring up towards her but not quite reaching her eyes.

"Quiet down, perv," she said. "You're worse than a new recruit."

"Well," Griffon said, "can we at least stop for a break? You guys realize that I have to walk twice as far as you because of my little legs, right? One step for you is like two for me. I'm doing double the work, just walking across this damned continent."

"Yeah, sure," LT said, "I can use a break too."

She stopped, unslung her satchel, dropped it to the ground, and plopped down next to it, sighing.

"Reggie," she said, looking up as the man walked back to them, "what do you think we're going to find at Akar?"

"I'm hesitant to guess," he said.

"Oh, come on, dude!" Griffon pulled off a boot—an upgrade from his sandals—and turned it upside down, dumping small rocks and dirt out. "Stop using so many words when you don't need them!"

LT rubbed her foot, both her boots sitting beside her.

"But," Reggie continued with a groan as he sat down, "it could be more lost folk, or it could be vriktiri, or everyone may be fine and going about their daily tasks."

"Who says things like 'daily tasks'?" Griffon mocked.

"That guy," LT pointed at Reggie, "him, right there. I just heard him say it. Weren't you listening?"

"Do you two want to stop for the day?" Reggie asked.

"What?" Griffon gasped, pressing his fingertips to his chest and feigning surprise. "Did I just hear what I thought I heard? Did Reggie—of all people—suggest we *not* keep going? That we sit idle without marching forward to conquer our daily tasks?"

"Actually," Reggie drew out the word.

"Oh, here it comes," LT chuckled. "I've had commanders like this guy."

"I was thinking it might be nice to get some training in with the spear, bow, and dagger for LT…"

"Yeah," Griffon agreed, "she pretty much sucks at it right now."

"…and that you get some magic practice in." Reggie grinned at the gnome. "You pretty much suck at it right now. An annoying laugh and a couple of fireworks aren't enough. If you're going to be an effective sorcerer, you're going to need to shape up."

"Is it a sorcerer?" Griffon asked. "I mean, elementalists who work with ley lines are wizards, the guys back in Allendale who used telekinesis were mages, alchemists are—well, crazy—but pretty much an alchemist, a conjurer and summoner are what they are, and priests are priests. But what is a sorcerer? What magic do they use? And what does illusion fall under?"

"Sounds like it would be a specialist mage," Reggie shrugged, "and perhaps sorcerer is the wrong term. Maybe that is the title for conjurors?"

"I know!" LT held up a finger, drawing their attention. "The simple truth is…you're both just delaying getting to work by talking about bidj that doesn't matter!"

"Oh, she called you out!" Griffon said in a sing-song tone.

"Yes, indeed," Reggie nodded, pushing back to his feet, "but it wasn't just me. You two rest while I set up the Citadel, then we'll get to work."

Griffon moaned and fell backwards onto the grass.

The day was overcast. Chilly drafts and bands of dark clouds heralded the rain that would soon arrive.

They'd left the rolling foothills of the Wandering Hills and entered the grassy plains to the south. In the distance was a herd of fanged deer, grazing as they watched for predators.

Reggie was fascinated by the creatures, knowing they existed in his world also, but these ungulates had evolved to use their fangs for more than battling for leadership of the herd. The beasts had become omnivores and used their fangs to drain the blood from anything that attacked them.

"Nature is incredible," Reggie murmured, and flipped the base of the Citadel open on the ground.

With a command, the magical tent popped to its full size and melted into the background. From the outside, it looked like a small, grassy knoll.

Fiddling with the sides, Reggie watched his two friends. Both were capable, but Griffon needed to build the mindset of what he had to do. LT had the mindset but needed to build the muscle memory of her new body to do what she'd been able to do in her old body.

The woman also had a lot of traumata going on inside of her. Coming from their world to this one was enough to deal with, but adding the training, and the challenge of dealing with having killed people she quasi-knew from this world…well, it was a lot to deal with.

"And how the hell do I train a mind mage when I know nothing about magic?" Reggie said, staring at Griffon as the gnome pulled a foot to his mouth to bite his toenails.

"Ew!" LT said, swatting the little man on the shoulder. "Don't do that, it's disgusting!"

"They don't have nail clippers here," Griffon said defensively. "How else am I going to trim them?"

"I don't know?" LT squirmed. "But not by chewing on them. Maybe use a knife or something. People had to have a way to do it before they invented in nail clippers, right? And I don't think they had toenail chewing saloons where you went to get a mani-pedi."

"Maybe they do!" Griffon said excitedly. "Like, maybe some grubby goblins are in a booth, just waiting to nibble on your toes, then paint them pretty colors."

LT sighed.

"I used to enjoy mani-pedis," she said. "It was one of my small pleasures. I loved getting cool patterns put on, or pumpkins and ghosts for Halloween. I had one friend, Maria, who was awesome at it. She was an artist, and self-taught."

"Yeah, okay." Griffon rolled his eyes. "I just bit mine off. No one ever looked at me anyway. Why should I care what they look like?"

"Maybe if you took care of yourself a little more," LT said with sincerity, "they would look at you. You know, if you feel good about yourself, take pride in your appearance, others see that confidence and are drawn to it."

"Are you drawn to me?" Griffon waggled his eyebrows, leaning closer to the woman.

"Ew, no!" LT laughed. "It'd be like horn dogging on my little brother. Very little in your case."

"Not all of me is little," the gnome grinned wickedly and waggled his eyebrows again.

"Okay," Reggie walked over to them, "that's enough rest. Let's get some training in before the storm hits us. I also saw some spring onions in the area. We might be able to pick some of those to spice up our dinner tonight."

"We're out of mutton," Griffon grumbled, then brightened. "You think we can take down one of those them over there?" He pointed at the herd of fanged deer.

"I don't think so," Reggie shook his head, smiling, "if we lose, those particular deer will suck our blood."

"What?" LT leaned back, sliding a boot back on. "Really? That's wild."

"Of course, they would," Griffon sighed. "Everything in this world is messed up, so why not vampire deer? Do they fly and turn into a mist, also?"

"I don't think so," Reggie noted the disappointment on the gnome's face, "but maybe. Why not? If it stops you from chasing them, let's say they do."

"Okay, let's get on with it," LT stood, stomping her feet to get her boots into place.

"Griffon," Reggie said to the gnome who was doing the same, "do you think you can show LT some more advanced techniques with the short spear? You're much better at weapons than I am, and I think she's ready for more than the basics."

LT beamed at the praise, pulling her shoulders back and patting her weapon, then caught herself and stiffened to a military posture.

"Yeah!" The gnome was excited again. "I can show her some cool spins and thrust combos, how to work a crowd and intimidate her opponent!"

"I don't know if she'll need that with vriktiri and lost folk," Reggie laughed.

"Look," Griffon said, hands on his hips, "maybe she will or maybe she won't, but it is an important part of using a weapon. If someone decides to hit on her, spinning the spear in a figure eight, around her neck, then tossing it in the air and catching it will put off a crowd of douchebags."

"Speaking from experience?" LT laughed. Seeing his hurt look, she added. "Aw, don't worry, I'm sure that deep down, you're a decent guy. Very, very deep down."

"Whatever," Griffon grumbled, "you're only making the training I'm about to give you harder."

"Oh, really?" LT raised her eyebrows in mock surprise. "We'll see about that."

"Here," Reggie held Marcid towards the gladiator, the rapier morphing into a silver spear, "use mine so the two of you don't need to keep handing hers back and forth."

Griffon stared at the magical weapon, his eyes running along the metal vines twining up the shaft. He reached for it reverently.

"You sure?" He stopped, his fingers twitching, almost brushing the shaft.

"Indeed," Reggie laughed, nodding. "Just make sure Raven Stealer doesn't get jealous."

"Oh, no!" Griffon snatched the spear from Reggie, pulling it to his chest. "She's not the jealous type. She's perfectly okay with me touching another man's—"

"Careful what you say next," LT grinned.

"Shut up, whatever," Griffon groused. "I wasn't going to say penis or anything. But I'm really sure my sword wouldn't mind me touching one of those, either."

"I hope not," LT gasped, "after all, you touch yours every night."

"What? I do not!" Griffon said.

"We do share a tent…" LT looked away, "but I think it's time to train."

"Indeed," Reggie nodded, turning away, "I think I shall go gather some of those onions I saw. Maybe I can find a few other herbs, as well."

His voice faded as he walked away, scanning the ground.

"Okay, you know the basics," Griffon said, spinning Marcid around him, "like the pointy end goes in—"

"That's what she said," LT giggled.

"Whatever, that's so 2010s," he sighed, "can we just be serious for a minute?"

"That's something I wouldn't expect you to say," LT teased, then her face became neutral. "Yes, carry on, I'm paying attention."

The woman shifted to a parade rest, one hand behind her back and the other on the shaft of her spear beside her.

"Good," Griffon continued, "you know the thrusts—no comments from the peanut gallery—and how to slice. Your balance is actually pretty good, but your stances are weak. There are offensive and defensive stances and ways to hold your weapon…"

The gladiator began demonstrating what he was saying, showing the woman cross-body blocks, and how to extend to a strike. He explained how every block should open her next attack, and the conservation of movement to make every action count in battle.

The two switched to sparring once LT had gotten the hang of the basic countermoves, taking turns striking at one another with slow, exaggerated motions.

A couple of hours later, sweating and working in a misting rain, they heard Reggie calling them in to dinner.

"My arms are quivering," LT said, holding her spoon out to show it was shaking. "That was quite a workout."

"Yep," Griffon nodded between slurps of the vegetable soup Reggie had put together, "and I bet your legs are like noodles."

"They are," LT laughed. "I haven't been like this since basic training."

"Speaking of which," Reggie looked up from cleaning Marcid, "you may want to start a calisthenics regiment."

"Or just a workout routine," Griffon threw in, "some basic sit-ups, pushups, squats. You know, a bit of cardio wouldn't hurt either."

"I know about that stuff," she nodded, mildly annoyed, "I am in the military, you know. It's just that this body is used to a hoe and a rake, not a weapon."

"You've got a great build," Reggie said, sounding technical. "Farming builds muscle. Your body is used to hard work and physical labor."

"Yeah," Griffon agreed, "you seen her legs? Like tree trunks. I couldn't sweep her legs at all today."

"Yes, you did," LT said. "When I was off balance, you took me down a couple times."

"Sure," Griffon shrugged, "but I couldn't even come close when you had your balance."

"I was a majorette in high school," LT explained, "and some of it came back. The twirling and the leg strength has a lot to do with that."

"But that wasn't in this body," Griffon said.

"That's true," she said, shrugging, "but the muscle memory was in me, so it helped."

The three finished eating while planning LT's training. They gathered the bowls and got the step stool out for Griffon so he could take his turn at washing the dishes, even though he whined about it the entire time.

"We can continue this tomorrow," Reggie said a couple hours later, closing a book about types of magic, "but we need to get some rest. We have four more days until we reach Akar, and Griffon has magic to practice since he deftly avoided it today."

"I don't know if I'm eager to reach the city, or dreading it," LT said from her cot.

"I know what you mean when you say that LT," Reggie agreed, blowing out the lantern. "I fear for the worst, and hope it isn't more than we can handle."

Chapter 9

"Damn it!" Griffon waved his hands at the cloud of illusionary fireflies dive bombing his head. "How do I make them go away?

"From what I've read in the books left behind by Aiyana," Reggie said, covering his amused smile with a hand, "you stop believing in them."

"Like Tinkerbell?" LT asked. "If you don't believe in them, they die? Now, Griffon, do you really want to be responsible for the death of a bunch of imaginary bugs?"

"Whatever," Griffon snapped.

The gnome called forth a bird, who snapped at the flying insects. The creature was about the size of a turkey, with tiny green wings, purple plumage, and a stunted neck.

"And what the heck is that supposed to be?" LT pointed, laughing around her hard tack. "And since we're on the subject, do fairies exist here?"

"I'm not sure," Reggie tilted his head, "but I'm sure they may. We just haven't encountered any. I know bipeds of immense size are real here. I've even battled an ogre once."

"An ogre?" LT crinkled her nose. "Like Shrek?"

"I don't know who or what a Shrek is…" Reggie paused to drink from his waterskin, "but this one was in a swampy part of a forest and living in a tower with the dead souls of my troop of men that he'd killed guarding it."

"Oh," LT said quietly, looking at her feet, "and did you have to kill your own men?"

"They were already dead," Reggie said, looking up at the sky, "but yes, I did. I had help, though. It seems a normal sword does little to the cold, dark wraiths they'd become. It took magic. Which is why I'm encouraging our friend here to learn a bit of it."

"This is stupid." Griffon threw his hands up to protect his face from the multi-colored feathered monstrosity that was now trying to land on him. "I don't want to do this anymore!"

The bird and the few remaining fireflies disappeared in a blink.

"Oh, that's better," Griffon sighed, dropping to the ground beside the others.

"If I have to practice my forms and stances," LT said, "as well as do aerobics and a workout, then you can play at being a magician."

"They suck." Griffon's voice was hard. "They die so easy in all the games. I'd rather have a sword any day."

"But you will have a sword," Reggie pointed out. "We're not trying to get you to give up what you know, just to add new skills and abilities to your repertoire."

"Why aren't you doing any training?" Griffon shot back.

"Because he doesn't need to," LT said. "He's not special, like you. You have an incredible gift, and I think it's tied to your imagination. You see the world differently than us and constantly picture things we wouldn't even think of. So, you're…special."

"Yeah," Griffon nodded, a small smile creeping onto his face, "I can do something he can't!"

"Well," Reggie raised a hand, "I don't think that was what she was trying to say…"

"Ha, ha!" Griffon poked a finger at the man. "I can do things you can't!"

Reggie rolled his eyes, and Griffon stood up.

"I'm going to try again," the gnome said.

The three had walked for three more days and expected to see the city of Akar tomorrow. The grasses of the plains were higher than their knees and up to the gnome's waist. The hum and chirp of bugs and birds filled the air as spring blossomed. The smell of new growth was everywhere, but there was an underlying taint of something rotting. They sat in a field of tiny white flowers; the bees were just beginning to explore the area, and fluffy white clouds dotted the pale blue sky overhead.

Griffon gritted his teeth, clenched his fists, squatted slightly, and made a low, wheezing noise.

"I think he's trying too hard," LT snickered. "If he's not careful, he's going to blow out his anoose."

"Anoose?" Reggie looked at the woman.

"Yeah," she nodded, "his butthole. Just going to cause it to explode outward. Or at least get hemorrhoids."

The ground rumbled, and LT put a hand down to steady herself.

"Did I do that?" Griffon asked, looking around excitedly.

"I don't believe you did," Reggie said, rising to his feet. "That was another tremor, and they're getting stronger."

"And more frequent," LT added. "Do you think we're getting closer to the source?"

"I pray to Jonath that is the case," Reggie said quietly, "otherwise it means they're getting more powerful over a wider area."

A cracking noise came from the ground, the sound of stone on stone.

"What was that?" Griffon asked, reaching over his shoulder and pulling Raven Stealer from her scabbard.

Nothing good, the sword said in the gnome's head. *I am feeling something unnatural in that direction. Faint, but definite.*

"Raven Stealer is nervous," he translated for the group, "says it wasn't natural."

"We should get going," Reggie said, standing and collecting his belongings. "We want to be on our feet if we have to deal with something heading our way."

"Yep," LT said, mirroring his movements, "and I can smell water. We'll probably see the lake soon."

"The High Tarn?" Griffon asked.

It once was a sacred place, the sword said, *the seed that fed the Great Desert before it was a desert and drained of all life.*

"What did she just say?" Reggie asked.

"How do you know she said anything?" Griffon pulled the sword closer, possessively.

"Because you get a look on your face," Reggie said.

"No, I don't," Griffon argued.

"Is that what that is?" LT asked. "I thought he was just constipated, or daydreaming of internet porn and finishing up, if you know what I mean."

"I don't get a look!" the gnome insisted.

"But you do," Reggie teased.

"What's that like?" LT asked, tucking away the last of her lunch stuff. "I mean, you both have magical weapons. Do they both talk to you? Do they tingle when you touch them? Is it like your own thoughts when they talk to you, or what?"

"It's like someone talking in your ear from the table behind you at a restaurant." Griffon explained. "You can't see them, but you hear them as clearly as if they were standing right…here."

The gnome waved his hand over his shoulder.

"Does how far away change?" she asked.

"No, not really," Griffon shrugged.

"Then it's like having a Bluetooth earbud," LT said, "and you can hear tonal change and emotion, but they're never far away?"

"Yeah," Griffon nodded, smiling, "exactly like that."

"Marcid doesn't talk to me," Reggie said, then looked surprised.

"What?" LT asked. "What happened?"

"She…" Reggie licked his lips, looking around, "made a…feeling. I felt her disagree. I don't know what the Bluetooth thing you mentioned is, but it was like hands on my shoulders, but with no physical sensation. She's never done that before."

"Maybe she's growing," Griffon shrugged dismissively. "It happens with these sorts of things."

"Like you know about such things," Reggie huffed.

"I'm jealous," LT said, and the two men looked at her.

"I don't have a magical weapon," she sighed, "and it sounds like you always have a friend with you. It's like my co-pilot. Charlie was always in my ear whenever I was flying. I didn't have to look over. She was always just there."

LT's face dropped.

"You may see her again, you know?" Reggie said comfortingly.

"How?" LT looked up. "You think she might come here, too?"

"Naw," Griffon said, "some dude named Jack Tucker offers a chance for us to go back to our world whenever we finish a major questline."

LT looked thoughtful as Reggie nodded.

"Were you two married?" Griffon asked.

"What? No." LT shook her head, smiling. "It's not like that. I guess we were a bit in love, but not sexually. You can fall in love with someone without it ever having anything to do with sex. Just look forward to seeing them, sharing your thoughts, and hearing theirs. The first person you want to talk to when something happens. That's like being in love, you know?"

"I'd settle for just the sex part," Griffon said, "not worried about the other stuff."

"You will be when it happens to you," LT said.

"Whatever," the gnome shrugged.

"Gather up your things, Griffon," Reggie said. "We're not your mother and going to do such things for you, and we need to go."

"You sound like my mother," Griffon muttered, but started doing as he was told.

They walked south, following the merchant road but staying in the tall grass in case they needed to hide. Single file, and a handful of paces apart, Reggie led, and Griffon took up the rear. LT, in the middle, practiced her spear twirling and thrusts while walking. Many flowering stems were decapitated.

You should practice your illusions, Raven Stealer said.

"Do you think I have a chance with her?" Griffon whispered back to the sword.

I am a sword, created long ago, and matters of the heart are nothing I have ever concerned myself with. I am a tool of Promethene, who teaches that love can be more pure when not consummated physically. The entire order is chaste.

"Chased by what?" he asked.

I knew you were going to say that. Do you really not know what the word means? I see in your head that you do not know. It means, and brace yourself, never having sex.

"What?" Griffon gasped.

LT looked at him, stopping in mid-spin and walking backwards.

"You okay?" she asked.

"Yeah," Griffon smiled, "my sword is just talking nonsense. Something about never having sex."

"Well, she is a sword," LT said, glancing over her shoulder to check the path, "and it might be a little weird if she had."

She makes a fair point, Raven Stealer said, *but you know that is not what I said. You know I dislike it when you purposely misinterpret what I said to others. It is false advertising.*

"Besides," LT got a sly look on her face, "have you ever had sex?"

"Sure," Griffon shrugged nonchalantly, "lots of times. The chicks love me."

"Ever do it without a mouse in your hand a bottle of lotion beside you?" LT grinned. "You know, with another person physically in the same room as you?"

The woman spun back to face forward and began twirling her spear again.

Griffon opened his mouth to say something, but another cracking sound cut him off.

"That one was to the north," Reggie said, stopping and peering in that direction, his hand shading his eyes. "What's that?"

He pointed to something in the distance.

"Was that there before?" he asked.

The other two turned to look.

A tall, slim mound of brown stood on the horizon.

"A small mountain, or a big hill?" Griffon snorted. "What's it matter?"

"Was it there when we were there?" Reggie asked. "That's in the exact path we've been traveling."

"I don't think it was," LT said slowly.

"And what about that one?" Griffon asked, pointing south.

They all turned to look. A dark silhouette sat in the distance.

"I would say that looks like another one," Reggie nodded, "but taller."

"Looks fresh, too." LT said.

"What's that mean?" Griffon asked.

"Well, hills are usually covered with grass," the woman explained, "and mountains aren't the color of fresh dirt. They're…weathered, and rarely do you get a single mountain. They form from geological shifts, tectonic plates pressing together, causing the earth to rise up and make a line of them."

"Okay," Griffon said, "but what's it all mean? Why are solo mountains all of a sudden growing up in the middle of nowhere?"

"I think," Reggie said, "that the sands in the hourglass are emptying quickly, and we have little time left."

"Don't they have clocks in your century?" Griffon looked up at the man.

"He's an archeologist," LT patted the gnome, "he likes old timey things."

"Just be glad I didn't make a sundial comparison," Reggie teased, "or a henge reference. We should get going."

The others nodded their agreement, and they set out again.

A few hours later, Griffon stopped and called to the others.

"Hey guys, hold on," he said.

They turned to look at him.

"Is our new friend smoking?" The gnome pointed south.

Turning to look, they saw the mountain had a dark plume rising from the center.

"Volcano?" LT said. "Well, that makes more sense than a new mountain, I guess. Is this region geothermally active?"

"I guess it is now," Reggie waved a hand, "I haven't been this far west, but hadn't heard about anything like this."

"And what's that?" LT pointed in the distance, a bit to one side.

Griffon shaded his eyes and squinted, trying to make out she meant.

"Is that," Reggie said, "a caravan?"

LT nodded.

"I think so," she said, "and they've got camels. Or whatever is the equivalent in this place."

"Nomadic tribe leaving the Great Desert?" Reggie sounded dumbfounded. "That does not bode well."

"Do we go towards them, or avoid them?" LT asked.

"Avoid them," Griffon said, nodding once.

"No," Reggie said firmly, "I think we should head towards them."

The other two looked at him.

"We might be able to gather information about what we may be dealing with," Reggie explained. "They've just left the area we're going into. If they left the land they were born and raised in, it must be something dire. It would be helpful to know what that was."

"Makes sense," LT agreed.

"What if they're cannibals?" Griffon asked, standing on his tiptoes to get a better look.

"Not much meat on you," LT nudged him, "they'd probably eat you last."

"Ha ha, hilarious," the gnome said dryly.

"It's a fair question, though," LT turned to Reggie. "It looks like there are a couple dozen of them. Are you sure we should do this?"

"Yes," he said, "and I think they will want information about what we've seen in the north, and where it might be safe for them to go. I think we can help one another."

"Okay," LT sighed, "I'll bow to your judgment."

"But," Griffon said as the other two started walking, "what if they're the evil minions of the mad wizard doing all this? What if they're lost folk with lost camels, looking for a snack? I'm snack sized! I mean, I'm also fun sized, but that's a whole different encounter. Oh, maybe they're into little people, and have like, a fetish or something, and I can get lucky!"

The other two ignored him and continued walking.

In another hour, the caravan was close enough to make out individual faces. The nomads had stopped in a long line, spread out across the road and surrounding grasslands. They held curved blades ready, and arrows set to bowstrings, waiting for the trio to approach.

Chapter 10

LT looked to Reggie for his reaction since they'd agreed he was the commanding officer. He raised his hands and looked down the line of desert folk, Marcid still in her scabbard on his hip. Griffon, slightly behind and to one side of Reggie, twitched nervously, but Raven Stealer remained on his back.

Not knowing what to do with her spear, LT leaned on it like a walking stick, leaving her bow unstrung on her back. She didn't like this idea of just walking up with no weapons ready and was glad to have hers in hand and could ready it at a moment's notice.

The nomads looked tired, but ready for a fight. Most had a pale blue cloth tagelmust wrapped in their turban around their heads and across their face. All wore long, loose, daraas robes that protected them from the sun and sands while still allowing airflow. LT had seen similar outfits in her time in the service and thought the clothing was beautiful and functional.

"Hello," Reggie raised his voice, allowing everyone to hear him, "we've come from the north, Allendale, and are traveling to Akar, and points south of that city."

The desert dwellers stared at the trio, and a camel let out a thick bray.

"I am Kazzek Tel Virian," Reggie said, using his name from this world, and LT assumed it was because it might carry some weight, "and this is Auric the gladiator."

"I hate that pemtie name," Griffon grumbled as Reggie gestured at him.

"Our third companion is…" Reggie hesitated, glancing at LT.

"Tamilda" she shouted, then hesitated before going on, "the farmer."

"Tamilda?" Griffon snorted. "At least my name isn't that lame."

A man near the end of the line kicked his camel and moved forward.

"Kazzek Tel Virian?" The man had an accent, but it sounded regional rather than the language he spoke in was a foreign one. "The freer of men?"

The three exchanged looks.

"Are you the same man who opened the aeifain Icon Hall?" the spokesperson continued. "And the man who journeyed to the Nine Towers with the dragon, Trinity?"

"Oh, well, yes," Reggie called back. "That was me. How is it you have heard of me?"

"Your dragon friend has spoken with our dragon of the desert," the man explained. "Felstonus was also at that place, fighting to free the magics. He returned to share the tales with our shaman. Your name was spoken with praise and high regard."

"Oh," Reggie said, surprised. "That's good. Would you trade information with us? And stories? I know a few."

"Yeah," Griffon mumbled, "and he won't shut up if you get him started."

The rider held up a hand, then turned his camel and returned to the line of desert people. A handful of others broke from their place and gathered around him. LT heard an argument but couldn't make out the words. She shifted her satchel, patting the smaller exterior pockets while watching the group discuss their fate.

"I hope you know what you're doing," she said to Reggie from the corner of her mouth, "because they have more bows than we have blades."

"Hey, Reggie?" Griffon squinted up at the man.

"Yeah, Griffon?" Reggie grunted, not taking his eyes off the men.

"Why have they heard of you, but not me?" the gnome asked. "I was at the Nine Towers, too, but didn't his dragon, Fah-stoner, talk about me?"

"Maybe it's because I'm human?" Reggie shrugged. "If we went to a rokairn or gnome stronghold, I bet they'd know who you are before they knew me."

"That's a bit racist," Griffon huffed.

"Yes, it is," LT nodded, "welcome to my world. People just praise their own quicker than other races. But—before coming here—have you ever actually dealt with that?"

"Well, I got picked on," Griffon said. "I know what it's like to be discriminated against. I wasn't included in lots of things and was even beat up more than once."

"But *why* were you discriminated against?" LT pressed. "Was it because you were annoying? Or because of the color of your skin? And when you got beat up, did you fear that every single day of your life? Or was it just for a few school years? Did those things happen because of who you are, or what you are?"

"Dude," Griffon glanced at LT, "calm down. We're about to die and you're getting all worked up about why people picked on me? And did you just call me annoying? That's racist."

"That's not how this works, Griffon," LT said. "And did you totally miss everything else I said?"

"Hush," Reggie grunted, "they're coming back."

An hour later the group sat around a firepit of wild grasses and dried camel dung, the Mauritania having welcomed them to their fires for the night.

"We are nomads," Jdeidou, the spokesperson, said, "as have been our people for many thousands of years. But we are what is left of the four tribes of the Great Desert, though we called it Burkina Faso, which means 'the land of honest men'. The Tuareg who once settled into the lands and walls of Rogen the Rokairn, once known as Rogen the Plague. The Haratin of the Crag Wastes in the north and west. The Haalpulaar who roamed the lands along the Sea of the Great Plague to the south. And the Amazigh, who rode the camel trails along the Straight River in the east."

"What happened to the others?" Griffon asked, then returned to tearing at the leg of fowl he held.

"Some decided to stay behind," Jdeidou said, "but most perished in the attacks of the vriktiri or became lost folk."

"You've seen the disease here, also?" Reggie leaned forward, elbows on his knees.

"Yes," Jdeidou nodded, "and we believe it started here. We had not heard of it from anyone we traded with before it happened to our people."

"When the vriktiri come," LT said, "do they appear from holes in the ground, and does a totem of insect figures rise before they come out?"

"Yes," their host nodded, "a totem of dark, burnt wood, roughly carved."

"You've had the chance to inspect one?" Reggie asked, his eagerness apparent.

"Of course," Jdeidou waved a hand dismissively, "we have looked at many of them."

"Could you describe them to me?" Reggie pressed. "Were they all the same? What style of carving was it?"

Jdeidou leaned back, studying Reggie for almost a full minute.

LT studied the nomad in return. He was sun browned and his skin showed the weathered texture that comes with living in the sands for decades. Smile lines surrounded his eyes, which were bright and sharp, leading LT to think he was intelligent and kind, but shrewd.

"Hademine," Jdeidou called to a passing woman, "please, come here and tell this man and his friends of the vriktiri totems."

The woman who joined them was young, surprising LT, and had the same eyes as Jdeidou, suggesting they were related.

"Your daughter?" LT asked, looking between the two.

"You can ask me directly, grasslander," Hademine said, her voice as piercing as her eyes.

"Daughter," Jdeidou laughed, "be kind, be polite. They are strangers, not enemies. Perhaps they are fools, or perhaps they are brave for what they will do, but could be both."

"And what is it you will do?" Hademine addressed LT, squatting down to look her in the eye.

"We plan to go south and enter the—" Reggie said, but the woman cut him off.

"Do you not let your women speak, grasslander?" Hademine said, keeping her focus on LT.

Reggie moved his open hand in front of him, gesturing for LT to lead the way into the conversation.

"As my friend was saying," LT said, "we go south to find the source of this disease."

"Why?" Hademine challenged. "Do you hope to destroy the source? That will not cure the people if this is really a disease, as you suggest."

"But it will stop the further spread of it," LT said with a small smile, "at least we hope it will."

"Daughter, I called you over to tell our *guests*," Jdeidou leaned into the word a little, "about the totems that precede the vriktiri arriving."

Hademine looked over the three, and LT felt like she was being measured inside and out.

"Fine, yes," Hademine said, "I will do this. They are wood, but petrified and solid as stone, and scored with flame and age. Ancient markings, like the ones our shaman taught us, came from Ez'rainia-fromton. They show a queen vriktiri on the bottom, three warriors stacked atop of her, and then a pyramid cap that might belong to an obelisk. The runes upon the base and top are ones of slavery and control, and the breaking from what had come before."

"Would your shaman be able to tell us more?" LT asked.

"No," Hademine shook her head, scowling. "He is dead, along with hundreds of others."

"She is our shaman now," Jdeidou said. "She trained under each of the ones before, and now will teach the next generation when it comes. If it comes."

"It *will* come, Father," the younger woman grunted, rising from her squat. "I have foreseen it. And heroes will rise to reclaim our ancestral lands, bringing the seed and fruit of plenty with them."

Hademine turned and walked away, sand kicking up under her sandals.

"She is angry," Jdeidou sighed, "but I think it is more because she has such a heavy burden to carry than anything else. I don't think I have heard her laugh in three moons, but I hope it comes back to her soon."

"Can you tell us of anything else that lies to the south?" Reggie asked. "Or where the best place to look for Ez'rainia-fromton might be?"

"That place was once a great city along the Straight River, the seat of a powerful empire," Jdeidou said, "but the center of it became the prison for foul creatures who drained the land, and their people, of life and spirit. You should seek where the Acute River joins the Straight River, then head towards the setting sun."

Jdeidou raised his hands to stop Reggie's next question.

"But you should know that the sand grows into the smoking mounds along that river and to the north," the man continued, "volcanoes are rising, and I do not believe there is anything natural about them. Strange creatures come with them, beings of the like that our elders had not seen since the Downfall and the days when the Talisman hung low in the sky."

"Demons?" Reggie asked.

Jdeidou shrugged. "I do not know. I only know that they're weird."

Griffon snorted. "That covers a lot of territory."

The three stood outside of the Citadel, which Reggie had opened as a small tent, using the magics to disguise it.

"I just didn't want everyone to see me unroll a tarp and then…boom…a huge tent appears," he explained, "but it's still the same size on the inside."

"So, we won't be all cuddled together in a sexy cuddle pile?" Griffon asked, sounding disappointed.

"Nope," Reggie shook his head, "sorry about that, chap."

"We could still cuddle," Griffon said. "You know that, right LT?"

"Just get inside." LT shoved the gnome towards the tent flap.

Once inside, the three spread out to their different corners of the large area. Reggie straddled a stool, opening the books he'd been reading and flipping through pages. He pulled his pipe from his satchel and packed it with tobacco. LT stretched luxuriously, intertwining her arms and reaching for the canvas ceiling. Griffon flopped on his cot, sighing heavily.

"You missed the chance to ogle me while I was stretching," LT smirked at the gnome. "Oh my god, I don't believe I just flirted with him. I must be going crazy."

"Yeah, whatever," Griffon mumbled. "I miss my Nintendo Switch. It gets so boring here with nothing to do."

"You could open a book," Reggie said around the pipe clenched in his teeth, tracing his finger along a page, "study up on your illusions. Learn something."

"That's work," Griffon muttered. "I want something fun."

"Then make your own video game out of illusions," LT suggested absently, looking over Reggie's shoulder. "What *are* you studying, Reggie?"

"Portals," the man said without looking up, puffing on the pipe, "Aiyana dedicated all her time to them, and I'm wondering if we can use them, as well. She theoretically unlocked an entire network of them, but I can't figure out where they are…"

He trailed off, distracted by his reading.

"Can't we just make one?" LT asked.

"What?" Reggie looked at her, blinking. "No. Not without the precise magical ability and training. But there are static locations where they were. She found a bunch of them, but I'm unsure if she wrote down the locations. So far, I've only found descriptions of what makes a place able to maintain one. I'm hoping that I can figure out where they are most likely to be, and then use them."

"Can I help?"

"Why not?" Reggie slid a tome in front of another stool. "Have a seat and start reading."

Griffon huffed from behind them. Bringing his hands together and pulling them apart, he created the illusion of a small dragon on his lap. It had very little detail and started cleaning itself like a cat.

"That's pemtie," the gnome said, clapping his hands and dispelling the beast.

He raised his hands and twiddled his fingers like he was flicking water from them. A miniature troll and a knight appeared, the first with a huge club, the second with a massive sword. The two illusions charged one another, slicing and bashing at one another.

Griffon giggled.

"They're a bit blocky and Minecraft-y," he said, "but I think I'm getting better."

The three worked for a couple of hours before Reggie looked up, rubbing his eyes.

"I think it's time for bed," he said. "We'll need to be rested when we go into Akar tomorrow."

LT stood up, stretching again, and looked over at Griffon. The gnome was gently snoring, a gnohl and a fanged deer cuddling in between his splayed legs. The illusions shifted as LT pulled a blanket over the man, rising through the blanket as it settled over him.

Once the lantern was extinguished and Reggie and LT lay in their separate cots, the woman turned on her side, propped on her elbow, to look at the man.

"Reggie?" she whispered.

"Hm?" he replied, sleepily.

"Are all swords named after women, like boats?" she asked.

"No," he mumbled, turning to get more comfortable, "they tell us what they are. We don't get to pick for them."

"How progressive," she smiled, and rolled over to go to sleep.

Chapter 11

The city of Akar spread out below them along the shore of the High Tarn. The lake was placid, small waves breaking on the shore in the distance.

"It has a blend of architectures," Reggie pointed out. "It's in the grasslands, and you can see construction in the sprawl that the northern lands have influenced, but it also shows the stacked stonework that comes from the people of the Great Desert. This is amazing."

"Its buildings surrounded by a wall," Griffon rolled his eyes, "so interesting."

The trio passed the burgeoning volcano between them and the city about two hours before, and the sun was high in a bright blue sky.

The ground rumbled, as it had frequently in the past week, but this time it didn't stop.

"Uh, oh," LT said.

The two men turned to look at her, and saw her staring back the way they'd come, her hand to her mouth, swaying with the quake's vibrations.

A loud crack, followed by an explosion, shook the air around them, and the mound to the north erupted. Lava burst into the clear sky, followed by thick black plumes of ash.

Another explosion made them turn south, and they saw another rising plume along the Straight River. Then another behind it. The clouds spread across the firmament and joined into a massive overhead highway of soot and ash. Red flakes rained down over them, and the ground continued to shake.

"What the chuz is that?" Griffon said, wide-eyed and dropping to put his hands beside his feet so he didn't fall.

Smaller explosions drowned out anything else he said as totems burst through the grass in a semi-circle behind them. Vriktiri flooded out of holes at the base of the talismans.

"I think those are portals," Reggie said, pointing, "not them coming up from underground tunnels. That would explain how they pop up at the most inconvenient—"

"Stop talking," LT shouted, grabbing his arm and pulling him in the opposite direction of the bug-men, "and start running!"

They stumbled down the hill, heading for Akar, picking up speed and balance with the continued rumbling of the earth. Griffon drew Raven Stealer, disappearing and reappearing a stone's throw distance ahead of them.

"How'd he do that?" LT puffed, her long strides letting her pull ahead of Reggie.

"His sword," the man panted, "has magics. Allows him to teleport…short distances, generally…in line of sight."

"You do," she said, "use a lot of words."

A group of figures on horseback rode out of the city below at full gallop, heading directly for them.

"Help," LT said hopefully, "is on its way!"

"Kazzek," came a distant voice from the horsemen, "you're a dead man!"

"Or not," LT said, veering to the west and away from the oncoming riders. "Griffon, go right."

"That clinches it," Reggie huffed, "bad things do…come in threes!"

The horde of insect creatures swarmed over the hilltop behind them, running on all six limbs, hissing, their mandibles clicking.

The riders raised a battle cry and swords, the pounding of their horses' hooves adding to the trembling of the plains.

The two groups closed on the trio.

"We can't outrun them," LT shouted, slowing to a jog. "Find a defensible place and we can make a stand."

"Rocks!" Griffon pointed at a stony area on the shoreline and ran towards them.

The three reached the place Griffon had indicated and cast around for somewhere that was better than the open.

"We'll box ourselves in," Reggie said.

"Better than them coming at us from all sides," LT gasped, one hand on her stomach.

She leaned her spear against an outcropping and pulled her bow from her back. Stringing it, she tested the pull and drew an arrow from her quiver.

"Six riders," Griffon said, standing on his tiptoes to see, "and maybe twenty buggies."

"Could be worse odds," LT nocked her arrow and drew the string back, "but let's see if we can't make them better."

She released the string, and the missile flew true, striking a man on horseback in the chest. She nocked another arrow as he fell, firing at a new target.

The vriktiri came into view behind the horses, moving in zig-zag patterns.

"Maybe we should get bows," Reggie muttered, drawing Marcid. "Because I don't enjoy playing against a stacked deck."

"Whatever, old man," Griffon stepped in front of the other two, raising his blade, "just don't get in my way."

The riders pulled up short, another falling to LT's precise shot. The four remaining looked back and forth between the cornered trio and the oncoming monsters.

An arrow sprouted from the lead horse, and the beast reared, turning and toppling to one side, throwing its rider. The horse clambered to its feet and bolted away; the man rising slower and looking around for his mount. His compatriots wheeled their horses and kicked them into motion, heading towards Akar.

The vriktiri turned, a handful launching themselves at the trailing rider in the group's rear, pulling the man and horse to the ground. Screams echoed off the rocks as they tore the thug to pieces. The horse scrambled away, following the other fleeing mounted men.

Another group rolled across the dismounted attacker, and he went down also, eerily silent as they dismembered him.

LT continued to fire arrows into the oncoming enemy, taking down three before the first of the vriktiri reached them.

When the first of the bug-men entered the rocky alcove, Griffon blinked out of existence, appearing behind the attackers. His sword was a white blur behind the creatures.

LT dropped the bow, grabbing her spear and moving into a low fighting stance. She thrust upward at the first one, piercing its thorax, and jerking her weapon side to side. Thick, white, viscous stuff oozed from the hole, and LT backpedaled with a startled squeak.

Reggie gripped Marcid with both hands. Pulling them apart, he held the rapier and a matching main-gauche. Batting away a pincered hand, he stabbed the vriktiri in its faceted eye with the rapier, and in the abdomen with the parrying blade.

Pushing the spasming body to one side, he lunged for another who was trying to flank LT, cutting into it. A third locked onto Reggie's forearm with its mandibles and tore away his bracer.

A spear thrust over his shoulder, into the beast's open maw, and out the back of its head.

"Stop trying to save me, damn it," LT growled, spinning to attack another.

Griffon was in his element, having years of experience fighting multiple enemies and not all of them human. He danced from one to the other, slicing through legs and ducking under their raised bodies, using his smaller size to his advantage.

The trio came together, forming a wedge, Griffon at the point, and LT using her spear's length to her advantage.

A few minutes later they stood among bug parts, still twitching, and finishing any enemies who looked like they still had fight in them.

"That wasn't so bad," Griffon giggled, wiping a bit of goop from his forehead.

LT sighed.

"Then what about them?" the woman pointed at the rise.

Dozens of vriktiri were pouring over the top of the hill and rushing towards them.

Reggie pointed into the volcanic dust blocking the sky.

"Look there," he said, "within the tephra…"

"The what?" Griffon squinted upward.

"What are we looking at?" LT asked.

"In the ash," Reggie said, "rock crows. They search out caves. I wonder if one is Captain Farrell, my old friend. Follow them!"

Reggie put action to words, running in the direction the ebony avians headed. The others followed, LT snatching her bow up before leaving.

The air was thick with detritus from the volcanoes and gave them a smokescreen to hide in as they followed the birds who were swooping and cawing.

"Here!" Reggie darted around a corner and disappeared between an outcropping of rocks.

The other two followed and found themselves in a natural tunnel leading down into the earth.

Reggie held his blades together, and they melted into one. He sheathed Marcid and looked around.

"You sure this isn't a bug hole?" Griffon asked as Reggie knelt, rummaging through his satchel.

"Looks like a lava tube," the man said, pulling a lantern from the bag, "which says this area once had volcanic activity. Guess whoever caused the new volcanoes to rise had something to work with."

"You think someone did this?" LT asked, astounded. "You don't think it was a natural occurrence?"

"No, I don't," Reggie shook his head, filling the lamp with oil, "it's too coincidental, and with the elemental magic I've seen in my time here, I think it's very possible." Lighting the lantern with flint and steel, he glanced at the gnome. "Guard our backs, Griffon," he said, the lantern flaring to life, "and we'll go deeper. I think it's time to use the portal stone Aiyana gave me."

"Why didn't we just use it in the first place," Griffon grumbled, "instead of walking for over a week?"

"Because I had to try and help Akar," Reggie sighed, leading the way deeper into the cavern.

"You know you're just one man, right?" LT asked.

"Not when I'm with you two," he smiled. "I've seen three people do incredible things."

"Yeah," Griffon retorted, "but those other people had magic that could melt buildings. We have a sword and spear."

"And spunk," Reggie said, "don't forget that. That makes up for a lot."

"I've got your spunk right here," Griffon quipped.

"Hey now," LT said, "don't go throwing that around. I'm still in my childbearing years."

"Oh, really?" Griffon grinned. "Is that something you'd be interested in?"

"No," LT growled, "and especially not with you."

"Aw, come on," the gnome chided, "the kids would be small. They wouldn't take up much room. And think how fun it would be making them."

"Ew," LT said, "just ew."

"This will do," Reggie said, stopping and setting the lantern down.

Pulling a stone from his bag, he picked up the lantern again.

"Everyone ready?" he asked.

"Depends," LT said. "Ready for what?"

"This," Reggie said, and the air around the trio flared a deep blue.

Ahken'ho-tek watched the figures disappear into the cavern. He waved his hand over the table and the scene made of sand melted into a flat surface, the vriktiri disappearing along with the terrain.

"They are coming," the lich said, rubbing his hands on his robes, an old habit from his living days.

"You did well, Chektar-ral," he said to the Mistress of the Ley, "our power network now extends from here to the Valley of Rykul."

Turning to the Master of Minions, he looked the lesser lich up and down.

"Kenal," he said, his tone threatening, "you need to control those beasts better. If left to their own devices, they would have overcome the interlopers, and we'd have them now. You failed me, and I will not accept that again. We can put your energies to better use if you cannot control your charges."

Kenal bowed low, backing away as Ahken'ho-tek swept past him.

The Lord of Liches strode through the throne room and into the passage leading to his chamber. He despised returning to it after being trapped within the room for centuries, but he needed privacy and time to think without simpering fools bothering him.

They knew their jobs, but still came to him for the most inconsequential of matters. Or hoping to garner some small scrap of favor for doing their expected duties. A thousand years old, but they still competed like children for the attention of a parent.

Attendant spirits and undead wandered the ancient halls, seeking a task to do, then forgetting in the space of a moment. They moved from Ahken'ho-tek's path, bowing their heads, and avoiding eye contact.

"At least they know their place," Ahken'ho-tek rasped, sweeping past a trio of wraiths.

The three ethereal hunters eyed the master of the ruins as he moved away.

Entering his chamber, Ahken'ho-tek waved at the doorway, dropping the magical curtain to ensure he had privacy. It was a wanton use of the arcane energies, but necessary.

Calling upon another spell, he opened the scrying mirror on the wall to spy on his servants. Lepat-fal, Master of the Unseen, stood close to Telvak-ral, Guardian of the Tomes, the two in quiet conversation. Calling up the clairaudience enchantment that Verl'zen-luk had placed upon the clairvoyance surface, he listened to their exchange.

Verl'zen-luk had been paranoid about Ahken'ho-tek's ambition—and everyone else's—and rightfully so. Each of the great liches had plans, plots, and schemes to rise to power. But Verl'zen-luk had outplayed each of them, using them for his own devices and rising to godhood.

Ahken'ho-tek had learned from him, and trusted no one within his court, or outside of it.

"His arrogance grows," Lepat-fal said, brushing at his shining robes, "but my pets watch him from the places he cannot see. We will have our chance; I promise you that."

"With the portal totems in place, and powered by Chektar-ral's line of volcanoes," Telvak-ral grinned through broken teeth, "we will have all the power we need when the time comes."

"Will she join us?" the first lich asked.

"I don't know," the other laughed, a grating noise from deep inside, "she's a loyal one with little foresight of what we can do together, but I have a plan in place if she doesn't choose correctly. Imagine what power we will hold if we control her magics in addition to our own."

"We would be unstoppable," Lepat-fal moaned, his clothing rippling with excitement.

"We already are," Telvak-ral rasped another laugh.

"Tell me what you are hiding," Ahken'ho-tek said to himself, leaning towards the magic mirror and casting a suggestive tendril of magic into it to compel the other lich to reveal the secret he hid.

"I have a special artifact at the ready…" Telvak-ral hesitated, his face contorting.

"What is it?" Lepat-fal leaned in, rubbing his hands together in anticipation.

The Guardian of the Tomes looked at the Master of the Unseen suspiciously.

"Do you think I am a pawn to be manipulated?" Telvak-ral spat. "You use something to compel me to speak my secrets!"

Lepat-fal took a step back, looking around.

"I do not," the Master of the Unseen hissed, "but perhaps someone else does."

Ahken'ho-tek waved a hand, dismissing the viewing before they tracked the thread of magic back to him. He wouldn't learn the information now, but he had at least inserted a seed of mistrust between the two conspiring against him.

"It will grow and one or both will come to me, prepared to betray the other." Ahken'ho-tek smiled, looked around his opulent room—his tomb—and rubbed his hands on his robes in anticipation. "But once the other three arrive, my traitorous lackeys will no longer be necessary."

Chapter 12

Reggie blinked in the haze of darkness, wondering if the magical stone had failed. He looked at his palm and saw the last glimmer of magic fading.

"Where are we?" Griffon asked, his dim silhouette shifting to look around.

Reggie did the same and felt his boots slide in sand instead of on stone. His eyes adjusted to the weak aura of light cast by the lantern—at least compared to the sunlight they'd left moments before—and Reggie wiped at his forehead, mopping away a sheen of sweat that hadn't been there before portalling.

"Well, we're in a desert alright," LT said. "I know this kind of heat. I was stationed in it for a couple years."

Pulling out a kerchief, Reggie tied it around his head, covering his mouth and nose. "You may want to do the same," he waved a hand at the others, "I don't imagine breathing this stuff in will be healthy."

A thick layer of soot coated everything, and was quickly covering them, making them look like snowmen made in hell. Sounds were muted. Their shuffled steps, when they dropped their bags to retrieve something to cover their faces, the small coughs as one of them sucked in ash were all muffled in the volcanic ashfall.

Waiting for the others, Reggie glanced around. His vision cleared enough to make out the shapes in the grey flakes. "The stone streets are arrow straight," he said in low tones, almost in awe, "as if they'd laid them out with a ruler and chalk lines. Look at the pillars, they're immense…and the artistry of the stone carvings…"

He trailed off, his eyes moving over the dozens of ash-coated, square structures laid out in a perfect grid. The streets were long avenues with knee-high medians down the center. Reggie guessed they once were the home for palm trees, aloe plants, and other greens that didn't need excessive watering. Every fourth column was an animal-headed statue holding a thinner column with a creature perched atop. Reptile- and feline-headed men and women supported chimeras and pegasus, canine- and avian-headed raised up hydras and hippogryphs, bovine and simian lofted coatls and mermaids.

The buildings were stacked and lined up as neat as the blocks of a child with obsessive neurosis. Each had three floors, the bottommost the widest, and the smallest. Each had the deliberate architecture of a religious structure, but the carved décor of individual personalities. The winds and grit of the desert had sanded both smooth from years of blasting.

Reggie returned to the moment, suddenly exhausted. Even in the dim light and thick air, Reggie felt the oppressive heat pressing down on him.

Griffon made small spitting noises, trying to dislodge the dust from his mouth as he tied a cloth across his face.

"I wish I had my NVGs," LT said, tying a second cloth over her hair. "The goggle part so I don't need to keep blinking this bidj from my eyes. Plus, the night vision part so I can see better in this flurry."

"I can make some illusionary ones," Griffon said, a steampunk-looking pair appearing on his face, "but I don't think that will do anything except make me look even cooler."

"Keep dreaming, short stuff." LT dusted her shoulder off, muttering, "It's like the worst case of dandruff ever."

"Well," Reggie said, picking up his satchel and shouldering it, "it looks like the teleport spell worked. Now, to find our way into the underground complex."

"Do you know how to do that?" Griffon looked around, his hands on his hips. "I can barely tell where the buildings are, and gnomes are known for seeing well in dim light…"

"I have the vision from Thomas," Reggie said, slightly muffled by the face covering, "and I think I can find the entrance. From there, I'll need to figure it out as we go until we reach a point we recognize from our last outing here."

"You've been here before?" LT asked.

"Sorta," Griffon said, "we portalled to the inside of a tomb. Opened a forbidden doorway. Stole a magical stick to get out. You know, the usual."

"I see," LT said dubiously. "Do you think we should set up the Citadel and camp for the night? I'm not sure if the things inside of wherever we're going are more likely to sleep during the day or be stronger at night."

"I don't think it works like that," Griffon laughed.

"It might," Reggie said, and the other two looked at him. "Think about it. The beings have set up a line of volcanoes. They're covering the entire area with ash, making it like twilight. So, LT's thought may have some bearing."

"So, tent and rest?" LT asked again.

"It has been a long day," Reggie nodded, "and I think there's wisdom in your suggestion. Let's find somewhere to set up the Citadel."

Sullen dust devils stalked the deserted streets, a chorus of ghostly howls keeping them company. The air was thick, turning the golden rays of the late afternoon into something from a cautionary tale. Wan beams of light filtered through the airborne silt, never reaching the ground.

The Citadel took on the appearance of the local buildings, looking like a short, squat building of sun-bleached stone, and was quickly covered with grey ash. No light or noise escaped from the magical structure, but the forces of nature haunting the exterior made themselves felt by the three inside.

"It's just the wind," LT nudged Griffon, "nothing to be afraid of."

"That's what they always say in horror movies right before they die." The gnome stared at the rippling walls of the tent. "Or as they're about to have sex."

He glanced at LT, expectantly.

"You have a much better chance of the first," she said, straight-faced, "especially if you try the second."

"Children, please," Reggie said, leaning over the table and tracing a finger along the rough map, "and would one of you get my pipe and tobacco pouch? I think it's over there." He waved vaguely toward his cot and footlocker.

Griffon was suddenly interested in something under his fingernail, so LT walked over and retrieved the requested items with a sigh. She set them in front of the preoccupied man and slid them closer.

"There you go, professor," she said.

Reggie looked up, smiling.

"Thank you, LT." he said. "You know, this brings me back, reminds me of happier moments."

"Being trapped in a desert, looking for the way into a city of the dead, and things outside that sound like wolves just had a baby with a banshee is some of your happier moments?" Griffon asked. "Man, I hope you got enough hugs as a kid, otherwise you're going to be the one that sacrifices us in our sleep."

Reggie laughed.

"There's nothing outside except the wind!" LT said, exasperated.

"No, but yes," Reggie interrupted. "I have been in a sandstorm in a city of the dead, twice. And such noises were common, but nothing more than architecture angles creating auditory aberrations."

"You did that on purpose," LT muttered.

"But what I meant was," Reggie continued, "is that I've taught archeology, and had students as assistants. They'd bicker and play to cover their anxiety. Almost always, one was the worried one, and the other played tough to balance it out. It's a wonderful give and take of interaction."

"Professor Betancourt," LT said, her voice holding an edge of sarcasm, "I'm not actually scared and trying to cover it up with bravado."

"Oh," Reggie nodded, picking up his pipe and opening the tobacco pouch, "I know you're not scared. The walking dead are easy to handle after seeing the monsters people can be during wartime. But I think you are…how do you kids say it? Freaked out?"

He paused, holding up a hand to stop any reply, then pushed a pinch of tobacco into the pipe bowl, filling it.

"You've entered a new world," Reggie said, puffing on the unlit stem to check the draw, "and just going to a jungle or a new country can be jarring."

"Yes," LT rolled her head to the ceiling, "and I'm covering all that by retreating into my professional soldier persona. I do have a degree in psychology and recognize my own behavior. It's a fair way to handle things, so I can process everything."

"I got back up hugs right here if you need them to help cope," Griffon patted his chest and held his arms wide.

"Kind of you, Griffon," Reggie said between puffs, lighting his pipe from a burning twig he kept for such purposes. "But no, thank you," he continued, blowing out a stream of smoke, "I'll be fine."

"Didn't mean you," the gnome muttered, and LT smirked.

"Look LT," Reggie went on, "you offered to help study the books for portal references, allowing me to look into Aiyana's notes on lost civilizations. That was her second passion, and has a plethora of information on them, but they're jumbled."

The man looked at the gnome.

"Griffon," he said, tapping the map on the table, "do you think you could make a three-dimensional representation of what I've drawn out using your illusions?"

"Maybe." Griffon scrunched up his face, looking at the partial layout of the city and buildings.

Wispy forms of the structures and terrain grew from the table, mimicking the lines on the hand-drawn map. They were incomplete and blocky, but recognizable.

"See?" Reggie winked at LT. "You're both very helpful."

Griffon beamed under the praise, his face wrinkling in concentration.

"How did you get this much detail?" LT leaned in to get a better view. "I could barely see what was around us, let alone half the city."

"Griffon may have enhanced parts of it with what he saw with his superior vision. But I got my drawings partially from the images I got out of Thomas's vision," Reggie said, tamping his pipe, "and partially from my own knowledge blended with Aiyana's notes and sketches. She copied multiple tomes of information into her notes from Icon Hall using magic. I think she may have done this for me, knowing I planned to come here."

"And you thought she didn't like you," Griffon said, wiping sweat from his forehead.

"I'm still not sure she did," Reggie laughed, "but she valued what I intended to do. She was always about saving the world. Whichever world she was in."

"Whatever," Griffon said. "Can we get on with this? How do we get into this place?"

"They originally built the structure as a palace," Reggie said, "but was later turned into a prison. So, it's not so much us breaking in, as us breaking them out. I think the advantage we shall have is that the traps, magical or mundane, will be set to stop anyone coming out, rather than coming in."

Reggie bent over the map, pointing out features and buildings, explaining uses and the path they'd most likely take to find their goal.

Rising early the following morning, they loaded useful items into their bags, collapsed the Citadel and stowed it. The air danced with thick flakes of ash, hanging in the sky like a threatening storm but falling like dirty snow. Each of them wore a face covering and carried their weapons drawn. They shuffled through grimy, ankle-deep drifts towards the main building.

Reggie looked around through rose-colored glasses. The lenses were magicked to show hidden things and lines of magical energy, but had lost that enchantment at the Nine Towers of Magic. Al, the Troll Lord, had re-enchanted them, and Reggie suspected he'd added a few bells and whistles.

The desert had reclaimed most of the city, and a few streets away, dunes covered most structures, corners of buildings jutting out of the sand. Winds kept the wide, flat areas relatively clear, but those same gusts scoured the details from carvings, scrollwork, art, and architecture with flying sands over hundreds the centuries.

Huge obelisks towered above the stairs leading up to the palace, and stone creatures—that Reggie thought resembled manticores—sat at the base of each monolith. The lion-headed creatures had wings folded along their massive backs, and scorpion tails hung over their heads, one broken off and laying half-buried in the ash.

They moved up the steps towards where Reggie thought the entrance lay. Entering a foyer sheltered from the wind and weather, the crunch of soot and detritus lessened, and the three spread out. None of them spoke, and Reggie wasn't sure if they were feeling the same awe and immense weight of history as he was, or if they just had nothing to say.

Reggie studied the walls, pulling a small leather-bound notebook from his satchel and consulting it. Running his fingers across a script that looked like cuneiform and hieroglyphics had a baby, he half mumbled words and phrases he recognized and slid past others.

LT stood in front of the enormous stone double doors, looking at the eroded relief carving that displayed an army in blocks of parade formation. Statues towering three times her height stood on each side of the doors, one man and one woman, each holding a wide, shallow bowl.

Griffon noisily cleared his nose, holding one nostril closed and blowing and then the other, while watching the wide causeway for anything moving.

"Only the living may pass," Reggie murmured, "but must give life's water to enter."

The other two—their curiosity caught by his words—turned and watched him. He turned in a circle, slowly inspecting the walls, floor, and ceiling, then moved. Walking along the perimeter of the foyer, Reggie looked up and down the walls before settling on the statues.

"I think I know what's required here," Reggie said, tucking the notebook into his bag and stepping beside LT. "Can you give me a boost? Lift me up so I can reach the bowl?"

"Sure," LT shrugged, and leaned her spear and unstrung bow against the wall. Cupping her hands together to create a stirrup, she said, "Up you go."

Placing his hands on her shoulders, he put his foot in her hands and rose so he could investigate the shallow vessel.

"Watch your eyes," he said, and dusted sand from the stoneware.

Reggie drew Marcid, and the sword shrunk to a short knife. Drawing it across his palm, Reggie cut himself and squeezed his hand into a fist, drizzling blood onto the surface.

"Now, the other one," Reggie dropped from LT's hands.

"You had to make a blood sacrifice?" LT asked, moving to the other statue.

"More of a token donation," Reggie said, hiking himself up in front of the other using LT's help, "and the stream must connect with the body to show it is living. And from what I read, if it's too much, it won't work."

"Why?" Griffon asked.

"I guess so a dead person doesn't just cut the throat of a living person to get in and release the imprisoned." Reggie said, squeezing his fist over the second bowl.

The blood dribbled down, coating the bottom of the vessel. After a moment, it bubbled, and an outlined faded script inside the bowl appeared, colored by the blood. A thin red line traced its way out of the bowl, up the statue's arms to its shoulder. The line continued extending up the figure's neck, behind its ear, then across its temples to the corner of its eye. The eyes filled with the deep maroon liquid and then lit up with an internal glow.

The statues shifted, grating in the small drift of sand at their square bases, turning in place to face one another, their bowls creating an arch overhead. With a grinding noise, the doors swung inward, revealing a wide, dim passage.

Murky yellow stones struggled to life, giving a sickly glow along the long, barren, sloping hall. Similar glyphs and sigils as the foyer covered the interior walls, and a layer of dust muted the colors on these.

Reggie stepped inside, LT reaching to stop him, and he shrugged her hand off.

"It's safe," he said, "for now. These symbols should show us the next safeguard."

Dozens of shoulder-height columns held large mirrors alternating with busts, and lined the passage, disappearing into the gloom ahead.

"Long-dead rulers and heroes of the land," Reggie murmured, "at least, that's what I assume they are."

"They like to put on a show for visitors, don't they?" Griffon said from Reggie's elbow, making him jump in surprise. "Nervous much?"

"I think the people who put these here," Reggie said, ignoring the gnome's jibe as he stopped and leaned close to inspect a bust, "did so just before locking the place down. Dead guardians to make sure the new dead never escaped."

Chapter 13

They stepped into a hall as wide as the foyer. The sandstone walls were wide enough that four men could walk shoulder to shoulder and still have room to draw a sword. Motes and spirals of dust glittered in the space between the shoulder-height columns and stone heads. A dull waft moved the thick atmosphere of the forgotten tomb, bringing the weight of stale air from the depths, as if the darkness below was drawing a long-awaited breath. Griffon's sword cast a clear, white glow around the three in the murky yellow haze of the ancient glow stones set in the head-height alcoves along the hall.

"Thank you, Raven Stealer," Reggie nodded and smiled in Griffon's direction. "Very helpful."

The light dimmed, then brightened.

"She said you're welcome," Griffon translated, patting the pommel of his sword. "So, what are we doing this time? You gotta flex at the heads? Or do a little dance in the mirrors? Maybe lop off an ear or finger and stick it on the faces?"

"Not sure yet," Reggie said, turning to inspect the closest markings on the wall. "But if you could stay close so I may use your light, or perhaps your ear, if required, it would be appreciated."

"Don't worry about that, old man," Griffon said, looking around. "I'm not going anywhere."

"It's adorable how he's guarding you," LT said, securing her spear to her back and bringing her bow around. "I'm beginning to think he genuinely cares for you."

"He's a decent kid," Reggie said absently, his hands gliding across the runes, "and I feel…the way is lit by…"

Reggie's words trailed off into a mumble, distracted by what he was reading.

Stringing her bow, LT nocked an arrow and stood sideways so she could look out the door or down the hall.

Minutes crept past, time seeming to slow as Reggie slid sideways, pausing his reading to move around a column. At the bottom of the long hall was a large open chamber with no floor and no ceiling. A glittering swirl of purplish mist floated in the open air, shifting across the space even though no wind was present. The other side was barely visible in the murky distance.

Griffon held Raven Stealer over the precipice, looking up, then down.

"No bottom or top," Griffon sighed. "But check this out…"

He waved his sword towards the mass of purple. The cloudy formation slid away from the white light, avoiding it.

"Looks like it's alive," LT said, "and it doesn't like your sword."

"The power of Promethene, baby," Griffon smiled, then followed Reggie.

The archeologist retreated to the open doors and began reading the opposite wall, referring to his notebook every few steps.

"This is mind blowing," LT said. "I mean, it's like being in a movie version of an Egyptian tomb, if it hooked up with one of the ancient temples in the jungles of Cambodia."

"You may be thinking of Angkor Wat," Reggie said, looking up from his notes. "It's one of the oldest on Earth, as far as we know."

"That might be the one," LT shrugged, "but it's amazing. I just can't get over the fact that I'm really here, living through this in someone else's body."

"Get used to it, babe," Griffon snorted, "because I got the feeling you ain't seen nothing yet."

"We really need to work on how you address women, small fry," LT said, but without any anger, as she stared at the relief carvings Reggie was studying.

They fell silent again. The only sounds were the moan of the wind outside, the shuffle of their feet, and Reggie mumbling and flipping pages to check or make notes.

"Well," Reggie sighed, once he reached the pit again, "it seems this open chamber without floor or ceiling is the challenge."

He walked back towards the entrance, and the other two followed.

"We need to create a bridge of light," he continued, "and that should show a path, or create one, that leads us safely to the opposite side of the chasm."

"Can we use Raven Stealer?" LT asked.

"I don't believe so," Reggie shook his head, "otherwise we'd have seen the way when Griffon waved her over the side. I believe we need sunlight."

"Hmph," Griffon grunted, tapping at his teeth with the nub of his dirty, chewed fingernail.

The gnome paced back and forth, looking at the walls, then the door, then down the hall.

"What are you thinking, little one?" LT asked.

"That we need to work on how you address gnomes, tall chick," Griffon said, then went on. "But, no, really…what I'm thinking is that this whole thing isn't much different from some of the stuff I've done in dungeons in my video games."

The gnome's face brightened.

"Hey!" He exclaimed, and the other two looked over expectantly. "I wonder if I could design a video game based on this world and my adventures if I ever get back home! That would be awesome. There's nothing like this on the market!"

"Focus, Griffon," Reggie said gently. "Did you have an idea to get across?"

"The mirrors, duh," the gamer said, pointing, "you're supposed to angle them, so they catch the light, bounce it off one another, and light up that pit. It's about the perfect time of day for it also. We started just after sunrise, so the sun should be at the perfect angle to hit the first one."

"One problem," LT pointed at the doors, "there is no sunlight because of volcanic cloud cover that makes it eternally dusk."

"Yeah," Griffon nodded, tapping on his teeth again, "I'm working on that."

"I've never seen him think this hard," Reggie whispered to LT.

"Think his head will explode?" LT grinned.

"Probably not," Reggie smiled back, "but there's a good chance he'll have a headache at a minimum."

"I can still hear you, dorks," Griffon said, chewing on his nail. He paced back and forth, squinting in each direction, then snapped his fingers. "I got it!"

He moved to the open doorway, and stood in the center, Raven Stealer in one hand and held low.

"Are you going to fill us in?" LT asked.

"I make sunlight," Griffon said, shrugging, "using my illusions. If I can make fireworks, why not one beam of light? You guys just position the mirrors, so it bounces from one to the other."

"I do see a small fly in the ointment," Reggie said slowly.

"What's that mean?" Griffon huffed.

"It means that there's a problem with your plan," LT explained. "What is it, Reggie?"

"How does he get across?" Reggie asked, and the other two stared at him. "Think for a moment. He makes the sunbeam—which may or may not work— and we get across. He has to move to cross the path, and he can barely hold an illusion while concentrating. Even if he can do it, once he's at the edge of the pit, the mirrors will be behind him, and the light won't be there."

"He's right," Griffon slumped. "I can't move and hold the light. I could just wait here for you guys to get back."

"No," Reggie shook his head, "we might need you, and you don't know what will be coming out and may need us."

"Right," Griffon sighed, "never split the party."

"Can't you teleport across the pit?" LT asked. "Your sword lets you do that, right?"

"He has to be able to see where he's going," Reggie said.

"No, she's right," Griffon brightened. "Once you guys are there, make sure you have some light and I should be able to see well enough to teleport to the other side."

Reggie stared at the gnome, considering.

"Can anyone think of another way?" he asked.

Both shook their heads.

"Then," he sighed, "I guess this is our best plan. Go ahead and do it, Griffon."

Griffon pulled his shoulders back and took a deep breath, preparing himself.

"But," Reggie said, "be careful."

"And don't drop us in the hole," LT warned. "If you kill me, I'm going to come back as one of these dead things and kill you. Or at least haunt you."

"Your beauty is haunting enough," Griffon said, smiling.

"Oh, that was pretty good," LT laughed.

"Yes, very well flirted," Reggie grumbled. "Now, can we get on with this?"

Griffon readied himself again, Reggie moving to the first mirror, and LT moving to the one across from the archeologist.

The gnome's free hand glowed, and a beam of yellow sunlight burst from his open palm. He held it up, aiming it for the first mirror. Reggie twisted the looking glass on its stand, catching the beam and directing it across the hall to the second mirror.

LT pivoted the reflective surface of the second one as Reggie jogged to the next one on his side of the hall. They continued playing leapfrog, pointing the mirrors deeper into the gloom.

Halfway down the hall, the beam wavered, stuttering in intermittent bursts.

"You okay?" LT called back to Griffon.

"Yeah," Griffon shouted, "my nose was itching, and I had to scratch it."

The beam wavered again, and Reggie traded concerned looks with LT.

"He sounds like he's pushing himself," Reggie whispered.

"Let's pick up the pace then," LT whispered back, and ran to the next mirror.

She bumped into the column and the looking glass wobbled with a loud clunk, clunk noise. She grabbed at it as it tumbled from the stand, catching it a fingerbreadth from the floor.

Letting out a slow breath, she set it back on the column and adjusted it. The beam hit Reggie's worried face at the next station, and he squinted and shook his head as he adjusted the angle of his mirror.

In less than two minutes, they turned the final mirror towards the pit. A golden pathway sparkled into existence, creating a walkway across the waiting darkness.

The purple cloud sparked and darted away from the path, but lingered close.

"We're crossing," Reggie shouted down the hall, and saw the beam of light waver, along with the bridge.

"I hope he was just nodding," LT mumbled, then turned to Reggie. "After you."

She gestured for the man to cross first, and Reggie didn't argue or attempt to be chivalrous. He ran across the golden span, being careful to stay in the center, his eyes darting to the purple haze lurking nearby.

His feet made no sound on the surface, and each step made a brighter spot when his foot touched it.

Reaching the other side, he spun and held a hand out to LT, who was close behind him. She took it, and the two fell to the ground.

"We're across!" She shouted back the way they'd come, and the light of the bridge winked out before she was done.

The energy cloud shot towards them, slamming against an invisible barrier at the edge of the precipice, and the two pulled their feet further from the pit.

The square of light of the open doorway was much smaller than they expected it to be, and it silhouetted a tiny smudge of the gnome in the center.

"I think he's catching his breath," LT said quietly.

"He did well," Reggie said, nodding. "He deserves a break. But I hope not too long."

As if Griffon had heard them, they saw the pure white globe of light from Raven Stealer growing larger. It moved slowly at first, but as it approached the edge, grew faster.

"Why's he running?" LT asked. "Does he need a running start to make it?"

"The light!" Reggie said, pulling his pack off his shoulder and scrambling through the contents. Lantern, oil, flint, and steel tumbled across the ground, rolling towards the edge and the waiting cloud.

LT snatched them up and unscrewed the reservoir on the bottom of the lantern.

"Not enough time," Reggie said, snatching up the flask of oil, uncorking it and pouring it on the stone floor.

LT grabbed the flint and steel, striking a spark and the ground flared blue, then burst into a bright yellow flame.

Reggie looked up to see Griffon almost at the edge, running at full speed, and the gnome leapt into the air over the chasm.

The purple cloud exploded into action, shooting towards the man, thin sparking tendrils launching from its mass towards Griffon. The gnome disappeared in a flash of white, accompanied by a dramatic, musical "bum, bum!". The energy tentacles closed on empty air, and Griffon reappeared in front of the two, and in the center of the flames. Letting out a sharp scream, the gnome danced backwards, his foot going off the edge of the ledge. He windmilled his arms, Raven Stealer leaving trailers of light in the air.

LT and Reggie lurched forward, grabbing at the gnome. They pulled him in, LT tugging him to her side, and the purple energy slammed against the invisible barrier again. She slapped at the flames on the gnome's boots, still gripping his belt with her other hand.

"You can keep holding that if you want," Griffon said, looking down at her hand curled around his belt buckle and down the front of his trousers.

"Ugh," she said, jerking her hand away, "you need to cool off, big guy, before I push you over the edge myself."

"Too hot to handle, amirite?" Griffon purred suavely.

"Pemtie," LT said, standing up and wiping her hands on her thighs.

Reggie dropped back down to the ground, and the flames of the spilled oil died down to small sprouts of fire dancing in the last of the puddle.

"Take a moment," he panted, "then we'll look around."

"Having a heart attack?" Griffon asked, moving around the remaining flames to sit down.

"No," Reggie breathed, shaking his head, "had those. This is not one."

"He was just worried about you," LT said teasingly.

"D'aw," Griffon drew out the sound, "he really does care."

"Damn right, I do." Reggie snapped. "Now, collect yourselves so we can get on with this."

Reggie saw LT studying him, and he waved a dismissive hand at her.

"I'm fine, really," he said.

"You're under a lot of pressure," LT said, "and you're doing great."

"What about me?" Griffon interrupted. "I was the brains this time, and I did the thing! I think I was pretty awesome."

The last sentence came out much quieter.

"You were dazzling," Reggie smiled at the gnome. "We couldn't have gotten this far without you. The world will owe you a debt if we survive this."

"Oh, good job boosting morale, Reggie," LT said dryly. "We'll be heroes, as long as we don't die."

"Naw," Griffon said, rising to his feet, "I get it."

The small man put a hand to his head and winced.

"You okay?" LT asked.

"Just a headache," Griffon nodded.

"Told you," Reggie shot a look and a pained grin at LT.

"At least his head didn't explode," LT grinned.

"Feels like it might," Griffon groaned, squeezing his temples.

"Drink something," Reggie said, standing and turning to inspect the walls, "and eat some of that hard bread you hate. It might help."

"Ugh, no thanks," Griffon said.

"He's right," LT said, digging in her pack and bringing out some hard tack, "and besides, he's going to need some time to look around and see what comes next."

Reggie bent and picked up his lantern and other things, then pulled out another flask of oil.

"I'll use this until you can stand without wincing," he said, filling the reservoir and lighting the lantern.

"I'll hold it for you," LT offered, "so you can scribble in your little book."

Reggie passed the light to her, glancing back at Griffon. The small man had sat back down and was tearing a chunk of bread off with his teeth and holding his head with his free hand.

The walls came together at an angle, like a funnel, a passage at the point. A few paces down that hall was a huge stone block. A small gap at the sides showed dozens of hands, black fingers with crusted nails scratching at the edge of the stone.

"Dead inside," LT murmured, and Reggie cast a startled glance at the woman.

Chapter 14

"So, it's a literal dead end?" Griffon snickered after they'd relayed the news back to him, then moaned and touched his head.

"Hold on," Reggie said, "let me check the walls to see what information the mages left there."

"First the blood," LT said, "then that thing and the pit…"

"I think it fed on living essence," Reggie said over his shoulder as he studied the carvings on the wall.

"Like the soul?" LT asked, moving the light so show the next section of symbols. "It was a soul-sucking energy cloud."

"Maybe," Reggie shrugged, making a note in his book.

"That's chuzzed up," LT shivered. "How would you even make something like that?"

"No idea," Reggie mumbled, "but it would drain anything living or dead it touched."

"Glad you weren't very clear on that before we crossed the pit," LT said. "Can't wait to see what the third thing is. And they always do it in threes, don't they?"

"Magic number, and all that," Reggie said, moving to the stone blocking their way and giving the dead hands a wide berth.

LT dropped the subject, letting the man do his work. She looked around, craning her neck to the ceiling and stretching. She stopped, raising the lantern higher to cast light on the overhead stone.

"Do you mind?" Reggie asked. "I can't read with you turning away like that."

"Oh, sorry," she said, "but I just noticed something."

The lantern lit Reggie's face as she swung it back to the wall, and the man looked haggard.

"What did you notice?" he asked, turning back to the symbols.

"They rigged the ceiling to collapse if that stone is moved," LT said.

Reggie froze, slowly turning towards her, and glanced up.

"What?" he asked, then shook his head to stop her from repeating the words. "I heard you, but are you sure?"

"Pretty sure," she nodded, pointing at spots above them. "Look there, and there, and over in the corner. Those are balance points. The ceiling is resting on that stone, and…"

LT lifted the light, moving it to illuminate the stone above them, then down the wall.

"Yeah," she nodded again, "there's a whole mechanism. Looks like it goes behind the walls, though. We'd have to break them down to get to them, but they might allow us to find the safety switch and winch the blockade up."

"And release a horde of undead into the room with us," Reggie sighed, "with an endless drop behind us with a…what did you call it? A soul sucker behind us, waiting for a meal?"

"Sure," LT nodded, "if you want to put it that way, it sounds pretty grim."

The white light of Raven Stealer crept across them, and Griffon stepped forward.

"I don't think that's our only problem," he said, one hand on his head, the other holding the blade, "but if we do this third impossible task, and then beat whatever is behind the wall, and shut down the magical disease factory…how are we going to get out?"

LT stared at the gnome.

Reggie cleared his throat.

"I am hoping there's a back door," he said guiltily.

"So, you thought of that?" LT turned and looked at Reggie. "This could turn out to be a suicide mission?"

"She's right," Griffon said. "It's not like we have a couple of spellslingers with us."

The three stood in silence for a minute.

"I'm truly sorry I brought you both into this," Reggie sighed. "But look at all we've accomplished so far. We've fought through vriktiri and lost folk, faced down bounty hunters, saved Allendale, and made it past two of the three obstacles in this forgotten ruin. I'm confident we'll be able to see this through and live to tell the tale."

"Do we have a choice?" LT snarled. "Look, I know you're under a lot of pressure, and I think we would've both come along with you even if we knew the odds…"

"I wouldn't have," Griffon grumbled.

"But not telling us," LT continued, "that's just bullbidj."

They fell silent again.

"In my defense," Reggie mumbled, "I didn't know about the traps."

"Whatever," Griffon said.

"Doesn't matter now," LT huffed, "we're here and either we see this through, or we die on this platform. Let's figure this out, and we can deal with you later."

"Now she sounds like your mom," Griffon giggled, then gripped his head.

"Stow it, pipsqueak," LT growled, lifting the lantern, "and don't say you have something I can stow, because I'll punch you."

LT stomped around the room, studying the walls. Glancing back at the two men, she sighed.

"Come on, boys," she said, "start reading the walls. Maybe there's something helpful there. I'll figure out how to stop the roof from collapsing."

"How you gonna do that?" Griffon asked.

"Engineer, remember?" she replied.

"Geez, this woman knows how to do everything," Griffon muttered.

"Maybe that's why she was chosen," Reggie said. "Now, can you hold that sword up so I can look at the writings?"

The three went to work, LT keeping her distance from Reggie. She drew a dagger, glancing at her bow near the edge of the pit to make sure it was still there, and tapped on the stone walls. She tilted her head, listening to the sound as she moved along the relief carvings.

"Here," Reggie said, "I've found something."

LT turned and looked at him.

"What?" she asked.

"This panel has no information of import relating to the prison. It details the history of the mages and warns to not release what's inside."

"Don't you think we should listen to a bunch of thousand-year-old mages who left a message?" Griffon asked.

LT walked over and tapped on the panel with the butt of her dagger.

"Hollow," she said. "Or at least not solid, not as thick as the other parts. Did you get any information about how to stop what's inside?"

"Erm, yes, sort of," Reggie nodded.

"Sorta?" LT raised her eyebrows. "What does that mean?"

"Here," Reggie put a finger on a line of hieroglyphics surrounded by ancient script, "I believe that says that there are thirteen liches within, along with their servants. Those servants would be what you think of as zombies, and some would be wraiths."

"Wraiths?" Griffon swallowed. "You mean the ghost guys that if they touch you, it drains your life from you and turns your brain to mush?"

Reggie nodded; his mouth drawn into a tight line.

"And thirteen liches?" Griffon asked.

Reggie nodded again.

"What's a lich?" LT stared at the pictographs.

"A spellslinger who is also the walking dead," Reggie explained.

"But with centuries of experience," Griffon added.

"The good news is that the most powerful is no longer imprisoned here," Reggie said. "Verl'zen-luk escaped and became a…god." He grew quieter with each word. "And he may have weakened the others when he did that," Reggie finished.

"It says that?" LT asked.

"No," Reggie shook his head, "but it would make sense."

"Does it tell us how to beat the ones left behind?" she asked.

"Bet they're gonna be pissed," Griffon said.

"No, it doesn't," Reggie said, rushing on with his next words, "but I think the light of Griffon's sword, and my own Marcid may disrupt them. It looks like the mages used the power of light and life to trap them here. Raven Stealer is a holy blade of Promethene, goddess of sound and light. And Jonath blessed my blade for protection and Senaria blessed it for life."

"And what do I have?" LT asked.

"I'll protect you," Griffon smiled innocently up at the woman.

"Wow," LT said, "you actually made eye contact when you said that. Progress. Maybe there is hope for you."

Griffon shifted his eyes back down to her chest.

LT put a hand on his face and shoved him back.

"Ow," Griffon yelped, stumbling back and putting a hand on his forehead, "my head!"

"Serves you right, perv," LT said. "Okay, what about the liches? Will your swords help with them?"

Reggie heaved a sigh.

"I don't know," he said, then quickly added, "but I hope so."

"Hope so?" LT stared at him, then nodded. "I guess it will have to do." She pointed at the panel Reggie had singled out earlier. "Break it down. I need to get to the mechanism behind it. It lines up with the chains and pulley system above. It should let us move the stone without dying."

"Why didn't they just blow this place up?" Griffon asked. "I mean, just kill everything in it. Again. So they were really dead?"

"Probably because it would have released their spirits," LT said, "and let them loose on the world."

"Enh," Griffon shrugged, "makes sense."

Reggie drew Marcid, and the thin rapier blade morphed and warped into a massive sledgehammer with a long handle.

He raised the weapon and swung it at chest level. It connected with the stone panel and the wall shuddered.

A collective groan came from the stone blocking the way deeper into the complex.

"Was that them," Griffon said, pointing at the gnarled hands jutting between the wall and the blockade, "or the building?"

"I don't know which answer I'd rather hear," LT said, then turned to Reggie. "Keep going, Pops. Let's do this thing."

Raising the hammer again, Reggie swung at the façade and the head of the weapon lodged in a hole created by his blow. He repeated the process, moving from side to side, and up and down, until the wall lay in rubble at their feet.

He stood up, stretching his back and wiping the sweat on his forehead.

"It's up to you now," he said to LT.

"Hope this doesn't kill us," Griffon breathed.

"Oh, don't worry about that," LT said, and hooked a thumb at Reggie as she walked past the man. "He may have already done that. And, in case you two didn't notice, the air seems to be affecting us in a weird way. We're all showing signs of it. Your headache,

Griffon. Your tiredness, Reggie. My temper is raging right now. Could be one more trap to keep people from releasing these things. A mental attack through the stale air. Or it could be a side effect of what lies beyond this third trap."

LT turned back to the opening. A series of levers were arrayed in the alcove, and LT studied them, tracing the chains connected to them. She followed them with her eyes and pointed with a finger, up the wall and into the holes that led into the depths of the structure.

"This one," she touched a lever, "should collapse this entire area."

"Don't pull that one then," Griffon suggested helpfully.

"This one should…" LT followed the lines with her eyes again, "should turn the door, so it opens like a secret passage."

She looked at the two men.

"I suggest you both get ready for a flood of zombies, or whatever," she said, then walked over to recover her bow.

"If they bite me," Griffon asked, holding his weapon horizontal over his head in an attack stance, "will I become a zombie?"

"I don't think it works that way," Reggie said, changing Marcid into a rapier and main-gauche.

"That's how it works in movies," Griffon pointed out.

"Necromancers need to imbue them with magic in this world. At least that's my understanding," Reggie said, bouncing on the balls of his feet. "If we're killed, then one of the liches would need to animate our corpses for us to become one of the undead."

"Well," LT said, returning to the levers, "that's reassuring."

She tucked an arrow between her fingers holding her bow and looked at the men.

"Are we ready, then?" she asked.

"Maybe we should eat first," Reggie suggested, glancing at her, "so we have energy and a bit of rest?"

"Too late for that," she growled and pulled the lever.

The enormous stone blocking the passage jerked, the building shuddering and sand drifting down from above, and slowly turned sideways.

Openings on each side appeared, and a flood of desiccated figures poured through. They tumbled over one another, scrambling towards the three, clawed fingers spasming and mouths open to show broken teeth.

"Oh," Reggie shouted over the dry rustle of dozens of undead rushing toward them, "to kill them permanently, we want to behead them or burn their corpses! Otherwise, they just reassemble and get back up in a few minutes!"

"Another thing you might have wanted to tell us before I opened the damned door!" LT shouted back, firing arrows into the mass as quickly as she could draw and nock them.

"They are inside the complex, My Lord," Karek-kal muttered into the sand at Ahken'ho-tek's feet, "and have overcome the obstacles that kept us locked within. We may leave at any time."

The Lich Lord looked down at the husk prostrated in front of him, his grey lips twitching. The once minor lord who prided himself on his ability to manipulate people—and bed anybody his whim fancied—hadn't seen a bed in longer than any human had been alive. Ahken'ho-tek had made sure of it.

Removing the sins, pleasures, and vices of his inferiors was a tried-and-true method of keeping them off balance, unable to release steam so they were twisted tight, and ready to explode with the slightest push.

Five other liches were arrayed behind the once powerful mage and were loyal to him, not Ahken'ho-tek. Today, they would learn the error of their ways.

Karek-kal had once been the third most powerful lich in the city, but had spent too much time and energy currying the favor of his lessers instead of competing against or undercutting his betters. The power-gap had widened, and he fell behind the others. They went on to gain position and the titles that came with it, while Karek-kal tried to play damage control with his squabbling underlings.

It was a fatal mistake, but one which Ahken'ho-tek could use.

"Then," Ahken'ho-tek said, "let us begin with the final preparations. You six shall be instrumental in my plans and allow me to rise above all the others."

The Lord glided down the steps from the throne, the semi-circle moving back and closing around him.

"Come," Ahken'ho-tek purred, "join hands in a circle surrounding me. Link your magics, creating a sphere around me strong enough to feed from my energy."

Karek-kal's eyes lit up, and Ahken'ho-tek pretended to not notice. The minor lich nodded his permission and encouragement to his flunkies, holding his hands out to the sides to form the circle.

"That's it," Ahken'ho-tek encouraged, "and dig your arcane fingers into my aura, burrow into my energies, seek the core of my power."

A single minor lich looked up, a shocked look crossing her withered face. Pulling away, she tried to free her hands from the others, but was locked in their grips and their greed.

The Lich Lord felt them delve into his spirit and knew when they'd hooked into his essence. He reversed the polarity of the spell he'd woven before they'd entered and felt it feed him.

The ethereal proboscises of the six were drawn in further, and rather than pulling the arcane energies from Ahken'ho-tek, it began pumping theirs into the Lich Lord.

The heads of the lesser liches collapsed, crumpling into themselves as their bodies shriveled, turning to wispy streams of dust. A ghostly form wavered in the place the beings had been a few seconds before, then those too shrank and were drawn into Ahken'ho-tek. The Lich Lord shivered and sighed, his face contorting into a smile.

"One more item on my agenda that must be addressed," Ahken'ho-tek said, "then I shall be prepared to change the very laws of nature."

Chapter 15

The dead littered the floor and Griffon felt his stomach turn. Broken, beheaded bodies were slowly becoming smoldering cords of corpse kindling. He kicked a wriggling hand towards the fires.

He didn't glorify in the deaths he caused in the arena or in combat in the field, but it was very different from slaying the undead.

Be honest with yourself, Raven Stealer said in his head, *you glorify in it a little bit. You take pride in it, to say the least.*

The remains of the undead were different than living creatures, as if some mystical taint was being released from them, and their very souls had rotted along with their bodies.

"I only have one flask of oil remaining," Reggie said, tucking the container he'd just emptied back into his bag. "I suggest we make some torches so we can destroy any others we run across."

"Do these things have souls?" Griffon asked.

"I don't think so," Reggie shook his head, "at least not in the way we think of them. The soul, from what I understand, is what makes us who we are. It's thoughts, emotions, memories, and experiences all wrapped into the spirit. That was all released when these people died, but the magic reanimated their corpses with something else. An energy from someplace else."

"That seems pretty well thought out," LT said.

"I was pretty old before," Reggie shrugged, "and had a lot of time to mull it over. Reading Aiyana's notes helped expand and reinforce the ideas I'd already formed. But I don't think we're fully capable of grasping it in our current forms. Our minds just can't encompass all of it."

He is correct, Griffon's sword said, *you do have an extremely limited grasp on the larger picture.*

"But I assume you know it all?" Griffon asked the weapon.

Not at all, Raven Stealer said telepathically, *but I have a more complete view than you and your friends.*

"No, Griffon," Reggie sighed, "but I try to make sense of what I've lived through, and what may come next."

"Not you," the gnome said to Reggie. "My sword is putting us down."

I am not, I merely have a larger perspective. The weapon clarified.

"Guys," LT said, "what is that?" She pointed at a dusky form floating down the hall towards them.

"Wraith," Reggie said, lifting Marcid towards the being.

"Allow me," Griffon moved in front of the man and the light from Raven Stealer made the creature flinch away.

The gnome charged forward, and the spirit slid to one side, trying to move past him. The weapon touched the ethereal form, and it screamed, sort of. The sound was inside Griffon's head as much as out, and the gnome gritted his teeth and swung again.

You are very angry, Raven Stealer commented, *and I cannot find the reason why.*

The wraith melted under the blows, a shadow staining the wall where it had been a moment before.

"My head hurts," Griffon growled, pressing one hand to the back of his skull and massaging, "and I don't really want to be here."

Stalking forward and breathing heavily, Griffon watched for more of the things to appear.

The dry air in the tunnels didn't have a scent, and the bacteria that created smells needed moisture and a food source. Both things had faded long ago. There was a grit in the air that settled on everything, and Griffon could feel it on his teeth, in his hair, on his skin, and in his lungs.

The murky yellow stones they'd watched light the way when they first entered the ruins were still present, but only one out of three shone, and they were dimmer than the ones in the entryway. The ceilings were the height of two humans, making Griffon wonder if it was to make the cramped space seem larger, or because giants once walked these halls.

The halls were wide stone passages, faded scenes painted every dozen paces or so, most of them too far gone to be recognizable. At intersections, directories were etched into the walls, reminding the gnome of how offices and hotels did the same so guests could find their way around.

It was eerily quiet, most sounds coming from their own breathing and footfalls. Any noise not from them made him stop and tilt his head to see if something was coming.

The others trailed behind him, Reggie taking up the rear. Griffon assumed that was in case something came up behind them. The swashbuckler would have a better chance against the mobs in this place with his magical weapon than LT would.

Turning the corner, Griffon checked the walls, looking for the carved signposts he'd used the last time he'd been here with Reggie.

"It's okay, Griffon," LT said, "you've got this."

The comment earned her a glare from the gnome.

"Do I have a choice?" he asked. "Do any of us?"

I have never seen you like this, and am not sure how to offer help, Raven Stealer said.

"Just watch my back and let me know if you see anything," Griffon muttered, as much to LT as the sword.

Griffon usually let his mind go when he was in combat, allowing the instincts of the body to guide him. Now it was different. He was in total control of himself, and it annoyed him. There was no autopilot to lean on, no other autonomous response, so he didn't have to think and deal with what was going on.

I do not think Auric ever had to deal with anything like this in his lifetime, Raven Stealer said. *Perhaps you are better equipped to handle this than the other part of you?*

"Whatever," he mumbled, "but it makes me think of the witches that were sacrificing me when I first got here, and the thing they summoned. I wonder if I should go look for them after all this is done."

"Is he okay?" LT whispered over her shoulder to Reggie.

"Probably," Reggie said, "but I imagine dealing with a magical sword in your head can be…different."

"You know she can talk out loud, right?" Griffon said, his voice echoing down the hall. "She's made noises, music and stuff, and I know she could make words if she wanted to."

"Tattle tale," Raven Stealer said out loud, a musical tinkling sound, her blade dimming and brightening with each syllable.

"Wow!" Reggie said, craning his neck to look around LT. "Think of what we can learn from her!"

"Not now," Griffon snapped, "we've got more company."

A trio of the spectral residents of the undead city materialized into murky solidity a few paces in front of the gladiator.

The gnome charged forward, slicing through the first, and spinning to cut through the second. The third crouched, reaching out with a glowing blue hand and gripped Griffon's calf. The gnome crumpled to the ground.

He swung the sword at the being's head, slicing through the misty form. The wraith dissipated into strands of fog and disappeared.

"I can't feel my leg," Griffon said, rubbing his calf with his free hand. "It's like it went super cold, then numb."

LT reached down and helped him up.

Struggling to his feet, Griffon tested his weight on the afflicted leg and stumbled. LT held him up and he grimaced at her.

"Ow, ow, ow," he breathed. "I think the feeling is coming back."

"Glad it didn't touch you on your chest," LT said.

The gnome looked up at her, paling.

"Bidj," he said, "I wonder if it could stop my heart."

"Anyone ever have blessed arrows?" LT asked. "They would be pretty damned handy right now."

"That makes me wonder," Griffon said through gritted teeth, "why don't vampire slayers use arrows instead of trying to stab Dracula with a stake?"

"Dramatics," Reggie said, "also, an arrow could pass through, thus being useless."

"Maybe," LT said thoughtfully, looking at the steel tip on the arrow nocked to her bowstring in her other hand.

"I think the throne room is just around the corner," Griffon said, pointing at the symbols on the wall, "but I don't know if that's where we want to go to stop this disease. Is it?"

He directed that last question to Reggie.

"I think it is," the man nodded, "because that was where the map room was located. I think the portal room we used to enter and leave might be the back door we're hoping exists."

"But can we get it to work without the Scepter Key we stole?" Griffon tossed a worried look at Reggie.

"You mean this?" Reggie asked, pulling a curved object out of his bag just far enough that the others could see it.

"Oh, yeah," Griffon said with apparent relief, "I forgot you grabbed that."

"How's your leg?" LT asked.

"Better," Griffon said. "I think I can walk on it. Or at least limp on it."

He tested his balance, LT still holding his arm, and nodded.

"I should be fine," he said, pulling away from the woman, "let's get this done. Maybe we'll get some treasure this time. These things haven't had a single copper sharp on them."

In a few minutes, they came upon the wide double doors to the throne room. Unlike the first time they'd been here, they were closed.

Griffon reached for them, but Reggie put a hand on the gnome's shoulder, stopping him.

"Let her look them over," Reggie suggested. "She has a keen eye, and it may be trapped or warded."

"That's ridiculous," Griffon rolled his eyes, "who puts traps inside of the place they live? Now who's been playing too many video games?"

"Humor me," Reggie said. "LT, would you please take a look?"

"You know, a group of guys used to play Dungeons and Dragons on base," she said, moving forward to inspect the doors, "and they'd spend an hour looking for traps and secret doors every time they did anything. It felt stupid then, but now, it kind of makes sense. People would lay tripwires that set off explosives in some of the places we went, so…"

She shrugged, standing up from checking out the doorframe and the latches.

"Looks clean to me," she said and pushed on the doors.

They didn't budge.

"But they might be locked," she said sheepishly.

"That's new," Reggie muttered, leaning in to look. "Anyone any good at opening locked things?"

"They open inward, so can't pop the hinges," LT pointed out, "and those are just handles, so no lock to pick. Could be barred from the other side. That means trying to lift the latch or whatever, or if they've used door stops or rods that go in the ceiling and floor, then we'll need to force the door."

She had her thin dagger out and slid it between the double doors and jiggled it up and down. Something clacked on the other side and the door swung open a hand-span. A beam of bright light spilled into the hall.

"Hey," Griffon said brightly, "she's got the makings of a pretty good rogue."

"Then maybe she should have put her eye to the crack before opening the door," Reggie murmured, pointing at the scene inside.

Griffon moved closer, leaning over to look inside.

"Oh," he said, "I withdraw my previous statement."

The throne room was as the two men remembered: a wide chamber with double columns lining the length, and a huge stone throne in the center. Fragments of crystal embedded in the walls and supports reflected light, and the room was well lit, showing the doorways on each side.

A withered husk of a man in tattered robes stood in front of the throne, three figures arrayed in front of him. Two others knelt on the floor at the foot of the steps leading up to the massive stone chair, quivering as intense rays of energy swirled around them. Their heads were thrown back, and their backs arched in a rictus of pain.

The thicker of the victims wore dazzling, shimmering robes, and the smaller one looked almost alive with pale skin that showed few traces of decay. Six other desiccated forms lay in wrinkled piles around the scene.

"That must be the liches," Griffon said quietly, licking his lips. "Is he…sucking them off?"

"Lepat-fal Master of the Unseen and Telvak-ral Guardian of the Tomes," the lich in the center rasped, his accent thick and almost undecipherable, "you have conspired against me, and for this I thank you. You have given up your rights in our coven, but still fulfill a useful purpose. I gratefully accept your sacrifice and your power into myself."

"Ahken'ho-tek, Lord of Liches," a female lich beside the Lord intoned, "has taken what is rightfully his by our laws, and we thank him for his mercy upon us. I, Venat-fal, Mistress of the Stables, pledge myself and my legion of undead to you."

She fell to her knees, her head bowed.

"I, Kenal, Master of Minions," the second said reverently, dropping to his hands and knees, placing his forehead on the ground between his splayed arms, "accept you as my master, and pledge my legions of vriktiri to your whim and command."

"And I, Chektar-ral, Mistress of the Ley, also pledge my power to your guidance and wisdom," the third said, lowering herself to a kneeling position and bowing her head slightly.

"Interestingly put, Chektar-ral," Ahken'ho-tek said, turning from the third lich, "but enough of this. Our liberators have arrived."

Pointing at the door, the lich continued to draw in the energies from the writhing forms in front of him.

"Let us welcome them, and bequeath upon them their eternal reward," Ahken'ho-tek said, "the keys to the kingdom, and their place as rightful rulers of Ez'rainia-fromton, City of the Dead, and their final resting place."

The other three rose from their subservient positions and turned towards the trio.

"I have the gift you left for us," Ahken'ho-tek said, holding a dull colored, fist-sized stone up, "the portalling stone you used to get here."

"Guess the jig is up," Reggie said, pushing the doors open, "I'll keep him talking. You two take out the others."

Reggie strode into the room, Marcid in his hand, and gave a small bow.

"You're welcome," Reggie said, "but it won't do you any good. It's exhausted, all the magic spent."

"But that is not completely the truth," Ahken'ho-tek rasped, "it is emptied, but can be recharged with the energies within this complex. All our plans shall come to fruition, because of you."

The arcane energies around the imprisoned liches fell away, their drained bodies falling to the floor with a click of bones and a whisper of parchment flesh and torn cloth.

The scintillating rays scattered across the chamber bent, turning towards the Lord of Liches, and piercing the stone in his hand. His dead face split into a grin, deep blue flames dancing within his sunken eye sockets.

"To hell with this," Griffon said. "I'm not waiting for the Voltron of liches—Vol-lich? No, Lichtron—to finish his plan while he keeps *you* talking!"

The gladiator raised his ivory blade and charged forward.

LT sighed, lifting her bow and firing to cover her smaller friend.

Arrows sailed over him and broke on an unseen barrier between the group and the throne, just outside of the circle of drained liches scattered on the floor.

Griffon covered the space in seconds, but crashed face first into that same invisible shield, bouncing off and landing on his butt.

"We shan't leave you without a fight," Ahken'ho-tek hissed. "In fact, you will never be alone again. Venat-fal call the troops, and I will summon the unseen forces of Ez'rainia-fromton. We shall give the new rulers a proper welcome."

A deep moan came from outside of the room, and dozens of forms lurched in from every doorway.

With a laugh like nails on a chalkboard, Ahken'ho-tek held the portalling stone up as it absorbed the last of the magic from the complex and the surrounding lights winked out.

A blue shimmering mist gathered around the four liches on the dais, and they faded from view, the last of their magical light disappearing.

Only the light of Raven Stealer remained, and it showed the shuffling legion of undead approaching the trio.

Chapter 16

Reggie and LT moved closer to Griffon and the light shed by Raven Stealer.

"Is the throne more defensible, or the map room?" Reggie asked.

"The throne lets them come at us from all sides," LT said, gripping her bow, "but a doorway makes them come in a few at a time."

"On it," Griffon said.

Having regained his feet, the gnome headed towards the door directly across from where they were, cutting through the legs of a handful of zombies between him and his destination, clearing a path for his friends.

Once in the door, he waved them past and took up a defensive stance to block the way from the dozens more moaning undead coming towards them.

LT took a quick inventory of her remaining arrows, fifteen, then pulled the spear from her back and leaned it against the wall beside her.

Reggie set his satchel on the map table and rummaged through it. He pulled out the lantern, flint and steel, and his last remaining flask of oil.

"If," Griffon said, decapitating the first undead trying to enter, "we're the new rulers, why are they attacking instead of kneeling?"

"That guy might have been lying?" LT gasped, her sarcasm apparent. "If you can't trust a dead guy who's been trapped for a thousand years or more, who can you trust?"

"LT," Reggie snapped, "don't shoot any arrows yet. Let me pour some oil on them first, then you light them on the lantern. Flaming arrows should work better than regular ones."

"I won't be able to get them back if they're burnt to a crisp," she said, then shrugged, "of course, I can't get them back if I'm one of them either."

She knelt, dumped her remaining arrows on the floor, and laid them out into a row.

Reggie carefully poured some oil on their tips, then the rest into the lantern. He struck the flint and steel, setting the wick ablaze.

Drawing Marcid, the swashbuckler moved next to Griffon.

"You know this won't work, right?" he said.

"Great," LT said, "more morale boosting."

She fired a series of arrows over the heads of her companions and the first line of undead. Flames erupted in the throne room as the arrows bit into the dry flesh of the undead.

"Get used to it," Griffon said. "This guy can be a real downer."

"What I mean is, we need to get to the chamber where we can get out, the teleporting chamber."

"Where will it take us?" Griffon asked, taking out two more undead. "Will it pop us over to the Nine Towers of Magic? At least we'd be safe there, or able to gather others to help."

"I don't think it would," Reggie morphed Marcid to a wide-bladed axe and sliced off the head of a zombie reaching for him. "Aiyana guided us there. But I think anywhere would be better than here."

"What about the disease?" LT asked. "Aren't we supposed to shut that down before leaving?"

"I'm going to step back, Griffon," Reggie said. "Get ready to cover the whole door."

Moving away, he morphed Marcid into a wide-bladed spear and set her on the ground at LT's feet.

"I need that light and your spear when you run out of arrows," he said.

"Great," she said, "just four left. Give me about thirty seconds."

When she fired the last flaming arrow, Reggie grabbed the lantern and her spear, and she took up Marcid and replaced him at the door.

Reggie stepped to the table, studying it, wondering if his plan would work.

"I think they used this to aim whatever they did," Reggie muttered, "directing the vriktiri and the disease. So, to stop it, I should just have to destroy this table…a priceless artifact created in a time of wonder and magic."

"Is he talking to us?" LT said to Griffon, slicing the throat of a zombie with a swing, and decapitating it on the return swing.

"Naw," Griffon said, "he talks to himself when playing with his toys."

"But how do I break a solid stone table?" Reggie went on, ignoring the others. "First, the sand."

He leaned over and scooped the sand across the table. The representations of structures and troops collapsed with contact, and sand poured off the side and onto the floor.

"Next," he said, lifting the lantern to look at the table and then the walls, "there must be magical focuses to use the energy. I just need to break them, right?"

The surface of the table was etched with runes and hieroglyphs. Reggie set down the light and scraped at the symbols with the blade of the spear. The surface crumbled under his vandalism and a gem popped out from under the sigil he'd just destroyed.

Flipping the spear, he crushed it with the butt of the weapon.

The room rumbled.

"That did something," Griffon panted, "but I don't know if it was good."

"Indeed," Reggie muttered, repeating the process.

When he broke the seventh gem he dug out from the table's surface, the map of the continents on the wall turned to a rain of sand and fell across the floor.

"Looks like I'm getting somewhere," he called out, "shouldn't be long now."

"Great," LT said, "hurry up, my arms are burning, and I don't think I can keep this up much longer."

Reggie picked up the pace, the chamber constantly shaking now in response to his destruction.

"Alright," he said loud enough for the others to hear, "I'm going to crush the last few gems, get ready to run for the teleporting chamber."

"If we can remember where it is," Griffon said, "and find it in the dark with hundreds of undead trying to eat our faces."

"Sounds," LT gasped between thrusts, "like a party."

Reggie smashed the remaining gems, the final map bursting into dust, and the table cracking. A large stone fell from the ceiling, crashing to the ground an arm's length from the archeologist.

Snatching the lantern, he dashed across the room to the doorway. Dozens of undead lay in piles just outside the room, and a few inside, and some still were moving.

"Trade me," Reggie thrust the mundane spear at LT.

She took her spear and the lantern with a grateful sigh and handed him Marcid. The magical weapon changed to a longsword the moment Reggie wrapped his hand around the hilt.

"I'll lead," Reggie said, taking a two-handed grip and stepping in front of Griffon. "You two do what you can, but don't die."

"The wisdom of the old," Griffon muttered, "so helpful."

Cutting through the line of zombies past the pile of their confederates, Reggie saw the rest of the room was mostly empty of the creatures, except for a few wandering mindlessly in the far corners.

He beelined for the door they'd entered through, slicing the arm of the single undead reaching for him, then cutting off its head on the return stroke.

Reaching the double doors, he turned right—the opposite direction from which they came—and moved down the hall. He heard the other two following and used Raven Stealer's light to guide his way.

The light was dim because of the distance, and his and LT's shadows kept making him jump, thinking it was something moving in the dark ahead of him.

A wraith materialized directly in front of him, and he skidded to a halt, LT bumping into him and knocking him forward.

Reggie's head and vision spun, his breath catching and his entire body going cold as he passed through the creature. Marcid flared with a silver burst, and the apparition burst into dancing motes of sparks.

He stumbled, throwing a hand out to catch himself, and realized he was on his knees, gasping for breath. A puddle of vomit spread across the floor, and he recoiled.

"Come on," LT said, "I've got you, but you have to stand up. Now. We need to keep moving."

"Of course," he rasped, pushing to his feet.

His knees popped and his joints ached, the familiar feel of arthritis flooding through him. It was like the worst case of body aches he'd ever had when he was sick.

He tottered upright, feeling like he'd aged fifty years in moments, and took a tentative step forward.

Small white flowers appeared on the metal vines along Marcid's cross guard, and berries appeared in the center, growing at an incredible rate. They turned from green to red, and Reggie felt the sword urge him to eat some.

He popped a few off and stuffed them into his mouth. The flavor exploded in his mouth and his head cleared a little as he swallowed.

Turning to the others, he pointed at the berries.

"Both of you," he said, "take some of these. Hurry! I forgot PepperGarten enchanted Marcid to do this. These berries should refresh you, and, well, just eat some, quickly."

LT looked at him dubiously but pulled a few off and put them in her mouth. Her eyes went wide.

"Wow," she whispered, "that's incredible."

"Move over," Griffon pushed her aside, pulling as many off as his he could grab in his small hand and shoved them in his mouth.

Chewing, he sighed and rolled his shoulders.

"Why haven't we been using those all the time?" the gnome asked.

"I forgot about them," Reggie said, taking advantage of the proximity of the light to study the directory on the wall beside him. "But Marcid didn't. It's this way."

The shuffling sounds of the creatures echoed in the hall behind them, and Reggie moved towards their goal.

In a few minutes, and a few turns, Reggie stopped at a stone door with a small alcove in the center.

"Ain't that going to chop off your hand when you stick it in to open the door?" Griffon asked. "I mean, that's what happened before, but Nathan made a stone hand or something, right?"

"Correct," Reggie nodded, and his weapon shifted, becoming shorter and thicker until a metal hand and wrist were in the place the blade was a moment before. "Light, please."

Griffon moved closer, the light from his sword illuminating the interior of the small opening.

Leaning down, Reggie studied the inside, then grunted.

Pushing the appendage into the hole, he twisted the makeshift arm and a metallic click sounded, followed by the door sliding to one side.

"Quickly, inside," Reggie said, pulling Marcid free.

He followed the other two in, forms appearing behind him, and he shoved the magical hand into an alcove on the other side. Withered arms reached for him and were crushed as the massive stone portal slammed shut. Severed limbs thudded on the ground, writhing, and blindly reaching for anything they could grab.

"Now, to get out of here," Reggie said, backpedaling from the undead arms and returning Marcid to her rapier form. He slid the blade back into her scabbard.

Pulling his satchel from his back, he rummaged through it to find the Scepter Key and drew it out reverently.

"Should I keep it this time?" he asked no one in particular.

"I always keep that sort of things in my games," Griffon shrugged, "never know when you want to go back to a dungeon."

Another tremor shook the building, and sand drifted down from above.

"I don't know if this one will be here for much longer," LT said, looking around with wide eyes, "but if you took it, that would mean you might be able to come back. But so could someone else. Do you want to take the chance of it falling into the wrong hands, and someone coming back to use whatever is in this place?"

"Very true," Reggie said quietly, "but I hate to lose the opportunity to study an ancient, lost culture. Remember, this was once an empire before it was a prison."

Sand drifted down around them, and Griffon lifted his feet to pull them free of the ankle-deep silt. "Better decide quickly," he said. "I think the whole place is sinking."

"Maybe into the space created by the lava eruptions," LT suggested, "because if all those volcanoes originated here, then there might be a lot of open space underneath the city. But can we go now? Just take it. You'll never sleep if you don't."

Reggie nodded and stepped to the magical receptacle made to hold the key. "Here goes nothing," he said and pushed the artifact into place.

Reggie blinked in the bright sunlight. His eyes adjusted, and he realized they were still in the muted dusk of the ash clouds overhead.

"Look," Griffon shouted, pointing down the dune they stood on, "it's going!"

LT and Reggie looked in the direction the gnome pointed and saw the collection of yellowed buildings slowly sinking from sight. Waves of sand rolled over the structures like an ocean.

"It's like a desert Atlantis," Griffon said. "And I'm pretty sure it exists."

"Jack Tucker hinted it did when we were in Central America," Reggie murmured quietly, "said it was part of something greater than I could imagine."

They watched the last remnants of a thousand-year-old culture disappear into the dunes, ash covering the ripples of the desert.

Reggie sighed. "That's it, then," he said, his voice rough.

"It could still be under there," Griffon said, "and you guys love digging stuff like that up."

"Except in this world," LT said, "the mummy's curses are real. I'd think twice before going back, Reggie."

After a few minutes, Griffon spoke up. "Can we go now?" he asked.

"Where?" LT said. "We're in the middle of the desert. The liches didn't kill us, neither did the zombies and wraiths, and we survived the collapse of the entire place, but the sun and dehydration can still get us."

"The river," Reggie said, pointing at the sludge packed waterway that cut a straight line from north to south. "We go there and follow it back to the High Tarn and Akar."

"Where do you think the liches went?" Griffon asked.

"Hush," LT shoved the gnome.

"I guess we need to at least warn people about them," Reggie said.

"Just warn them, right?" Griffon asked. "Because I don't think we have what it takes to find them and stop four power-mad and fully pimped ancient dead spellslingers."

"We'll see," Reggie muttered.

LT shoved the gnome again.

"See?" she growled. "This is why you should keep your mouth shut."

They made their way down the sandy slopes to the river and set up the Citadel on its banks. They fell into their cots after a small meal of dried fruits and some heavy drinking.

"Tomorrow," Reggie said into the blackness, "we take the next step into the future, and try to bring hope to a world steeped in darkness."

"Whatever," Griffon murmured sleepily.

"Both of you shut up and get some shuteye," LT's voice came from across the tent, "those berries are wearing off and I don't think I can put up with anymore…"

Her voice drifted off, and a soft snore followed.

Reggie rolled to his side and stared at the canvas wall, thinking of Ez'rainia-fromton and the lost souls left behind in time.

Chapter 17

The crocodile bumped the boat again and Griffon squeaked.

"Was that reeds creaking?" Reggie asked, dipping the paddle shaped Marcid back into the water.

"Nope," LT said, "it was him."

The three sat single file in the reed canoe LT constructed, paddling up the Straight River. Griffon in front, Reggie in the middle, and LT in the back to act as the rudder or to paddle when needed. They'd constructed a few paddles, including an extra, from fallen date trees and spent long days on the water, working their way north.

Gathering fruit from the trees—mangos, figs, and dates—to supplement their dwindling supplies, they also caught and smoked a few fish, fowl, and turtles. They wanted to spend as much time moving and as little time waiting to see what predators thought of them as food.

"That thing must be as long as the three of us end to end," Griffon said, trying to look over the side without leaning his head over the water, "and remember the one we saw the other day? It must have been fifteen meters long! I mean, it was almost the size of a white-trash trailer. I swear I heard gator banjos!"

"That one was positively prehistoric," Reggie said with a wistful sigh.

"Don't say it like that!" LT jabbed the man in the back with a finger. "That thing almost knocked down the Citadel. I thought it was supposed to be camouflaged or something."

"Nothing is perfect, my dear," Reggie mumbled, "and nature always finds a way to outdo man. After all, we're nothing more than children of Senaria and part of her tree of life."

"Did he just compare life to a god in this world?" LT asked. "That's not like him."

"I think he just quoted Lion King and Jurassic Park without knowing it," Griffon snickered.

"Reggie, you okay, old man?" LT poked him again.

"Hm?" Reggie mumbled, looking over his shoulder. "What? Yes, yes, I'm fine. Just loving this part of the journey."

"Are you kidding me?" Griffon turned back to look at him and splashed water across himself. "You're loving that we're sitting in the heat all day, paddling through ash and muck, and tempting alligators three times longer than our canoe—which, may I point out, it made of weeds—to come over and check us out like a buffet?"

"They're crocodiles," Reggie said. "Their snouts are pointed, they're slimmer and larger, they have visible teeth on the bottom jaw. They're more aggressive and their teeth are made for tearing rather than crushing. The differences are obvious to anyone who looks."

"I don't want to experience that last thing. But aren't crocs saltwater though?" LT asked.

"Usually," Reggie shrugged, "but these may have adapted. You can also see a color difference. These are patterned rather than just a very dark green or black."

The craft rocked again, and Griffon jerked his paddle from the side and onto his lap.

"Don't worry," Reggie said, "she's just trying to figure out what we are."

"Lunch," the gnome said, "that's what we are if she tips us."

"Maybe we'll get picked up by one of those river boats Reggie claims do trade on this river," LT said.

"I hope so," the antiquarian said, "but I'm wondering if they'd stopped their routes because of the ash and volcanoes."

"There's like fourteen of them," Griffon said. "They're everywhere."

"Fourteen that you can see," Reggie said. "They can stay submerged for an hour or so."

"That's not helping my anxiety," the gnome muttered.

"Paddle, Griffon," LT said from the rear, "we're drifting towards the shore, and that's where they hang out waiting for things to eat."

Griffon moaned and delicately put his paddle back in the water and stroked.

The ash cloud still hovered above the landscape, covering everything from horizon to horizon, causing plants to wither. They fell into a routine, getting on the river early when it was a gentle current, and hiking overland when the water was too swift or rough.

They camped away from the river at night, usually just a few minutes' walk from the shore, but far enough away to avoid being in the path of nocturnal predators looking for a drink.

LT was feeling better every day, her usually aching body becoming used to the strenuous activity of being outdoors, as well as the weapon practices. She'd slimmed down, her doughy frame becoming lean and muscled.

Reggie assured them they were making good time, but the sands slowed walking, and paddling a reed canoe wasn't much faster than walking. It would take a few weeks to get to Akar.

The first week was grueling as they found their rhythm, but the second week went better. In the middle of the third week, they left the river and entered the lake. Akar was on the northeast shore of the High Tarn, and knowing their trip was almost done, lifted spirits.

Ditching the canoe, the three hiked along the shoreline. The sands turned to scrub grass, which became fertile lands that had a lot more plant and animal life than the desert.

It was late afternoon of the twenty-third day they saw the sprawl of the buildings of the city. The once whitewashed surface of the wall surrounding the city was now a dull grey of ash and soot. The farmlands around Akar were covered, as well, and only a couple of shepherds with their flocks were in sight. Thick, black smoke rose from a half dozen dark heaps outside of the walls.

"Do we go in now, or camp in sight of the walls?" Reggie asked.

"Where is everyone?" Griffon asked.

"Yeah," LT agreed, "shouldn't there be farmers in the fields doing the spring planting and stuff like that?"

"I assume the ash has put a damper on spring plantings," Reggie said. "And they may be being extra careful after the raids from the vriktiri."

"Or they're all dead," LT said.

"Or worse, they might have all been hit with the lost folk disease," Griffon pointed out. "Still, that's kinda dead."

"None of this answers the question though. Do we head into the city now, or set up the Citadel and wait until morning to go in?" Reggie said.

"It would be nice to have the protection of the walls," LT said, "and maybe pick up some information about what happened in the weeks since we went into the desert."

"And to not have to cook and do dishes," Griffon added.

"You both realize," Reggie said, still eyeing the city, "that those walls might also trap us from getting out if there are problems, right? Is it worth the risk?"

"Well, with that kind of thinking," LT said, "we'd never go into another city anywhere ever again."

"Sounds like we're going in then," Griffon said, hiking his backpack up and walking towards the fallow fields.

"Alright," Reggie said, following with LT, "but we get some place near the outer gate, and be on the lookout for anything dangerous."

"When has there not been something dangerous, Reggie?" Griffon called over his shoulder. "Since coming to this world, there's nothing but danger. Maybe you should figure that out and accept it, and then you'll be much happier rather than worried or disappointed when everything goes to bidj."

"Griffon," Reggie sighed, "that's actually very wise advice."

"It was bound to happen sometime," LT said, "just don't get used to it. It just leads to that disappointment thing the little perv mentioned."

"I got your disappointment right here, babe," Griffon said, his hand moving in front of him. "Hold on, wait, that didn't…"

"Too late," LT laughed, "you called it on that one, *babe*."

The group passed near a flock of sheep. A man, a woman, and a smudged teen with cudgels and crossbows watched them with sunken eyes and suspicious glares.

"They don't look related," Griffon muttered even though the people were a bowshot away.

"I don't think they were," LT said, watching them. "I bet people are just grouping together right now. Safety in numbers and all that."

Arriving at the gate an hour later, a middle-aged man stood on the arch over the gate, his hands shaking as he held a bow drawn and an arrow nocked.

Four other men stepped into the road, one from each of the two guard towers, and two from behind the wall. Each held a spear and looked haunted, like they hadn't slept well in weeks.

"Show us!" the man shouted from above.

"Show you what?" Griffon shouted, his hand on Raven Stealer's pommel.

"They respond," one of the four spearmen growled, "that's one."

"Don't be pemtie," the bowman called down, "let us see them, now!"

"What are you looking for?" Reggie asked, stepping in front of Griffon. "Are you robbing us? We don't have much, as we've just come from a long journey in the Great Desert."

"Your armpits and the back of your knees," one spearman, a thick, greying man, said, "and lift your chin so we can see your necks."

"What the hell is going on?" Griffon looked back and forth between LT and Reggie.

"Glands and lymph nodes," LT said, tilting her head up and pulling her shirt collar open to expose her throat, "they're looking for the sickness."

"Ah," Reggie said and copied her actions, then started unbuttoning his doublet.

"So, they want us to strip in the middle of the street?" Griffon complained. "I don't mind showing off my body. After all, it's an amazing, sculpted work of art, but this is just demeaning."

"Griffon," LT sighed, rolling up her pants legs to above her boots, "just do it and quit bitching about it. Or would you rather not have a warm meal and bed at an inn tonight?"

"Fine," the gnome sullenly flashed his neck at the spearmen, "whatever."

The older man who spoke nodded a thanks at LT, then nodded at Griffon to show he'd seen that the neck was clear of marks or swelling.

LT and Reggie untucked their shirts, lifting them up to expose one side of their ribs up to the armpit, then the other.

The gladiator locked eyes with the older man, then slowly reached up and unstrapped his pauldron, letting it slide down his arm to fall into the sooty street. Peeling his shirt up, he exposed his abs and ran a hand across them, then pulled it over his head, only breaking eye contact with the man for a moment. The shirt hung on the pommel of Raven Stealer, flapping in the warm breeze.

The gnome spun in a circle, hands above his head, his hips moving up and down with each step.

Reaching down, Griffon unbuckled his belt and let it drop. His fingers fumbled at the ties of his breeches, and the gnome had to look down to undo them, then jerked his head back up to stare at the man.

He shoved his trousers down, exposing his small-clothes, turning them inside out over his knee-high boots. Taking small steps, the gnome turned in another circle, stumbling on the pant laces.

"Wow," LT said, tucking her shirt back into her belt, "you really showed them, and me, and the sheep, and the people down the street. I guess it's the small things that make you happy."

She pointed at Griffon's crotch, smirking.

"Good," the older spearman said, "and thank you for cooperating. Now, what's your business in Akar?"

"Just passing through on our way north," Reggie said, buttoning up his doublet, but leaving his shirt untucked. "We just want a place to sleep without ash, maybe a meal and a bath. If we can find news of the north, that would help us as well."

"I can take you to one of the few inns still open for business," the man said, "but I make no promises on the rest of what you're hoping for. Things have changed here, and the city isn't what it was a month ago. It's like the Downfall all over again."

The other men stepped back into their respective places, and Reggie and LT moved forward. Griffon gathered up his things in his arms, and waddled forward, gripping the waistband of his pants in one hand.

"Really?" LT said, "you're going to do this? What are you? Twelve?"

"Whatever," Griffon snapped.

"Whatever, indeed," LT nodded. "You do you, have your tantrum. Just try to keep up without tripping."

"I'm Galdrak," the remaining man said as he turned and led the way through the gate. "Once a farmer, then a guard, and now the makeshift mayor of Akar. Like I said, things aren't what they once were. But better me than some others. I tend to keep a level head."

"What happened here?" Reggie asked, stepping beside the man. "We passed the city a month ago and everything seemed pretty normal."

"It wasn't," Galdrak said, "but it was closer to normal than it is now. A few months ago, some people got sick. Well, they didn't show any symptoms, but woke up one morning and were the lost folk. Mindless and murderous. We did what we had to do and once they were burned, we thought it was done."

They passed shops as the man talked, most of them empty, a few boarded up, and occasionally a burnt husk. A handful of people came out to watch the strange procession, clutching axes, pitchforks, or other various weapons while children clutched their legs and peeked out from behind.

"Less than two months ago," Galdrak continued, "those bug things showed up, attacking farmers and herdsmen outside of the walls. People flocked to the city, hoping to find protection inside the walls. It didn't matter, though."

The man waved at a group of four spearmen trudging past in the ankle-deep ash, and the lead man saluted.

"A couple weeks after that," Galdrak continued once the men had passed, "the bug holes began appearing in town. It was at night, and they didn't attack the city. Just broke into homes and businesses and roughed up folks. Didn't kill them, just beat them up a bit. We didn't know what to make of it, until we realized the scratches left on the people attacked carried some disease with it."

Galdrak sighed.

"That's when it got really hard," he said, shaking his head, "because once people realized they were sick if they'd been attacked, they started hiding the attacks. The city watch and government had no way of knowing who had been infected, and who was just scratched doing their normal, everyday things. People started accusing their neighbors of being sick, and the city jails were overflowing with common citizens as we watched to see if they changed."

"A witch hunt," LT muttered, and Galdrak nodded.

"But with everyone locked together," he went on, "the ones who were affected contaminated the ones who weren't. So, even if we pulled the lost one out before they attacked anyone, everyone would eventually catch it from close contact. We burned bodies, but it didn't seem to help."

"It looks like you got it under control, though," Reggie said, his voice sympathetic.

"Sure," Galdrak shrugged with a sad smile, "but it wasn't until we'd lost most of the people in the city that the lich showed up and offered us the cure in exchange for our loyalty."

Chapter 18

"Oh, bidj!" Griffon shouted, dropping his gear.

A cloud of ash puffed upward into the gnome's face as he bent to pull up his drawers. Coughing, he hurriedly laced them.

The group had stopped in the middle of the street, and Reggie cocked his head to study the man, LT standing behind him with her spear held in both hands in a cross-body position.

"What does that loyalty entail?" Reggie asked.

Galdrak sighed and shook his head.

"They own Akar," the man said, "and we all answer to them."

Griffon pulled his shirt back over his head. One arm got caught in a sleeve that had turned inside out. The fabric ripped as he forced his arm through, and the sleeve flapped behind his back. The gnome dipped back down for his belt.

"And visitors to the city?" Reggie asked. "What happens to them?"

"Yeah," Galdrak held up his hands. "I was waiting for this question, which is why I wanted to tell you this tale before you got to the inn. As far as I'm concerned, if you don't live here, then you aren't under the rule of the city. As long as you don't break any laws, you should be okay."

Griffon slammed his pauldron over his head, fumbling at the buckles.

The two men stared at one another for a long moment, Griffon frantically trying to pull Raven Stealer free of the sleeve she was tangled in.

"Alright," Reggie nodded, "and thank you."

"Aren't you going to ask us about where we were? Why we're here?" LT glared at Galdrak.

The makeshift mayor shook his head.

"I think I'll go on the assumption that your business in the Great Desert was for trading purposes," Galdrak said, "and you just came into Akar because it's the end of the river merchant line. If I thought you meant us harm, I wouldn't have brought you to Kirtal's place, the Rusty Wheel. You would've been delivered to Fneud's establishment, the Baked Fowl instead. Kirtal will do what she can to treat you like we treated folks a year ago, Fneud would dispose of your bodies in the night."

Griffon struck a defensive pose, Raven Stealer held ready.

"Stand down, boy," Reggie shot the gnome a look. "There's nothing here to fight. We're just going to go into the Rusty Wheel, ask for Kirtal, and tell her that Galdrak highly recommends her inn for strangers passing through."

Galdrak nodded and held out a hand to Reggie.

"I hope your road leads to better places, Kazzek Tel Virian," Galdrak said, "and your companions, Auric the gladiator, and, um, your lady friend with the spear."

Reggie took the man's hand, shaking it.

"Mayor Galdrak," he said, "there will be brighter days and good health again for Akar, and soon. I promise you that."

The man looked at Reggie, his brow furrowed, then nodded and released his grip.

"I pray it is so," Galdrak said, turning and walking away.

They watched the man leave, and in three blocks, his shape disappeared into the ashfall.

"So," Griffon said, "I'm not going to kill anyone?"

"Pemtie ass," LT smacked the gnome on the back of his head, "get in the inn."

The three turned and saw a woman standing on the covered porch of the inn, drying a dented tankard with a grey-stained cloth. She smiled at them and nodded.

"He really is a good man," she said, gesturing in the direction Galdrak had gone with her chin. "Why don't you folks come in and we'll see what we can scrounge up for you. Dust yourselves off on the porch before coming in, would you? No need to track this bidj through my place."

She turned and disappeared into the inn.

The three followed her, pausing under the eave to shake off most of the ash on them.

"Been a month since we've seen the sun," Kirtal called from behind the bar to the right, setting the tankard down. "Three weeks since we've seen rain, and two since we've seen a wagon train with beer. I can't offer much, but I can offer enough without trying to rob you of everything you own. Not that coins do any good to anyone right now. Can't spend money if no one has anything to sell, can you?"

The common room was on two levels: a balcony with tables circling the lower floor. Two bars dominated opposite walls, to the left and the right, and the kitchen had a large open counter directly ahead. A dour woman and three younger women watched the three enter from behind a butcher block, the oldest gripping a cleaver.

On their left, stairs led to the upstairs dining, and stairs on the right led to an addition to the building.

Seven people sat at tables in the center of the room, all next to each other. Two men with dice were at one, a man and a woman holding hands at the second, and three teens—two boys and a girl—watched them from the third.

"Pick anywhere," Kirtal said, "and don't mind them. You can understand that we're a bit wary of strangers. But Galdrak brought you here, and he's a great judge of character, and of livestock. Though I guess there's not much difference sometimes."

"May we sit at the bar?" Reggie asked from the doorway, gesturing to the stools across from the proprietress.

"Of course," she smiled, "come on over and get settled in. I think we have porridge and maybe some leek soup if you like. Oh, and cheese. We brought out our last wheel of cheese earlier this week. Maybe you'd like some of that?"

"That sounds wonderful," Reggie said, moving to the bar.

"Are we just going to ignore—" Griffon protested but was cut off by LT's hand squeezing his shoulder. "Ow, what was that for?"

"Hush," LT hissed. "Just be quiet for once and use your ears instead of your mouth."

"Gnomes, eh?" Kirtal chuckled. "I do love them, but they can be like small dogs. They tend to yap a lot until they get comfortable with you. Just to let you know they can bite, so you shouldn't step on them."

"Did she just threaten me?" Griffon whispered to LT, trailing after her.

"Be a good boy and quiet down, Fido, and climb up a seat." LT said, swinging her leg over a stool. "Kirtal, I think we have some extra dates and fruit. Can we offer that to you to help cover the food we're taking?"

"Aw, that's sweet of you," the woman said, "and I think some of us here would love some fresh fruit. What can I bring you, now?"

"Um," LT looked at the ceiling, considering, while watching the room in the polished silver mirror behind the bar, "I think a bowl of hot porridge would be wonderful."

"The leek soup sounds delightful," Reggie said.

"Is that really all you have?" Griffon whined.

LT jabbed him with her elbow.

"Fine," he said, "I'll have one of each."

Kirtal looked at LT, her mouth drawing into a distressed moue.

"Pick one, Griffon," LT said through gritted teeth.

"But I was really hoping for something I could chew," he said, then saw the look on LT's face. "Okay, okay, I'll have the, um, soup. Oh, and a stout and a whiskey."

LT jerked her head towards the gnome and was surprised when she heard Reggie say he'd have the same.

"In that case," LT looked at Kirtal and shrugged, "make that three."

"Great," the hostess smiled, "easier to serve from kegs and bottles than the kettle and pot right now."

She poured the drinks, passed them out, and brought over bowls from the kitchen, along with wooden spoons.

"Enjoy that," she said, "and pardon me while I check on my other custom."

The three watched the woman in the mirror as she moved through the nearly empty common room, talking to the locals and wiping down empty tables.

"Why'd you offer our food to them?" Griffon hissed at LT.

"Because it was the right thing to do," she hissed back, "and because last night you were just complaining about eating the same thing every day. Now, you can complain about something different, not having anything every day."

"Stop it, you two," Reggie muttered around his spoon. "Eat up and let's get to our room, which we will share tonight. We need to finish here quickly, and then get out of town before sunrise."

He shook his head when Griffon opened his mouth to say something.

"Not here, not now, Griffon," Reggie said curtly. "Later, in private."

Kirtal came back around the bar and Reggie smiled up at her, complimenting her on the soup.

They ate their meals and made small talk, sharing the last of their supplies with everyone in the inn. Reggie paid the woman more than she asked for and was shown to a single room with two cots. They carried buckets of murky water, sullied by the ash, to wash up with.

"I'm not sleeping on the floor," Griffon said once they were alone.

"And you don't need to," Reggie explained in a quiet voice, "because only two of us will be sleeping at a time. We're going to set a watch and bar the door."

"What?" Griffon said in mock surprise, putting a hand on his chest and staring at Reggie with wide eyes. "Now who's the paranoid one?"

"What's going on, Reggie?" LT said, searching the man's face.

"This," he said, pulling a folded paper from his satchel and setting it on the small table.

The other two crowded close to it, squinting in the dim light.

The paper had a sketch of the three of them, a written description, and the offer of the reward of favor of Ahken'ho-tek, Lord of Ez'rainia-fromton, The Great Desert, Akar, the Wandering Hills, and all surrounding territories and settlements.

"How'd you get that?" LT asked.

"Pulled it off a wall when Griffon was putting on his little show," Reggie shrugged. "The point is, even though Galdrak and Kirtal have been very nice, I prefer to err on the side of caution, and be gone before the sun rises. We can sleep here for a while, wake the next person after two hours, and leave before anyone is the wiser. I'll offer to take the middle shift so you two can get a longer bit of sleep."

"It's probably twelve hours to sunrise," LT pointed out, "so why only get six hours of sleep?"

"Better safe than sorry," Reggie shrugged one shoulder.

"Well," Griffon huffed, "I can't just fall asleep on command."

"Great," LT said, "because Reggie and I are old campaigners, and we can. So, you take first watch and wake him in a couple hours."

"But," Griffon said as the two began stripping down to their small-clothes.

"Nope," LT said.

"What? I didn't even—" Griffon started.

"Nope," LT repeated. "No talking. We're washing, sleeping, then leaving. All without talking. Got it?"

The gnome pulled his baldric from over his head and leaned Raven Stealer against the wall beside one of the two chairs around the table. He jumped onto one, crossed his arms, and pouted.

"Wake up," LT said, shaking the gnome, "get dressed. We need to go. Now."

"I just fell asleep," Griffon moaned, rolling over and pulling the thin blanket over his head, "just five more minutes."

Something scratched at the outside of the door and a low breathy moan came from the other side.

"What the chuz?" Griffon bolted upright, wide awake.

"Yup," LT said, "time to go."

"And I think we'll be leaving by the window," Reggie said, buckling Marcid to his waist.

"Why do you never see anything except human undead?" Griffon asked, swinging his legs over the side of the bed and dropping to the floor. "I mean, we haven't run across a single gnome, rokairn, or aeifain zombie."

"Racist affliction?" LT suggested. "Or maybe because we've been in human territories?"

"I think some of the wraith things were aeifain," Reggie said. "I believe there may be a correlation between that sort of creature and an affinity for spell casting, but I'm not positive about that."

"Maybe you can ask the next one we meet?" Griffon tugged his trousers up and tied them. "Mister dead guy, before you suck out my soul, let me ask you…were you an elf or use magic of any sort?"

"We don't call them elves," Reggie said, opening the shutters and looking out the window.

"We don't?" LT asked. "Why?"

"It's a racial slur," Reggie whispered over his shoulder, "so is calling a rokairn a dwarf. The street has about a dozen lost folk wandering about; I think. Hard to tell in the dark and ash."

"Where were they hiding them all?" LT wondered aloud.

"Probably under the command of Anchor-head the Lichtron," Griffon shrugged into his shirt, "waiting for someone to tell them to come out and eat people."

"Once we're outside," Reggie said, drawing back into the room, "we should find an abandoned store. Restock our supplies. Arrows, oil, and maybe even get some horses."

LT and Reggie gathered their remaining belongings while Griffon finished getting dressed. Once they were all ready, the three crept out onto the porch roof overlooking the street.

Reaching the corner, they waited for a group of lost folk to wander past, then dropped to the ground one at a time. Griffon went first, drawing Raven Stealer while still crouched. LT came down next, spear in hand and her bow secured to her back.

Moans came from the murk, coming closer, drawn by the sound. Galdrak lurched out of the murky night, blank eyes and slack jaw showing his mind was no longer his, along with a handful of townsfolk.

Reggie dropped to the ground beside the other two, then back pedaled.

"They turned the entire town," Reggie gasped, his back hitting the porch railing as he stumbled away from the man who'd greeted them at the gate, "murdered them all, because of us."

"Then it will be a mercy to release them to their final death," LT said, running the razor edge of her spear across the man's throat from the side.

Reggie's words from over a month ago echoed in his ears as he watched the newly changed zombie's blood pour out and splash on the silt at his feet.

Griffon burst into motion, Raven Stealer a blur as the gladiator cut through the calves of the closest zombies, severing tendons and ligaments. The creatures collapsed to the ground, unable to support themselves.

"Come on, dude," Griffon whispered harshly, "handle your bidj, and whip out your sword. Don't make us die here too because you got all the feels."

Reggie sucked in a breath and a few flakes of ash, breaking into a coughing fit. New groans came from the murk, and the sound of shuffling feet drew closer. Reggie pulled Marcid from her scabbard and pulled his shoulders back.

"Let's show some mercy," he whispered, mostly to himself. Turning to the others, Reggie raised his voice enough for them to hear him. "Follow me. I saw a blacksmith shop beside some stables on the way here."

Leading the way, Reggie walked down the center of the street. He moved with fierce speed, spurred by grim determination, whenever they encountered someone, attacking anyone that came into sight. Reggie had cut down more than a half dozen lost folk when he felt a firm hand grip his arm. He spun towards whoever, or whatever, had grabbed him, blade ready.

"Whoa, there!" LT released his arm and leaned away. "Reggie, this isn't the way to do this. We'll exhaust ourselves. These things aren't very smart. We should sneak past most of them, not engage them."

Reggie hesitated, opening his mouth to argue, then snapped it shut and nodded. He turned away and moved closer to the buildings, ducking behind a horse trough as another group of lost folk trundled into sight. The three crept towards the stables and smithy.

Chapter 19

Ahken'ho-tek strolled down the middle of Dragon Staff's main thoroughfare, Venat-fal, Kenal, and Chektar-ral trailing behind the Lord of Liches. The three appeared collected and equal to their master, and in no way subservient or inferior to the man they'd pledged themselves to a month ago. Each wore an opulent outfit of fine silks, dazzling jewels, and the best leather goods. They walked with an ageless grace at a stately pace, interrupted only by the occasional lurch from atrophied muscles or the intermittent twitch caused by spasming shrunken tendons.

They had cleared the ash from the street, but like a snowfall, it didn't stop new flakes from gathering underfoot. The tall buildings were of dark woods, and the second story was offset to create a covered walkway for the lower floor and provide shade to the street. The third story jutted out even further, connecting to buildings across the street with thick bridges, creating a manmade valley of the street.

People gathered on each side of the road; spring flowers gripped in their hands, waiting to be thrown at the feet of their saviors. But no one did. No one cheered or clapped. No one moved. A baby squalled—a gurgling cry—as the entourage passed, and the mother clutched her child tighter but didn't take her eyes from the liches.

Vriktiri skittered along the rooftops, eyeing the people below. Two weeks ago, the buildings had been overrun with the creatures as they swarmed the city. Since then, the masters of the city had sent the bulk of the insect army to the next conquest.

A loose triple line of lost folk trailed behind the liches, their blank stares making the assembled townsfolk along the parade route flinch and look away. The mindless undead were the city patrol and the militia who'd shown resistance to the conquering liches and their host of vriktiri.

"This stroll is much less eventful than our last," Kenal said. "Not a single person has thrown anything rotten, swore at us, promised retribution, or tried to slay us in vengeance for their losses. It's almost a shame."

"We won't be nearly as sated at the end of this walk as we were the last," Venat-fal nodded her agreement, "and our coffers shan't swell under the weight of claimed properties. We glutted and fattened ourselves in many ways last week."

"Neither of you have gone out among them, have you?" Chektar-ral said from behind the two. "Listened to them and learned from them."

"Why would we do that?" Venat-fal sneered, not bothering to look at the Mistress of the Leys.

"Mistress of the Stables," Chektar-ral said to the woman, then shifted her gaze the Kenal, "Master of Minions, you are both in the practice of using people as a herdsman uses his livestock. Never considering that every reaction of those you command adds nuance to the results you see. These are not unthinking beasts…"

The Mistress of the Ley waved a hand at the silent assemblage on the side of the street.

"...they are intelligent, thinking, planning, cunning beasts with hopes, fears, plans, and emotions. They may be inferior to us in every way, but that doesn't mean they're docile animals to be prodded in a direction without them changing the plan at least a little."

"Perhaps," Venat-fal conceded, "but why should that concern us?"

"A shepherd should always be concerned with the health of their flock," Chektar-ral said. "But what if your herd could talk? What if you could sit and listen to their hopes and fears? What if you could know what they wanted? Learn what would make them behave more docilely, or make them rebellious?"

Venat-fal scoffed and Ahken'ho-tek turned his head slightly, as if noticing them for the first time.

"Chektar-ral speaks with wisdom," Ahken'ho-tek said over his shoulder, "and it is the same things I did with each of you over the past centuries. I listened and waited, encouraging you here and influencing you there. The way you see these people is how I see you, as something to care for. In turn, you shall care for me and mine, helping my interests to grow and expand, so you also may increase your holdings."

The three behind the Lord of Liches fell silent again, but Chektar-ral watched the back of each of the others. Her undead eyes saw the threads of magical energy connected to—and passing through—each of them. A thick strand led from each of them to Ahken'ho-tek, showing the control he had over them, but Chektar-ral's thread was fraying.

She could see the five magics weaving through her colleagues, becoming a necromantic tapestry that combined to keep each of them housed inside their current forms. Once they were all humans, but she was more than that. She mutilated and demeaned herself in life to get close to the rulers of Ez'rainia-fromton, entering their world as a slave, though she was much more powerful than any mage or elementalist who held her chains. Verl'zen-luk may be out of reach for the moment, but these three weren't, and she'd already orchestrated the death of the others through her manipulation of Ahken'ho-tek.

She'd pushed at Kenal and Venat-fal to make them dig deeper into their arrogance and security in their situation, make them draw further from the common people. Ahken'ho-tek blatantly saying he'd manipulated them, when she'd been doing the same with him, was carefully done. Chektar-ral was amused that neither of the other two had realized what their Lord had meant, only that they were above the common folk.

She'd be patient, biding her time, and when everything was in place, she'd make her final move and have her revenge for what they'd done to her people.

The farce of a parade ended, and Chektar-ral glided away from the others, her magical senses watching their movements throughout the manor house that once served as the city's municipal headquarters. They had cleared it for their use, the entire staff drained of life and taken in by the liches as an example of the futility of resisting their rule. It also took away the very people that most of the population would have rallied behind to reclaim the city.

Dragon Staff was an ancient city established thousands of years ago, destroyed a dozen times, and rebuilt on top of the ruins of the last city. Tunnels and sewers wound through the bedrock below, and

Chektar-ral made her way to those through the basement of the building. It was also a minor nexus point for ley energies, three different elements converging under the city.

Once, dragons had lived here in harmony with the humans and others of the land. The city was the gateway to the Valley of Rykul, and the beginning of the road to Dargaon's Hole, the mythical resting place of the arcane reptiles' ancestors, and the key to their power. Controlling this city opened many doors, but Ahken'ho-tek didn't realize all that was hidden here.

Ahken'ho-tek was a master schemer, but Chektar-ral had lived a half a millennium before the man that became a monster had even lived and rose to power. Her people, the Intreponian—translated as the First Born—had been around when the first races had built their huts from mud ten thousand years ago.

She came from the archipelago in the center of the oceans, using magics that were already ancient when the aeifain were just learning their first spells. Her people remembered the time before the first gods, when the Troll Lords first split the races, and before demons from other realities discovered this world. They knew where the Troöds came from and why they couldn't leave.

Chektar-ral wound her way deeper into the bowels of the earth, seeking the chamber she could feel hidden below the city.

Ahken'ho-tek, the Lord of Liches, sought power. He wanted to take the force of nature embodied in Rykul the Great Bear and change the rules. He planned to use that power to claim what he considered his rightful place among the gods, dethroning Verl'zen-luk and taking his place.

Chektar-ral had different plans, but a few things had to be put into play before she could be confident of overcoming Ahken'ho-tek and taking the arcane energies he'd stolen from Ez'rainia-fromton and the lesser liches. He'd also taken control of the unseen dead—the ghosts, banshees, wraiths, specters, and more—when he drained Lepat-fal.

She felt the nexus point flare around her, her mind opening as it spun into the vortex created by multiple ley lines converging. Her abilities flared internally in reaction, and her awareness shot outward in a sphere, then drew back in.

Looking around, she saw a collapsed tunnel, with hints of corners long eroded, and a psychic echo of the room that once existed here. Chektar-ral grabbed the earthen ley line and pulled in the fire line, linking the two and recreating the long-lost alchemical laboratory that once existed in this space.

The wall melted, creeping away from the woman in waves, then rose to join the rippling ceiling. Tables carved from the rock, rose, and shelves stretched along the edges of the chamber. A mirror of silver crackled outward from the surrounding stone until the smooth, polished surface was from floor to ceiling, and three times the width of Chektar-ral's shoulders.

Her elemental magic blended with her conjuring, and small magma elementals sprouted from a lava pool in the corner, and the creatures ran about the lab, setting things to right. The conjuration connected with her alchemical abilities, and jars and bottles popped into existence on the shelves and tables.

Turning to the mirror, she layered it with water from the closest ley line, and poured her mind mage strength into it, seeking a voice she hadn't heard since she'd been imprisoned.

"Tolliver?" she breathed, her voice sounding closer to a human than it should. "Is that you?"

Ahken'ho-tek gazed into the scrying pool he'd constructed from the rock-ringed fishpond in the garden outside of his chambers. He'd watched Chektar-ral show incredible amounts of skill and ability a few moments before as she rebuilt the ancient chamber.

"Had you been in that room before?" Ahken'ho-tek asked, "Or did you envision it from scraps of memory imprinted in the stone? Either way, I'm impressed, and you make my suspicions grow with each move you move in this game we play."

Ahken'ho-tek cast the arcane energies, enabling clairaudience to repeat each sound in the chamber he was observing.

"They've trapped me," Chektar-ral was saying, "and hadn't been able to get anything out of the tomb in centuries, not even a single magical thread."

"Did you kill them all?" the man in the gazing wall asked. "Were you able to remove them permanently?"

"No," she said, "there were…complications. One named Verl'zen-luk escaped the ruins and achieved great power. He is now what these people think of as a god."

"Ah, yes," he said, "we've heard of him. That was nearly a century ago, though. Why didn't everyone else escape at the same time?"

"The usual reason, politics and power plays," Chektar-ral sighed, "and it's still going on. One named Ahken'ho-tek has plans to overthrow an additional source of energy and claim it. Then he wants to challenge the lich who escaped."

"How did they survive this long?" the man in the reflection asked.

"Animation of necrotic tissue, Tolliver," Chektar-ral waved a hand at the question. "It was the only way they could figure out how to not die."

"Does this woman think the feat of staying in this body for hundreds of years is something petty to be waved away?" Ahken'ho-tek asked aloud. "What does she and this other man know that this task seems frivolous?"

"Wait, Chek," Tolliver interrupted the woman, "did you do this also?"

"Tolliver," Chektar-ral's tone dropped to a very serious level, "you know I don't need that. But I had to make some alterations to my basic physiology. My body might live for more than a thousand years, but these creatures would have slain me if they thought I wasn't one of them."

"Are you still you?" he asked.

"Mostly," she shrugged, "I had to make some basic changes, or be discovered."

"Can it be reversed?" the man asked.

"Shouldn't be too hard," she said confidently. "Just a purging of the necrosis, then a dialysis of fresh energy from a wellspring, and I should be back to normal."

"She has the secret to reverse becoming undead?" Ahken'ho-tek breathed. "I cannot slay her until I know that ritual."

"Let me send you assistance," Tolliver said. "It will help you win out over these monsters and complete your mission."

"You can't send a ship, but maybe a small pod?" Chektar-ral stroked her chin.

"Yes," Tolliver nodded, "let me just get your location…"

Ahken'ho-tek flinched, and raised his hands to the scrying pool, pouring energy into it, blocking the communication between the woman and her coconspirator.

"Tolliver?" Chektar-ral raised her hands towards the image, which was blurring and jumping in intermittent pulses. "Something is interfering, it could be a surge, hold on while I—"

Twisting the energy, Ahken'ho-tek shoved a flood of arcane power through the connection, and the chamber he was observing shook, chunks of the ceiling tumbling down around the Mistress of the Ley.

The scrying pool went dark, ripples flowing across it, becoming small waves.

"No," Ahken'ho-tek grinned, "you won't do anything but run."

The Lord of Liches turned and paced across his chamber.

"So, she thinks she can overthrow me," he said, "and take what is mine. But she now has a new use, and one I cannot pull from her without her telling me what I need to know. This will be a challenge."

He stopped at the table along the wall, looking over the magical artifacts he'd collected at each place he and the other liches had stopped.

"I will need something special for this," he murmured, "and I think I know exactly what she will be susceptible to if I can get a small piece of her flesh."

Chapter 20

"Why not?" Griffon asked, bouncing on the back of his stolen horse.

"Because," Reggie said, "we're in a hurry. We need to find out if the same fate has befallen Allendale, and how far these monsters have spread their influence."

"They have almost a month head start," LT said, "and I bet they haven't been idle."

Griffon looked over at her and huffed.

Reid grinned, knowing the gnome was annoyed with how well she rode. Griffon was tossed around on the back of his mount, having never ridden before in this world or the other.

But Reid was experienced on horseback, in both worlds. Her host body, Tamilda, didn't ride much, but was raised with horses and livestock. Back on Earth, though, Reid had a horse growing up. She'd even done some competition riding in her teens.

It had been a passion, bonding her with the animal, learning to work together.

Reid had been the who'd one picked the horses back in Akar, when they'd crept into the stables in the middle of the night. They'd taken two horses for each of them, so they could switch mounts and not tire one animal too much.

They rode at a trot now, a pace the animals could sustain for a while on the relatively flat ground, though they were entering the hilly territory as they drew closer to Allendale. Reggie led the wedge formation, with a long lead to the spare horses behind each one of them. The sky was a dingy grey, the line of volcanoes still spewing ash into the firmament. The tall grasses were brown and wilting, and the spring growth of the trees was withered and pitiful.

Animals were scarce, as well. They'd seen a fox and her kits hunting in the ash drifts, jumping and diving after a mouse or something, like they did with snow in the depths of winter. Migrating herds moved to the west, seeking literal greener pastures, and birds were doing the same.

The weather had grown colder with the constant cloud cover, and a snow flurry mixed with the soot from the fiery mountains. A constant odor of rotten eggs coated everything, and Reid didn't think she'd ever get that smell out of her clothes, hair, or skin.

All three of them kept a bandana or scarf across their mouths and noses, stopping most of the detritus from being inhaled, though she still had to clean out her nasal passages multiple times a day.

"What's our plan once we get to Allendale?" Reid asked. "And we're getting low on feed. These poor horses can't eat the grass, well, not if they don't want to get sick. And fresh water has to be scavenged for, and then boiled."

"It still tastes nasty," Griffon said.

"That's the sulphur in the ash," Reggie said.

"Whatever," Griffon grumped, "it tastes like ass."

"Eat a lot of that, Griffon?" Reid teased.

"Hey," the gnome grinned, "if that's what—"

"Let's drop to a walk for a little while," Reggie interrupted, reining in his horse. "Ol Bessy needs a break."

The other two followed his example, Reid leaning over to stroke Kimmy's neck and making soothing noises. The horse snorted, jerked her head, and rolled her eyes.

Reid had named the mare after her favorite childhood horse, the one she competed with, and her second mount she'd named Monty. Reggie, always the practical one, named his Number One and Number Two. Griffon, on the other hand, stayed true to his nature and called his Warrior and Tank.

"The plan," Reggie said, "is to see what's there, and then make a plan. If it's overrun, then we pass through and keep going—"

"To where?" Griffon asked, pulling a strip of jerky from his bag and tearing off a bite. "And I'm going to need a bio break soon."

"Dragon Staff," Reid said, answering the question, "where I suggested we go when this all began."

"Yes," Reggie nodded, "to both of you. There's a stream a bit ahead of us. I saw the water a while back. I think it's moving fast enough that we might be able to let the horses drink directly from it. And we know you said that LT, and I'm truly regretting not listening when you suggested it."

"But we had to stop the disease, right?" Griffon asked. "If we didn't, then it would've kept spreading?"

"Yes," Reggie sighed, "but we released the very beings who controlled it. So, it may not be spreading on its own now, but the liches can spread it wherever they go now."

"Sounds like a no-win situation," Griffon shrugged.

"Life is a no-win situation," Reggie mumbled.

"There you go again with the inspiring words," Reid glared at the man.

"Just calling it like I see it," Reggie said.

"She's right, though," Griffon said. "You used to be a lot more optimistic. You always looked on the bright side and talked about how things would get better."

"That's before things were his fault," Reid pointed out, "and he was cleaning up someone else's mess instead of his own. It's the guilt that makes him pessimistic."

"Oh, look at her," Griffon snickered, "analyzing the chuz out of you."

"Stow it," Reggie said, shooting the gnome a glare.

"Reggie," Reid sighed, "I'm sorry. I know you were trying to do the right thing. You always do. But sometimes there isn't a right thing to do. Sometimes there are only bad choices followed up by damage control."

"Speaking of damage control," Griffon said, sitting up taller in his saddle to scratch at his rump, "we've been riding for three days, and my butt hurts. But I don't wanna walk in this stuff. And on other topics, how do we stop these things?"

"I don't know, alright?" Reggie snapped.

Griffon jerked and looked at the man.

"Griffon," Reggie said between clenched teeth, "I'm making this up as I go. I have no idea how to stop them. I assume a sword in the guts will do it or burning them. But how do we get close enough to them to do that? Or how do we even find them to begin with?"

"One step at a time," Reid said, trying to calm things down, "we go to Allendale, and then decide what to do next, just like you said."

The three fell silent, heading towards the stream.

They camped that night within sight of Allendale, streams of smoke rising to meet the grey clouds hanging in the sky. Setting up the Citadel, they raised an extra tarp for the horses.

"It's a shame we can't bring them inside," Reid said. "I'd feel better. I worry about predators here."

"I wouldn't want to be the one to clean that litter box," Griffon groaned, tying a rope across the opening to create a makeshift corral. "I can't even image what size scoop you'd need."

"A pitchfork usually," Reid said, brushing down Monty, "but that's why we tie them out here."

"You think we can do this?" Griffon asked, pausing and looking up at Reid. "And do you think he'll be okay?"

"Griffon," she said without stopping her brushing, "I think we have to see this through. We can run off, but this is more of a duty we signed up for."

"Heh, you said doodie," the gnome giggled. "But seriously, I never signed up for a duty. I thought this was supposed to be an adventure. I expected some fights, some gold, and some glory. I got the fights, but we haven't found much treasure, and all the people are dead or dying. Hard to get a cheering crowd when they're all zombies trying to eat your face."

"Adventures are what duty becomes when you tell the story afterwards," Reid said, "and I think Reggie will be okay, but it'll take a while. Being in charge and responsible for others weighs on you. Add in world-ending cataclysms like a zombie apocalypse and mad undead wizards who want to enslave or kill everyone and, well, it can be a lot."

"Uh huh," Griffon agreed, tying off the last line. "Think we'll get some fame and stuff when this is all over, and we're telling people about our duty turned adventure? Or at least some gold?"

"No idea," Reid sighed. "The real world doesn't work that way most of the time. Heroes in stories are created after the fact, by the people who write the histories. Usually, they're just people doing the hard stuff, and if they get lucky, someone else sees them and tells others."

"That's going to be hard to do if they're all dead," Griffon said. "At least there's stew tonight."

The two went inside, and Griffon warmed himself in front of the potbelly stove while Reid washed up.

Reggie set the bowls on the table and sat down, not looking up. The three ate in silence, Griffon looking back and forth between the other two.

"Well," the gnome said, "not much meat in this, but I really like the potatoes and carrots. And the seasonings."

Reggie grunted, and the room fell silent again.

"Is there any more?" Griffon asked after lifting his bowl to lick it clean.

"No," Reggie said, "we have to ration what we have until we can buy more. Hard to hunt and forage from the land right now."

"Right," Griffon nodded, staring at his empty bowl. "Because all the animals ran away, and all the plants are dying."

"Griffon," Reid said, a warning in her voice.

Looking up, Griffon looked back and forth between the others.

"Ah, right, okay," he sighed, "I guess I'll do the dishes."

Collecting their bowls, the gnome moved to the washbasin to clean up.

Reggie got up from the table and settled in a chair, opening a book and packing his pipe.

Reid moved to the center of the room and began her exercises. She'd grown toned in the past weeks, the walking and weapon practices melting away the extra weight and building muscle. After an hour, she washed up again, picked up the book she'd been reading, and dropped onto her cot.

Looking at Griffon, she watched him make fairies dance across his knees, swaying seductively. He was getting better at it, even if he was doing it in ways that weren't rated PG, or PC.

Turning her attention to her book, she started reading where she'd left off the previous night. The words blurred, and she realized she'd read the same passage three times and had dozed off in the middle of it.

Griffon was snoring gently, a fairy twitching on his belly. Reggie had moved to his cot, and was rolled on his side, facing away from her.

Reid sat up, stretching, and caught Griffon peeking at her through slitted eyes, still snoring.

"Perv," Reid mumbled, and stood to tap the magical globe, casting the room into darkness.

She crawled back into bed and fell asleep instantly.

Jerking awake, she wondered what had woken her. She sat up and listened in the dark. A horse whinnied, and something slapped the side of the Citadel, the canvas wall rippling.

"Guys," Reid hissed, "something's outside and trying to get at the horses."

"It's okay," Griffon mumbled, "this place is camo'd out the yazoo, and no one can see it, remember?"

"But they can see and smell the horses," Reid whispered, sliding from her bunk, fumbling for her boots.

She heard movement from Reggie's side of the tent, the sound of clothes being slid on and the jingle of buckles.

A piercing equine scream ripped through the night, and Griffon's bunk burst into twinkling lights along with his shout.

"What the chuz was that?" he shouted.

A globe of light flared to life, and Reggie stood silhouetted in it, drawing Marcid.

The man walked to the door and pushed into the night.

"Damn," Griffon said, jumping to the floor, "I think I prefer him talking too much. He's scary when he doesn't say anything."

Reid finished dressing, grabbed her spear, and headed for the door flap. "Hurry up," she said, looking back over her shoulder, "we need your mighty sword, not your mighty mouth."

Ducking outside, she looked around, her eyes adjusting to the gloom.

Figures scurried around the tent, a dozen surrounding the horses. Three of the beasts were lying on the ground, legs kicking weakly, and the other three pressed against the wall of the Citadel.

"Vriktiri," Reid breathed, and moved towards the bug-men attacking the mounts.

She whirled her spear like a staff, smacking two away from the horses still standing, then her foot slipped in something wet and warm.

Going down to one knee, her leg twisted as it shot out from under her. The other vriktiri turned towards her, their eyes catching the minute moonlight breaking through the volcanic cloud cover.

Then Reggie was there, standing over her, his blade flashing in the night. He grunted as he skewered one enemy with the rapier, and his main-gauche pushed up into the underside of another's head.

Using her spear to help, Reid climbed to her feet and felt her knee pop. She winced and shifted her weight to her other leg, stabbing out over Reggie's shoulder to impale another vriktiri through its faceted eye.

The insect creature hissed, pulling away, and their mandibles clicked a rhythmic tattoo of noises. The night came alive with movement.

Reid limped in a circle, turning away from Reggie, who stepped towards her until they were back-to-back.

"Ready for this, commander?" Reid whispered over her shoulder.

"Helluva way to end the night," Reggie grunted.

"Or start a new day," Reid said, not having time to say anything else.

The vriktiri poured towards them, dozens of the monsters tumbling over one another to get to them. It wasn't coordinated or a team effort the way Reid expected it to be. It was a chaotic, frenetic mass of bodies boiling towards them.

She struck out with her spear, swatting away the first few enemies. They were taller than her, but they were probably half her weight, and her solid body weight let her toss them back.

Reggie moved behind her, staying close, but she could feel him lunge then step back to her, each of them protecting the other from being attacked from behind.

When working out—here or in the military—they'd trained her to hyper-focus on what was in front of her, to zone in on what she needed to do, and not let the outside world distract her. This mindset let her see what was going on around her, beyond her immediate vicinity, but still be totally in the moment.

She tried to put herself in that place now, to not let her mind distract her from what her body was doing. She could be a machine when she needed to be, and that's what she sought to do now.

Ignore the aches and pains, the biting chill air, and the terrified noises coming from the horse pen. She knew where Reggie was, used him to provide cover on one side, but using the range she could.

Her spear grew slick in her grasp. She couldn't tell whether it was from her sweaty palms or from the visceral goop of the impaled enemies.

The tent flap burst open, and Griffon's compact form exploded from the interior, a battle scream ripping through her focus. Her foot slipped again, and she caught herself before falling, bouncing up on her good leg and thrusting into the torso of another attacker.

Griffon and his ivory blade danced in a whirling circle around his two friends—the gnome shouting insults and obscenities the entire time—and cleared some breathing room for them.

A short time later, the three stood panting in a circle of carnage, vriktiri limbs and sections of bodies littering a wide swath around them. Sounds of others came from the distance, but nothing nearby moved except them and the remaining horses.

"Pack it up," Reid said. "I'll check the horses. If I can saddle them, I'll do that. If they can't, then I'll cut them loose and hope they can get away. We ride for Allendale, now."

Chapter 21

They rode as the morning light turned the dark grey flakes of ash into a lighter grey. A boom followed by an earth-shaking crack came from behind them, and Griffon looked back to see the bright red gash of a lava geyser in the distance.

"It's like Mount Doom had a litter," he shouted through the rushing wind as they galloped, "and I can't decide if Anchor-head the lich is scarier than Sauron or not."

Allendale rose out of the ashfall, and the source of the smoke they'd seen rising from the town became apparent. Heaps of burned corpses smouldered outside of the waist-high palisade, and dozens of buildings in the town were still in flames.

Small groups of vriktiri scurried through the streets—circling the dark totems and the bolt holes that preceded their arrival—and lumbering bands of lost folk moved throughout the town, ignoring the bug people.

"Do we go around?" LT asked, slowing Monty to a walk.

Reggie and Griffon reined in to keep pace with her.

A flash of light and an explosion caught their attention two streets in. Furtive movement and shouts came from the area.

"Damn it," Reggie said, "there's still people in there. And it looks like it may be the mind mages."

LT sighed and Griffon looked at the woman.

They were exhausted, and LT couldn't raise herself in her stirrups when galloping because of her messed-up knee. Reggie had a wild look about him, and Griffon didn't think the man was thinking straight.

"So, do we go in and try to save them?" Griffon asked. "I mean, they have magic and might help LT with her leg. On the other hand, we could die. Is it too late to just turn west and go to the gnomish territory? I have a cousin, Beeble Dozentoes, who would probably let us stay with her."

Reggie glared at the gnome, then shook his head.

"We have to help," Reggie said.

"Can't we figure out a way to get rid of the bugs, then?" Griffon asked. "I know! I can use my illusion of that high-pitched noise that scares insects and rats away. Or do either of you have a huge can of bug spray?"

"There's still the lost folk." LT waved a hand at the scene in front of them and nearly lost her balance.

Gripping the horn on her saddle, she looked around to see if anyone had noticed.

"What's controlling these things?" Griffon asked. "What makes them come up out of the ground at these specific places?"

"The totems," Reggie pointed at one with a handful of vriktiri around it.

The totems, Raven Stealer said in Griffon's head, *they emanate magic.*

"I know the totems are magical," Griffon said, "and the liches make them pop up…"

His words slowed, and he tilted his head.

"Can we destroy one?" he asked.

"What?" LT asked, rubbing her knee.

"What happens if we destroy one?" Griffon pressed on. "What if it's like an antenna to send commands to them?"

"Kriksi, the priest," LT said, her voice strained, "said his bug god wouldn't do anything like this."

Reggie stared at the two, his forehead wrinkled.

"I'll be a monkey's uncle," he muttered, "that makes sense. Khelikian isn't the type from everything I know, and…yes. I think that's the beginning of a plan."

"Who knows?" Griffon shrugged. "Maybe that's how they're controlling the lost folk also, or even spreading the disease."

"No," Reggie shook his head, "the disease showed up before the totems, but they might send out commands as you suggested."

"Imma genius," Griffon said, grinning at Reggie's newly recovered enthusiasm.

"Okay, genius," LT said, "then why didn't you think of this a month ago?"

"No time to talk about it right now," Griffon said, "we have a totem to take down."

"Leave the horses here," Reggie said, dismounting, "let LT watch them."

The woman opened her mouth to object, but Reggie held up a hand to stop her.

"We have magic weapons, you don't," he explained, "and you're the one who's good with the animals. Also, you can barely walk, and your knee is so swollen that it's trying to break out of your breeches. I'm not leaving you behind. This is just the best way to do this."

"I was going to say," LT said, nodding, "hand me the extra arrows so I can provide some cover for you.

I'm not too proud to give backup, and don't really want to be bait, anyway."

Griffon slid from Tank, rubbed his butt, and then held the reins up to LT.

He walked towards the town, bowlegged, and looked over his shoulder.

"You coming?" He called back to Reggie.

Reggie looked up at LT, then over at Griffon.

"Yes, be right there," he said to the gnome, then turned back to the woman. "LT, watch your back. And if this doesn't work out, head for Dragon Staff."

"Shut up and get going," LT said, tying off the three reins on the pommel of her saddle.

Griffon watched her ready her bow, and Reggie caught up to him. The two jogged towards Allendale, weapons in hand.

"So, what do you think the best way to destroy one of these things is?" Griffon asked.

"If they're like petrified wood, as Jdeidou and Hademine described," Reggie puffed, "then that means they're hard as stone, and not much is going to be able to destroy them except for perhaps a seven-kilo hammer and some strong backs."

"Well, I got one of those things if you can supply the other," Griffon said. "Turn that thing into Thor's hammer and pass it over."

"I think you mean Mjolnir," Reggie corrected, Marcid reshaping herself in his grip, "but this will be more like John Henry's hammer."

Reggie tossed the meter long maul to the gnome, who tossed Raven Stealer to him in return. Griffon inspected the head, blunt and round on one side, and coming almost to a wedge on the opposite.

Twirling it in a circle at his side, Griffon felt his muscles tighten and ripple, and he couldn't help but stare at his biceps in admiration.

"I look good," he crowed, refocusing on the rapidly approaching totem. "Cover me while I do some damage, boss!"

Griffon leapt through the air—feeling like how Chris Hemsworth looked in the Marvel movies—the massive silver hammer held above his head and flying across the landscape in one jump.

He landed three steps ahead of where he started and brought the blunted end down on the totem. The hammer slammed into the magical guidepost, and both shuddered.

"Um, Griffon," Reggie said, and the gnome looked up at him, "turn it around. Use the other side first. The wedge part may work better to split this, then the flat part to break it up."

Reggie pointed, then twirled a finger, indicating that Griffon should turn the hammer around.

"Ah, right, thanks!" Griffon smiled. "And, um, Reggie?"

"Yes, Griffon?" Reggie smiled back.

"Bug things," Griffon pointed, then twirled a finger, indicating Reggie should turn around, "right behind you, and looking pissed."

Reggie dropped low and spun, Raven Stealer an extension of his arm, and the vriktiri charging him slid to the dirt in two pieces.

"Wow," Reggie said, looking at the ivory blade, "she's impressive. It's like she guides your hand, no wonder you do so well with her. Oh! And she just spoke in my head! Well, you're welcome. Not only impressive, but beautiful and witty? You have it all, don't you?"

"Stop," Griffon grunted, smashing the totem, "flirting with my sword, and get with the bug stomping."

The frenzied vriktiri came at the gnome as the hammer hit the arcane focus. Reggie stepped between the attackers and his friend, Raven Stealer flashing in the dim light. Segmented arms flew and faceted eyes twirled as heads fell to the ground.

A group of lost folk turned towards the disruption, and lurched at high speed towards the two, throaty, gurgling noises escaping their throats.

An arrow cut down one of the living dead, sliding between sagging eyelids and piercing the brain. Half the group peeled off and headed towards where the arrow came from. Griffon glanced toward LT, and saw her lining up her next shot, focusing on the approaching zombies.

"They sound worried," Reggie said, adjusting his stance for a concentrated mob of attackers, rather than the loose formation he'd faced a moment before. "Keep it up."

"Really?" Griffon puffed, slamming the wedge into the post repeatedly, splitting it lengthwise. "Thank goodness you were here to talk about that and coach me. I thought I was done and could go get breakfast."

"And you say I talk a lot," Reggie leaned into a thrust, cutting the interior of one foe's left thigh, and then the right as he drew back.

"If I can type bidj-talk in chat while tanking a boss fight with adds," the gladiator chuffed, flipping Marcid to batter the broken totem with the blunt end, "I can talk while—"

The totem shattered, an explosion of magic tossing the men backwards. Both scrambled to their feet, shaking their heads, and wiping splinters from their faces. Pinpricks of blood blossomed along their foreheads and upper cheeks above their bandanas.

The lost folk hesitated, turning in random directions, then wandered off individually, no longer in a clump.

"Okay, chief," Griffon said, "do we go after them, or the next totem?"

"Totem," Reggie answered without hesitation, "once we break their ranks, we can pick them off easily."

"Great," the gnome said, propping Marcid against his shoulder, "there's another one to the east."

"Lead the way," Reggie gestured for Griffon to lead, bending and collecting any serviceable arrows he could find.

LT rode up, reins in one hand and her bow in the other. She leaned a little more, and her boots showed scratch marks from the last attack. Reggie held the shafts up, and she took them.

"Same plan," Reggie said, then turned and jogged after the gnome.

Arrows arced over their heads as they approached their next target, LT having followed at a distance, piercing the vriktiri first.

"Why isn't she going for the zombie people?" Griffon asked, ducking under the swing of a lost folk, then slamming the sledge into its kneecap, giggling as it did a broken somersault.

"Arrows rarely take them down," Reggie answered, beheading another. "She's aiming where she can do the most damage."

Griffon fought his way to the next totem, moving like a man laying train tracks. He crushed knees like slamming ties and shattered heads like pounding in railroad spikes. Each time he took out a stricken townsfolk, he winced and giggled to cover the spreading sickness in his gut.

Reggie moved to take the brunt of the attack, and the gnome went to work on the magical antenna, repeating the process he'd done before.

"I feel bad," he said between blows, "killing them. They're not the dried husks I think of with zombies. They're still…juicy."

"They've only been like this a short while," Reggie called over his shoulder, facing off with two lost folk and a vriktiri, "and you're a decent person. But they're lost and you're doing the right thing."

He's right, Raven Stealer said in the gnome's mind, *but I understand your trepidation. Keep it up, and soon we will be past all this.*

It took almost an hour to circle the town, taking out the totems. Griffon and Reggie moved with deliberate and focused steps, their arms aching and exhaustion setting in. LT teetered on Monty, rubbing her injured knee.

"Think there's some in the town?" Griffon asked.

"Yes," Reggie nodded, "but I saw a group of the locals moving around in there. I think they saw what we were doing and took care of them. Shall we go say hello?"

"And maybe they'll cheer for us showing up to rescue them!" Griffon brightened. "Give us some food that isn't wrinkly, a hot bath, and a warm bed."

The sun had risen, but the sky was slate grey. Occasionally, a dirty finger of light pushed through the ashen clouds and touched the land, feeling like a sign of hope. The smell of burning bodies and buildings tempered the idea, though.

The trio mounted and headed into Allendale. When the three saw the faces of the group of people waiting to meet them, Griffon's hope of glory faded.

"Chuz me," he moaned, "they look pissed."

"You're not welcome here," Talien said, her voice hoarse. "You need to move on."

"But we just saved you," Griffon shouted across the half of a block distance, "we broke all the totems, and that made all the bug guys and dead guys…bugger off."

"Why do you think they were here in the first place?" Talien asked, leaning heavily on a staff. "Your friend here told us all about your plans. It's only because of what you just did that we aren't killing you at this moment, and letting you leave in peace."

"What friend?" Reggie asked. "What plans?"

A tall, thin man stepped from the shadows of a porch, tugging his lace cuffs down.

"I told them," Dandy Rym said, "how you played the system in Arena. How you rushed here, and everywhere you went, the lost folk appeared. When you went to Akar, the volcanoes erupted, and you released the Lich Lords of Ez'rainia-fromton and sent them here."

"How could you know about the liches?" Reggie asked.

"See?" Dandy Rym raised his voice and an accusatory finger, pointing at Reggie. "He told us he was going there, told the entire council of Allendale, and now he admits he released them. He'll try and turn this around. Don't listen to his excuses. He brings death with him wherever he goes."

"We're trying to stop them, you pemtie mother-chuzzer," Griffon shouted, his voice going shrill, "and went south because you said we should!"

"And I feel like a fool for being a pawn in your game," Dandy Rym shook his head. "If I'd known what you were planning to do, I would've slit your throats myself. In fact, that's what I think we should do right now."

"No," Talien held up a hand, stopping the small crowd surging forward, "we'll not kill more people. We don't have proof that they did all this, but we know trouble follows them."

"But we didn't do anything!" Griffon shouted.

"You did plenty," Dandy Rym shouted back, "and I'm tired of being caught up in your schemes for power and glory!"

"Griffon," LT said quietly, sidling next to him on her horse and putting a hand on his shoulder, "stop. It won't help. We should go while we still can."

"But we didn't…" the gnome started.

"She's right," Reggie said, "we need to go."

"But what about my armor?" Griffon said defiantly. "We paid for that, and it's mine."

"Yes," Talien nodded, and gestured behind her, "bring them what they are owed."

The leather worker they'd commissioned to make the gnome custom armor stepped from the crowd and tossed a cloth-wrapped bundle into the street.

"Take it and go," Talien crossed her arms, staring up at the trio, "before we change our minds."

Griffon moved his horse forward and slid from the saddle, grumbling. He dropped to the ground, snatched up the bundle, and climbed back up into the saddle.

Turning Tank, he moved beside LT and Reggie again.

Griffon saw Reggie about to say something, his eyes on Dandy Rym. The swashbuckler shook his head, spun Number One to face the opposite direction, and trotted away.

LT kicked Monty into motion, and Griffon followed the two, glaring back over his shoulder at the group in the street.

Chapter 22

"That's bullbidj," Griffon said when they were out of earshot, "that guy is totally full of it, and I want to take it personally. What'd we ever do to him?"

"It is personal," Reggie said, "and I'm sorry you two are suffering from my shortcomings."

"What shortcomings are those?" LT asked. "The bitterness? The drive to leave your mark? Your obsession with making things right?"

Her tone sounded light and teasing, but Reggie felt an underlying current of bitter honesty in the words.

"You're right," Reggie sighed. "I've led you both from one disaster to the next. I could've stopped the disease when I first went into the ruins with Griffon and Aiyana…"

"But we had to do that," Griffon interjected, "because to stop it, we couldn't have left and saved the world."

"Doesn't matter," Reggie snapped, "going back set the next things into motion. The disease was out, and we might have been able to contain it with standard methods."

"That's stupid," LT interrupted, "because you couldn't contain it in every town and village. That's impossible in a day and age without mass communication."

"And hell," Griffon said, "if COVID taught us anything, it's that people won't listen to quarantine rules. They just go out like they're immune and get everyone sick."

"COVID?" Reggie asked.

"It's the Spanish influenza of our century," LT explained, "and even with better medical facilities and information, people are still the key to not spreading the disease. People are pemtie and self-centered and will do whatever they want with no regard to the greater good."

"Yep," Griffon agreed, "it's like humankind is trying to kill itself."

"Some would say it's the natural order," Reggie said, "and the strong survive."

"Whether or not that's true," LT said, "people are people and do pemtie things."

The three fell silent, guiding their mounts in a wide circle around the city to head north. A lone figure broke away from the shadows of Allendale, walking towards them and lifting a hand for them to stop. They reined in, waiting for the figure to get to them.

The bleak landscape rumbled, piles of tephra tumbling into the grey soot on the ground. A stark red line appeared to the north, showing lava erupting into the atmosphere. A hare bounded away from its nearby hiding place, disappearing into a stand of wilted trees and withered bushes.

"Is that the bug guy?" Griffon asked.

"I think it is Kriksi," Reggie squinted in the falling ash.

The priest stopped a half dozen paces away from them, looking up from under a hooded cloak.

"Kazzek," the man said, looking at Reggie, "I wanted to warn you, and thank you."

"About what?" LT asked.

"For what?" Reggie asked at the same time.

"Chuz off," Griffon added.

"When you broke the totems," Kriksi said, ignoring their questions and comment, "I was able to commune with Khelikian. She sends a warning about servants and Rykul, the Great Bear."

"What is it?" Reggie asked, leaning forward in his saddle, resting his elbows on his thighs.

"I wanted to thank you for releasing the vriktiri here in Allendale, but it's not done yet. Khelikian's children are still under the spell of the liches in the north," Kriksi went on, "and they are heading into the Valley of the Bear to slay the creature. If the liches can destroy Rykul, they'll drain his magic and reshape nature in ways that would allow them to spread their disease further and faster. Right now, only the vriktiri carry it, but that will change if they succeed."

"Oh, is that all?" Griffon said, his voice dripping with sarcasm.

"No," Kriksi shook his head, "if you can free her children, Khelikian will grant you a boon. You carry her symbol, is that correct?"

Reggie fished in a pouch on his waist and withdrew his chain of holy symbols. Flipping through them, he held one up.

"Right here," he said.

"Then if you free her children," Kriksi said, "pray to Khelikian, and she will hear you and lend what aid she can."

Silence fell across the group, the only sound the soft fall of ash and Monty snorting and stamping.

Kriksi cleared his throat and looked around. "I should return now, but you have my apology for how

I acted before, and my gratitude for doing what you've done."

"Hey, wait," Griffon said, "can you bless us now? You know, give us bug powers or telepathy? Maybe make it so we're not freaking whipped and about to fall over?"

"And our horses?" LT added.

Kriksi cocked his head, and Reggie thought the man resembled a praying mantis in that moment. Reggie also knew that those insects were predatory.

"I will try," the priest said, his hands moving under his cloak.

The man bowed his head and made a series of noises. Foreign syllables separated clicks and hisses, which didn't sound like a language. After a minute or so, he raised his head.

"My god will bless you when you need it," Kriksi's body twitched, his head tilting and turning to one side, "but now is not the time. I pray for your survival and offer you this advice: act as a single hive, working for the survival of your nest, and you shall prevail."

The man turned, his body moving in stunted steps as he retreated towards Allendale.

"Weirdo," Griffon mumbled at the priest's back, "and I'm glad his prayer didn't work. I imagine it would've felt like little, tiny bugs crawling all over my body, getting under my clothes. Itty, bitty pincers biting at my—"

"Okay, stop!" LT shivered. "That was a little too detailed."

"We should get moving," Reggie stared into the gloom of the north. "I think the ash is thicker that way, and it's a long ride to Dragon Staff. We need to find a place to camp, because I don't think any of us are going to be able to handle a full day's ride."

Reggie clucked his tongue and kicked Number One in the ribs to get the horse moving. The other two caught up in a few moments, and Griffon sighed.

"So, to recap," the gnome said, "we're heading to a city the liches probably control and is overrun with bug guys and zombies. And it's a week ride in hilly country with volcanoes exploding, with very little food and no clean water anywhere. And we're trying to make our way into a valley surrounded by mountains to find a mythical bear that is the key to controlling how nature works before the already mentioned dead wizards kill us or beat us to it. Does that about sum it up?"

"And according to the people in my village," LT said, "all the entrances into the valley are destroyed. Collapsed from earthquakes decades ago, with maybe the exception of the one inside of Dragon Staff."

"Great," Griffon threw up his hands, "so there's that to deal with, too!"

"Yup," LT said, "all without beating up the annoying gnome who talks too much."

"Oh, bring it sister," Griffon said. "I taught you everything you know. I can block anything you throw at me, and take you out in the same breath, all without breaking a sweat."

"We shouldn't be fighting among ourselves," Reggie said, his voice hard.

"Yeah, gramps," Griffon said, "preach it. Because you'll beat yourself up enough for all of us. The only time you talk is when you feel the need to whine about what a horrible person you are. Why don't you just chase us off, tell us to go our own way, and that you'll do this all by yourself?"

"That's a fair point," Reggie reined in, turning to look at the gnome. "Why don't you leave? You've constantly been nagging me to go west and leave this entire mess behind. Why don't you do that? You can go anytime you like. All you have to do is shut up long enough to turn your horse and ride away."

The whistling sound was the only warning Reggie had before an arrow ripped along his bicep. His hand reflexively grabbed the injury, and he winced. He turned to look at LT, his eyes wide with surprise and confusion.

The woman was staring back at him, confusion on her face and her bow strapped beside her saddle.

"Oh, chuz," Griffon shouted, "it wasn't you that shot him!"

The three traded looks, then jerked around to see where the attack had come from. More than a dozen figures stood in the murky haze of ash, a few dozen paces away, bows drawn and releasing a barrage of arrows.

Pulling the reins of their horses, they turned them away from the attackers and broke into a gallop, arrows hitting the spot they'd been a moment before.

"Do we run or fight?" Griffon asked.

"They'll follow if we run," Reggie said, "then ambush us when we're totally exhausted."

"Or we could lose them in the ash," LT suggested.

"They'll track us easily in this mess," Reggie pointed out, "and the horses can't keep up a gallop for long. We've already pushed them to their limits."

"Head for those trees the rabbit went," Griffon said, turning Tank in that direction, "and Reggie, get your horse on the other side of LT."

The swashbuckler did as the gnome said. Arrows thudded into the ground, only missing because of the sudden change of course. More hit the trees as they entered the copse.

"Now, give her the reins," Griffon pulled alongside of LT, tossing his reins to her, "and slow down so we can drop off."

The gladiator stood on his saddle as LT did as he said, and jumped off the back of Tank, rolling into some bushes.

Reggie pulled his legs into a side saddle position and slid off. He was determined to make this turn out right, but it seemed like the gods themselves were against him helping the world. At every turn, there was a new obstacle blocking the way and trying to kill him.

LT kept moving, struggling to control the three horses. Reggie watched her for a moment, making sure she put the trees between herself and the attackers. He didn't want to see her hurt. She'd dealt with enough of that in her life already.

"But then again," he muttered, "Jack doesn't bring folks here who can't handle it."

"Do you think he's a god?" Griffon whispered, crouching in the hilly folds of earth, the stand of trees offering extra protection.

"Not sure," Reggie said, "but I'll be sure to ask him when I see him next. If I live to see him, that is. Now hush, we're setting an ambush, you annoying little scallywag."

"Since when did you start talking like an old British schoolmarm?" Griffon asked. "At least you're using a bunch of words again, that must mean you're feeling—"

Reggie cut off the man's words by shoving him to the side and diving in the other direction, three arrows slicing into the space they'd been in a moment before.

Griffon leaned back towards where he'd been, and flicked all five fingers in an outward burst, and the Wilhelm Scream cut through the air, muffled by the finger deep ash covering everything.

"I got one!" a rough voice called out, followed by the crunch of boots coming closer. "Hope it was that bastard, Tel Virian. I want to be the one that gets him, even if we split the bounty."

"Well, one thing I can say about the Bounty Hunters of Kresk," an odd voice called out from the far side of the brush, "is that they are much too stone headed and dry witted to ever know when they should give up. Even if it means their doom and that they're going to get their collective arses handed to them in a lovely basket wrapped with a pretty bow, and a spritz of perfume."

Reggie turned towards the sound, wondering who else could show up in this god-forsaken land, and then he realized it was his voice.

"I am using so many words," the other Reggie said, drawing out the sentence in a sing-song tone, "but I can make it easy for you pemties. You're gonna get your collective asses kicked."

"You five go that way," a deep rumbling baritone called out, "you five go this way, and the rest of us cut right through the middle of the trees. They ain't getting away this time."

Reggie glanced back at Griffon and saw the gnome cup his hands, whispering into them.

"Your mothers didn't want me to get away either," the other Reggie shouted through the haze. "In fact, they paid me to stay the night with her. All of them. At the same time. Hungry little tarts, aren't they now?"

A line of five men stomped between Reggie and Griffon, and the gnome caught Reggie's eye, winked, and held up a fist, indicating they should hold position. When the third man passed the two, Griffon stood up and swung Raven Stealer, cutting into the man's midsection.

Reggie surged forward, drawing Marcid and slapping his hands together, and drew them apart, holding the rapier and main-gauche. He thrust the long blade into the fifth man's throat and stabbed the parrying blade into the man's guts.

The other three spun towards the noise of the attack, and Griffon was turning to face them. Swiping up with his weapon, he smacked away the third man's sword, and reversed the direction of his blade to open a crimson line from the foe's collar bone to hip.

Spinning past the man—who dropped his sword to clutch at his open wound—Griffon squared off with the second man, who brought down a huge club towards the gnome's head.

Griffon stepped to one side, the club crashing to the ground where he'd been a moment before, and slashed across the man's midsection. Soft wet sounds preceded the man's scream.

Reggie rose to his full height, flipped his main-gauche in his hand—the blade morphing into a solid rod—and threw it at the man who'd led the way through the brush. The blunt rod hit the man square in the forehead, and the man's head jerked back. He stood still for a moment, his hands falling to his sides, then he fell backwards into the ash, a cloud puffing up around him.

"Don't kill this one," Reggie said, striding past Griffon and recovering the item he'd thrown. "We need one alive to question."

Surprised shouts came from the far side of the trees, accompanied by the whistle and thump of arrows.

"LT," Reggie said, "let's get to the rest of them before they get their bows out and return fire on her."

Chapter 23

Reid plucked another arrow from beside her, set it to the bowstring, and fired. It flew true and embedded itself into the core of another man, the fifth she'd hit since the ten of them had come around the trees in two groups.

The men weren't out of the fight, but putting a shaft into someone's chest or belly generally kept them preoccupied. At least, it allowed her to focus on the others who were coming towards her hiding place.

She was nestled in between a fallen tree and a large stone on a hillside; the horses tied on the other side. She brushed at the flakes of ash hitting her face and pulled another arrow from her stash.

Arrows clattered around her, one sticking into an exposed root directly over her head. A hand-span lower and she'd have one hell of a headache. She aimed for the person who'd fired it, and released at the same time the man shot another one in her direction.

Both arrows found their mark, and the man screamed, but Reid just grunted and looked at her calf. The feathered flights quivered on one side of her leg, and the wide metal arrowhead bobbed on the other as her muscle spasmed.

Gritting her teeth, she debated on breaking it off and pulling it free or firing another shot. She reached for her stockpile, and the movement made bright splashes of light fill her vision.

Another arrow thunked into the tree, this one beside her. They were getting closer.

Shouts rose, and she recognized Griffon's and Reggie's voices, followed by steel on steel. Her vision cleared, and she saw her friends clashing with the four remaining men. She sighed and leaned back, wincing at the jiggling arrow.

"Same leg," she muttered, "so that's a small blessing."

Setting the bow beside her remaining arrows, she reached to steady the missile. Steadying herself with long, deep breaths, she reached both hands to the back of her calf and gripped the shaft with one hand and the arrowhead with the other.

She snapped the head off with a grunt and a whimper, then took a moment for the stars to subside and her spinning head to slow. She tugged her bandana off, readying it to wrap around the wound, and then reached to the front of her leg and pulled the shaft out the way it had gone in.

Tossing it away, she wrapped the bandana around her calf, tied it off one, then made a knot and pulled it tight enough to make her scream.

Reggie stood over her then, and she blinked in confusion.

"I must've blacked out," she mumbled, "but I'm glad you're the one standing over me. Did we beat the bad guys?"

"Griffon offered to handle the cleanup," Reggie shrugged, "but I think we'll have one left to question."

"How'd you get to the outer edge so quickly to distract them?" she asked.

"That was Griffon," he said, kneeling in front of her and looking at her leg, "using an auditory illusion."

"He's getting better," she said, her words cut off with a grunt as Reggie touched her injury. "Calm down Brutie McBrutus, that's tender."

"I see that," Reggie said. "You did a decent job of tying it off, but it's going to need to have a bit more done to it. Shall I see to that now?"

"Yeah, sure, why not?" She rasped. "I don't have any other pressing plans."

Reggie swung his satchel around and rummaged through it, pulling out a waterskin, a knife, a flask, and some cloth.

"Have a drink?" he held the flask towards her.

"Don't have to ask me twice," she said, taking the flask and opening it.

She threw it back and swallowed twice, then leaned forward.

"That's pretty smooth," she said, surprised.

"Yup," Reggie nodded, and pressed some berries into her hand, "it's my private stock. I don't believe in keeping the rough stuff. Eat those while I tend to this."

Wincing as the man unwrapped her calf, she popped the berries into her mouth and chewed. Warmth bled its way down her throat to her belly, and she felt her leg twinge as Reggie cut away the cloth above her boot.

Pouring water on one side, then the opposite side, he looked up at her.

"You ready for this?" he asked.

She nodded.

Reggie splashed some alcohol on the open wound, blood oozing out of the hole, then jammed a wad of cloth over one hole. He pulled a longer cloth around to hold it in place, then pressed another wad against the other side, wrapping the cloth around the leg a few times before tying it off with a jerk.

Reid grunted and leaned back, nausea rolling across her as her head spun.

"LT," Reggie said gently, "I'm going to look for a branch that you can use as a crutch, okay? Will you be alright for a couple minutes?"

Nodding, she looked past him and watched Griffon move between the prone forms on the battlefield. *The bastard's looting them!* She thought. *He's going through their pouches and packs, tucking various items into his backpack and pouches.*

It made sense to her, logically, but made her cringe internally. They needed food and water, as well as other supplies, and since they couldn't go into town and pick up groceries, this was a reasonable way to get what they needed to survive.

None of them were moving, and Reid wondered if they were already dead or if Griffon had needed to finish the job. That was another thing that made sense, but she didn't want to think about. This was war, and you did things in these situations that civilians never considered. It was also things that you never really talked about later, not wanting to admit you did it, even to yourself.

It messed with a person's head to end another person's life, and even more if they were injured when you did it. But the other option was to leave an enemy alive who could come after you later.

Reggie came back, a tall, straight-ish branch in hand. The smaller branches had been hewn off, and he'd wrapped the crooked "y" at the top with more cloth.

"You've done this before," Reid said.

"Once or twice," he smiled, but it was a tight expression with no joy. "You do what you must to survive. Do you want to try and stand?"

Reid nodded, taking the makeshift crutch from him and using it and him to help her get on her feet.

"You said there was one left alive?" she asked, tottering as she pushed the support under her armpit.

"Yeah," Reggie said, still grim, "back in the trees."

"We should get to him before he wakes up and gets away," she said, "but what are we going to do with him after we finish questioning him?"

"Ah, yes," Reggie drew his lips into a straight line, "the eternal question. And best brought up before we have him in front of us. The best answer I can give is…I don't know. I'm prone to let him go, but realize the downside of that choice. But I'd rather risk that than murder someone in cold blood."

"And is that what Griffon was doing in the field down there?" Reid asked.

Reggie winced, then shrugged.

"Honestly, I was avoiding thinking about that," he sighed. "How about I go get the…prisoner, and send Griffon to fetch the horses. You just see how you can do with that crutch and leg. Sound good?"

"Avoidance," she nodded, "got it."

"Thank you," he said, turning away so she couldn't read his expression.

She watched him move down the hill and stop to talk to Griffon. His posture was weighed down. He shuffled instead of standing straight and walking tall. He didn't like this.

Reid had seen the man win a dozen fights, killing when necessary, but it wasn't something he ever wanted. She could see he'd been ground down by circumstances beyond his control, and she felt the same.

Limping, she carefully made her way towards Griffon as the gnome trotted towards her.

"Oh, ouch," Griffon said, pointing at her leg with his chin, "looks painful."

"Yup," she nodded, wobbling to a standstill. "Get anything good off of them?"

"I was gonna share," the gnome said, sounding defensive.

"Did you get their water and food?" Reid asked. "Extra medical supplies? Herbs? Anything besides money?"

"I got a new knife," Griffon pouted, "but I can go back and get the other stuff."

"Start with the horses," she said. "We'll need to repack things anyway to distribute the weight."

She hobbled past the gnome, picking the path of least resistance to the field, and Griffon huffed and jogged off in the direction where she'd tied their mounts.

Resting at the halfway point, Reid saw Reggie coming out of the trees, dragging a man who was bound at the hands and feet. Reggie had his hand on the ropes around the prisoner's wrists and was bent as he lugged him into the open. Looking up, Reggie met her eyes, then looked away.

She started moving again, limping past the looted bodies and heading for her companion. When she reached him, she looked at the prisoner. The man had a huge red welt on his forehead, and his face was covered in ash and dirt.

"How about I watch him," Reid said, "and you go check those guys for things that are actually useful. I don't think our little friend took anything except money and shiny things."

Reggie nodded, dropped the man's wrists, and trudged away.

In ten minutes, the three stood around the prisoner, who now had his hands tied above him around a tree branch. The horses pawed at the ground, trying to find something they could graze on.

"Are we going to camp here?" Griffon asked.

"No," Reggie answered before Reid could, "we will wake and question this man, then ride for a few hours before making camp. Scavengers and predators will be here soon, attracted by the scent of carrion."

"Not to mention the townsfolk," Reid added, "they could come out to see what's going on. This would not raise their opinion of us."

"You know you could stay with them, right?" Reggie asked.

Reid looked at him, tilting her head and scoffing.

"No, I can't," she said flatly.

"They offered it before," he continued. "Said you should stay with them instead of coming with us. It would be safer, especially with your leg."

"Worried about me slowing you down?" She tried to make it sound playful, but it came out harshly. "No, I'm in this until the end. Whatever that might be. End of discussion."

"What about you, Griffon?" Reggie turned to the gnome. "Care to take Tank and ride west with whatever you took from these bounty hunters?"

"That would be the smart thing to do," a new voice interjected. "Run away, as far and as fast as you can. Heading north and fighting a bunch of liches is suicide."

"Fillion," Reggie turned to the man tied to the tree, "welcome back to the world of the living. And if you'd like to stay that way, you're going to give us information."

"You were always pemtie like that, Kazzek," the prisoner went on as if Reggie hadn't spoken, "helping others. It's not that kind of world, kid. Hasn't been for a long time."

"Maybe I just like to bring hope to folks," Reggie shrugged, "let them know there's something still worth fighting for."

The big man on the ground snorted and shook his head.

"We don't have time for this," Griffon said, drawing Raven Stealer and jabbing it under the man's chin. "Why were you trying to kill us?"

The prisoner glared up at the gnome, almost eye level with the smaller man, even though he was sitting.

"Wrong question, runt," Fillion said.

"Griffon," Reid put a hand on the gnome's shoulder, and felt him push the sword closer to the bound man's throat, "he's a bounty hunter who thinks he has a debt to settle with Reggie…um Kazzek. That's why he was hunting us."

"No," Fillion shook his head at them, stopping as Griffon pushed again, "it's just business. The money was good. Dandy Rym added his own bounty on top of what was already being offered back east. Plus, if we took you out, then it might look good for the new overlords of the land."

"You'd work for the liches?" Reggie drew back, and Reid saw a look of horrified amazement on the man's face. "They don't want you, or anyone."

"Not true," Fillion grunted, trying to move away from the blade at his throat. "They're offering deals at each place they take. They did it here, in Akar, and probably did it in Dragon Staff."

"They've turned the entire city of Akar to lost folk," Reggie spat, "they turned them all without even being there."

Fillion lifted his eyes to study Reggie's face.

"Kazzek," the man said after a moment, "you were always too honest to be in this line of work, so I think you're telling the truth. If you let me live, I'll tell you something that can help you get to that valley quicker."

"Sounds fair," Reggie said, holding up a hand to forestall Griffon or Reid from saying anything. "I promise none of us will harm you further if we find your information helpful."

The bounty hunter shifted his eyes to the other two, waiting for each to nod their agreement before speaking.

Griffon stepped back at Reid's insistent tugging, lowering Raven Stealer.

"Okay then," Fillion smiled, "I can tell you that there's one mountain pass on the eastern side of the valley that you can still get through when the snows are melted. It's rough going, but it's passable."

"Go on," Reggie said, "that's not enough. How do we find it?"

"Follow the main road for about a day," Fillion continued, "when you're in the morning shadow of the mountain ring, a small track heads east while the main one goes north to Dragon Staff. Follow it for a couple days and look for some old ruins. It's like a guard post, but bigger. You'll find a settlement just beyond it, right on the roots of the mountains. Look for the peaks that look like a woman's breasts, and head in between them."

"You've been there?" Reid asked.

"I've been between a lot of breasts," Fillion leered at the woman. "I can show you if you're up to a roll."

"Griffon," she said, "stab him."

The gnome stepped forward again, raising his ivory blade.

"Wait, I was kidding!" Fillion went on quickly. "I haven't been there, but a man I trust said there's ancient markers every kilometer or so that shows the way. The setting sun makes them glow like stars. I swear it, and that's all I know!"

Reid and Griffon looked at Reggie, who was studying the captive.

"Good enough," Reggie said, nodding. "Let's mount up and get moving." Turning on heel, Reggie moved to stand beside Monty.

"I'll help you up, LT," he said, and gestured for her to come over.

"Wait," Fillion said, sounding a bit panicked to Reid, "what about me? You said you'd let me go if I helped."

"No, I didn't," Reggie glared at the bounty hunter. "I said we wouldn't harm you, but that doesn't mean we need to help you. Maybe I'm being soft by not killing you, but as you said…I never was good for this sort of thing."

"Yeah," Griffon said, "take that bidj-bag. Maybe the coyotes or whatever lives in these parts will gnaw you free."

"Griffon, stop," Reid called over her shoulder as she made her way to her horse, "let's just go. And don't kick him!"

"How'd she know?" The gnome grumbled and lowered his foot.

Portals: Book 6 – Legions & Liches

Chapter 24

They camped a few hours later, finding shelter in a ranger's safe camp carved into a hillside. Griffon had spotted some markings on a stone in the slope, and Reggie had translated them as "haven". They found the entrance by chance, concealed behind overgrown shrubs, and a jutting stone larger than them. But it was large enough for them and the horses.

It looked like no one had been here in years, and the only thing of use was the bubbling spring in the corner. A sturdy wooden chest held moth-eaten blankets, and most of the foodstuffs that had been in sealed jars had long turned into a sludge that was no longer consumable. There were a few jars of oats, and they split it between the mounts and the people. Even the hardwood bunks were unstable after years of insects gnawing at them.

Each of them drank their fill, including the horses, and bathed as best they could. Reggie cooked a small meal in the firepit, the first proper fire they'd had in a long time. The light was hidden from the outside, and LT was happy to not be sleeping in the cold.

Reggie checked her wound, re-bandaged it, and then tended to the horses. He brushed them down, talking to them in a low, soothing voice.

LT curled up near the fire, rolled up in her blanket, and murmured in her sleep, her hand gripping her spear. She was pale and shivered, but Griffon didn't think she was sick, just dreaming.

The gnome sat in a corner, Raven Stealer across his lap. He wiped at the blade with a cloth absently, staring at his crossed legs.

Something troubling you? The sword asked.

I don't know, Griffon answered her in his head, not wanting to share the conversation with the others. *Maybe. I guess.* He shifted, stretching a leg out in front of him. *It's just that this whole thing isn't like the video games, you know? I mean, not just the getting hungry and going to the bathroom, but I don't feel like a hero. I don't feel like I'm winning.*

Real life does not usually feel that way, Raven Stealer said gently, *and sometimes you have to face hard times to become who you really are.*

But this isn't real life. Griffon insisted. *It can't be. The stuff here is impossible. And it's not fun. There's so much boring stuff. Like riding a horse across the country sounds awesome until you're actually doing it. And I'm always hungry now. I swear I'd stab Reggie for a can of Pringles. Or even just a piece of fresh fruit. Who knew those things were seasonal? I used to be able to have my mom pick them up at the grocery any time of the year.*

Do you miss being there? She asked.

Sure, but I can't do the kind of things I do while I'm here, you know? Griffon cocked his head. *Not the killing, but the other things. I never rode a horse before coming here. Or camped out. Or even really had friends, not like these guys. And I'm a badass with a sword. I mean, I really kick ass, you know?*

You can be like that in the other world, too, you know? Raven Stealer chuckled in his head.

"Yeah," Griffon said aloud, "but how do you get from where I am now to there?"

"We should find the split in the road tomorrow morning," Reggie said, looking over at Griffon, thinking the gnome was speaking to him. "We'll find that guard post, the markers, and get into the valley."

Griffon watched Reggie, the wheels turning in his head. "Dude," he said, "you look so tired. I guess this adventure isn't turning out like you thought it would, huh?"

"Not at all," Reggie smiled sadly. "It just keeps on coming, never really resolving. There's always one more thing to do, and I feel like I'm failing. Even with you two—"

"I know what you mean," Griffon interrupted. "I imagined a huge gladiator tour through different arenas. Winning matches, getting hurt, then having a sexy priestess heal me, and then…"

"I get the picture," Reggie said.

"But do you?" The gnome went on. "The places here are so far apart, and we spend most of our time doing nothing but training. Then there's like twenty minutes of something exciting, then a bunch more nothing."

"Griffon," Reggie sighed, "that's how real life is. The trick is to enjoy the journey. Look at the landscape and see things you wouldn't have time to appreciate in the exciting times. Recognize the milestones and markers for the high points, and the low points, but relax when you can and enjoy the quiet times to help when you can't rest."

"So, your advice is," Griffon tapped the sword, "learn to love being bored, because you might die tomorrow."

"Well, not exactly what I was saying," Reggie said, "but that's a reasonable bit of something, too."

LT moaned and rolled over to look at the men.

"Can you guys appreciate some sleep right now?" she muttered. "Isn't this something we can talk about on the long, boring horse ride tomorrow?"

"Of course, sorry about that," Reggie chuckled. "How's the leg?"

"Throbbing," LT said, rolling over with a sharp intake of breath, "hurts like hell every time I move. I think the berries helped, but now that I'm relaxing—and trying to sleep—its complaining with every little movement."

"Need a few more?" Reggie asked.

"Oh, can I have some, too?" Griffon chimed in. "I don't have a leg with a hole in it, but I'm achy from this morning and smashing all those totems."

LT moaned again.

"Was that really just this morning?" she asked. "Feels like a week ago."

"So, yes, to the berries?" Reggie smiled.

"Yeah, sure," she said, "berries all around, you damned berry pusher. You're my berry dealer."

When they woke, the mild gloom outside announced morning had arrived. They ate boiled oats, and packed up in the chilly spring air, made even colder by the cloud cover.

"Let me check your bandages again," Reggie insisted, "switch them out for clean ones while we have fresh water. And I'd like to do it before the horses stick their heads back into it."

"I can do it myself," LT said.

"I can see it better than you," Reggie said, squatting down in front of the woman, "but I wish I had something to stitch it up. Needles are hard to get here."

"And so are sanitary conditions and anesthetic," LT complained, "and I think I'd prefer to just avoid sepsis."

"Isn't there something in the Citadel?" Griffon asked, and the other two turned to stare at him.

"Duh," LT shook her head, "why didn't we think of that?"

"Exhaustion?" Reggie suggested. "We were just so happy to not need to set it up last night. It wasn't even something we considered."

"What can I say," Griffon sang in his best Dwayne Johnson voice, "but you're welcome!"

LT rolled her eyes, and Reggie looked clueless.

"Should we set it up now and see if we can find something?" Reggie asked.

"Maybe wait for tonight?" LT said, and it sounded more like a question than a statement. "If you didn't see any signs of infection, I should be okay until then."

Reggie looked doubtful.

"We really should get moving if we want to find the turnoff," LT pressed, "and I'm fine. I really am. Just stiff, that's all."

"Alright," he said, handing her the crutch. "Let's get you up on that horse, then. I took the liberty of whittling a bit more on your brace last night. Smoothed down the arm rest and straightened the shaft."

"That's what she said," Griffon snickered.

They packed up the remaining gear, loaded the horses, and set out to the north on the main road. Thunder rumbled and lightning jigged its way through the thick clouds overhead. Ash turned to a slippery sludge in the misting rain, and the trio took to riding beside the road instead of on it. All three had pulled out their rain cloaks, helping keep them relatively dry and much warmer.

After riding for a while, Griffon looked over at LT.

"Your horse is beginning to look like a porcupine," Griffon said. "You've got your spear and bow, and now the crutch is sticking up, also. If you add anything else, we're going to need a bigger horse. Want a flag or anything?"

"I'm not as lucky as you two," LT said. "I don't have a magic weapon that can shapeshift into anything I want it to."

"Mine doesn't do that," Griffon pointed out.

"No, she doesn't," she answered, "but she teleports, is a huge glow stick, heals you, and talks to you. And if I had a Marcid, I could use her as a spear, a crutch, and a bow."

"Reggie can't use Marcid as a bow," Griffon argued.

"I'm afraid he's correct," Reggie agreed.

"I don't think you've tried." LT sniffed. "If you can make two weapons from the one, then why not make a bow? The string could be attached and made of metal, because it wouldn't be much thinner than the vines on your hilt wrap guard thing. And I've seen you throw your main-gauche, which means you could make arrows and fire them. They wouldn't break like normal arrows, and the flights wouldn't be any harder to create than the leaves on the vines I already mentioned. You just need to recover them after, which should be easy as long as you don't shoot them over a cliff or into a dragon or something. Or just use regular arrows if you don't want to risk losing part of Marcid."

"Um," Reggie mumbled, staring into the middle distance as he considered this. "I think you're on to something. I really do. That all makes sense. I've just never tried it. Never even considered doing it."

"Crossbow might be harder because of the moving parts," LT went on, "so that one might not be possible. And you could even make a long spear with a reach two or three times more than my short spear. Or a javelin like the women in Black Panther use. They seem pretty versatile."

She looked at the men, smirking.

"What about a shield?" she asked. "Could you make one of those? A personal battering ram? Those spiked gauntlets that Griffon has that he almost never uses? What about turning it into a piece of jewelry so you could wear it without appearing to have a weapon? Can you do any of that?"

"Now you have my mind working," Reggie smiled. "This is the beauty of a different point of view. It brings ideas to the forefront that I would have never considered on my own."

"Shovel? Rake? Garden hoe?" LT went on.

"Okay, already!" Griffon said. "We get the idea. Reggie is unimaginative and didn't use his toy to its full potential. He could've been working the garden in his downtime. Pemtie."

"More like I was stuck in a rut," Reggie said, "and I pigeonholed poor Marcid."

Drawing his blade, Reggie concentrated on her, and she pulled back into herself, and flowed over his hand, forming a bracer on his forearm and wrist. Vines decorated the silver surface, and the swashbuckler held his arm in front of him to admire her.

"Amazing," he said, sounding genuinely pleased to Griffon. "It's like when I turned it into a gauntlet in Ez'rainia-fromton."

Another hour of riding brought them to a turnoff towards the east. They steered their horses in that direction, and rode on, hunched in their saddles in what had become a torrential downpour.

"Glad we found it before the bottom fell out," LT said, raising her voice to be heard over the rain.

"Fillion said it was a couple days down the road," Reggie said, "and I'm debating if we should stop soon, or go until we lose the light. Considering your leg and the freezing rain, I want to stop sooner rather than later. But I do feel pressed for time. The longer it takes us to get there, the more time Ahken'ho-tek and his flunkies will have to hunt Rykul."

They spent the next two days following the trail and setting up the Citadel in the evenings. The rains continued, and LT's condition deteriorated. They'd treated her wound with herbs and poultices they'd found in the laboratory, as well as stitching the wound closed, but she was getting worse.

"There's the barbican," Reggie said, rising in his stirrups and pointing. "I think we should camp here, instead of going into the place when the sun will be setting shortly. Another couple of days and we should be in the Valley of Rykul."

"You'd think that bear could take care of itself," Griffon said, "because it's supposed to be an aspect of nature, or a force of nature, or something like that."

"But folks say Rykul died," LT said, her voice quavering with shivers, "and it's possible that his power is just waiting for someone to come pick it up and use it. Or there could be a new bear, who's just learning the bear ropes of being a demigod and would be easy to beat up."

"Alright you two," Reggie said, "we need to find a place to set up the Citadel. LT can barely ride, or talk, because she's shivering so hard, and I'm concerned with infection festering in her leg. So, keep an eye out for someplace clear and flat enough."

The other two nodded, and Griffon thought that LT must be feeling pretty bad if she didn't even argue with Reggie.

By the time they found a spot, LT was hunched in her saddle, her teeth chattering and her body shaking. Reggie and Griffon rushed to set up the Citadel, the former taking LT inside when they completed it, and the latter staying out in the rain to erect the makeshift horse stall.

"Why do I always get the bidj jobs?" Griffon muttered, affecting a shiver of his own to show he was cold.

"You know," Raven Stealer said out loud, "you're not actually cold. Reggie will know it, too. You spent half the winter walking around the Nine Towers in sleeveless shirts."

"Griffon," Reggie's sharp voice barked from inside, "get in here, now."

"Oh bidj," Griffon moaned, "I'm in trouble now. I forgot you can hear everything inside the tent and drop the protections to be heard outside."

The gnome tied off the last of the lines, turned and trudged inside. He bent to pull off his boots, not looking up at Reggie.

"Don't worry about that," Reggie said, his tone ominous, "we need to get her into the tub and use cold water. Her fever has spiked, and she's delirious."

Chapter 25

Reggie opened the water keg's spigot and water drizzled into the claw-foot tub. He soaked a cloth under the flow and hurried back to the cot where LT shifted and mumbled.

Griffon stood just inside the entryway, one boot half off, looking lost. The gnome followed Reggie's movements, his eyes shifting back and forth between the tub and LT.

"Help me get her out of these clothes," Reggie said, giving Griffon something to focus on. "And no creepy stuff. We're trying to save her life. We're going to bring down her fever, then get her bundled up for the night."

The gnome didn't move, staring at the scene.

"Now, boy!" Reggie snapped, wiping the cool cloth across the woman's forehead, face, and neck.

Griffon jumped, startled from inaction, and rushed to the bedside to help. "What do I do?" he asked in a small voice, sounding lost and worried to Reggie.

"Take off her boots," Reggie said, this time more gently.

Reggie unclasped her cloak, then worked at the buckles and straps of LT's leather chest cover. The two peeled off layers until she was down to her small-clothes.

"Grab her legs under the knees," Reggie said.

He moved to the top of the cot and slid his arms under her armpits. He stood, lifting, and LT thrashed.

"Sh, sh," Griffon said, and slid an arm under her knees and the other under the small of her back.

The gnome lifted, and Reggie was amazed at the smaller man's strength, and not for the first time. Griffon was built solid, and for all his bluster he could be caring when he wasn't putting up a front.

Reggie helped, though his efforts were minimal, more guiding than lifting. They waddled sideways to get her off the cot, walked to the tub, and lowered her carefully into the water.

"I got this now," Reggie said. "Go to the herbs. Crush some elderflower, ginger, and garlic with the mortar and pestle."

Wetting the cloth, Reggie wiped LT down, focusing on her neck, armpits, back of the knees, and groin. The tub only had a hand-span of water in it, but it was enough to do the job.

Reaching up, he turned off the tap, and watched Griffon work as he administered to LT. The woman shivered and moaned, struggling weakly. Reggie put a hand on her shoulder, soothing her.

"How much of each?" Griffon asked, looking at the earthenware jars he'd set on the table.

"Two spoons of each, crush them up well, and keep them separate." Reggie instructed.

A couple of minutes later, Griffon asked, "Okay, now what?"

"Boil some water," Reggie said, "won't need much, just enough for a cup or two. It'll be quicker that way, as well. Once you have the kettle on, come help me carry her back to bed."

The gnome was at his side in short order, and Reggie looked at him with a serious expression.

"I need to undress her the rest of the way," he explained. "We can't put her to bed in wet underthings. You can look away if you want, but you're going to see everything when we move her back to the cot."

Griffon nodded, and Reggie went to work removing LT's undershirt and drawers.

"Alright," Reggie nodded, "same process to get her back. I'll need to dry her off before we get her covered, so let's bring her to my bed first and get her sitting up for that."

Swallowing hard, Griffon nodded.

They repeated the carrying process, got her to Reggie's cot, and Griffon moved behind LT and propped her up. Reggie toweled her off, nodded at the gnome again, and jerked his head towards her cot.

"One more time," he said.

They moved LT to her bed and laid the woman down on top of the blanket.

"Go pour the hot water in a bowl," Reggie said, "only enough to dissolve a spoonful of each of the ingredients, then fill it a bit more with cold water. Make sure the bowl is only about half full."

"Wait," Griffon said, "a cup or a bowl?"

"Bowl," Reggie said, covering LT's naked form with a second blanket. "It's easier to pour into her mouth in little sips. Cups make you tilt their head back too far, and she may choke."

"Okay." Griffon darted away as Reggie arranged her legs and arms.

Reggie stepped to his cot, pulled the blanket from it, and returned to LT, tucking his blanket around her.

Returning with the bowl, Griffon passed it to the other man, then helped him sit LT up. Reggie tilted the vessel to the woman's lips.

"LT," he said, "you need to drink some of this. Just little sips."

"Where's Charlie?" LT mumbled. "Is she okay?"

"I'm sure she's fine," Reggie soothed. "Now drink a little of this."

She sipped at the mixture, sputtering a little. Reggie made her drink the entire bowl, then they helped LT lay down again.

"She's out," Reggie said, adjusting the blankets again. "She might sleep through the night, but I'll stay awake to watch her. You go get some sleep."

"Okay," Griffon said quietly, "but you can wake me up if you get tired. I can take a turn watching her."

"Thank you, Griffon," Reggie said. "You really are a decent fellow."

He watched the gnome cross the room, looking lost again now that he didn't have a specific task to do.

Rising to his feet, Reggie stretched. He moved around the room, tapping all but one of the magical light globes, turning them off. Settling on his bunk, Reggie pulled off his boots, removed his doublet, and got a bit more comfortable for his vigil.

LT wasn't any better in the morning, and Reggie paced nervously. He heard Griffon sit up on his cot and turned to look.

"Thanks for taking over last night," Reggie said. "It was helpful. And the use of your blanket."

"Well, you needed it," Griffon shrugged, "and I wasn't sleeping so great, anyway. How is she?"

"No real change," Reggie sighed. "Still feverish. I've been trying to keep her cool and give her the tea and alternating water when she'll take it. I wish there was something more I could do."

"What about the berries?" Griffon asked.

"Doesn't seem to do much," Reggie said, "though she sleeps a little after having a couple."

"Maybe pray to that bug god," Griffon laughed bitterly. "Creaky, the bug priest, said she'd do you a favor. Wouldn't this count?"

Reggie stopped pacing and stared at Griffon.

"What?" the gnome asked, looking around. "Did I say something wrong?"

"No," Reggie said quietly, "you may have said something right."

"Achievement unlocked!" Griffon crowed softly, pumping his fist in the air.

Reggie moved to his pouches and rummaged through one until he found the ring of holy symbols. He returned to LT's bedside and knelt, holding the ring in clasped hands, the symbol of Khelikian jutting out from between his fingers.

"Um," Griffon swung his legs over the side of the bed, "want me to go out and check on the horses or something?"

Looking up, Reggie shook his head, then shrugged. "You can," he said, "or you can come pray with me. Or you can just sit there and watch."

Reggie saw Griffon lick his lips and look around, unsure what to do. The kid was nervous, Reggie had seen it before. He wanted to be useful, just not have to do it here, where any action could determine if a friend lives or dies.

"Why don't you put on the pot for oats?" Reggie suggested. "While it's cooking, check on the horses and bring them water. I should be finished by the time you are."

"Great," Griffon jumped to the floor and scrambled for his clothes, "I'm on it. You do your thing, and I'll do…all the other things."

Reggie bowed his head again, trying to focus on a prayer and not get distracted by the racket the gnome was making as he rushed around the Citadel. Pulling the coin-sized charm from the ring, Reggie placed it on LT's breastbone, and tried again. Griffon finally went outside, and Reggie leaned back on his knees, sighing.

"Marcid," he breathed, standing.

Walking back to his cot, he picked up the bracer shaped artifact and willed her to the shape of the insect deity's symbol.

"Alright, Marcid," he whispered to the disk, "I figure the help of many gods made and shaped you, so perhaps you can help me with this prayer, and focus on what I want better than I can do alone."

He returned to LT's side and knelt again, bowing his head. His mind ran in a thousand directions, and after a couple minutes, he blew out his breath and looked up.

"I can do this," Reggie said to no one. "I've studied belief systems and cultural methodology of worship all my life, in both worlds. Holy people, priests, gurus, and wise men have instructed me. Just…settle your mind, calm your thoughts, and breathe."

He fell silent, staring at the far wall and letting his eyes go slightly out of focus. Reggie stopped thinking about a billion different things, and instead concentrated on his breathing—in through the nose, hold it, out through the mouth, slowly—and allowed his muscles to relax.

He repeated this process for long minutes, trying to find the tricky space between awareness and the timeless floating of those moments before you drifted off to sleep.

Griffon set a tin plate of oats in front of each of the horses and began rubbing down Number One. He affectionately called Reggie's mount "European", because of that old joke about being Russian when going into the bathroom and American coming out, what were you in between? European!

The rain finally stopped, but thunder rumbled far away. Or maybe it was the volcanoes. Griffon wasn't sure. The ground had puddles, and he looked to see if any of them were rippling. They weren't. Looking up, he studied the low-hanging pregnant clouds, and then looked east towards the rising sun. A mountain was between him and it, and he knew it would stay dim and murky until almost noon. He shrugged and moved to Tank, petting him along the barrel of his chest.

This was the last of the oats, and once Reggie and LT had theirs…

He stopped mid-stroke on Tank's flank, the thought of "if" floating through his mind. If LT had any. *She could keep getting worse and never eat again, because she would be…*

He mentally trailed off again, then laughed. It was funny, because he could walk into a field of wounded men and end their lives without thinking twice about it but let someone he knew die of an infection and a cold, and he gets all weird.

A horse whinnied, the sound tumbling down the mountain rising above him, and Griffon looked at Tank, Monty, and Number One. They each had their ears up, swiveling to catch the noise. Monty knickered a reply, lifting his head to scent the air.

The sound of muted voices came from above, high on the mountainside, and the clatter of falling pebbles clacked down the stone slope and pattered on the overhead tarp.

The gnome crouched down and crept to the edge of the lean-to, peeking up to see who it was. He saw the muzzles of horses, but couldn't tell who was on them.

"Raven Stealer," he whispered, "think I could use an illusion to hide the tarp?"

You could, she answered, *but I think they've already seen it, and will come looking for it even if it is invisible.*

"You think I could turn myself invisible?" he asked, his voice rising in wonder. "Then we could teleport above them and get a look at them!"

It's possible, but I do not know if you're quite to that skill level yet with your illusions.

"Let's try it!" Griffon giggled.

He scrunched up his face and pushed his will at his concentration.

You're going to burst a blood vessel, the sword said, *relax. Let it flow.*

"Like pooping?" Griffon asked. "Just let it go?"

He said the last three words in a sing-song voice.

Did you just quote Frozen in reference to a bowel movement? She asked.

Griffon giggled again and breathed in deep. He closed his eyes and let out the air, trying to let the idea of not being there wash over him.

The sensation of teleporting washed over him, and he opened his eyes. He was squatting at the edge of a ledge, and a dozen horses were below him.

Recognizing two of the figures, Dandy Rym and Fillion, he sighed.

"I'm getting tired of these guys," he moaned, "and how'd they get here so fast?"

His voice echoed off the cliff-side and the group below looked up.

"There's the damned gnome!" Fillion said, pointing.

"That's right," Griffon said, standing and holding up his fist, one finger jutting upward, "and your asses are in trouble now!"

The men below pulled bows from their saddles and began stringing them.

"Oh, bidj," Griffon shuffled backwards a single step until his back the wall, then crouched, "now what do I do?"

I'd suggest teleporting again, Raven Stealer said, *either into the middle of them, or back to the Citadel.*

"Not much room down there," Griffon said, leaning over the edge to check, "and I think it would be a bad idea."

He jerked backwards and arrows struck the stone below and above him.

"Okay," he puffed, "I think we head home and warn Reggie. Maybe they'll try coming up here first and give us some time to get ready."

Raven Stealer teleported him again.

The tent flap burst open as Griffon faded into view, surprising Reggie. The gnome was flushed and puffing, and the sound of voices shouting came from above the Citadel.

"What's going on?" Reggie asked.

"Dandy Rym and Fillion are here, with a bunch more guys," Griffon said hurriedly, "and I distracted them so they're looking for me up the mountain, but they've seen the horses, so will be down here, eventually."

The gnome looked around the room, then at LT.

"Did it work?" Griffon pointed at the unconscious woman. "Is she all better?"

"No," Reggie shrugged, his face twisted in confusion, "I don't know. I prayed, and I felt…something. I saw something. So, I think it worked, but think it's going to take some time."

"Chuz," Griffon said. "In my games, it's always instant. Why can't this be like them? I guess we aren't running then." Griffon winced. "We better get ready for our company, because they are hot for you, man."

Chapter 26

Reggie led the horses into the Citadel, and Griffon dragged the tarp in behind him. The gnome tossed the heavy cloth in a pile, and the two turned and headed back outside.

Calling upon the magic of the tent, Reggie secured the door and stepped back to make sure it was blending with the terrain.

The two made their way down the trail, heading for the barbican, sidestepping puddles and slicks spots.

"Whoever thought that ash would turn slippery when wet?" Griffon muttered.

"Get ready with some fireworks," Reggie said, "we want to draw them away from the camp."

"Maybe I should do something better?" Griffon said. "I mean, doesn't that feel like an obvious distraction? Maybe I should do dragon flame and a roar? Think that would scare them away?"

"No," Reggie jumped a rivulet of water streaming across the road, "Dandy knows you do magic and probably wouldn't be fooled. But it would draw them here as much as fireworks. Do either, or just do a bonfire. The trick to fooling people is to show them something they'd believe. A dragon is a bit too unbelievable."

"Why?" Griffon asked. "We hung out with a bunch of them. Bidj, they chuzzing talk about us to other people. Like they did with the sand people."

"Griffon, you had a problem keeping a steady beam of sunlight a month and a half ago. Do you think you could make a dragon now? And make it roar and shoot fire?"

Griffon stopped, turned towards Reggie, and his face went smooth. He cupped his hands in front of his mouth and his lips moved.

"Hey, you chuzzing pemties," Griffon's voice echoed from in front of them, in the direction of the ruins of the guard post, "we're waiting to kick the bidj out of you! If you can pull your head out of your asses long enough, maybe you can come over here and face us like true warriors, instead of hiding like little children!"

Griffon smirked up at Reggie, and the taller man rolled his eyes, looking up at the grey sky.

"Think you could have waited until we were hidden in the ruins before doing that?" Reggie sighed. "And you just told them it was more than you, taking away that little element of surprise."

"Whatever," Griffon shrugged, "but I guess we should get a move on."

Shouts rose from the mountain slope and behind them. They picked up the pace, heading for the looming structure in front of them. A fog had rolled in, but it wasn't a normal one.

"This fog is weird," Griffon said.

"It's vog, volcanic fog," Reggie explained, jogging towards a set of broken doors in the dual guard towers. "It's blending the rising moisture with the ashfall. Makes it thicker, and, well, weird."

They stopped in front of the dilapidated buildings, Reggie craning his neck to follow the stone walkway that connected them. Griffon peeked inside one, then the other.

"No exits," the gnome said, "think we should go past it and into the compound in the pass?"

"This is a bottleneck point," Reggie said, "and I don't want to get lost or run into a dead end in a place we don't know. Maybe hide on the other side, and then make some noise past the towers so they think we went into the larger ruins?"

"Sure," Griffon shrugged, "sounds good. But we should hurry. I hear them coming."

Reggie cocked his head, listening, and heard horse's hooves approaching at a trot.

"You go right," he whispered, pointing, "and I'll hide over here. Let's finish these guys quick and get back to LT. I don't want her waking up alone."

They moved through the arch, heading for the spots Reggie indicated, and settled into a crouch as the first horse came into view, slowing to a walk.

Reggie caught Griffon's eye, and pointed further into the broken compound behind them, pointed at his ear, then held up his pointer and thumb close together.

Griffon nodded, and relaxed, his face going smooth.

A torch flared to life about ten paces past them and bobbed away like someone was carrying it deeper into the ruins.

"I see the bastards," a rough voice whispered, Fillion, "and I want that chuzzing gnome. I'll show him what it's like to have a blade at his throat."

"That's fine," came Dandy Rym's voice. "The rest of you use your bows if you can, then run them down with the horses. Don't get into sword range if you can help it. They'll tear you apart."

Fillion rode past, bow in hand, and ten other riders followed him, heading for the bobbing torch. Once they'd all passed, the light winked out.

"They're onto us," Fillion called, slowing his mount and setting an arrow to the string.

The other men followed his example, leaning towards the shadows where they thought their quarry was hiding.

Catching Griffon's eye, Reggie pointed at himself then at Dandy Rym. Griffon smiled, nodded, and moved towards the others in a crouched run.

"Hey," Griffon's voice came from an alcove in a loud whisper, just ahead of Fillion. "Do you think they saw us?"

The horsemen rose in their stirrups, firing arrows into the murky vog. At that same moment, Griffon swung his sword at the rear ruffian and Reggie darted towards Dandy Rym, Marcid drawn.

Reid floated in nothingness but didn't feel alone or even worried. The feeling of something greater surrounded her, comforted her, and blanketed her with a presence unlike anything she'd ever experienced.

After an eternity of tumbling nightmares and dreamscapes, where even mundane events had shaken her to the core as world-shattering moments, this was the bliss of a lack of anxiety. It was being whole, accepted, and part of a community where you knew your place, your job, and your worth. It was like being in the military but lacking the sharp edges of social politics, and of worrying about the egos of others or yourself.

"Where am I?" she thought.

She'd meant to think the words, but they rang in her ears as if she'd spoken. It had that wavering sound like she had water in her ears, but was still sharp and crisp.

Looking around, Reid tried to figure out where she was. It was dark, but warm. She could see an emanating warmth, but not with her eyes. It was an ambiance, an atmosphere, and an aura. Her mind compared it to entering carnival grounds and being wrapped up in the welcoming smells. There are always a dozen scents of food, animals, and more. The smell of the stables, the allure of the fried sausage, the wafting, buttery tang of the popcorn, the crisp, sweet, greasy smell of funnel cakes covered with powdered sugar, the bite of gasoline mellowed by the fatty gentleness of oil on countless rods, joints, and gears. All these things were separate, but together.

"You are safe, my child," the words came from all around her, but from nowhere, "and you are home."

They weren't words as much as that combination of scents in a particular order that let her know that information. It showed her images in smells that meant a nest that was protected, and a hive with a working order, and a colony that had others to help.

"Who are you?" Reid asked.

"I am Khelikian," came the answer, "the Queen of the colony that is this planet. I am the one who joins all of my children into one family to keep the ecosystem stable.

"You were injured by my children," the voice went on, "and you have the fungal infection that will control your brain. I've seen this used before, but never against your species."

"Why am I here?" Reid felt an urgency, but it was distant and muted.

"Because your drone prayed to me, you were struck down using my hand, though someone else guided it, and you have a gift and potential that I have never seen before. I answered a call of beseeching, of duty, and of potential."

"What's going to happen to me?" Reid asked. "Am I going to become a lost one?"

"You could, if you choose," Khelikian answered. "Or you can accept my blessing to once again be whole. But there is a third option I would like to offer you."

Reid waited for the deity to go on, her scent coming off as impatient.

"I see," Khelikian sounded amused, "I shall tell you then. When a hive is full, or when they need to expand, they send out a new queen and part of the nest follows her. Since Ahken'ho-tek subverted part of my colony, I find the need to grow again to maintain the balance. But to keep that equilibrium properly primed, I need one of the species most affected to help with this expansion. Would you be willing to cooperate with me?"

"What?" Reid jerked in the space that wasn't quite real, but much more substantial than a dream. "You want me to go out and have a bunch of babies to make up for all the humans that were killed or turned into zombies? I don't even know if I want a kid, let alone repopulate the continent single handedly. Or single uterus-edly in this case."

"No, you misconstrue my suggestion." Khelikian had an amused scent again, and it was beginning to irk Reid. "I offer a bond with your small hive, your drone and worker—the Reggie and the Griffon—and also a bond with my children."

"I don't know what that means," Reid said.

"You would know where they are," Khelikian explained, "and be able to communicate basic information through scent, pheromones, and body movement."

"So, I could speak to the vriktiri and my friends without words?" Reid asked.

"Yes, and more, but that is close summation," the queen of insects said. "It is similar to how we are communicating now."

"Would I get armor plating like the vriktiri?" Reid asked, sending out a puff of suspicion.

"Would you like that?" Khelikian asked. "I do grant that boon on some of my high priests. Or sometimes extra limbs, and the ability to climb surfaces, or extra strength. Kriksi, who you know, has some of these abilities in a limited fashion. He is a very loyal drone, but he is saturated with aggression, and I am not sure if he is ready for more."

"I wouldn't want to change physically," Reid said, "so no extra limbs. As for the strength and climbing, can I get back to you about that?"

"Of course," Khelikian said. "I shall heal you, and you shall carry the immunity to the fungus that controlled you to become a lost folk that will be passed down your family line. I will bestow the gift of communication upon you and let you decide on the rest in the future."

"Sounds good for now," Reid said.

Sitting up, Reid gasped in a deep breath and reached down to scratch her leg. It burned and itched below the surface of her skin.

She could sense her friends, Griffon and Reggie, not too far away. Tilting her head, she knew they were in danger. She also felt vriktiri, just beyond the two, waiting for the moment to swarm.

Swinging her feet to the floor, she noticed she was nude, and reached for her clothes.

Reggie plunged Marcid towards Dandy Rym's midsection, and the tall man slapped the blade away with an absent gesture. Falling into an offensive stance, the swashbuckler attacked with a flurry of blows, and the fop weaved around all of them.

"Fool," Dandy Rym sneered, "do you think I am defenseless?"

"I had hoped," Reggie said grimly, "but there was the chance you were something more."

The two men fell away from one another, Reggie holding Marcid across his body defensively.

"I've thought about it a lot," he went on, "you never have a weapon, but have a goon squad at your disposal. And you somehow managed to get here, and that's pretty incredible. So, spellslinger?"

"You're not a complete pemtie," Dandy Rym nodded, "and my allies want you disposed of, so here I am."

"You're the servant of Ahken'ho-tek," Reggie nodded.

"Don't be simple," Dandy Rym spat, "there is more at work here than just that fossil. I serve a greater power than him. I am, or will be, the commander of the forces of the Mistress of the Ley, Chektar-ral. She shall slay the liches and bring order to the chaos on this continent."

"But she's a lich herself," Reggie pointed out, "how is that any different?"

"No, my dear simple pawn," Dandy Rym shook his head, "she is something very different from them. She's been biding her time to put her plan into action."

"And you've been using the Bounty Hunters of Kresk to herd me towards whatever she needed done, while making it seem like it was Ahken'ho-tek's plan," Reggie sighed, "while you access portal points to move around, staying one step ahead of me. You're a mind mage, then? And using your magic to increase your speed, strength, and skin density?"

"Something like that," Dandy Rym smiled, visibly preening.

"I speak from vast experience when I ask, do you know the problem with talking too much?"

"You do talk a lot for a—" Dandy Rym's words cut off, his hands darting to his midsection.

Reggie watched the man look down to look at the silver spear jutting from his abdomen, his bloody hands clutching at the shaft.

"It interferes with anyone else getting the point across," Reggie smiled, "but I think you got mine, even without words."

Twisting the haft, Reggie separated Marcid into two weapons: the short spear currently in Dandy Rym's guts, and a half halberd with a slim axe blade at the end. He swiped the second blade across the mage's throat and winced as the man's head folded backwards, twin gouts of blood spraying across the area.

A shout of combat came from behind him, and Reggie glanced in that direction.

"Griffon," he breathed, pulling the spear free from the collapsing form in front of him.

The sound of hooves came from the opposite direction of the battle, and Reggie hesitated, unsure if he should wait for the new threat or help his friend.

Chapter 27

Griffon was in the thick of it, Raven Stealer in one hand, and the cestus on the other. He bashed at the flank of the closest horse and the beast reared throwing its rider. The man crunched to the cobblestone road on his neck and shoulders, crumbling into a heap.

Darting past him, Griffon cut into the calf of the next rider, slicing the Achille's tendon. The man screamed and tilted towards the gnome, scrambling to stay in the saddle. Slamming the cestus into the man's jaw as he dropped low enough to reach, Griffon ran past. The man collapsed into unconsciousness, hanging from his mount by his one good leg, and the horse bolted past the others and into the murk.

The third man turned towards the gnome, nocking an arrow and firing. Raven Stealer teleported the gladiator, and Griffon reappeared on the back of the horse of the bowman. Punching the man in the back of the head, the sound of vertebrae crackle like bubble wrap popping was heard. He followed up the blow with the pommel of his sword to the man's temple. The rider slid off the horse, hitting the ground with a wet noise.

Calling upon the power of Promethene, Griffon clenched his eyes shut and flared the light from Raven Stealer, blinding the men for a critical moment.

It was at that moment when everything went horribly wrong. The horse beneath him bucked and bolted, throwing the gnome high into the air. The illumination of the sword winked out as she teleported him at the apex of his short flight, and he appeared a hand-span from the ground, landing in a crouch.

Not many of those left, Raven Stealer said, *so don't rely on teleporting. I need sunlight to recharge, and we have had little of that lately.*

"Three down," Griffon said, "and a bunch to go."

Three horses barreled towards him, and Griffon rolled to the side, tangling in the trampling legs of the outer mount. The steel shod hooves didn't get him, but his head slammed hard against the stones of the road.

Bursts of stars flooded his vision, and he heard the clack of arrows around him. He rolled again, his gorge rising, and hit a wall. Putting his gauntleted hand on the wall, he pushed to his feet, bringing his sword in front of him.

He sicked up, pouring the last of the oats across his feet, and an arrow punched him backwards. His head slammed against the wall, and the world spun.

Griffon could hear charging hoofbeats, but he couldn't tell from what direction.

A woman's shout cut through his awareness, confusing him. He didn't remember any of the riders being a woman.

Trying to call upon his fireworks, he held out a hand to fire a distracting burst towards the sound. The effort made his head scream, and he fell.

"Handle them," he heard Fillion shout, "the gnome is mine."

Heavy boots thudded to the ground near his head, and Raven Stealer urged him to lift her. Griffon did, and something slammed into the blade, the sound of metal-on-metal scraping through his brain.

"Griffon," Reggie's voice cut through the sound of battle, "on your right!"

Not knowing which direction was which, the gladiator lifted Raven Stealer above him on one side, and the cestus on the other, protecting his head. The wrist encased in the battle glove cracked and went limp inside the protective sheath. Griffon screamed, and his vision swam back into blurred shapes. A form stood over him. Behind that person was a scatter of horses and people engaged in a free-for-all melee.

A blur dropped towards his head, and he raised the arm holding Raven Stealer to block it. A sword battered against his blade, hammering into it again and again, bringing it lower with each strike. Still on his butt, Griffon kicked out towards the looming shadow over him, and felt his boot connect. The sound of cartilage popping let him know he'd hit a knee, and the man hacking at him let out a shout and tumbled forward.

Griffon rolled to the side, swinging his ivory blade in the opposite direction. It bit into flesh, and the man's shout turned into a scream, his weapon clattering on the ground. Stumbling to his feet, Griffon clutched his injured wrist to his belly and turned towards his attacker.

Fillion knelt, his hand pressed to his bicep, thick red liquid oozing from between his fingers.

"The bigger they are," Griffon said, raising Raven Stealer.

Lashing out with his bloody hand, Fillion punched Griffon in his exposed belly, forcing the air from his lungs. The gnome collapsed to his knees, putting his hand out to catch himself. The jarring force of his shattered wrist hitting the ground made him squeak.

"Damn it!" the gnome screamed and thrust with Raven Stealer.

The blade bit into Fillion's chest at the shoulder of the hand that he'd just used. He fell face first onto the street, both arms and one leg useless.

"Stop hurting me!" Griffon said and brought his blade down again.

It cut deep into Fillion's shoulder, getting caught so Griffon couldn't pull it free. He kicked the man's face, and Fillion went limp. Griffon continued kicking, screaming curses at the man until he couldn't catch his breath.

"Hey, buddy," a gentle voice cut through the haze of anger, "come on, it's over. He's not moving. I think you got him."

Griffon looked over his shoulder and saw LT. She looked worried, and it made the anger well up again.

"I don't need your pity!" he screamed at her, turning to square off, then pivoting back to his fallen enemy.

Fillion wasn't moving and Raven Stealer jutted from between his neck and shoulder. Grabbing the handle of the sword, Griffon jerked on it, trying to free it. But he couldn't see as the world went watery. His breath came in ragged spasms, and he tried to wipe his nose with his free hand, causing pain to shoot up his arm.

"It's okay now," LT said, laying a hand on his shoulder. "You beat him, and no one is pitying you. We're worried about your arm. Did you hurt it?"

Griffon looked up into her face and snorted back phlegm.

"I saw you naked," he snuffled at the woman.

"Yup," Reggie said from behind LT, "he's going to be alright."

"Don't make me punch you," she growled, but without real force behind it, "I don't think you'd could take it right now."

Looking past the two, Griffon saw the carnage of the fight scattered across the wet cobblestones. A half dozen horses milled around, the rest missing, but none of the men moved.

"Pity, huh?" LT teased.

"Shut up," Griffon mumbled, "whatever. My wrist hurts."

He looked down at his arm, held tight against his belly.

"We should take a look at that," Reggie said, standing back from the two.

Movement caught Griffon's attention, and he looked past his friends. Dozens of vriktiri were climbing down the walls, coming towards them.

"Oh chuz!" he shouted, reaching for Raven Stealer again. "There's a bunch of bug-men!"

"It's okay," LT said, pulling him away from the sword. "They're with me."

"What?" Griffon jerked his head towards her, and bright stars erupted in his vision again. He spun in place and fell on his butt.

"You might have a concussion," LT's voice was thick with concern. "But yes, it's the blessing of Khelikian. These are the locals, and they're going to help us through the pass and to find Rykul."

The army of Ahken'ho-tek marched. Hundreds of lost folk shambled at a slow walk, interspersed with dozens of vriktiri. They poured out of the hewn tunnel of stone that led from Dragon Staff under the mountains and into the Valley of Rykul.

The jungle closed around the column, the air thick with humidity and the temperatures well above what they were outside of the valley. Birds and small animals called from the canopy, darting about in the wide leaves of tropical foliage. The ten mountains that ringed the valley blocked outside interference of the magical and mundane variety.

Kenal and Venat-fal walked among the creatures under their control, maintaining their grip on the minds and actions of the mass of foot soldiers. The Master of Minions held a tight grip on the lost folk, and the Mistress of the Stables pressed her will over that of the vriktiri. She'd placed a totem in the center of the valley, which was more than a hundred kilometers across, to assist in the task.

Ahken'ho-tek rode in a palisade carried by citizens of Dragon Staff who also served as porters and servants. Chektar-ral walked behind the Lich Lord, her eyes constantly on his back.

The woman had slowly changed, becoming less like the other liches and applying makeup to cover it, lest the others grow suspicious. She'd barely made it out of the collapse, and she still wondered if Ahken'ho-tek had anything to do with it. The elemental magics weren't his forte, but he had skill with most of the arcane arts.

Kenal and Venat-fal had powerful talents with mind magic and conjuration, which is why they controlled the mass of the army. Their master,

Ahken'ho-tek, was most skilled in alchemy, but also mind magics and elemental. His weak points were conjuring and holy.

Chektar-ral was skilled with elemental, or ley magic, but was a natural mind mage. She wasn't as good at conjuring as the others, but could hold her own. Alchemy was something her people did naturally, so she never bothered to master it. Holy magics made her shudder in revulsion. She had no desire to worship a god, begging for scraps of arcane energy based on how much they liked her.

Calling a halt to the procession, Ahken'ho-tek gestured his personal valet closer and ordered the camp set. The man ruled by fear and intimidation, insinuating he knew more than he did. It drove people to paranoia, and when that happened, they were prone to make mistakes, or grovel to prove their loyalty.

Kenal sent out the lost folk to form a loose perimeter, and Venat-fal ordered the vriktiri to hunt. The insect men would bring back food for the living and themselves. Chektar-ral's job was to keep the sun's rays away, because it would eat away at the bodies of the liches, weakening them.

That wasn't a simple task in this valley. There was a super-nexus of ley lines, pumping in so much power it could burn her out if she wasn't careful. On the other hand, she could focus it and take out the others if needed. She wasn't sure if she wanted to do that yet.

The ash from the chain of volcanoes she'd raised wasn't heavy here, the odd wind currents keeping most of it away. But there were some, and she pulled on the air and water ley lines to thicken the cloud cover. Chektar-ral knew she couldn't maintain control over the lost folk, the vriktiri, gain control over Rykul, and also fight Ahken'ho-tek and the other two liches. So, she had to wait.

Something struck her from behind, knocking her prone, and twisted ropes of magical energy formed around her throat, wrists, and ankles. She was dragged backwards across the jungle floor, wet leaves and detritus clumping in her robes and under her chin.

Her body spun and was pulled upright to her knees. Blinking the dirt from her eyes, she saw Ahken'ho-tek standing in front of her, holding the other end of her magical leash.

"Chektar-ral," Ahken'ho-tek said, "you are a betrayer, and in turn have been betrayed."

The Lich Lord settled into the chair he'd rode in all day; servants having set it up under a garish pavilion. He slid into a pose, one leg raised on the footrest and his arm resting across the knee. It gave him the look of kneeling, but still looming over all those around in judgment.

The remaining two liches—Kenal and Venat-fal—stood on each side of the makeshift throne, bracketing him, but a step behind. Neither looked comfortable, standing ramrod stiff, not making eye contact, almost appearing truly dead.

"You see," Ahken'ho-tek continued, "I've known you were planning this little farce of yours since before we went to sleep—"

"Stop talking," Chektar-ral spat, "and get on with it. Unless you plan to talk me to true death, I have no desire to listen to you. You are pathetic and weak and only have power because you—"

The bindings around her neck tightened, cutting off her words. Her arms pulled upward, high behind her, and she fell face first into the wet earth.

"I was speaking," Ahken'ho-tek sneered, "and my lessers must know when to listen."

The ground around Chektar-ral boiled, turning red as rivulets of lava broke the surface. A streak of lightning cracked overhead and shot down, striking the woman. She glowed with the intensity of the bolt and rose into the air on a gust of wind. The bonds surged with power, lines of electricity tracing their way towards the lich lord.

Kenal and Venat-fal stepped back, their faces showing fear and surprise. The human servants scattered in all directions, and cries of animals erupted in the surrounding trees.

Ahken'ho-tek looked worried for a moment, then his face hardened, and he drew in the power coursing towards him. The energy hit a shield and enveloped it, cocooning the lich in an egg of brilliant sparks.

"You cannot hurt me," he said, sneering at Chektar-ral, "and I will use your own magics to bury you…forever."

The ground shuddered and split, a crevasse appearing under the floating woman. Ahken'ho-tek pushed his power down the bindings, and Chektar-ral screamed. The winds lifting her disappeared, and she fell into the waiting abyss. With a wave of his hand, the lich lord closed the earth around the woman.

Energies coursed along the ropes holding the interred woman, and Ahken'ho-tek leaned his head back, a look of ecstasy on his features. He threw his arms wide, and lightning pelted down, bolt after bolt, turning the remains of the small trench to glass.

The rumbling subsided, the winds stilled, and the clouds above parted. The jungle fell silent.

"Kenal, Master of Minions," Ahken'ho-tek said, his voice thick, "and Venat-fal, Mistress of the Stables, I require one final service from you before I begin my last task of claiming the power of Rykul. Step forward."

He gestured to the area in front of him, a dark, glassy gash of destruction.

The two liches came around the sides of his throne, each standing on one side of Chektar-ral's ultimate resting place.

"What can I do, Master?" Kenal said, bowing his head and looking at Ahken'ho-tek feet.

"How may I serve you, Master?" Venat-fal fell to her knees, prostrating herself before Ahken'ho-tek.

"I need all the power I can have for this final challenge," the lich lord said, "and this shall be the last thing I ask of you. It will also assure me that you will never betray me as the others have."

Ahken'ho-tek raised his hands, and the magical rope in his hands shot towards the subservient liches, wrapping around their wrists, ankles, and throats.

"I shall remember your loyal servitude and sacrifice when I ascend to godhood," he said, smiling, and began taking what was rightfully his.

The groveling liches screamed.

Chapter 28

Reid, Griffon, and Reggie rode, dozens of vriktiri running on each side, as they entered the Valley of Rykul. The cloud cover thinned, though it was still heavy in the northwestern part of the valley, lightning streaking through the nimbus.

Daylight was limited inside the ring of mountains, morning coming later as the sun crested the mountains and evening early as it sunk below the western peaks. They'd started their journey at dawn, moving through a high-walled canyon in shade for hours, and entered the jungle basin as the sun was passing the western wall of the vale.

"This is incredible," Reggie said, looking around with wonder. "Jules Verne and Edgar Rice Burroughs wrote about places like this. A closed ecosystem, with its own weather patterns, animal life, and entirely different species of plants. It was all fiction, but I did love the stories. Always dreamed of being someone who discovered such a place when I was an archeologist."

"And doing archeology?" Griffon asked. "Were you doing science? Were you science-ing? I bet you could science the hell out of things."

"Did you just quote The Lost Skeleton of Cadavra?" Reid gave the gnome the side eye.

"Think we might find any atmospherium?" Griffon asked.

"You're a dork," Reid said, grinning.

"What are you two talking about?" Reggie asked.

"Old movie," Griffon said.

"Not so old," Reid said. "I saw it when I was in my mid-teens. It came out in 2001."

"Yeah," Griffon agreed, "and I was still in diapers. Like I said, old movie. Classic. Retro. Vintage. Old."

"Still in diapers?" Reid asked. "So, you just saw it last year? Quiet down, baby boy, the grownups are talking."

"Screw you, boomer," Griffon said, "or else I'll take you back to the nursing home and tell them you can't have any Jell-O."

"Boomers were born just after World War II," Reid corrected. "You're using the word wrong."

"Only a boomer would say that, boomer." Griffon sniffed.

The ground shuddered and thunder rumbled from the north, lightning arcing through the distant clouds. Steam gushed upward over the trees, adding to the thicker clouds.

"That was close," Reggie said, reining in. "maybe a dozen kilometers. What do you think it was?"

He slid from his horse, dropping the reins to let Number One free graze. The other two followed his lead.

"Our competition, Anchor-head?" Griffon shrugged; his tone glib but he looked worried.

"Guys," Reid pointed to the north, drawing the others' attention, "I can feel a bunch more vriktiri in that direction. Their minds just aren't…right. I think Griffon could be correct this time."

The vriktiri traveling with them stopped when they did, and every single one of them stared in that direction.

The group had just entered the valley, and were on a rise, able to see the treetops in the distance. A ripple moved across the foliage, leaves changing from vibrant greens to dull browns.

"Are they…" Reggie sucked in a breath, "draining the life from the jungle?"

"I think we need to pick up our pace," Reid said, nodding.

"Are we going towards them?" Griffon asked, drawing Raven Stealer with his good hand. "Oh, she sighed. The sun, she's…drinking it like we drink water when dehydrated."

"I don't think we should go after them," Reggie said. "If they can do that, then we probably aren't a match for them. We should head towards their goal, try and stop them from getting it and increasing their power. We should head for Rykul."

"Yup," Reid nodded, "and he, or they, should be in the center of this valley. That's what I'm getting from my hive mind with the vriktiri. They can smell something there, and they've lived in and around this valley for generations."

"Very well then," Reggie nodded, "and thanks for explaining what went on between you and Khelikian. What's the plan, Lieutenant?"

Reid didn't miss the title, spoken in its entirety. She also noted Reggie was passing the command to her.

"You sure you want me to do this?" she asked him.

"Do what?" Griffon asked. "What're we doing? What'd I miss?"

"You have the open line of communication with the legion troops," Reggie said. "You have organized military training and experience, including officer training. I have some loose affiliation with the French Foreign Legion, where some guys listened to me a few times. I think this is the right decision."

"What?" Griffon asked. "Did he just pass party leadership to you? I was next in line!"

"Griffon," Reid held Reggie's eyes for a moment longer, nodded, then turned to the gnome, "you're a gladiator. You're a walking weapon, but not a strategist. Giving you command would hinder you. It would stop you from doing what you're good at and take away one of our most powerful tools. We are not selfish enough to do that to you. Besides, I need you beside me to protect me, and to take down the BBEG in the boss fight."

"Okay," the gnome said slowly, "that makes sense."

"And I fight from the back of the group," Reid went on, "doing ranged DPS. I can see the entire fight and am better suited to call out where we need backup and support roles."

"Yeah, okay," Griffon nodded, "this makes sense now."

"Plus, I'm better at it than you," Reid added with a smirk.

Griffon opened his mouth to argue, but Reid raised her voice loud enough for everyone to hear.

"We ride for the middle of the valley," she called out. "We go fast and hard. If the trees get too thick or the horses get tired, we go on foot. I estimate it's about thirty or forty klicks, and we're in a race with the enemy. We should be able to get there before morning with the vriktiri guiding us."

"We're riding through the night?" Griffon asked. "We're going to be exhausted and useless."

"I know," Reid agreed. "Reggie, the three of us are going to need some of those berries from Marcid and some for the horses."

"What about the vriktiri?" Reggie asked.

"They're going to scout ahead and eat along the way, so they'll be fine," Reid said.

"Don't they need to sleep?" Reggie asked. "I don't think Marcid can make enough berries for all of them. She can only make a couple dozen every few days, and we're already pushing the limit with what we gave Griffon for his wrist."

"They're napping now," Reid gestured towards the few visible soldiers, who stood unmoving. "I've learned they take a dozen short, five-minute naps every day. It lets them keep moving when we can't."

"Very good," Reggie said. "Shall we take a quick meal while they nap?"

Reid saw how he asked her, making it a suggestion instead of a command.

"Good thinking," she nodded, "let's do that, and then we'll get started. I think the enemy stopped for the night, and we have a little extra time."

"Quick question," Reggie said, and Reid looked over at him. "If the vriktiri were napping, and you communicate with them without words most of the time…why did you raise your voice when going over the plan?"

"Oh, that?" Reid smiled. "I just wanted to stop Griffon from getting the last word in."

They rode through the extended twilight and into the night. The vriktiri scouted, and predators avoided the large group moving through the jungle.

When the sun tinted the sky to the east, staining the western peaks with dappled light, they'd arrived at a large indentation in the center of the valley.

"The construction almost looks Greek," Reggie said, pointing at columns protruding from the low-grown plant life, "and abandoned for…" the archeologist hesitated, cocking his head, "maybe centuries?" he said, unsure. "Maybe decades. Things age differently in this kind of humidity."

"Did you guys notice that the ash isn't as thick?" Griffon asked, peering into the sky.

"It hasn't been since we entered the valley," Reid shrugged.

"No, look," Griffon pointed at the southwestern line of peaks, "it's thinner than before. I think the volcanoes have stopped blowing their tops. Also, I haven't felt a single tremor since the one yesterday that happened with all the lightning, and then all those trees died."

The other two looked around, raising their eyes to the sky.

"I think he's right," Reggie said. "It does look like…wait, there!"

The man pointed to the south where the clouds had parted, showing a patch of blue.

"Open sky," he breathed. "It's been a while since we've seen that."

"Something changed," Reid said, her voice worried.

"First good news in more than a month," Griffon put his injured hand on his hip and cocked his head, "and you're sounding like it's bad news?"

"Why did the volcanoes stop?" Reid asked. "There's something more to this. The liches wouldn't have stopped doing something that helps them. And look there, in the west…"

Thick, dark clouds roiled and tumbled in the direction she pointed. The leading edge of the front was close, and thick tendrils reached out to the east, the longest one almost overhead.

"Wow," Reggie said, "it's like they pulled all the ash over them, and it's moving this way. For it to be this close, they must have traveled through the night, like we did."

"We need to get moving," Reid said, turning in a circle. "The vriktiri tell me that the other vriktiri under the liches control are coming this way, along with the lost folk, but what we need is further in. They can feel a totem nearby, and that's how the other soldiers are being controlled. Reggie, what do you think is the best path from here?"

She watched the man look from the sky down to the jungle to the west, then east into the shallow depression with the ruins jutting upward like bleached bones.

"I go into the ruins and try to find Rykul," Reggie said quietly. "You two go find the totem and destroy it. That should free the remaining vriktiri. Maybe they'll join you, but even if they run, it'll be better than fighting them."

"Um," Griffon held up a finger, "I'm going to need Marcid to break the totem."

Reggie nodded, unstrapping his sword belt. Griffon reached up to remove Raven Stealer.

"No," Reggie stopped him, "you'll need her more than me. Just give Marcid to LT when you're done with her."

Griffon hesitated, his hands on the buckle of his baldric, then nodded.

"I think we should leave the horses and all our supplies here," Reid said. "We can move faster without the extra weight, and we're not going to need the Citadel or anything we're not carrying. Besides, the horses are large, noisy, and exhausted. They can't keep going."

The three set up a partial camp, roping off a trio of trees in a makeshift corral with a tarp over it. They went through their packs, sorting what they needed to carry versus what they could leave behind. Ten minutes later, they were ready to go.

"Be careful out there," Reggie said, "and…well, be careful."

"Go bag us a bear," Reid said, and pulled Reggie into a bearhug.

"Rawr," he muttered, clumsily patting her on the back.

"Can I get one of those?" Griffon said, tugging Reggie's sleeve.

"I didn't know you were a hugger, Griffon," Reggie said, turning to the smaller man and kneeling.

The gnome pushed past him and threw himself at Reid. She caught his forehead with her open palm and stopped him at arm's length.

"Nuh uh," she waggled a finger at him, "we're not going to play motorboat."

"Motorboat?" Reggie asked.

"Nothing, never mind," Reid said, shoving Griffon back a step.

The gnome grinned up at her mischievously.

"Come on, short stuff," Reid gestured for Griffon to lead, "we've got a mission."

"Ladies first, hot stuff," Griffon mimicked her gesture.

"Nope," she shook her head, "you lead so you can protect me, and not just stare at my ass. Besides, I need a meat shield."

"I got a meat sword to go with it," Griffon said, turning to lead the way into the jungle.

"I think you're a horrid little bastard," Reid teased. "You know that, right?"

"So, what you're saying is that you do think about me, then, right?" Griffon said over his shoulder.

The vriktiri moved in the tree line like ghosts, shadowing the two. Some ran along the ground, and others through the treetops, the chatter of wings breaking the hum of insects and birds.

"Hold on," Griffon stopped and looked up at the noise. "These guys can fly?"

"These are a different breed from what we encountered before," Reid explained. "The ones that the liches enslaved were burrowing vriktiri. These are jungle vriktiri. That's also why their carapaces are more green and brown, instead of red and brown. Also, if you look, you'll see that their abdomen is slimmer than the other species."

"They all look the same to me," Griffon shrugged.

"You can't say that." Reid cuffed the gnome on the shoulder. "It's racist."

"What? They're bugs!" Griffon's voice went shrill. "It's not like they have feelings like we do."

"You don't know that!" Reid said. "You can't know that. But I *do* know that they're intelligent creatures with an entire society. Comparing them to bugs is like comparing dragons to yard lizards, or those satyrs and minotaurs you talk about in your sleep to goats and cows. They're an evolved species and complex. Maybe they don't have feelings the same as us, maybe they do, but they're thinking and independent and deserve respect."

"Okay, already, geez!" Griffon threw up his hands. "You've been hanging out with Reggie too much. You're starting to use almost as many words as him."

They fell into a rhythm, Griffon hacking at leaves and branches with Marcid in the form of a machete, and Reid giving him directions toward the last totem.

"I just realized," Griffon said, "Marcid is a transmog."

"What?" Reid asked.

"A transmog," Griffon repeated. "You know, like in video games, where you make one weapon or piece of armor look like a different weapon or piece of gear? Transmog? Transmogrification?"

"Isn't that from Calvin and Hobbes?" Reid said.

"What's that?" Griffon wrinkled his nose.

"Comic strip from the late 80s and early 90s," Reid smiled, "focused on imagination and stuff. I grew up on it."

A cracking noise cut off their conversation, and they both drew up short.

"What was that?" Griffon whispered. "It sounded like a tree breaking. A big tree."

"Sh," Reid put a hand on his shoulder, "they're checking."

"You mean the bug guys are checking?" Griffon turned to look up and over his shoulder at her.

Another creaking noise cut through the haze of rain forest noise, followed by a snap, and the rushing noise of leaves and branches hitting others as a tree fell.

Reid shoved Griffon forward and dove to one side. A thick trunk crashed to the ground where they'd been a moment before.

The jungle erupted with a flurry of movement, hundreds of vriktiri swarming towards them.

Chapter 29

Reggie moved through the ruins, running his fingers along the moss-covered architecture. The structures were mostly open-air affairs, but small chambers through archways—which he thought of as sleeping quarters—lined a sunken area.

A circular, chest-deep depression had doorways evenly spaced around it, ramps leading down to the area on each side. In the center was a stone table, with pillars rising around it.

"Simply exquisite," he muttered, talking aloud to himself. "It could have been their place to have meals together. Just outside of their sleeping quarters. The pillars would've had a cloth covering for the elements."

He'd become so used to having the others around, their absence was like a weight of silence and emptiness. Not even the steady pulse of warmth and company of Marcid was there anymore. He was alone, and it made him talk to himself, an old habit from his days of archeology.

Ducking into an opening, he crawled up a short ramp into a room that was just slightly taller than a person sitting.

"The chambers all slope upward to this flat area. Oh, there's a square, metal insert in the center, and a chimney above it."

He turned in a circle, still squatting, light filtering in at the corners.

"The edges of the rooms have vents in the ceiling and a trench along the outer edge to drain any rain that came through and into the room. Ingenious!"

He exited the way he'd come in and stood, stretching. A feeling of peace and contentment washed over him.

"It was like a true commune," he said, smiling, "and I bet they were druids, or some nature-based magic. I can almost feel it all around me."

Closing his eyes, he breathed in deep, and his lungs caught, causing him to cough.

"Something," he opened his eyes and looked around, "has fouled the area. But that's why I'm here, isn't it?"

Shifting the satchel on shoulder, he walked up the ramp and moved deeper into the…

"What are these?" he asked himself, strolling along a marble causeway as wide as his arms held out to each side. "Ruins, to be sure, but not quite a city."

The path meandered, and a sense of urgency pressed down on Reggie. He picked up his pace until he was jogging.

It took more than an hour to reach the center, walking and running. He'd passed dozens of open-air places separated by long abandoned gardens and vineyards. Small animals scurried across the paths, neither afraid of him nor friendly. He was just another creature in the ecosystem. He saw groups of deer-like beasts, only knee high, and occasional predators that reminded him of foxes.

The epicenter of the complex was a still, shallow pool fed by small streams. Fish darted in the water, and frogs and birds hunted the insects buzzing about. A rise in the middle of the water showed an immense skeleton covered with moss and sunken into the loamy earth.

"Rykul?" Reggie asked aloud. "Could that be you? You look ursine, but of prehistoric proportions. Albert, the Troll Lord, mentioned you. Said you'd tease him about people calling him 'Great One', so I assume you had a sense of humor. But now you're gone. I think Al would be sad to know this."

Nothing is ever truly gone, something said, sounding like dozens of voices speaking as one.

It was a whisper in the wind, nothing more, and Reggie wasn't sure if he'd heard it or if it was nothing more than his own thoughts and imagination.

Looking around, Reggie's hand went to his hip, where Marcid usually rested. He smiled sadly and patted his belt.

"Marcid was attuned to nature," he sighed. "She'd probably recognize you, or something akin to you."

He circled the pond slowly and felt comforted by being there.

"Looks like you're dead, though," he said, talking to himself more than the bones. "I can only imagine the knowledge you had, the things you've seen, and the people you met. A force of nature, that's what they called you. A child of Senaria, put here to help the civilized races work with nature, instead of dominating it. Looks like they did the latter, though."

"Would you help, then?" A deep, throaty rumbled asked from behind him.

Reggie spun, half expecting to see a talking bear, and found only a half dozen frogs on blossoming lily pads.

"Sure," he laughed, partially because he was talking to voices of things that weren't there. "If it helps the land and I can explore lost places and civilizations, I'm game. Deal me in."

The bones on the small island shifted, rising from the moss-covered disc of land, and Reggie froze in place.

"Run!" LT yelled, shoving Griffon. "Head to the north. That's where the vriktiri said the totem is!"

The two plunged through the underbrush, thorny vines ripping at their clothes and skin, Griffon leading the way. Marcid glinted in the murky daylight, slashing at the jungle to clear the way. Dry branches crumbled beneath the blade, the surrounds changing from healthy to brittle and brown.

"I think we're getting closer," Griffon shouted.

Glancing over his shoulder, he saw LT falling behind. Vriktiri were everywhere. Green-brown forms dropped from above onto the backs of the red-brown enemies, but a few dozen were no match for hundreds.

The jungle stopped suddenly, Griffon breaking through in a circular clearing of dead and decaying trees and bushes. In the center stood a blackened column of carved petrified wood, the familiar symbols interlaced along its rough sides.

The allied bug-men formed a line on the perimeter, two deep and staggered. The surge of the enemy force knocked them back, tightening the defensive ring.

"I'm calling for more of the local vriktiri," LT grunted, stabbing at the attackers with her spear, "but nothing is answering. And this close to the totem, I can't influence the other ones at all."

Griffon morphed Marcid from the machete to a huge double-handed mallet and laid into the magical pillar in the center of the clearing. He wanted nothing more than to join in the melee, but knew if he didn't take down the arcane focus, none of them would survive.

The first hit with the enchanted hammer made the totem ring out like a metal bell. The second deflected into the dirt, as if the target had smacked it away. The third hit with a solid thump, and chips of wood flew in all directions. Griffon could see a small crack winding its way down the column.

He struck again and again, ignoring the sounds of battle behind him. That was where he wanted to be, where he was meant to be. In the middle of the action, not on the sidelines beating up a glorified log.

His frustration made him want to beat on something, break something, and he almost laughed when he realized that's exactly what he was doing. But it wasn't making him feel better, and that only made him angrier.

Use it, pemtie. Raven Stealer's voice in his head was barely a whisper, the long absence of the sun weakening her. *Harness what you feel to do what you need to do. But control it, do not let it control you.*

"I don't know what that means," each word was grunted through gritted teeth and punctuated by a blow to the totem.

That focus helps, the sword said. *Let me try to put it into terms you can understand. When fighting a boss with adds, if everyone just runs around doing their own thing, you wipe. If everyone focuses on the same mob, you can take them down quicker. Harness your feelings like a raid group, and do not let them go everywhere, or you will get overwhelmed.*

"Whatever," Griffon grunted. "Sounds stupid."

I can hear you thinking about it… Raven Stealer's voice grew weaker and faded in mid-sentence.

"RS?" the gnome said, his voice cracking. "Raven Stealer? You there, you pemtie sword?" Griffon suddenly felt alone and scared. Not for himself, but for those around him. Not the bug guys. Those weren't like him and the others.

Raven Stealer had been a voice of wisdom that knew to give advice while teasing him. LT was like a big sister—maybe a stepsister, a sexy one—who looked out for him and made sure he didn't screw up too badly. And Reggie had been a mentor and a father figure, something Griffon needed. They were all his best friends, and they would all die if he couldn't take down this one simple mutant telephone pole.

Reining in his fear, his anger, and his frustration, Griffon set his feet, checked the totem, and focused on the single, small crack he'd created. He willed Marcid to split into her current form, but also a wedge, and pulled the silver slice from the artifact.

Slamming the piece into the slit, he pounded at it with the flat of his hand. Stepping back, he refocused on the line in the wood, lifted the maul, and swung sideways with all his might. The mallet met the wedge, and the air exploded with a resounding crack, shards of blackened petrified wood raining down around the gnome. The totem fell apart into pieces.

The sounds of battle dimmed behind him, and he watched the silver triangle reabsorb into the giant hammer. He willed Marcid into the shape of a spear, and turned to check on LT.

The woman stood, her palms flat against the sides of her head, and a broken spear haft in one hand, the other half on the ground in front of her. She was panting hard, and Griffon moved to her side.

"You okay?" he asked her.

"Yeah," she nodded, her voice barely audible, "there's just so many of them, and they're all listening to me."

"That's good, right?" he asked. "We won, didn't we?"

Looking at the two factions of bug-men, he saw them all standing perfectly still, faceted eyes staring at LT.

A distant rumble rose in the jungle, coming closer. The dappled shadows in the distance broke into lumbering forms as thousands of the lost folk came into sight.

"Not quite yet," LT mumbled, each word broken into separate sentences.

Reggie fell backwards, the ghostly form of a gigantic grizzly bear towering over him. The bones stood on the island, in the exact pose as the pale blue specter in front of the man. Reggie scrambled away, grabbing for Marcid and coming up empty.

"Calm yourself, man," the ghost bear said, his lips not moving, "We are Rykul, and came because you called us."

"You're dead," the words came out of Reggie's mouth, half question, half statement.

"We are eternal, and only our body died," Rykul intoned as if it were a ritual, "and one spirit has called to ours to grow anew."

The bones creaked, falling to all fours and splashing into the water, heading towards the shore.

"Does that mean you can reconstitute yourself?" Reggie asked, still lying prone in front of the spirit. "You can rise again to fight the liches and their legions?"

"You can do that," Rykul's ethereal head bent to look down at the man, "We need willing flesh to live again."

"A sacrifice?" Reggie whispered. "You need me to die, so you may live?"

The bear tilted their head, their thick lips parting and baring their teeth.

The skeleton reached the edge of the pond, rose to its hind legs, and stepped inside the incorporeal form of Rykul. It created an eerie double image that moved as one, the bones slightly out of sync with the soul.

"We don't think we can explain it," Rykul said, "but we will try. Life requires something to grow. We need fertile and healthy ground to plant that seed. You have offered yourself to us, so we may do that."

"If I do this," Reggie panted, "will you fight the liches? Will you save my friends?"

"We will do everything we can to make this place, this world, safe again and able to grow anew," the double image nodded.

"Then," Reggie breathed out, "I guess this is my last adventure."

The man nodded, agreeing to what needed to happen.

The bear fell to all fours—the skeleton a fraction of a second behind the spirit—and lunged forward.

The jaws parted wider, and massive teeth pulled Reggie's legs into its maw.

Reggie felt himself being torn apart, stretched and twisted, his body going limp and his mind exploding with sensation. He tried to scream, but his broken ribs had punctured his lungs and he couldn't get his breath.

The world went dark, and the sensations of his body faded. His mind was still there, though, but there was something else there as well. A dozen other voices spoke with him, putting words to his thoughts.

"Are we dead?" Reggie asked, his final thought coming out in the voice he'd been talking to moments before. "We are Rykul, and we have been renewed."

Rykul turned, scenting the air to find their friends. They could smell the rot of the undead, and the confused spoor of the vriktiri. The aroma of fear came from a human and a gnome, and they knew where they had to go.

Calling upon Senaria and the winds, Rykul raised their voice in a roar, and began moving heaven and earth to set things right.

Chapter 30

All the minds and scents of the newly freed vriktiri washed over Reid, overwhelming her. Lost and separated from their queen and hive, they didn't know where their nests were. They all reached out to her, seeking guidance. She was their de facto queen.

Griffon stared past her and her hive at the mass of undead, Marcid held towards her in a loose grip.

"Looks like you get to fight after all," Reid said, reaching down and taking the silver spear from the gnome. "Suck it up, soldier. It's time to earn your keep!"

Though she'd been talking to Griffon, the vriktiri reacted to her command. They drew up to their full heights and turned as one to face the oncoming legion of lost folk.

"I thought it was bad when it was dozens against hundreds," Griffon murmured, drawing Raven Stealer, "but now it's hundreds against thousands."

He held the unicorn pommel in a two-handed grip, the once ivory blade now dull, off-white. Swirling the weapon in a figure eight and passing it from hand to hand, then around his back, and falling into an attack stance, the gnome grinned.

"Let's do this," he said, and moved forward towards the wall of living dead rolling towards them.

Reid felt the weight of command on her. She'd known this before in the military, but here it was different. There she had a squad of trained soldiers who'd chosen to join the armed forces and fight for their own reasons. Here, now, in this world, she had an elite fighting force that was bred for the task, and though they could fight independently, they looked to her to guide them as a battalion.

The weight was almost physical as the blessing of Khelikian pressed down on her, giving her the gift of communicating with the vriktiri through scent and a hive mind—not a direct telepathic link, more of an empathic link—and send her intentions to the soldiers who would live or die on the battlefield, all based on her decisions in the next few minutes.

Then there was Griffon, who would never take an order, unless it was to break it out of spite. He would rush, doing whatever he wanted, not coordinating with others in the least.

"Griffon," Reid called, "I'm giving you your own platoon. They'll go with you, follow your lead, and fight to the death beside you. Don't lead them into a trap."

She knew she was taking a risk, putting the lives of her soldiers in the gnome's hands, but she'd seen enough of Griffon to know a few things about the man. One, he was much more reckless when he didn't have any responsibility. Two, given responsibility, it scared him into thinking rather than following his impulses. Three, he really was a decent person, just terrified of showing it.

Reid had known others like him. They made you think they were a dick right away, that way they had control. They never had to wonder if you liked them or not. They knew what you thought of them, because they dictated your reaction to them. But she knew that trick, and how to overcome it.

"My own…" Griffon looked around as two and a half score of vriktiri moved to surround him, about half from each tribe. "Wow, really? You sure about this?"

"You're a natural," she smiled at him, "take them. They're your elite force now."

"You three," Griffon turned to the green-toned vriktiri with wings, "get in the trees to scout our way. You five, we need weapons that can cut through flesh without getting close. Find some. The rest of you green ones, I want you up in the trees and attacking. Use stones, coconuts, and anything else you can throw."

Turning to the reddish-brown vriktiri, he looked them up and down.

"Okay," he called, stepping forward, "stay in a diamond around me, but let a few of the zombie things in…"

Reid watched him marching forward, the sound of his voice trailing off as his platoon moved further away. Reaching out with her senses, she drew in information from the scouts she'd sent to the treetops. She needed to know where the liches were, how extensive the lost folks forces were, and if there were any other troops involved.

"There's only one?" Reid's head snapped up, surprised. "What do you mean there's only one lich left? Geez Charlie, what's that mean?"

One of the green-tinted vriktiri looked at her, then over his shoulder. A bifurcated hand came up to touch his chest questioningly.

Reid laughed as she realized the soldier thought she'd been talking to him. The vriktiri looked…offended? Did she hurt his feelings? She checked his scent and felt confusion, disappointment, and frustration.

"Yes, you," she said, tapping his chitinous chest plate, "you're Charlie now. Why not? I need a wingman I can trust. And I know I can completely trust you, you are male, and you have actual wings."

She raised herself up to her full height, which was considerable, and still had to look up into the new Charlie's faceted eyes.

"You stick with me," she said, "stay by my side, and help deliver my commands. Cover my six and keep an eye out for enemies I miss. You're my co-pilot now."

The vriktiri nodded as if he understood her words completely, and maybe he did. She didn't know he didn't, so she chose to believe he did. She called out commands, automatically using words even where they weren't needed.

"You don't need to use words," Charlie said, but not in words. "We can feel your intention, and that guides us better than a voice command ever could."

The vriktiri didn't speak, though he clicked his mandibles and made whistling wheezing noises by pushing air out between his clypeus and labrum. When she felt that information come across their connection, she sent comfort back to Charlie and went on verbalizing.

"I know, Charlie," she said, "but it helps me organize my thoughts. I also know that it's a messy way, but it is the way of my species. We're noisy little bastards."

Returning to directing her battalion of insect warriors, she focused on the information coming from her scouts. The single remaining lich walked under the shade of a pavilion carried by lost folk. She could feel the creature trying to wrest control of the vriktiri back, and she defended the warriors' minds by pushing the sense of community and nest on them, staving off the urge to wander away as a rogue vriktiri without a hive.

Sending wave after wave of her soldiers across the scattered lost one forces; she saw how disorganized the enemy was. The lich may be a powerful spellslinger, but he was no strategist. Either that or directing the lost folk was like trying to plant cooked spaghetti. Something the original Charlie used to say. You could anchor one end, but the rest just falls where it will.

She tightened her legion, using squads to execute surgical strikes in the enemy ranks, dividing one mass from another. They came together to decimate a group of lost folk, then split apart to find their next target.

Reid felt like she'd been born to do this. Planning large-scale tactics was her thing. She's played enough tabletop strategy war games. She should be good at this. She didn't think she was good because she'd played the games, rather that she'd played the games because she was good at it.

As a young girl, she'd watched her uncle with his group of college friends gather around the ping-pong table—sans the net—in the basement of her parents' house and pull out huge boxes with tiles to create the board and a million little pieces that looked like the armies. Game nights with Risk led to Conquest of the Empire, and that turned into multi-night Axis & Allies games.

She'd loved them all and by the time she was in high school, she could take out any single player. If they wanted to win, they had to team up and take her out first.

The army she faced had nowhere near the skill of her uncle and his friends. The troops were haphazard and clumsy, and their general was an overconfident egotist.

Griffon was a wild card, cutting through one group, and then circling around another. He moved with deliberate speed, executing guerilla warfare type attacks, taking out swaths of the enemy then disappearing.

But none of that mattered when it came down to sheer numbers. She had a couple hundred vriktiri, at best. The enemy had ten times the numbers. Slowly, but inevitably, her troops were being overrun.

Reid made her way to a rise, giving her a better view, and the high ground, and decided that was where she needed to make a stand. Calling Griffon back in, she set up a three deep rotation of soldiers, giving the back row a five-minute rest before bringing them forward. But it didn't matter. Their numbers dwindled into double digits.

A roar rent the air and trees bent out of the way, clearing a path for an immense, hairy, brown form. A bear that was larger than any grizzly she'd ever heard of ripped into the ranks of the enemy. Within minutes, Reid expanded her circle, the giant bear circling the perimeter of the vriktiri and tearing apart the lost folk.

"We are here, my friends," the bear said, his voice echoing in a chorus by itself, as if dozens of people spoke in unison. "We are Rykul, and your Reginald has guided us to you."

A single bolt of lightning flashed down, striking the beast, and it flung them over the hilltop, and the gathered force, to tumble down the other side.

"Then you are the one I've been waiting for," a new voice rasped, "and I shall claim your power for my own."

A single, withered man limped forward. He looked small in the crowd of lost folk, but they parted to let him pass.

"I am Ahken'ho-tek, Lord of the Liches," the man said, stopping a few paces from the circle of vriktiri. "And I thank you for once again bringing me the one thing I need to succeed."

From the opposite side of the hill came a throaty growl, and Rykul the Great Bear rose to their haunches and stood towering above the gathering. The beast shook their head, as if trying to clear it, then let out a guttural roar, lips curling back over teeth longer than Reid's hand. Rykul fell to all fours, lost folk and vriktiri scattering out of the way, and charged around the base of the hill to get to the lich.

Ahken'ho-tek's lips drew back also, showing yellow and brown teeth, and he threw his hands out in front of him. Red streams of lava erupted from the earth, solidifying into ropes, and wrapping around the bear as they came towards the lich. Flesh sizzled as the volcanic bonds tightened around the creature's neck and legs, pulling them to the ground.

Roaring, Rykul jerked his head up to the sky, and the trees leaned away, the clouds parting. Sunlight poured across the hilltop, and Reid saw it reach Raven Stealer, held high in Griffon's hand. The blade drank in the sun's energy, bleaching and glowing with a pure, white brilliance.

Griffon shouted something unintelligible and launched himself at the bear. He sliced at the lava bonds, cutting through the first one he reached and freeing Rykul's foreleg.

The lost folk surged forward, and Reid gave the command for the vriktiri to protect the bear. A thick cloud of ashen dust hung over the lich, blocking the daylight from reaching him, and he cackled a laugh.

"Griffon," Reid shouted, "light him up!"

She drew Marcid from where she was wrapped around her arm, and the artifact took on the form of a thick, silver spear. Reid thrust it towards a group of lost folk, and the weapon elongated, the middle becoming a chain, and the head shooting forward to pierce three of the living dead through their throats. The chain became a solid shaft and withdrew, retracting back to the woman's hands.

A group of the enemy force broke through the line behind her and lurched up the hill. Reid spun, changing Marcid to a shield with razor thin ridges along its outer surface, and swiped across the leading lost folk. Flesh shredded from bone, but the creatures didn't stop coming.

Griffon fought his way towards the lich but was in the middle of dozens of lost folk, his honor guard dwindled down to a handful of vriktiri.

Ahken'ho-tek threw his hands forward again, and the earth erupted around Rykul, shafts of stone spears piercing the beast in a half dozen places.

Reid drew in a deep breath, knowing this was their last stand.

Chapter 31

Griffon bit back a few choice swear words, not wanting to waste his energy or breath. But Raven Stealer could hear his thoughts, and she let out an audible laugh.

What are you laughing about? Griffon thought, slapping away hands trying to drag him down. *Reggie is still missing, but a rabid bear showed up. Reid and her bug squad are being torn down. My arms are on fire, and I can barely catch my breath, and we're all about to die, but you're laughing?*

I am just happy to be back, the sword said in his head, *and feel the sun once again. And you will not die. You are too pemtie to know when to lie down and die. Besides, you have an entire book of tricks you have not even pulled out yet.*

"Did you notice," Griffon switched to talking out loud, parrying an attack and then slicing the hands off two lost ones grabbing at him, "that Rykul is tanking? I'm in a support role! I'm supposed to be the tank, not some lame DPS."

Maybe you are growing up a little? She suggested. *Expanding your skill set? But you have not even tried out my second forte on this bunch.*

"Healing?" Griffon stabbed another one in the face. "Teleporting?"

No silly, Raven Stealer almost felt like she was shaking with laughter, or excitement. *My patron goddess has dominion over light and sound. Which is exactly what your illusions are. Did you think she chose you for your fighting skill?*

"But illusions don't work against these things," Griffon growled, back pedaling as the mass of lost ones surged forward, "so I don't think it really applies to this situation."

But Ahken'ho-tek is pulling in all the magic right now, Raven Stealer whispered in his head. *He is sucking up everything he can. Maybe even the stuff he does not want. And LT did say to light him up.*

"Are you saying…" Griffon looked around.

The lost ones clustered around the gigantic bear, and another mass of them were about to overwhelm LT. A cluster of bug guys surrounded her, but they were dropping…well, like flies.

Then he saw it, a path around the two massive groups that led almost directly to Ahken'ho-tek.

"Okay boys," he shouted to the few remaining vriktiri in his personal guard, "run interference, we're going in!"

Do not tank it, Raven Stealer said, *play the support role, just this once.*

"But I don't wanna," Griffon whined, then huffed. "Fine, whatever. Change of plans, guys. Just cover me."

The gnome took a deep breath, seeking the calm that allowed him to cast his illusions. The din of the battle faded slightly, and he felt the sun on his face.

"Okay, I got this," he muttered, then pulled all the sound to him through Raven Stealer.

A shrill shriek pierced the noise of the fight, the Wilhelm Scream, and the lost folk hesitated, their balance wobbling. A few tumbled to the ground, unhurt but disoriented.

Griffon thrust Raven Stealer up, calling upon the light above to create a massive, but simple, illusion. A giant magnifying glass appeared above him, the sun striking the massive convex lens. A tight beam of light, laser thin, traced its way across the grass, igniting the flora and the lost folks it touched.

The gnome directed the beam towards the lich, who was focused on his attack upon Rykul, and his robes burst into flame before he realized what was happening. The concentrated ray moved up Ahken'ho-tek's leg and struck him in the center of his torso, and the undead master erupted into a raging inferno. The focused conflagration flailed, a rusty scream coming from the center.

Rykul was up and charging through the disoriented mass of lost folk, their forms flying up and away from their path as they passed. Winds followed the force of nature or moved with them. Griffon couldn't tell. It ripped away the ash as the bear hit the lich, and the gust hit the cloud. The lost folk that the scream hadn't affected earlier tottered, the magical control held over them appearing to slip as Griffon watched Rykul maul the lich lord.

The bear took out the spellslinger's throat with one swipe, then bit off half of one of the lich's arms. Dropping the other paw onto the undead caster's chest, Rykul knocked Ahken'ho-tek to the ground, crushing his chest. Griffon kept moving the laser pointer of light running across the lich's form, trying to hit the spot that Rykul wasn't shredding.

Glancing back, the gnome saw LT on the hilltop. The woman was a flurry of silver and anger, vriktiri surging around her like an extension of her thoughts. The bug-men ripped the heads from the lost folk, and once decapitated, the living dead were no longer a problem.

Turning back to the clash of the two titans in front of him, Griffon saw the lich had lost both arms, and his legs were bent at unnatural angles.

"Guess he won't be walking away from this fight," Griffon snickered.

Rykul pressed Ahken'ho-tek's body into the soft loam, a puddle of lava rising around the undead caster. A small bridge of rock grew across the lich's chest, holding him in place, and the bear stepped back.

"You two should run," said the myriad voices from the Great Bear. "We will give you a few minutes, then we shall cleanse this land in the same way Ahken'ho-tek injured it."

A ring of rock rose around the lich, creating a basin with him at the center, lava shooting up in small jets of red.

"Right," Griffon said, "got it. Come on, LT, grab your bug force. We're out of here!"

At a gesture from the woman, the vriktiri formed a wedge with her at the center and moved to the west. The line opened as they reached Griffon, bringing him and his group inside. He fell into step with the main force, jogging through the jungle.

They followed the swath of dead flora left by the lich and his army, following it back the way they'd come. There were only a few dozen of the insect army left, and they moved steadily forward, but Griffon could see that even they were exhausted.

A few minutes later, the ground quaked. A rumble that Griffon had become all too familiar with over the past couple of months.

"Another volcano?" he breathed. "Really?"

"Rykul did say that the lich would die in the same way that he was killing the land," LT said, running in a limping lope. "I think we should head for the horses soon; they should be a bit south of the highway the undead army created. I'll send a few scouts out to help locate them, and that should be far enough away to stop for a little while."

A cracking boom shook the jungle, and a wave of heat rolled across their backs, knocking them face first into the dirt. Rolling over, they looked in the direction they'd come from.

A geyser of lava shot into the sky, a circle of ash rushing away from the epicenter. Birds, bugs, and animals fled. A herd of deer ran across the path in front of them, and a prickle of hedgehogs waddled out of the trees to cross behind them, two adults leading a line of hoglets. Squirrels and monkeys leapt across branches overhead, and a wedge of colorful parrots passed across a pale blue patch of sky.

"We should get moving," LT said, pushing to her feet, "we can rest when we get to the horses."

"Yup, yeah," Griffon gulped, following her example. "Sounds good."

After recovering their horses and supplies, and having a short rest, they camped the night on the path of destruction left behind. The following morning, they ran across the first stragglers from Dragon Staff that had been brought into the valley by Ahken'ho-tek.

They heard the story of how the lich lord had murdered his underlings, burying one alive (if that was the right word) using her elemental powers against her. As they traveled back through the tunnel leading to the city, they found other people. They were told how the liches had come to Dragon Staff, drained most of the people to create their army of lost folk, or to feed their own undead needs, and enslaved the remaining population.

It took three days to reach the city, two in the jungle, and one in the tunnel under the mountain. The volcano in the center of the valley erupted in fits and starts, but never as intense as what they'd seen before. By the end of the second day, as they headed into the tunnel high on the slope of the mountain face, they could see a single peak in the center of the canopy. It was already calming down; the ash pulled away by the winds.

The city had lost nearly two-thirds of its population and felt like a ghost town. Some people were packing up to leave, heading west to the Rolling Mountains, or east to Dargaon's Hole. Most were staying, though, and beginning to rebuild.

But what had to be rebuilt wasn't buildings, farms, and businesses. It was people. The liches hadn't attacked in the traditional sense. There was almost no property damage. They'd taken what was most important, the neighbors, friends, families, and loved ones of the citizens.

In the weeks following, LT helped consolidate businesses to a smaller circle within the city. She helped the broken government take control of people who'd lost all hope and assisted them in restructuring their lives. It meant clearing shops and homes of those who were gone and redistributing the wealth among those who remained.

Griffon mostly stuck to the outskirts of town, unable to handle the politics as people vied for position and power in the vacuum left behind. He organized patrols to watch the city's borders, hunt down remaining lost folk, and burn the bodies when they were found.

In the first week of Surem, the first month of summer, Griffon and LT sat at a café in the shade of the mountains on the eastern side of Dragon Staff. The gnome had a fruity drink with bits floating in it, and LT had a whiskey and this world's equivalent to coffee.

"Think he'll come back?" Griffon asked.

"No," LT said, "I think if Reggie was coming back, he'd have been here weeks ago."

"Think he's still in there," Griffon said, sniffing at his thick ceramic mug, "gently caressing some moldy table, and whispering to a broken column how beautiful it is?"

LT snorted into her coffee.

"Yeah, probably," she laughed, then grew serious. "I bet Rykul knows what happened to him."

"Think he'd tell us if we asked nicely?" the gnome looked up at the woman, closing one eye in the sunlight.

"I don't know if the bear lived through the birth of a new volcano," LT sighed, "but if he did…well, people said he helped in the past."

"So," Griffon drew out the word, "do we want to make one more trip into the Valley of Rykul, the Great Bear?"

"What about fame and glory?" LT looked over the rim of her mug at the gnome. "Shouldn't you be heading out so you can get gold and girls?"

"I think that can wait a little bit longer," Griffon shrugged. "I kinda feel like friends are more important and need to come first."

Epilogue

Summer was coming on strong, and the cloying humidity spiked as they left the shade of the tunnel that led to the Valley of Rykul from Dragon Staff. The ridge line at the end of the passage was stacked with crates and barrels, tools scattered across the containers.

"Damn bugs," LT said, slapping at her neck as the two walked down the path, "I don't remember them being this bad a month ago."

"They're not bugging me," Griffon said, then laughed at his unintentional joke. "Ha! See what I did there? I didn't even mean to be funny."

"Oh?" LT looked down at him. "Good thing, then. Because you weren't. And maybe they aren't biting you because you taste horrible."

"It looks like Rykul may be helping." Griffon jerked a thumb at the supplies by the tunnel entrance. "What do you think everyone is doing here?"

"Could be mining," LT shrugged, "or just cutting down trees for building materials."

After a couple minutes, they arrived at an outpost. Canvas canopies were erected for shade and walls of fine mesh allowed air flow while limiting the mosquitos and other biting insects. The makeshift shelters were attached by hallways of the stuff, tented so people didn't have to leave their protection.

The jungle was alive with sounds and smells. The insects were just a small part of the atmosphere. Birds called from overhead, and small creatures chittered from branches. Something that looked like a tapir waddled along a muddy rivulet, her two young following behind.

The smell of cooking food cut through the scents of the jungle—roasting game and baking bread—overpowering more subtle aromas. A trickle of laughter came from the furthest tent.

The two moved around the encampment, looking through the layers of the hazy material, trying to find an entry point.

"Is that a sign?" LT asked, pointing at an oblong piece of wood swinging in a faint breeze.

"I'll be damned," Griffon said quietly, "The Traveller's Inn. Looks like it's your turn to meet Jack Tucker and his crew."

"Sounds like a pirate," LT muttered, "bit out of his depth, if you know what I mean."

Griffon slapped at the netting beside the sign and slid between layers. He faded from view, moving further in. LT followed the gnome, mimicking his motions to find the entrance.

They came through the other side, where thin wooden plank tables lined an area cleared of foliage. Extra impromptu tables were set around the larger ones, most of those were nothing more than a barrel. A dozen people watched the newcomers, and a few raised drinks in welcome.

A stack of crates with a panel of wood across them acted as a makeshift bar, and a tall man with a very round head nodded at them from behind it.

Stoneware mugs and tankards were laid out on a sideboard. A cooking pit stood beyond it, a slowly turning spit displaying some sort of wild pig being prepared. A brickwork oven had been built to one side of the spit, and small loaves of bread were cooling beside it.

"Welcome Griffon," a man said, "good to see you again."

Turning to look, LT saw a rather plain man smiling up at her. He was the forgettable sort, looking neither young nor old, and he wore neutral-colored clothes in a style that blended in with everyone else.

"Jack!" Griffon almost shouted the man's name, thrusting his hand towards him. "Good to see you, too! Is Reggie here?"

The gnome shook the man's hand, standing on his tippytoes, craning his neck to see if he could spot his friend.

"Sort of," Jack smiled again, "but give it some time before we have that discussion. And you must be LT? Heard so many good things about you."

Jack turned to LT, holding out his hand in greeting.

"I'm good," she said, meeting his eyes. "What is this place?"

Gesturing with the hand, he waved it across the room. "This is the Traveller's Inn," he said, smiling, "and we're more of a wandering tavern than anything else."

"Wandering tavern?" LT echoed. "What's that even mean?"

"It means what it means," Griffon chortled, but not answering the question. "But he pays for the meal and drinks, so right now it means we get to stuff ourselves and get drunk for free. Sound good?"

"No," LT pulled her hand from Jack's. "I'd like to know a bit more. I mean, we just dealt with an army of undead swarming across the land using an enslaved second army. I think it's reasonable to want to know what's going on."

"Sounds perfectly reasonable to me," Jack agreed. "Would you like some roast boar and grilled veggies while you get those answers?"

"Um, sure," LT said, allowing Jack to lead her to a barrel set up as a small standing table. "What else do you have? I've just spent weeks helping to rebuild a shattered government, and in that light, I'd like to celebrate life after…what we just went through."

Grabbing Jack by his shirt collar, she pulled him close until their faces were almost touching. "Then I *really* want to know what happened to Reggie. Am I understood?"

The last three words came out slowly and separately.

"Um, LT?" Griffon gently placed a hand on hers, drawing it down and away from Jack's shirt. "I wouldn't do that. He might not look like much, but he's got pull in this place."

The gnome indicated the very quiet room around them, every head turned to watch the interaction.

"It's okay, folks," Jack held up his hands with a chuckle, "she's had a rough road. Everyone here can understand that, can't they? She just wants answers, and she'll get them."

Jack looked directly at LT with the last words, and she nodded her understanding and let Griffon pull her away.

She set her hands on the scarred wood of the barrel acting as a table and stared at them. The burnt symbols on the wood—probably telling the alcoholic contents of the vessel—meant nothing to her. Raising her eyes, she looked around the netted area that reminded her of Reggie's stories about the African continent and his adventures there.

A tall man with an open shirt watched her, and she recalled her friend mentioning Nomed, a demon bastard, that fit that description. Seeing the short man with tousled brown hair beside him—indubitably Wanderly—cinched it. The bartender would be Cogsley, and he wasn't human, according to Reggie. A golem that her friend had described stood next to the bartender, off to one side, glaring at her.

A gnome sat on the bar, a half-ogre towering above him, both looking her way. An old man in robes and a younger man paused over an odd-looking typing machine watched her from a table. Others also stared, waiting to see what she would do.

Reid reached out with her mind, feeling the vriktiri warriors surrounding the camp, waiting for orders or a pulse of panic or worry from their commander.

"That won't be necessary," Jack said, his hand on her wrist bringing her back to the present. "You're safe here, I promise. And think of this, who does Griffon ever greet cheerfully?"

LT looked at her friend, who was smiling and waving his pewter goblet towards anyone looking his way and let out a breath.

"He's a pemtie," she breathed, "and just because he's comfortable with…whatever this is, doesn't mean it's a good thing."

"He's got good instincts," Jack tilted his head to the gnome, "he's just young, a diamond in the rough, if you will."

"And," she drew the word out, "that's what you'd say if you were trying to…"

"Military training and years of dealing with assholes," Jack said, stopping LT's comment in its tracks, "and you're suspicious. Let me stop you there. Look, LT or Tamilda or Reid or LT Ripper or Lieutenant Pierce…I get it. But like the military you served, I'm looking at a larger picture. And that means sacrifice, while trying to maintain the individuals doing the things I set into motion."

Jack stopped, sighing…and looked at Reid.

"Eat something," he said, "have a drink. Water if you must, something stronger if you want. Then we'll talk. I promise. And you will find out about Reggie and what happened to him."

Jack turned away, moving towards the kitchens looking like the weight of the world rested on his shoulders. He turned back for a moment, meeting her eyes.

"Your vriktiri friends are welcome in," he said with a smile, "or you can call them into the camp if you're worried about what's going on here. Your call. You could also invite Kriksi to join you."

Jack flapped his hand towards a corner of the room as he retreated, and Reid looked in that direction. The thin priest sat by himself, crammed between a tent pole and sideboard laden with a clutter of dirty dishes. He had his hood down, showing a high forehead and thin hair brushed back against his scalp. His cloak was pulled tight around him, even in the oppressive heat, like he was cold.

Reid waved at the man, trying to get his attention. When he didn't notice her, she stood and crossed the room to him.

"Kriksi," she said, jarring him from his daze as he stared at the jungle outside the mosquito netting.

He started, looking up at her. She noticed changes in him, or perhaps they were always there, but she'd never noticed. Indented lines along the sides of his forehead disappeared into his hairline, and his bony hands clutching at the cloak had an extra knuckle on his three fingers and thumb. It was Reid's turn to startle as he smiled at her.

"My Queen," Kriksi said, dropping from his stool to his knees, pressing his head to the dirt floor at her feet, "you honor me."

"Get up," she hissed, reaching down and grabbing his robe to pull him to his feet. The cloth opened, and she saw small, vestigial arms under his normal arms. She could feel hard plates of flesh under the garment, and she stepped away quickly, releasing him.

"Yes, my Queen," Kriksi said, standing. "How may I be of service?"

"You can stop calling me your queen," Reid said. "LT is fine. And then you can come join Griffon and me at our table, or barrel, whatever."

"As you wish," Kriksi nodded in quick jerking motions.

Reid sighed, turning, and leading the way back to the table. Kriksi followed. Griffon saw them coming and raised his glass in one hand and a ceramic mug in the other.

"Kricket, you ol cranky bastard!" Griffon cried, then took a drink from each of the glasses in his hands. "Rub your legs together and meet any sexy praying mantises lately?"

"No," the priest grinned, his jaw clicking, "but I have received other gifts from Khelikian for the help I gave our Quee—Mistress LT. I need less sleep, can lift twice my weight, and I have these!"

Thin arms opened the center of his robes, dark hairs bristling along their chitinous lengths, and two fingers at the end of each pinching the air in greeting.

"Holy bat-bidj bug stumps!" Griffon shouted, scrabbling to stand on his stool. He stopped, leaned in, set down one of his drinks and reached out, grabbing one of Kriksi's new appendages and shaking it in greeting. "Well, how do you do, you buggy little priest?"

"I am well," Kriksi smiled like a kid making a new friend, "thank you for asking, you annoying braggart."

Griffon threw back his head with a braying laugh, which went on much too long and was much too loud. While catching his breath, he threw back the whiskey he had in his hand, then traded it for his beer mug and drank it down.

Reid slid onto her stool, watching the exchange and the room's reaction. More people stared at the gnome than the priest. *He's the perfect distraction, that's for sure. Kinda reassuring that he freaked out a bit, too.* She found herself smiling.

"So," Griffon said as the other two settled around the makeshift table, "what've you been up to? How's Allendale?"

"It is well," Kriksi nodded with a twitch, "before I left, I spoke with the grassland vriktiri and arranged for them to help the town. They will herd animals back for hunting, catch lost flocks, and help clear the river now that the volcanoes have fallen quiet."

"How did the Talien and the council take that?" Reid asked.

"They have a new relationship with Khelikian and have been promised her protection for a while," Kriksi said, turning a faceted eye towards Reid, the other staying on Griffon. "The local vriktiri will establish trade with the other tribes and help reopen roads in all directions for commerce."

"You're telling us," Griffon leaned forward, "that between you and your goddess, you arranged for your bug guys to become important in restoring all the cities from here to the Great Desert? Clever!"

"It is an ecosystem," Kriksi turned both eyes to the gnome, "and insects are essential to any ecosystem. We will also build hives, modeled after human cities, along the route. We hope to be accepted by the other species and grow with them."

"That reminds me," Griffon waved at the server for more drinks, "did I tell you about our trip from Ez'rainia-fromton to Akar to Allendale?"

The following hour was a blur for Reid as food and drink flowed and the gnomish gladiator chatted animatedly like he was the man of the hour. Griffon recounted the adventures—once dull and monotonous chores—to Kriksi and the other patrons. The crowd reacted with cheers, jeers, and the expected responses.

Reid couldn't help to think how Reggie would have told it. That man could tell a story, giving dull tales of history a flair that brought them to life. Griffon regaled the room, while standing on the small barrel that acted as a table, with a recounting of battles and encounters. But it didn't have the depth and history that Reggie found a way to weave into his accounts.

Reid leaned back, taking in the downtime, and listening to the vriktiri outside begin their twilight song. She could feel them on the edges of her mind, smell their pheromones, and knew they were content.

A while later, when the Traveller's Inn had quieted and only a few souls remained, Jack came out with dessert. He carried a tray with a half dozen muffins topped with creamy confectionary. Setting them on the barrel, he looked at Griffon and Reid in turn.

"Ready for the big reveal?" Jack asked.

"Isn't it anticlimactic if you ask?" Reid replied.

Thick layers of mosquito netting fell away on one side of the makeshift tavern, revealing a bear of immense proportions. The beast stood on all fours but still towered over everyone in the room. Beside him was a thin man who was as tall as the bear.

Reid felt emotion swell inside her, reaching her eyes and throat. She wheezed a gurgled sob, squeezing her eyes shut and feeling tears run down her cheeks. She felt a hand on her shoulder gripping gently, and she looked up to see Jack beside her.

"Reggie's still with us," Jack breathed. "He's with Rykul now. A part of him, but no longer just himself."

"The man, Reggie," Rykul said in a deep rumble, "is now part of the history he loves so much."

"Al, the chuzzing Troll Lord!" Griffon shouted, jumping from his perch to the floor and rushing to the Troll Lord with his arms held wide. He stopped in front of him, his arms dropping. "Well, I guess no hugs. I'd look like a chihuahua humping your leg."

"Not at all, little one," Al said, kneeling and pulling the gnome in.

"D'aww," Griffon said, throwing his arms around the Troll Lord's neck and thumping a shoulder in a drunken, manly fashion.

Al hugged him back carefully, and scooped the gnome up into his arms, standing. "Better Griffon?"

"Um," Griffon looked down and around the room, "not really. Now I'm like a two-year-old being held by his grandpa or something. Can you put me down? Maybe near the beer?"

The Troll Lord chuckled and took a few steps forward to set the gnome back on his stool.

"Okay," Reid said, clearing her throat of her emotional reaction, "that's the reveal. What happens now?"

"Is this when you offer to send us home, Jack?" Griffon asked, pouring a whiskey with a beer chaser.

"Well, um," Jack rubbed at his neck, "about that. I was hoping I could ask you to stay. Things have happened, and I think the two of you could be…useful."

"Useful?" Reid asked, squinting at the man. She sighed and rolled her head, a series of small audible pops following. "Yeah, Jack. I get it. Like the military, you're going to ask us to take a mission that you don't want to send anyone to do. But we have skills that may help, and you have no one else to ask."

"Actually," Jack was nodding, and looked more hopeful, "I know a few others who might be perfect to go with you."

"Another new person from our world?" Griffon chimed in, then threw back a shot.

"Not new." Jack shook his head. "I was thinking of the Kid, Torrents, and Kajuun. They all came here from your world, but chose to stay."

"A five-man dungeon party, eh?" Griffon mused, rubbing his chin with his free hand. "What's the job? Another undead temple? Evil elementals? Angry fairies that need some gnome loving?"

"The liches…" Al began, but Reid cut him off.

"Are dead." She said. "The liches are dead. We saw that."

"Yes," Rykul rumbled, "but Ahken'ho-tek could not kill one of the others, Chektar-ral, since she was not a lich. He could not drain her power as he did the others. Instead, he buried her and imprisoned her within the same elements that she controlled."

"Let me guess," Griffon interrupted, "but she got out, right? I knew it!" The gnome pumped his fist in the air, wobbling on his stool and almost falling. "So, you need us to find her and kill her. See? Evil elementals!"

"Not quite, my little friend." Al placed a hand on the gnome to calm him, the hand covering most of Griffon's back. "She is a member of a hidden civilization in the ocean to the west and south of Teurone. The Phydrian Empire."

"They're coming here, then?" Reid asked and Jack, Al, and Rykul all nodded. "And you want us to stop an army?"

"They are old," Al continued, "older than me, older than Rykul, and older than…" he paused, looking at Jack, "they are old."

"They have technology that's better than your world," Jack picked up the story, "and they use science in their magics."

"So, they have laser guns and a different kind of magic?" Griffon asked.

"Sort of," Jack scrunched up his face, "they write their own laws of magic using science. But no to laser guns, though they do have things like them. And that's why we think you and the others we mentioned would be best suited to do this. Technology won't surprise or scare you."

"Why don't you guys do it," Reid asked, "since you're all so powerful?"

"We cannot," Al's shoulders slumped. "Rykul cannot leave the valley. They would harvest me to control magics, and Jack is bound by his word to no longer directly interfere in matters of this world."

"But you have my sword, Marcid." It was Rykul who spoke, but it was Reggie's voice, with the echo of many other voices. "LT, you are an incredible woman. You are a natural leader and never give up. You point out people's strengths to encourage them and call them out on their bull-bidj when they won't listen. And you have Marcid, your very own magical weapon."

The massive bear turned to Griffon, who sat on the stool, wide-eyed, his drink halfway to his mouth.

"Griffon," Reggie went on through Rykul, "and Raven Stealer, you are an incredible team. Griffon, you are passionate about everything you do and do not know how to give up. And we would bring Kajuun, a diplomat and elementalist spellslinger. The Kid is a mind mage, but also an old and wise soul. And Torrents is a master of weapons who has an overwhelming desire to help others. This is the best possible group for something like this."

The room fell silent.

"Do you want to sleep on it?" Jack asked. "It's your choice."

"If not us, then who?" Reid whispered, staring down at her hands. "Yeah, we can sleep on it, but you already know our answer, don't you?"

"Of course," Jack gave a sad smile, nodding. "We can begin making preparations for the invasion in the morning."

End of Portals, Book 6

Calendar

The basic calendar is a lunar calendar. There are thirteen months in each year. Each month there are twenty-eight days. There is a new moon on the first day of every month. The first day of spring is on the equinox.

Seasons	**Months**	**Days**	
Spring	Loen	1.	Ginof
	Hapok	2.	Bestuf
	Axara	3.	Midā
		4.	Therin
Summer	Surem	5.	Uthr
	Santara	6.	Dunwith
	Xaco	7.	Lasin
Autumn	Harton		
	Thon		
	Ault		
Winter	Witen		
	Maleo		
	Frear		
Thaw	Milwen		

Glossary

Aborgas: Small hamlet near Red City.

Aeifain: Willowy race of beings with almond eyes, pale skin, and slightly pointed ears. Often more advanced in arts, culture, and magic than the lesser races.

Akar Lake: Body of water near Ruger Whitley Estates.

Ault: Ninth month of the year, and the third month of the autumn season.

Axara: Third month of the year, and the spring season.

Bestuf: Second day of the week.

Bidj: A swear word meaning waste or offal.

Binaple: a fruit that grows on binaple bushes used for make red, orange, and yellow dyes.

Changing Wheel, The: The god of cyclical change who all the other gods bow to.

Chuz: A harsh swear word.

Dangrazio: Subterranean metropolis and trading post.

Dasism: A race who follow the path of elements and nature. Physically, they are slighter than humans, with olive skin, pointed ears, and almond eyes.

Dioneze City: A broken city on the eastern part of the continent run by slavers. Known for its gladiatorial ring.

Dragon Estates: An ancient castle rumored to have a dragon residing in the caverns below it.

Dargaon's Hole: Ancestral home of dragons in the Wandering Hills.

Dunwith: Sixth day of the week.

Durgan's Keep: A city-state in the far east that was founded by a rokairn and his adventuring companions.

Edgewater: Medium port town on the coast of the Sea of Seron.

Everyway: Largest city on the continent of Teurone.

Ez'rainia-fromton: City of the dead located in the eastern part of the Great Desert, the city in which Verl'zen-luk had been imprisoned before his rise to godhood.

Fate's Run: Dockside gambling hall in Tarnish. Run by a woman named Fate.

Frear: Twelfth month of the year, and the third month of the winter season.

Ginof: First day of the week.

Glass Valley: A valley made of glass in the slim desert that was formed when a stone dragon fell from the heavens.

Grey Lands: Home of the Aeifain.

Great Desert: A large desert east of the southern Rolling Mountains, which is home to Rogen the Plague and the Great Desert Empire.

Great Desert Empire: A civilization built by Rogen the Plague and his nation slaves, located in the Great Desert.

Hapok: Second month of the year, and of the spring season.

Harton: Seventh month of the year, and the first month of the autumn season.

Highest Spire: A structure that is fifty kilometers at the base and spirals upward. Doors that lead to other places in time and space are spaced every six meters. The height of this tower in unmeasured.

Hope's Hollow: A small village on the on the borders of the Black Wood and the Wandering Hills.

Humbrey: A Kingdom of thirteen houses that embodies nobility and honor.

Icon Hall: Aeifain home on the eastern portion of Teurone.

Jonath: God of justice, protection, strength, and earth. His symbol is a trident and balanced scales.

Kez'et-dual: A demon enslaved by the Troöds.

Khelikian: Goddess of Insects.

Kord: A twisted gold wire that is the standard currency.

Land's End: A demon-ridden peninsula on the south-eastern most portion of the continent.

Lasin: Seventh day of the week.

Ley lines: Elemental energy currents, invisible to the naked eye, from which wizards can draw energy.

Loen: First month of the year, and of the spring season. It begins on the spring equinox.

Mage, Mind: Practitioner of the art of psychic magics such as body alteration, telekinesis, telepathy, etc.

Maleo: Eleventh month of the year, and the second month of the winter season.

Malvor: Duchy in the Kingdom of Trysteria, south of the Kingdom of Humbrey. Run by Duke Malvornick.

Midā: Third day of the week.

Milwen: The thirteenth month of the year, and the transition month between winter and spring.

Nine Towers of Magic: Abandoned during the Wizard Wars, this secluded and elite university was dedicated to teaching magic. Located east of the Black Wood.

Nomed: A demon-human-aeifain hybrid.

Northwood Community: The largest city in Northwood, founded by humans, dasism, and other races.

Obsidian/Onyx: God of Magic who came to power when the Talisman appeared in the sky.

Obsidian/Onyx Towers: Black towers raised by the God of Magic to distribute magical tools, goods, and weapons.

Ocean Wood: Lands reclaimed by the Dasism from humans under Kala the Black.

Olde Kingdom: A fallen Kingdom in the southern portion of the Everyway Plains.

Oracle Plain: Grasslands north of the Common Wood, east of the Slim Desert, and west of the Rolling Mountains. Home of the mystical order of the Oracle.

Pantageas: City run by mages and wizards in the northern Everyway Plains, just south of the Kingdom of Humbrey.

Paradise Island: An island created by a dead volcano. Now a refuge for pirates and seagoing folk. Run by small governments and individuals, known for its waterfalls.

Parsay Gevies: God of Luck, Chance, and Dreams. Referred to as Parsay by adults, who pray to him for luck, and as Mister Gevies by children, who pray to him for dreams to come true.

Pek: A silver coin, worth one-tenth of a gold kord.

Pemtie: A moron, ignorant, or stupid person, idea, or event.

Phaz, Day of: A day that happens once every four years. Shrouded with myth and superstition.

Promethene: Goddess of Song and Light. Her clergy is almost always women. Wife of the Walking God, Mother of Chanian and Senaria.

Pyridom of Power: A landmark on the east coast of the continent that focuses magical energies.

Red City: Run down city once plagued by lycanthropes and undead. Located on the coast of the

Red Wind: Located in the Red Plains, this city is known for its crime lords and drug trade.

Rock Crag Wastes: a rocky area geographically located west of the Great Desert and east of the southern Rolling Mountains.

Rogen the Plague: Rokairn slave master and lord of The Great Desert Empire.

Rokairn: The Stone Folk. A short, stout race known for their attention to detail, organization, and dedication to fine craftsmanship. Both sexes are known to have beards.

Rolling Mountains: An immense mountain range east of the Oracle Plain, and west of the Northwood.

Rondarius the Foul: Insane Necromancer

Royale Bay: A bay north of the Sea of Seron and east of the Everyway Plains.

Rugber Whitley Estates: A small community known for the mind mages born there.

Rumay Bay: A shanty town on the shores of the Broken Sea that was once a hub of trade before the Downfall.

Runsk: A warlord-controlled city nestled between the Grey Forest and Diaz Wood.

Santara: Fifth month of the year, and the second month of the summer season.

Sea of the Great Plague: A body of water south of the Great Desert.

Sea of Seron: A body of water south of the Everyway Plains.

Seawall City: A fortified city run by spellslingers in a military fashion, located on the east coast of Teurone on the Eastern Ocean.

Senaria: Goddess of nature, innate honor, and woodlands. Daughter of The Walking God and Promethene.

Sharp: A brass coin, with one one-hundredth of a gold kord.

Shuglak (shug-lak): Horse-sized herd creature with large round ears, a single nose horn on a flat hog-like snout, and two tusks jutting from the bottom jaw of males.

Shulyar City: Dasism name for Silver City.

Silver Castle: One-time home of the god, Jonath, who built it.

Silver City: Also known as Shulyar City, a city built by the god Jonath.

Sinking Swamp: A swamp that hides the Library of time, west of Trysteria and north of the Everyway Plains.

Slim Desert: A thin desert between Everyway Plains and Oracle Plain.

Spellslinger: A generalized term for a wielder of one of the five types of magic; alchemy, mind magic, holy, conjuring, and elemental.

Stadia Isle: A pirate island in the Sea of Seron.

Surem: Fourth month of the year, and the first month of the summer season.

Talisman: A comet that returns on a regular basis, but now is in orbit around the planet.

Tarnish: Run-down desert city on the coast of the Sea of the Great Plague.

Tarra: Goddess of water and healing. Twin of Torr.

Teurone: Continent detailed in this book.

Therin: Fourth day of the week.

Thon: Eighth month of the year, and the second month of the autumn season.

Torgoth: God of Trade and Commerce.

Torr: God of fire and combat. Twin of Tarra.

Transvartius: A wise and benevolent man sometimes known as the Traveller, the Hidden Diplomat, and disciple of the Walking God.

Traveling God, The: God of innate magic, such as mind mages and wizards. Also known as the Walking God.

Troöd: A race from another dimension, that are reptilian in features. They have two distinct species, greys and greens. The former deal in summoning magics, and the latter are chameleon like soldiers.

Trysteria: Kingdom in the northern portion of the Everyway Plains.

Uthr: Fifth day of the week.

Vallenwood: a wood harvested from Vallenwood trees that is strong and beautiful.

Velentian Brandy: A strong alcoholic drink.

Verl'zen-luk: God of ritual Magic.

Witen: Tenth month of the year, and the first month of the winter season.

Wizard: Practitioner of elemental magics which tap into the energy of ley lines.

Xaco: Sixth month of the year, and the third month of the summer season.

Author's Note

This is coming out on February 13th, 2024, and is the sixth and final book (for now) in the Portals series. Book one came out in July 2020 and took me twelve days to write in January of the same year. Book four came out in November of 2022. Book five was published three weeks before this book.

It's been a fun and frantic road. Six books in four years in this series alone, but more in other series. Two Silver and Smith books came out in that time, plus three 27 Thoughts books, and two of my children's books in the Kids & Monsters series under my Joe Wilson pen name. Oh, and Journal of a Stranger, Volume II. That's fourteen books in four years, plus working my day job and maintaining more than a half dozen podcasts I write, record, engineer, and publish, and my live stream on twitch.tv.

I do this because I love it, and I hope to pass something on to folks that entertain them, makes them think, or just helps them feel that they're not as alone as they thought. I'll be publishing sixteen more books in 2024 (one every three weeks), if I can keep my planned schedule.

I'm appreciative of all the support I receive. Some from the viewers of the live stream, most from a few close friends, my editor, and my wife. It's these interactions that convince me to keep doing this. I'm making a concentrated effort in 2024 to build a reader base that allows me to do this full time. But whether that happens or not, I'll be changing how I do things once I've completed my current writing schedule. I'm going to slow down and enjoy the process, as well as making each book better.

It's that simple. I love this and will constantly strive to improve. And I appreciate you reading my books, and I hope you found something of value in each one.

Travis I. Sivart

About the Author

Travis I. Sivart writes Fantasy, Steampunk, Cyberpulp, Social DIY, and more. You can find him live streaming the writing and editing of his latest project from his home in Central Virginia, surrounded by too many cats.

You can find Travis on Amazon, Barnes and Noble, Books-A-Million, and other literary retailers.

Travis I. Sivart